Advance praise for *Sheltered Lives*:

"Charles Oberndorf writes with a firmamental sincerity and honesty. This book is one from the heart. It's a mighty and indignant book. There are a few, just a few, books that leave you a changed person when you have finished them. This is one of them."
—Ian McDonald, author of *King of Morning, Queen of Day*

"Oberndorf's futuristic vision contains both beauty and horror. In his unabashed use of the first and his unflinching use of the second, Oberndorf has achieved a powerful effect—in *Sheltered Lives*, the beauty heightens the horror, and the horror makes what is beautiful even more so. *Sheltered Lives* is a book you will remember."
—Karen Joy Fowler, author of *Sarah Canary*

"*Sheltered Lives* should not be judged as a first novel, but as the work of a controlled and mature craftsman. Charles Oberndorf is an important talent, and his book is a splendidly honest, wonderfully achieved examination of what remains of our future, what is left of the American Dream."
—Lucius Shepard, author of *Life During Wartime*

Sheltered Lives

charles oberndorf

BANTAM BOOKS
NEW YORK · TORONTO
LONDON · SYDNEY
AUCKLAND

SHELTERED LIVES

A Bantam Spectra Book / March 1992

SPECTRA *and the portrayal of a boxed "s" are trademarks of Bantam Books, a division of Bantam Doubleday Dell Publishing Group, Inc.*

All rights reserved.
Copyright © 1992 by Charles Oberndorf.
Cover art copyright © 1992 by Oscar Chichoni.
No part of this book may be reproduced or transmitted in any form or by any means, electronic or mechanical, including photocopying, recording, or by any information storage and retrieval system, without permission in writing from the publisher.
For information address: Bantam Books.

> If you purchased this book without a cover you should be aware that this book is stolen property. It was reported as "unsold and destroyed" to the publisher and neither the author nor the publisher has received any payment for this "stripped book."

ISBN 0-553-29248-X

Published simultaneously in the United States and Canada

Bantam Books are published by Bantam Books, a division of Bantam Doubleday Dell Publishing Group, Inc. Its trademark, consisting of the words "Bantam Books" and the portrayal of a rooster, is Registered in U.S. Patent and Trademark Office and in other countries. Marca Registrada. Bantam Books, 666 Fifth Avenue, New York, New York 10103.

PRINTED IN THE UNITED STATES OF AMERICA

RAD 0 9 8 7 6 5 4 3 2 1

To my parents
for providing shelter
for my first twenty-four years

And to April
for sharing shelter
in the years that
have followed and will

They that can give up essential liberty to obtain a little temporary safety deserve neither liberty nor safety.
—BENJAMIN FRANKLIN

You told a half-truth? They'll say you lied twice if you tell the other half.
—ANTONIO MACHADO

Part 1

the job

> *The eye that you see*
> *is not an eye because you see*
> *it, but an eye because it sees you.*
> —Antonio Machado

1

THE CLIENT'S LOVER had killed himself.

On April 1, as if that were the best day to take stock of his life, Sauro Contini jumped from the roof of a five-story apartment building in Ohio City. On April 15, when everyone I knew was worrying about outputting tax forms, Anna Baxter walked to Personal Services and applied for a hired companion. The next day I was handed her file.

Half the file, one whole crystal, contained footage and documents dated April 1 and later. Marked *Thursday 1 April 1731:00* and counting, the first sequence featured Anna in her apartment living room. She was lying on the couch, head propped up, book open on her belly. It's not clear why she was reading a book, or if she realized that Contini had left her for the roof. While she read, shouts drifted up from the street; a child began to cry. Anna Baxter looked up from her book, seemed to decide that the commotion had nothing to do with her, and returned to her reading.

Tricky Dick, Personal Services' artificial *un*intelligence, had saved that moment for Baxter's file. But Tricky Dick had erased the good parts. There was no footage of Baxter and Contini's last conversation, the one that might have driven him to the roof. There was no footage of Anna seeing the dead body or dealing with the police investigators.

There was no footage of the funeral in the small stone church (one that had long ago been incorporated into the

University Circle mini-Construct); the Catholic Church had barred monitoring in all churches. However, the reception afterwards, held in Sauro's parents' flat—leased from a privately owned corporation that required monitoring—was on file. Sauro's parents, dressed up and looking awkward, did their best to include Anna as part of the family, even invited her to move in with them until she felt better.

On Monday, Anna called into the art gallery where she worked and, between sobs, took an indefinite leave of absence. Her friend Joan at the gallery must have hit the phone immediately, because within an hour some friends showed up at Anna's apartment and continued to show up in shifts throughout the week. All of them told her that it wasn't her fault: certainly Sauro had been depressed, but *no one* had expected this. They listened politely while she played his crystals of remastered twentieth-century jazz and when she opened his thick writer's notebook and read aloud from his unpublished poetry. Every now and then she would pull out one of his books on life in the relocation camps, and a friend would gently reshelve it, telling Anna to worry about it later. A rotund friend from the Heights visited, urging Anna to get out of the apartment and stay with her. Her aunt Lorena, who had established Anna's trust fund and had gotten her a job at the gallery last July, suggested that if Anna wasn't feeling well enough to work then maybe Anna should come and stay with her out in Hunting Valley. A telegram from her family in Boston expressed condolences and asked Anna to come back home where she belonged.

I reviewed that last moment several times. The image began at *Wednesday 14 April 944:25,* when the telegram was delivered by a white woman in a blue uniform. The telegram was her family's expensive, anachronistic gesture. Anna closed the door, stared at the envelope, and then almost skipped to the couch. She projected the same aura of energy that had been visible in earlier footage but had died out with Sauro.

Anna Baxter was not a beautiful woman by holovision standards. Her shoulders were too broad; her torso too solid. Only tightly worn clothes revealed her feminine figure. But when she was happy and the energy flared, men turned their heads as she passed by. Sauro Contini had called her a cuddly, sexy teddy bear. Now, full of this renewed energy, Anna tore open the telegram. She hadn't heard from them, certainly not from her father, since she had run off to Cleveland with Sauro last June, right after their graduation from college. As she read the message, her expression twisted, her thin lips pressed together. She squeezed her eyes shut as if that would erase the words. Her hands first tore up the telegram, then they tore out the barrette that held up her long brown hair, and finally they tore at her hair.

"It's like a judgment," she told her friend Joan from the art gallery that evening. "If I'd only loved him better." Two weeks earlier, according to the file, she'd told Joan how badly she'd wanted out of the relationship: "I just want to be on my own for a while. I never learned how to live on my own."

Now, on her own, she cried. She sat on the couch in front of the apartment's only monitor and cried and wailed and stomped her feet and shouted at Sauro and at her father and at her mother for going along with him and at her sisters for never calling her or showing up at the funeral. Tricky Dick saved it all. I fast-forwarded over a lot of it. She was treating the pitiable like it was tragic. With a ninth grade education, I knew the difference; you would think that college had taught her something.

I stopped fast-forwarding when her sobs subsided. She was still on the couch, her hands held loosely between her knees, her shoulders hunched forward. She stared toward the window, but I don't know if she was seeing anything. I got the sense that she was thinking, turning something over and over in her mind. The silence in the apartment was unnerving.

The next morning she called her friends and asked them to stay away; she wanted to break out of her rut. At this point Tricky Dick decided to make use of its Orson Welles long-take program and followed her as she left her apartment, hiked through Ohio City, and across the Hope Memorial Bridge. By the time she reached the Construct, she was sweating. I wondered if she was just saving the hundred-dollar transit fare (I'm amazed by what some people will do to save a buck) or if the walk involved some kind of inward journey from one world to another.

Inside the Construct she shivered visibly even though the climate control doesn't keep things that cool. Following the arrows to Personal Services, she seemed spooked by all the bug-eyed lensed monitors hanging from where corridor walls met ceiling; she kept looking up at them as if someone might care enough to pass judgment.

She made her way to the Prospect Corridors and the main outlet for Personal Services. After a good amount of time lingering near the SexyShops, the Sensory Arcades, the Brokerage Service, and the entrance to Direct Services, she finally, with a visible sense of resolution, entered the offices of Leisure Services.

An adviser sat down with her in a small cubicle. The adviser handed Anna a flatscreen with a standard questionnaire lit up on it. While Anna pressed out her answers, the adviser explained the purpose of the Personal Companion Program.

At one point Anna looked up from the flatscreen. "I don't know if I should be here," she said.

"You shouldn't worry. The contract would bind you to only one session; if you don't care for the companion, you can hire another or cancel entirely." Anna tried to hand the flatscreen back to the adviser, but the adviser's hands remained on the desk. "You know," the adviser said, "this is the most acceptable and natural thing in the world."

"You don't know my father," Anna said in a voice soft enough for the adviser to ignore it and loud enough for the monitor to pick it up. But Anna finished the questionnaire.

"Now, Ms. Baxter, would you like a personal companion to be on call for a four-hour daily shift or for the entire day?"

"How many other shifts would he have?"

"Just one other."

Anna shook her head violently. "I don't want to share." She glanced up at the monitor; she appeared appalled by what she'd just said.

The adviser barely noticed. Instead she got down to the details. "Employing a personal companion will cost eight thousand dollars a day, ten thousand dollars if you would like to contract out his or her exclusive sexual rights, fifteen thousand dollars if the companion moves in with you."

"What do you mean by exclusive, um, rights?"

"I'm sorry. I thought I'd explained that earlier. The companion would engage in no other sexual relationships. Our blood testing is thorough, so such a step is truly unnecessary. However, some clients prefer to stipulate that as part of the contract."

"Oh."

The adviser went on to explain the rest: the contract would be for an unspecified though limited period, to be terminated when the personal companion and the client agreed that the client could return to a world of two-way relationships. If the client was to get a release form signed by a psychiatrist, her medical insurance might cover up to 20 percent of the cost. The client would also have to sign papers releasing her complete file to the companion's care so he or she could study footage of her along with a computer-prepared psych-file. That way the companion could learn her tastes and needs.

Anna murmured agreement on all points. She asked for a male companion and decided she wanted someone intelligent, with artistic understanding, but not an artist. The adviser showed her photos, but Anna didn't want to see any nude shots or any of the advertising footage. "I don't want anything strange or kinky, just someone normal." Since all those formally educated in art appreciation were unavailable, she chose me.

I had seen enough. I knew all the other questions they'd asked her, and how they'd walked her through the main clauses of the contract, and that in the end she'd paid a nonrefundable deposit of ten thousand dollars to cover the first day. All that was followed by complete blood testing. I knew that Anna would somehow make it home and immediately regret her decision. I ejected the crystal from the terminal, and the screen went blank.

I left the cubicle and found Marie, my supervisor, and told her I didn't want the job. I hadn't been trained to service a woman who'd been born famous, who went to expensive schools, who had a summer home in Martha's Vineyard, and a trust fund to keep her going. Marie, who had been my trainer four years ago, assured me I'd had more than enough training. She went through my files and pointed out several shift-janes who had been from wealthy families, all of whom I had handled well. I told her that a woman whose lover had committed suicide was just too much, that it went beyond the training. She told me it was time to flex new muscles. She then handed me a crystal with software that would help me improve my grammar and my etiquette.

Several hours later Anna Baxter's blood was declared clean. They had drawn some of mine, just as they did every Friday morning, client or no client. On Saturday my blood was declared clean. First thing Monday morning Anna's adviser phoned her to confirm the seven o'clock meeting at her apartment. Anna hesitated, reminded herself out loud that she'd already as good as paid for one visit, then asked the adviser if she could change the hour to five o'clock, if that wasn't too early. The adviser assured her that it wasn't.

2

I CAUGHT THE westbound rapid transit at the Prospect Corridors. Two men in suits got on with me. My father would have said that they looked like accountants, even though most accountants had been replaced by software before I was born. The two men probably had stopped in at Direct Services for a half-hour quickie after work. They didn't look like they worked in the Business, and they did look embarrassed every time I glanced over at them.

The quality of their suits suggested that they were heading to lakefront houses in Lakewood or Rocky River. I was just crossing the Cuyahoga River to nearby Ohio City for a date, with Anna Elizabeth Baxter, scheduled for seventeen hours.

My supervisor had reminded me that Anna Baxter would say five o'clock, not seventeen hours. I had spent the whole afternoon going through etiquette and speech software, learning the when to use who or whom, relearning the difference between a salad fork and a dinner fork, and practicing propositions that didn't end in prepositions.

I was nervous, to say the least, and these were not just the usual butterflies in the stomach I felt before I met a new client. In four years I had learned how to prepare a role, play it for the four-hour shift. This was my first all-day jane. This was my first jane who all her life had gone to schools outside Cleveland that *I* had heard of; whose father had been on the cover of *Time* magazine; whose family probably looked at your bloodline and breeding before they even got to your individual flaws. I didn't want her to look at me and see someone as cheap and tawdry as she expected. I kept looking at myself in the transit car's window, my face reflected back by the glass and the underground darkness, and I kept straightening my tie.

Above me an official poster warned that panic was more dangerous than terrorists. The fine print advised that in case of electrical black out, passengers should remain on board and wait for further instructions. Half the regular riders of the RTA probably couldn't read the message, but voice-ads were legal only in the commercial neighborhoods.

The rapid came out from under the Construct and rose into the daylight. I left the businessmen behind and got off at the West Twenty-fifth Street stop. The air outside was cool; the long-range forecast threatened freezing rain or snow, by the end of the week.

A sign at the exit said: "Welcome to Ohio City: Saving the Best of the Past, Adding Only the Best of the Future." The best of the past contained the smell of splattered fruit and vegetables that the garbagemen were picking up alongside the West Side Market, overflowing trash receptacles at street corners, the feel of dust, the sound of cars. The best of the future was limited monitoring and limited computer service, at least in the buildings whose landlords listened to the local tenants' association. Sauro, in the footage I had seen of him, had liked to pontificate upon and proclaim the freedom he and Anna could still find there. "If nothing else," he had said, "if they black out Ohio City, we only have to open our windows if we want to breathe." When he spoke, his hands cut through the air with each idea, a finger—index, middle, ring, then pinky—popped up with each point, and, while listening, he rubbed his hands through his night black hair while his right leg jiggled up and down with the pent-up energy of his thoughts.

I walked past a mixture of upscale and seedy storefronts, crossed West 25th, and headed a couple of blocks west on Bridge. On the corner of West 28th and Bridge began a row of brownstones transplanted there during the postwar boom last century. They looked almost as rundown as the brick apartment buildings that ran alongside them on Jay. But both sets of buildings made the surrounding brick and clapboard houses look shabby and the century old projects on West 25th look shabbier. Anna had probably moved into the neighborhood because it was antithetical to what her grandfather had started.

Anna lived in Apartment 41, 2830 Bridge, the corner brownstone. The entranceway was tiny, room enough for several rows of mailboxes—obsolete status symbols of the good old days—with tiny black buzzer buttons below them. There was no monitor, not even a speaker for the visitor to identify himself.

I turned to the glass doorway and tried to catch my reflection. Sauro had dressed simply, almost somberly, usually in synthetics. For formal occasions he dressed in nicer synthetics. Cottons and wools were too expensive for a poet and West Side Marker janitor. I wanted to dress a bit more colorfully, but not too much. I wore black leather shoes, cotton slacks, a cotton shirt, and a wool jacket. I combed my hair, straightened my Beijing tie. I hoped I looked classy enough.

I searched the mailboxes for her name, then pressed the button below it. The buzzer seemed an angry reply, and I jumped to pull open the inner glass door in time. She lived on the fourth floor, and it felt like a long hike up. The lack of an elevator kept out the elderly and handicapped. Why was it always people my age who wanted contact with the past?

There was no doorbell by the door, but it didn't matter. She had been waiting for me. The thick wood door swung inward, and she smiled out at me.

It was hard to believe that men had ever turned their heads to watch her pass by. Her face was still puffy from two weeks of crying. The brightness in her eyes had burned out several weeks ago. The upturned nose now gave her a haughty, lost look. Her lips were pale. The smile wavered, uncertain. The contract gave her the option to keep me around for twenty-four hours a day, any five days of the week. I was less than delighted by the possibility.

But I regretted the thought. After all, she was dressed to make an impression. Her light blue pants and tight yellow shirt were as smooth as silk. I guessed the sandals were made from real leather. A pearl was clipped to each earlobe; a diamond pendant hung from her neck. If Tricky Dick's file on her could be trusted, Anna hadn't dressed up like this for Sauro since last January.

"Hi." She shrugged, as if she were supposed to say something more and couldn't remember what.

"Hi. I'm—"

"I know who you are, and I know why you're here."

"I'm not with the IRS."

She put on the formal, congenial smile that she told Sauro she'd inherited from her mother. "I'm sorry. I'm just not used to this. Come on in."

I offered her my own smile and slipped past her and through the doorway.

I'd seen footage of the apartment before, but I still felt as if I were walking into a place that had been made familiar in unknown, previous dreams. My dreams had been more colorful. The place looked like an old movie before a computer reprocessed the faded hues of brown, green, and white. The wood floor was unfinished, a dull brown. The wooden chairs looked uncomfortable, the tables unstable. The couch was long and upholstered in a fabric that had once been green. There wasn't a smooth line in the place; it all felt dim, colors fading into each other like an old animal fading into death.

"Would you like something?" she asked. She stood awkwardly, as if she'd forgotten what to do with her body.

I perked up, found another smile. Rule One: Never let a client think she is uninteresting. Too bad she hadn't asked an interesting question. "Juice," I replied, "if you have it."

"I'm sorry. We don't have any." Her voice began to drift off as if it were a leaf caught by a breeze. *Sauro never liked it*, was what she'd said to a commiserating friend who'd made the same request. *He said it was too bland.* The breeze stopped, and her voice fell. "I've got grapefruit juice if you want it."

My mouth puckered at the memory of its taste. "No . . . thank you. How about some water? Please."

"How about some beer?"

"Even better."

She hastily started for the kitchen before stopping and turning. "Please . . . make yourself at home. Sit down. I'll be right back." She turned and finished her awkward voyage to the kitchen. She reminded me of a holofilm about a robowaiter whose social programming had lapsed into a state of grumbling disrepair.

While glasses chimed together in the kitchen, I quickly searched the room. She had cleaned the place, of course, expecting me. Nothing was visible except the furniture—she had left no extra traces of herself in books, letters, or chairs absently misplaced. Sauro Contini's music crystals, along with a few of hers, were stacked neatly in the shelf below Sauro's stereo. Old-style bound books were arranged alphabetically by author in a shelf below the picture window. From the march of white bindings with green-printed titles, it looked like Sauro had bought the entire set of books that Americans for Social Democracy had put out about the relocation camps. Alongside the shelf were the armchair and footstool where Sauro had done most of his reading. The apartment's only computer terminal sat in the dark corner, its metal and plastic out of place among the wood floor and antiques. The model was obsolete, at least five years old.

I glanced up at the smooth one-eyed camera that hung from the ceiling corner. Sauro and Anna had joined the tenants' association to get the landlord to remove the monitoring; instead he had agreed to up the rent only 5 percent.

Anna returned with a tray that bore a plate of cheese and crackers (a brand advertised on the holovision by some out-of-work actor), a glass of beer, and a cola that looked diluted with rum.

She seemed to be regaining her poise, a protective mechanism from childhood. She sat, slapped her hands on her knees, and looked at me with a smile. This time the smile was real: it was the smile of a warm, cuddly cartoon chipmunk, but not from the kind of cartoon you'd show children. Dimples showed; eyes lighted. "Okay, Mr. Serviceman," she said. "Where do we go from here?" She wasn't drunk; that was her style. Loudness to cover the fears.

"We could go out for a drink," I said. "Maybe dinner."

"Not bed?"

"There are cheaper ways to get a bedmate, Anna."

"But none as respectable as this way."

I didn't want to take her to bed, and I doubted she wanted to go. She needed company, guaranteed companionship, not another excuse to feel guilty.

"Then why don't we go," I suggested, "and be respectable in some restaurant. It'll do you good to get out of here."

She looked relieved: finally, someone who understood her. Then the muscles on her face tightened, and she looked away from me. She must have remembered that I was being paid to do this, to fix her broken heart.

3

WE WALKED TO A nearby restaurant, the lengthening shadows and deepening chill making me nervous. I had seen too many shows on the holovision where people who moved out of the Construct met up with all sorts of danger. We passed a brownstone wall where a Hispano janitor was scrubbing away graffiti that someone had spraypainted: IF YOU HAVE NOTHING TO HIDE, YOU HAVE NOTHING TO FEAR. Below it was chiseled into the brownstone: MONITORING EATS OUR SOULS.

"Sauro inscribed that a month ago," Anna said. "The monitor on this street was out, so no one caught him."

On the corner of Bridge and West 30th was a facsimile Victorian house that, according to a plaque, was based on the design of a house built in 1895. In the house was a restaurant called Murmuring Brooks—what the wealthier Ohio City residents probably thought was a quaint name for a quaint place. The entranceway and the opposite wall were made of real wood. Above the entranceway was a single-lens monitor that was at least as old as the one in Anna's apartment. On the walls running the length of the restaurant was the holographic image of an expansive meadow; a holographic brook coursed at the level of the tabletops. The sun on the west wall was setting, casting an orange glow across the room. The sound of running water was quiet, but pervasive.

"I've always wanted to eat here," Anna said. "My father would take my aunt Lorena here for dinner whenever he came to Cleveland. Sauro and I could never really afford it." She almost lost her composure, but the maître d' arrived, and Anna became a model of social efficiency, informing the elderly man who spoke with a Middle Eastern accent that they had reserved a table for two under the name of Lawrence.

We were seated right where wood wall and murmuring brook met. The water that ran by us looked more ghostly than real. The table had been laid out with cloth napkins, a full array of silverware, including two spoons and two forks, three kinds of glasses, and an arrangement of flowers set around a lit white candle. The menus were etched into wood, and though I knew the prices would be high, I still felt a trace of shock. Anna Baxter, daughter of James Baxter and granddaughter of Harold Baxter, founder of Baxter Construction, began to worry about the meal's cost. I reminded her that she was here to enjoy herself. She looked hesitant and muttered something about how she shouldn't be spending principal. She meant her trust fund.

She cheered up a bit when she went through the menu and recommended what I should order.

Wine came, then salad, then soup. She gulped down the wine; I sipped it. "Tell me about yourself," she said.

It was a job interview; I elaborated on the story I had come up with four years ago when I had transferred from Direct Services to Leisure Services. I grew up in Cleveland Heights, went to Heights High, attended college at Cleveland State, majored in mathematics. My parents moved to San Antonio, Texas, when I was eighteen; my father was a banker; my mother was a nurse. Rule Two: Invent a past that is mostly truthful but without elements of tragedy; you are to sympathize with your client, not the other way around.

"How old are you, again?" she asked.

"Twenty-five."

"So you've been out of college for like three years." She made it sound like a long time. "How did a math major end up . . . doing . . . what you do?"

"It's a long story. I'll tell it to you sometime."

She leaned forward, eyes twinkling. "What kind of story is it? Funny? Sad? Sexy?"

"Funny," I said. In retrospect, of course. She'd think it sad and a bit too sordid for her tastes.

"Is making love with all those women sexy?"

I tried to smile as if remembering past pleasures. "Sometimes it's very sexy. And sometimes it's just a job." She was realistic enough to know that it wasn't always sexy; she was romantic enough not to want to hear all the details.

"How do you think I'll be?" She asked it in a low voice, as if she expected the answer to confirm whatever doubts had brought her to Personal Services.

I didn't know what to say. She sounded so sincere that, for a moment, I wanted to tell her the truth. "Pardon?" I said.

"How do you think I'll be? Sexy or just a job?"

"Sexy," I said.

"Would you say that if I wasn't paying you?"

"I'd more likely say that if you weren't paying me."

She shook her head. "I don't get it."

I leaned forward and took her hand. Her arm tensed, as if she were going to pull her hand away, but she changed her mind and let her fingers relax in mine. "Anna, do you want me to tell you it's just a job? It's not. I enjoy my work. I enjoy making other people happy. And I don't have to lie to do it."

"How do you know I'll be sexy, then?"

"When you smile," I said, "when you smile for real, a spontaneous smile, you're sexy."

She knew that much about herself to nod in agreement. She held my hand, and we listened to the quiet sounds of the water until dinner arrived. The room had grown dim, and a full moon was rising when the waitress, an Asian woman, brought me a steak and baked potato, and Anna swordfish and rice. The food was too rich, too spicy, as if one flavor wasn't enough for each item. We each had a half-bottle of wine: I drowned my distaste with red; Anna drowned something else with white.

"You know, with you here, I keep thinking about sex, and I keep feeling like I'm betraying Sauro."

"Don't think about sex, then. Talk about other things. After dinner we can go see a film, have a drink, go dancing.

I can then take you home, kiss you good night, and catch the rapid back to my place."

"Sort of like a date."

"Exactly."

"Except you'll never say no."

"To one or two things, I might. Now, isn't it my turn to hear your life story?"

"You know it. They gave you my file."

"Which was prepared by an artificial unintelligence. I don't know Anna Baxter according to Anna Baxter. And I'd like to hear it."

"Sure," she said. She thought for a moment while chewing on swordfish, swallowed, pursed her lips as if on the verge of saying something, then shook her head. "I don't know where to start. I've never done this before."

"Start with your childhood."

"It was awful. You don't want to hear about it."

"Sure I do."

"What do you want to hear? That I was the oldest of three daughters?"

"Sounds good."

She smiled. "I was meant to follow in my father's footsteps, being the oldest and all. I was his little girl, the apple of his eye. I was supposed to set a good example for my sisters—and for my classmates. It was like being in training. A good boarding school. An Ivy League college. Then business school. Then an important role in Baxter Construction. Build elaborate prisons for the poor and relocation camps for the hivers." She sounded like Sauro at his worst, and she must have realized it. She shook her head, poured herself some more wine. "I sound like UHL propaganda against my father."

The moon seemed to be in midair. Anna's face glowed orange in the candelight, her profile touched with the moon's silver. "My father's not that bad a person," she went on. "He means well. 'Mr. Morality in Business.'" She was quoting *Time* magazine. "He meant to be a teacher, and he was for a few years. I was just a baby then, so I don't remember anything. My father talks about it like it was the time of his life. Then Uncle Harold died—that's Harold, Junior, you know—and granddad Harold threw my father into Harvard Business School. Within fifteen years, by the time I was in boarding school, Granddad had retired and Big Daddy was running Baxter Construction.

"You know, my father probably believes I'm doing the same thing. Sowing some wild oats, unconsciously preparing for the day when I'll return to the fold. When Sauro died, all he did was send a telegram asking me to come back home. He thinks that my clitoris got the better of my judgment. That Sauro was the first guy I slept with and so I got all carried away, ran off with Sauro but left my brains behind in Boston." She shook her head. "He never knew about all the other guys I slept with. Lots of break-heart bastards. Sauro was the best thing in the world to come along. Honorable, dependable."

She shook her head, and her eyes seemed to cloud up. "That's not really true. I was the first woman *he'd* ever slept with. At first all he seemed to want was someone to teach him what to do in bed. He didn't like it that I felt so close to him right from the start. He barely talked to me the day after we first slept together." She picked up her wineglass, raised it in a toast. "Here's to believing whatever you have to believe to get to sleep at night."

I raised my glass to hers, and she leaned hers forward. The striking glass chimed.

"They must use real crystal here," Anna said.

The bill was for three thousand dollars, and Anna looked relieved when I offered the waitress my bancard. Thirty bucks shouldn't have mattered to someone with a six-million-dollar trust fund, and I realized her relief had less to do with money than with the need to have someone take care of her. But it was all an illusion. The thirty bucks would be tagged onto her bill.

I walked Anna home, the streetlamps casting more shadows than light, the real moon nowhere to be seen. Even with the wool jacket I felt a bit chilly. I looked around expecting some holovision Hispano to jump out of the shadows, knife in hand.

The wine had turned Anna soft, and a mild glow had risen to her face. She leaned against me, and I put my arm around her shoulders. We had to let go to hike up the four flights to her apartment. She hesitated at the doorway, as if she were trying to decided if she should invite me in or not.

"I'll call you tomorrow," I said.

"Thanks for listening to me blabber."

"You didn't blabber, and I was glad to listen."

She pressed her thumb against the lock, and the door unlatched. She walked in, turned, and smiled, her face framed by doorjamb and door. "Call me," she whispered, as if she might wake up someone. The door closed; the lock clicked shut. Not even a good-night kiss.

4

HARRY WASN'T WITH Kevin in the Admiral of the Port, the bar where they would normally be nursing beers, shots of dark rum, and arguments about politics. So I knew I would find him back home watching some old film on the TV. He refused to buy a holovision, complaining how little the government paid its workers. But he always smiled more sincerely when he said that old movies didn't look any good on the holovision. It was the only thing Harry and the New Puritans agreed on: holovision was terrible. It seduced us away from reality and God. And it fucked up old movies.

"There's a six-pack in the fridge," Harry called out as I hung up my wool jacket. It smelled; I had begun to sweat the instant I got off the rapid at Broadway and Harvard and headed up the corridors to Slavic Village, which was mostly government housing. Some people had stared at me in my clothes, no doubt thinking I had strayed too far from the business or pleasure neighborhoods.

"I'll bet it's a four-pack by now."

"Three-pack."

I walked into the section of the apartment we called the kitchen and pulled out a bottle from the fridge. Purchased bottles were expensive, but Harry didn't like the taste of the beer the synthesizer produced. I twisted off the top and tossed it into the disposal chute by the sink. Taking a swig, I walked over to the study, flipped on Albert Einstein, and checked for mail. Personal Services had sent several fliers about etiquette courses to be offered in May, to make sure

I knew when to say "Hello" and "How do you do." My bank had notified me of bills automatically paid. And my brother Arthur, who lived with our mother in Traverse City, Michigan, had left a message for me to call.

I then called up my access to Tricky Dick. Once he was on line, I inserted my bancard and transferred the three-thousand-dollar meal charge to Expenses and Billing. Once the transaction was completed, my card was returned. I placed my thumbs on special pads. Just after we had sat down to dinner, I had activated the implants in the balls of my thumbs in order to record Anna's skin temperature and heart rate anytime I touched her. The pads fed the data to Tricky Dick before erasing the implants' memory. I had held her hand only once—and maybe had touched bare skin five or six times—so there hadn't been much to record.

I adiosed Tricky Dick and flipped off Albert. I considered calling my brother, then I considered the liquor cabinet, which Harry had built with our friend Kevin, and decided to skip both my brother and the dark rum this evening. Beer in hand, I joined Harry in the TV room. The TV room, the study, the dining room, and the kitchen were really all one large room divided up mentally. On either side of the apartment were our tiny bedrooms, each with a tiny closet and a smaller bathroom.

"I didn't expect you home until tomorrow morning," Harry said as I sat down beside him. "Did you drop the case?"

"What film is this?" Robert Mitchum, wearing a suit rather than a trench coat, was meeting Mrs. Grayle, a woman with a smile he could feel in his hip pocket.

"You're avoiding the question."

"All you Cubanos are so nosy."

"My father wasn't a Cubano. So answer the question." Harry finished the bottle and went to the fridge for the second to last.

"I can't drop her. I told you that. Marie won't let me. She says I'm supposed to flex some new muscles."

"But you're home early." He plopped down into his chair and smiled his big toothy grin. "You didn't flex your old muscle tonight, did you?"

"I was home this early when I worked shift-janes. It's not big deal."

Robert Mitchum was now on the couch with Mrs. Grayle, kissing her. A feeble, old rich man, her husband, stumbled into the room, apologized and left. Robert Mitchum found it difficult to continue kissing Mrs. Grayle.

"Did you even kiss a little?"

"It takes time to get things going. You know that. If they were hot and heavy lovers, they wouldn't be hiring me."

"That's for sure." Harry finished his beer. "Do you want me to save the last one for you?"

"You can have it."

Harry returned with the last beer. We watched a bit more. During the commercial he plucked at my shirtsleeve. "I guess you can learn to like clothes like this. I guess I'd like them if they didn't cost so much." He sipped his beer. "I take it you might want to see the file on her ex?"

"You sure that's a good idea?" Last December, Monitoring Services had hired an ex–army man as their antiterrorist consultant. Since the Kansas City Black Out last month, he'd gotten Monitoring to tighten up some of its regulations about public access to Monitoring files.

"I think it's a great idea," Harry said. At a certain point in the evening, Harry's generosity grew geometrically with each drink.

"The guy's dead. I can get a big chunk of his file through regular channels."

"You won't get much. Right-to-privacy laws still apply to those in the file who are living. Let me get you the file tomorrow."

Although Harry had never told any of us, we all knew that he'd been skipped over for a promotion back in January. Our friend Kevin, who lived across the corridor and worked at Waste Management, had heard it from an ex-lover of his who worked at Monitoring ("and you're not hearing a word I'm saying," Kevin had declared). The antiterrorist consultant was a New Puritan and had found out about Harry's past; he had lost out on the promotion on moral grounds. When Harry had graduated from college he went on to teach for two years before going on to law school. His first year he'd fallen in love with one of the senior girls.

"You're not curious about this Italiano guy," he said.

"Yeah, of course."

"Her file's thin." Harry had watched some of the footage with me. Tricky Dick was good at preserving the sex scenes intact. "You need to know more about her. It's not going to be like the shift-janes. You won't be able to fake it with this one."

"It's not worth getting you in trouble."

"Hey, what are fellow bureaucrats for?"

I was too curious to say no. "Do we want to get lunch tomorrow?"

"Sure. I can give you a copy of the file then. Where do you want to go?"

"Have to go someplace where they take a govcard," I said. "Can't afford much else."

"Not if you keep Baxter as a client."

"Still don't get paid until the end of the month."

"Cleveland Cafeteria then?"

"Sure." I finished my beer and went to the liquor cabinet.

"By the way," Harry called out, "your brother called."

"I'll call him tomorrow."

"That's what you said last time."

I ignored him and poured a shot of dark rum. I raised it in a toast to the bug-eyed camera that hung from the nearby ceiling corner. It captured all our movements and words from the various angles of its complex lens, and Monitoring's AI decided what to file, what to erase. Harry had told me he edited out the footage of these conversations, but I couldn't help but wonder if they'd known for two years that Harry had been letting me go through nonclient files. It saved the hassle of filling out a large form declaring that so-and-so's file would help in the service of such-and-such a client, plus the extra hassle of only receiving the information that is allowable under the Public Right to Know Act.

What the hell, I thought, Harry and I both work for the government.

On the news that night they announced that Paul Flower, Director of Research at Greater Kansas City Monitoring Services, and one of the suspected ringleaders responsible for blacking out Kansas City five weeks ago, was found today in his apartment, dangling from the end of a rope.

"I guess he was hanging out with the wrong people," I said.

"Yeah," said Harry. "Like the police."

"I guess you could say someone nipped that Flower in the bud."

"You harvest what you sow."

We both had had enough to drink to think we were funny.

"*I guess I had* a little too much last night," Harry said to me at lunch the next day. He was talking a bit loudly because the place was filled with other bureaucrats.

"No. You were your usual kindly self." The macaroni and cheese tasted like paper, the coffee like flavored water. The rice and beans on Harry's plate looked like something organically recycled.

"Before you got home, Kevin and I were in the Admiral, throwing back shots of dark rum." Harry sipped his milk. "Betsy thinks she's pregnant again. Kevin went out and bought a mitt."

"He should have bought a soccer ball." You can play soccer in the corridors. You have to leave the Construct and walk through a local shackville until you find a big-enough playing field for real baseball; or you can take the rapid to Euclid and East 40th to play in the city's only large public park.

"Who knows?" Harry said. "Maybe they'll build bigger parks."

"You should have taken some Hangon last night." Hangon, went the ad, and don't hangover.

"I don't like Hangon. Or taking aspirin and lots of water. It defeats the purpose of a hangover, which is to remind you that you drank too much the night before. That way, if you're smart . . ."

". . . you'll drink less for a while," I said, finishing the monthly lecture.

"That's right. And drinking too much can make me forgetful. I made you a promise I can't keep."

For a moment I couldn't remember what promise Harry might have made. "You forgot the file."

"I can't bring the file. They upped the classification. The file can't be removed from the premises. I had looked at the file yesterday, you know, curiosity and all, but I forgot about the security change."

"What security change?"

"Watch my lips: they upped the classification."

"On Contini's file?"

"Did we change the subject, or were we not talking about Mr. Italiano?"

"What for?" I asked.

"Who knows. My guess is it's the work of our antiterrorist consultant. The one who was such a big deal during the Spanish War."

"The guy with a bug up his ass?"

"That's the one. Edward," said Harry slowly, as if swearing carefully, considering a new word for asshole, "Lang. He's the type who looks under his bed for hivers and terrorists. Actually, he probably thinks they're one and the same."

"Contini wasn't a terrorist," I said. "As far as I could tell, he had enough trouble being a radical."

"He was in the Close the Camps Campaign. Everyone who's signed a petition is probably classified. I'll give you odds that Lang thinks they all turned terrorist."

"Maybe it's for the best," I said. "It sort of felt like cheating, you know, looking at these extra files."

"It's bullshit is what it is. The Cleveland Construct is so haphazardly built that no one is going to black out the entire city. Not like they did in Kansas."

"I can live without the info."

"Don't worry. I'll get you in. Lang usually spends his afternoon hours out of the office. I'll sign up for an examination room and bring you in for your own private viewing."

"I don't want to get you in any trouble."

"Why not? Don't you want to see how this guy ran her programming? I'm not you, but I'd just stop and think about it. Mr. Italiano has no ambition to be a doctor, lawyer, or Indian chief, but he gets this woman. He wants to close down the hiver camps, and he starts sleeping with the daughter of the man who built them. Then he gets depressed and jumps off a roof. I'd like to know just what this guy was like. You know, in the name of human curiosity."

I called Anna to arrange a meeting for this evening. Her phone chirped like some tropical bird; a recorded Anna didn't come on-screen to take a message. I flipped on Albert Einstein, called up both the U.S. Postal Service and Tricky Dick, and sent a message to 2830 Bridge, Apartment 41, that I would be honored to have Anna Baxter accompany me to dinner and that I would pick her up at six o'clock, if that was convenient. Actually, I had written something simpler; Tricky Dick's etiquette program formalized it.

Not knowing if Anna would be honored or not, I considered taking the afternoon off and shooting hoops down at the Personal Services' gym. Instead I opened the drawer where I had placed the packet containing Anna's file.

I inserted the first crystal and went through it again. First, there were the Basics. Anna Elizabeth Baxter, born twenty-three years ago this past March 15, a social-security number, a draft-registration number, a B.A. in Economics, current employment at Mutangi's Art Gallery in Cleveland Heights.

At a glance, the first crystal—everything from Anna's birth to Sauro's death—had as much footage as the files of most of my shift-janes. But most shift-janes hadn't been involved in the kind of things that gets footage filed for posterity. Tricky Dick's programming had edited out a lot, or other monitoring AI's had filed little on Anna Baxter.

There weren't too many scenes from her youth. She had grown up in Newton, outside of Boston, in an environment that was largely unmonitored. Starting with first grade, she spent weekdays at a local boarding school. When she was fourteen, she went to a boarding school in New Hampshire that also had little monitoring. Same went for her college in New Hampshire, one that was prestigious enough to get most monitored events erased.

Her college life had gone largely unrecorded. There was no evidence of her collegiate break-heart bastards, and there was hardly any indication that she had slept with Sauro. There had been no monitors in any of the dorms, just in the fraternities due to some line-em-up fucks that may have been gang rapes (and these students are the best and the brightest?).

I jumped to documentation to learn that during her senior spring she had interviewed with three business schools, four businesses, and the CIA recruiter, but she had filled out no applications and had taken no tests. There was no documentation of when she had joined Americans for Social Democracy. In the footage there were three sequences of Sauro and Anna walking hand in hand to public ASD meetings. There was a shot of them sitting in the back of a conference room, glancing at each other, Anna's face flushed, Sauro looking embarrassed, both their minds obviously on another kind of politics.

In a flash of insight rare for Tricky Dick, Anna's file included footage of Anna after her graduation exercises, in what looked like a hockey arena: metal chairs where the ice should have been were disarrayed, and kids in robes were filing away with their parents. Anna held her cap in her hands and kept her eyes on her father.

James Baxter, built much like his daughter, but with the layer of flab and the pudgy cheeks of a former athlete who had no more time for exercise, shook his head as if he'd been slapped. She must have just told him that she was going to Cleveland. Papa Baxter was saying, "I was worried that this would come about. I had hoped you'd reach the right decision. I had always thought you had more control over your desires. I had thought you could truly identify your destiny and work toward it."

The next sequence showed Sauro and Anna in Cleveland, but there wasn't too much to look at, which was odd since their living room was monitored. I had to consult a chronology Tricky Dick had prepared to find out that they'd come to Cleveland a day after graduation, that Anna had stayed with her aunt Lorena, Sauro with his parents. There wasn't even footage of them moving into the apartment: the way they had handled that chore would have told me a lot about their relationship and about Anna.

Fortunately Tricky Dick had included some footage of Anna alone: Anna having lunch with her aunt Lorena Smith, Anna working as a clerk at the small art gallery, Anna organizing the food and drink at a monitored ASD gathering. There was some ASD stuff the two did together, but I fast-forwarded through that.

After watching all the footage for the second time, I still couldn't see why she was with him. Sulky when on the edge of things, animated—face alive, hands slicing air—when discussing ideas, opening a book, or writing a poem, he was so different from Anna: alertly listening, eyes twinkling, engaged, taking people by the arm to include them in the conversation. Her presence could be felt on the screen; some quality that held the eye was caught by the monitor, recorded for posterity.

For my job, of course, Tricky Dick had preserved the fuck footage, but there wasn't too much of that, either. I had forty-five seconds of them at a friend's apartment in downtown Boston, but Anna had turned off the lights so the monitor wouldn't see. The only apartment footage was of the few times they had screwed in the living room, in view of the monitor. Still, I knew more about how they fucked than why they did.

In November things between them started to fall apart. The Supreme Court had ruled that shipping hivers off to camps was constitutional. I remembered how the papers had declared that ASD was at the end of its rope. Sauro and Anna bickered more than touched. I had a shot of her hesitating before she kissed him. In January, when all they argued about was the newly formed Union for Human Liberation and the acceptability of violence, et cetera, as a political tool, Sauro began to look as if he were at the end of his own rope. He slouched around the apartment. His face was always downcast. He talked with his hands in his lap or, when standing, in his pockets. He touched Anna tentatively, as if his fingertips were electrically charged. There was no fuck footage dated after January 9. On February 23, Sauro demanded to know why their love life was in such a shambles. Anna demanded to know why he was so concerned with sex when everything they dreamed about was falling apart, everything she sacrificed, all for nothing. On March 5 Anna told him that she didn't like sex anymore, that she never really had.

Something about her confession depressed me, so I returned to the documentation. Symbols, percentages, and pyschobabble lifted from school aptitude tests told me Anna was intelligent and talented: could sing well, dance well, liked to act, high percentile ratings for spatial arrangement and math computation. And so what? It didn't tell me why she had loved Sauro, why she had slept with him, why she had stopped, why she had hired a servicer if she disliked sex.

I was used to shift-janes. You saw them several times a week for four hours per visit. I dressed the way everybody dressed, I found out topics of "mutual" interest to research so I'd sound compatible. I'd avoid major dislikes. For those who were having sexual problems, I had been trained in all the techniques and questions to get them more comfortable with their own pleasure. I was good at keeping the talk centered on the jane, to shift the conversation to her abilities, her accomplishments, her attractiveness, until it was all nothing more nor less than romanticized fucking with lots of talk.

Anna needed something different, but I didn't know what. All I could do was continue as I'd planned. I'd dress like Sauro refused to. I'd speak carefully and sanely: I'd make no sweeping pronouncements the way Sauro did. I wouldn't moralize the way her father was famous for. I'd listen, the way she felt neither man had. I'd offer little advice. I'd keep sex on the back burner, because she'd made a big deal that men thought only with their penises (she had stoutly denied that her mind had ever jumped into a correspondingly small place of her anatomy), but I would offer all sorts of offhand comments that made her sound sexy, because she worried too much that she wasn't. And for as long as she felt that she was betraying Sauro, I'd make sure we just talked. That way we'd never have to spend the whole night together. Once we got past the talk and her sense of guilt, we could get into some romanticized fucking, go dancing, go to some of the cultural events she liked, and wrap up the whole thing as something very sweet, but something that someone with her breeding would end. In the end, I hoped, it would be just as easy as the shift-janes. A bit more research, a few more hours, but it wouldn't be all that difficult. Besides, I thought, if I handled this well, it could open up all sorts of possibilities.

The idea depressed me. Nobody liked the horses who trotted their wares through the Heights. Whenever they reported in downtown, they were arrogant, talked as if they had eaten a dictionary or two too many, got picky about their food and who they hung out with. I didn't want to be like them.

There was still no answer at Anna's, so I went to the Personal Services gym to work off the feeling. I lifted for a bit, then swam a mile in the pool. The water felt heavy, and swimming seemed like too much of an effort. It was as if something were nagging at me, pulling at my thoughts.

Anna Baxter, I thought, didn't *want* romanticized fucking. Maybe, I thought later, she didn't want anything at all.

Our apartment door and three others were arranged in something of a circle, divided by a corridor, so that the four doors roughly faced each other. Maureen from across the corridor invited everyone over for a beer or two before she and Maggie went out to celebrate their third wedding anniversary. I was about to accept when Anna called. If I was still available, she would enjoy accompanying me to dinner. On the vid she was Ms. Congeniality, acting as if we were setting up a business lunch. Sauro had accused her of deep down being Daddy's little girl; on the vid she was.

Maureen frowned. Harry assured her I'd make it up to both her and Maggie. After I had changed into a coat and tie and before I left, Harry playfully punched me in the arm. "Maybe you'll get to flex the muscle tonight," he said.

5

ANNA WAS WEARING a loose dress that had been popular five years ago when Americans for Social Democracy was promoting a cross-cultural renaissance. The dress was colorful and faded; it looked foreign, but not distinctive enough that you could tell what country it came from.

"Sauro gave it to me," Anna told me as we walked to a different restaurant. "About two months after we first slept together. My parents hated it when I wore it at home. This kind of dress had pretty much gone out of style, and most people thought of ASD when they saw it. I think it was like half a year before I joined."

The Appletree was a tiny restaurant overlooking Lake Erie. This one was all wood, no technical wizardry, and the menu was printed on paper. Again, the reservations were under Lawrence, a table for two in the far corner. Anna ordered curried chicken; I ordered the normal kind. We agreed on beer for us both. She ordered Bass Ale; I ordered a Thirty-Three.

"You haven't asked me why I put reservations in your name."

I should have asked, even though I knew the answer. "So I'd know I was eating here too?"

"You're being silly."

"Then I don't know why. I'm not very good with small details."

"Most of the men in my life don't seem to be. I think that's why my father married my mother; he'd found someone to take care of the small details." She sounded bitter.

"Then why the reservations?"

She blushed. She wanted to tell me, but then again she didn't. "You know who Mary Hasselbacher is?"

"Sure. A columnist for the *Plain Dealer*."

"She made a big deal about me coming to this town. My aunt—Lorena Smith"—she dropped the name as if it were important; among certain circles it was—"called in to complain that the column was so outrageous. Hasselbacher wrote that I was living with a janitor who worked at the West Side Market. She didn't mention that Sauro wrote poetry, or that he was with ASD, or that he had been a national-merit scholar, that he'd graduated magna cum laude—that, in fact, he'd graduated from the same Ivy League college I did. She didn't mention anything like that. I think my father subscribed to the *PD* and had his computer call his attention to any articles that mentioned me or Sauro. Because right away I got a letter from my mother asking me to come home and patch things up. Then, on top of that, Mary Hasselbacher finds out that I was signed up on a bus to go out west to show solidarity with the rioters in Camp Seven. . . ."

Even though I'd skipped over political stuff in her file, I would have remembered a bus trip out west, especially one to join the riots. Until we'd seen the pictures of the dead from the Kansas City Black Out, our minds carried the news images of the National Guard firing tear gas into the crowds, of hivers and protesters being separated, of protesters placed in quarantine. "Did you go?" I asked. I half wanted her to say yes.

She shook her head and looked disappointed. "Sauro got sick. I stayed home with him." She must not have liked the topic, because she changed it immediately. "Anyway, Mary Hasselbacher's column says I went, and I got a letter from my sister Susan. Susan usually would write these really bland letters, but this one was different. I think my dad dictated it. Or maybe my mom. It was a bit more emotional than logical. My dad gets emotional when you talk about Ethics, or Morality, or Faith, or any big noun you might want to capitalize. My mom gets emotional when her kids get in trouble."

"What did the letter say?"

"Oh, just how lucky I was not to be dead or in quarantine until they found out if I had hives or not. I should reconsider what I was doing and who I was involved with and maybe I should come home. . . . Then when ASD broke up, Hasselbacher called to find out how James Baxter's rebellious daughter felt. When the UHL said it'd use any means necessary to close the camps, she called me up. When Sauro died . . . you get the point, don't you?"

"Yeah. Your dad likes to be in the news. You don't."

She looked wounded. If I'd been Sauro, it would have become an issue, but because this was our second evening together she said, "Yeah. That's pretty much it."

"Since you don't want to be in the paper, how'd you like to go dancing?"

Her face lit up. She sat up straight in her chair and leaned forward. "I'd love to." Second thoughts pulled her back into her chair. "But I don't think it's a good idea. Someone might recognize me."

"Are you being paranoid, or are you that important?"

"You have a way of taking my biggest fears and making them seem real tiny." She smiled against her will. "I should mind that, but I sort of like it."

"You don't have to. They are your fears, and that makes them valid." That was a stock line from training; people liked hearing it.

"Maybe, maybe not. I'm still responsible for my actions, just like everybody else, but I don't want to hear anybody's opinion about any of this. I don't want to hear how I'm surrendering in the face of life's challenges."

"You're not surrendering. You're taking a vacation."

She smiled again, but this time it was for real. "I like that. I'm taking a vacation." She looked me directly in the eyes. I almost felt as if we were playing emotional chicken, seeing who'd look away first. I did. She asked, "Do you plan on making sure I enjoy the vacation?"

"Of course."

"And will I return home safely?"

"You bet."

"Do you think the waitress will bring our food before I die of hunger?"

"I have a feeling we'll go hungry for a bit longer."

"So much for a perfect vacation."

"No one promised a perfect vacation," I said. "I just promised that you'd enjoy it."

"And that it'll be safe."

"As safe as they come."

After walking Anna home from dinner and taking the rapid back to the Construct, the alcohol from the after-dinner drinks settling into my system, I met Harry and Kevin in the Admiral of the Port to drink some more. Harry was drinking beer and trying to fill me in on Maureen and Maggie's impromptu anniversary and their subsequent fight. Kevin was still going at the dark rum; Betsy still hadn't taken a pregnancy test. Kevin told us how he'd bought a portable generator and some oxygen masks just in case terrorists blacked out Cleveland like they did to Kansas City last month. Before either of us could get a word in edgewise, Kevin went on about how he didn't want to raise a son in the Construct, not anymore, and how there'd never be enough money to buy a real house, not with the salary he made working for Waste Management. Maybe, he thought, he'd go into one of the oxygen forests, cut down some of the trees, build himself a house for Betsy and the kid. If he went far enough in, no one would ever know.

Before Kevin could start in about building a boat and sailing the Caribbean, I headed home. I called up Anna's file, along with index and cross-references. I searched for anything Anna might have said about ASD, UHL, the Camps, or hivers. I found the related *PD* articles. There was ten seconds of footage of her at a rally in Public Square. There were three five-second shots at the train station; I presumed she was offering moral support to some hivers being shipped out to a camp. There were a few minutes of her serving food at a buffet fund-raiser: she was dressed up, smiling and chatting with the people in line as they stepped forward to be served. It wasn't much, and politics had been a big part of Anna and Sauro's life together. There should have been more.

I considered calling up Tricky Dick and asking him to contact some other AIs, but it didn't seem worth the time or the money. Since politics had no bearing on the relationship, I couldn't yet justify the expense. I didn't want to pay for footage that might not tell me much more than the *PD*. Besides, Anna Baxter's politics were her problem; if they were bad politics, then they were Monitoring's problem, not mine.

I still had trouble going to sleep.

6

THE HEADQUARTERS FOR Cuyahoga County Monitoring Services was located in the Terminal Tower, the would-be center, and now the heart and mind of the metropolitan area. Sauro had told Anna that the Terminal Tower, an engineering feat in its time, had been built upon quicksand. Every year, in spite of reinforcements in the foundation, the Tower was sliding bit by bit into the quicksand beneath it. Sauro had thought that was a powerful metaphor.

I met Harry in open-air Public Square after lunch, and he took me up to the thirtieth floor. From the windows you could see the Construct radiate outward, like the bent spikes of a twisted half wheel. Each spoke was a long line of concrete, brick, and (where people could afford it) glass, all in blocks, tunnels, domes, newer concrete structures mixed in with old brick buildings and stone buildings and glass and steel buildings, almost all of it from the last century. The spokes spread out irregularly, following what had been the main arteries of traffic: Ontario, Superior, Chester, Euclid, Prospect, Carnegie, and Broadway. In the distance mini-Constructs could be seen, and eventually their haphazard structures would be clipped on like dangling modifiers to a long, awkward sentence.

The Construct hadn't extended over the Cuyahoga River, which split east side from west side. Much of the west side had been torn down, cleared for corporate farming and replanted forests. Its population had left homes for free housing and several years of reduced taxes.

From where I stood, you really couldn't see the small clusters of shackvilles that clung to the edges of the Construct like barnacles. They just melded into the landscape.

A secretary who recognized me from previous visits joked with me while Harry logged in my presence. The secretary had recently seen *Truest Love,* and he wondered if I had yet found the true love who would turn me straight. I told the straight that Harry was my secret true love.

"And you never even told me," said Harry, and he led me to a small cubicle.

Harry sat me down, and leaned over to call up the Contini file. Adolf asked for Harry's security clearance and password; Harry typed it in. Contini's face and several lines of the Basics flashed onto the screen. "He's all yours," said Harry.

"Are you sure about this?"

"It's good of you to ask *after* I used my password." Harry smiled. "Look. Lang's out of the office. If Contini was that important, I wouldn't be able to call up the file. And besides, would your one true love get you in trouble? How much time do you want?"

I checked the table of contents. The file was fat. There was no way I'd get through it all. "Give me two hours."

Harry flipped a switch and reminded me that a red DO NOT DISTURB sign had lit up on the other side of the door. Harry left, and the door's lock clicked into place. I took out my ChemKit, and found two K-pills. The amphetamine derivative would help me focus on the material and get through it faster.

The Basics. Sauro Frederico Contini was deceased by his own hand at age twenty-three on April 1 of this year. No kidding. He had a social-security number, a draft-registration number, a B.A. in political science, employed by the West Side Market as a janitor. Baptized a Catholic; declared religion at age eighteen: atheist. He had registered as a Democrat at age eighteen, then as a Pluralist at age twenty. Just after that election he joined the Americans for Social Democracy. It was unknown if he'd become a member of the Union for Human Liberation. His whereabouts on March 15 were unknown.

I'd never seen a file like this before. I'd never read a Basics that included religious and political information. Important dates were birthdays and, if any, important anniversaries. March 15 felt like an important date, but all I could remember was that it was Anna's birthday.

I called up Sauro's life summary. He was born in Little Italy. His father ran a dessert shop; his mother was an office worker. They both campaigned against Little Italy's incorporation into the University Circle mini-Construct, an odd fact for Contini's life summary to highlight with dates and details.

At elementary school Contini scored well on the Otis Lennon IQ, usually doing better with English expression than math. His school adviser wrote letters home suggesting that Suaro was acting out some problems and that he perhaps should receive professional treatment. There was no record of such treatment.

In high school, people seemed to see a different Sauro. His academic reports were glowing. His sophmore year adviser worried that Sauro was too introspective. Two years later the same adviser addressed a letter to Sauro congratulating him on his acceptence to a prestigious college and suggesting that Sauro take advantage of the opportunity to take risks and try new things.

I wondered if Anna gave Sauro the same advice. They had gotten together sometime during the Spring of their junior year, and it was then that Sauro joined the college paper and had a poem published in the college *Quarterly*. The file included articles by Sauro, but they only seemed to be ones that dealt with ASD activities on campus, about aid raised for New Palestinian refugees, and medical supplies collected and sent to one of the hiver camps in Utah.

There was some footage of Sauro in restaurant or bar or dining hall conversations with ASD buddies—enough to give the gist of the conversation and for the viewer to read names of the participants in the tiny white letters superimposed on the screen. When he had similar conversations with Anna, the New Hampshire AI filed away even more footage—it was as if the AI had been programmed to take a college student's pontifications on politics and love seriously. I listened to Sauro talk to her about the camps her father had built, about monitoring and the information panopticon, about human rights. Sauro's enthusiasm imbued him with a real presence on the screen; Anna was intimidated by his lectures and jokes. But several filed conversations later—who knows how many went on in the unmonitored dormitories where they were probably sleeping together—Anna started rising to the challenge, countering with her father's arguments about the individual's self-discipline, about the rights of society, the cost of necessary human progress. Finally, there was an Anna with a screen presence to match Sauro's, raising her hand as if to stop Sauro's flow of words, interrupting with new ideas, until they were discussing Jefferson and civil liberties, listing wrongdoings by the CIA abroad and the FBI at home, discussing if protesters had the right to employ violence, all this leading to talk about society and the role of the family, the role of love, the purpose of sex, social context, and personal content. It all started to sound like a class, and I'd forgotten my shovel.

Anna's energy was something new. It wasn't the energy of playing a new kind of role. It was instead something from deep enough inside that Anna must have felt she had come in contact with a part of herself she'd lost somewhere along the path to being Daddy's little girl.

The file cut to a spacious office where Anna was speaking with a woman in a business suit. The white letters across the bottom of the screen told me it was a recruitment interview with some multinational out of Beijing. This should have been in Anna's file. I hit the fast forward. Another interviewer. I called up the contents: all three business schools and four business interviews were there, plus the interview with the CIA recruiter. The inclusion of all this in Sauro's file didn't make any sense until what followed two hours after the CIA interview when Anna and Sauro had dinner at a local restaurant. Sauro, hands unsteady, his voice wavering, demanded to know why she was doing all this interviewing if she was going to come live with him in Cleveland. Worst of all, how could she interview with the CIA, knowing what she knew about them? He started to list atrocities in Spain, in New Palestine, in Pakistan.

"The CIA couldn't have done all of that," Anna said.

"Is this where we start talking about your uncle Ed?"

"He wasn't in the CIA. He was in the army."

"Sure. Fighting for the Spaniards' right to live like Americans."

She shook her head and looked down at her plate. I don't think she knew why she had gone to the interviews. The recruiters, even the CIA man, all had asked her if she planned to eventually work at Baxter Construction.

"Well, I don't want to hear about Uncle Ed. You know what kind of stuff he did in Spain. You know what kind of things they're willing to do to anyone they think's the enemy. If you really want to be with them, why don't you hire on as an informant and come to our meetings with all sorts of new equipment?" With a careless wave of his hand, he knocked over his glass of beer.

I glanced at my watch, realized I had twenty minutes left before Harry returned.

I called up the contents page and jumped forward to their arrival in Cleveland. The table of contents gave me no idea what I wanted to look for. I'd seen so much that everything had stopped making sense. I got glimpses of Sauro in his parents' flat located in the University Circle mini-Construct, which had now engulfed Little Italy. He wondered aloud how his mother could stand to be monitored, while his father leaned back in his chair and looked like Sauro's energy exhausted him. Sauro was talking about the information panopticon when I fast-forwarded. Anna and Sauro, infrared shot, in Sauro's bed saying something about the Fourth Amendment and monitoring. *Fast Forward*. Anna and Sauro standing in the empty room of what was soon to be their apartment. Anna was staring straight at the monitor. "Every apartment we can afford has at least one," she said. "I don't want to live in a place with monitors," Sauro said. "It's just one," said Anna, "and it's not in the bedroom." *Fast Forward*. Sauro with one ASD buddy who looked a bit older and wore a leather jacket. They were talking due process and hiver camps. *Fast*

Forward. Sauro and an old woman wondering how all the information filed and stored by the AI could ever mean anything, so much of it and edited together by programs that made human intuition look like rational genius. *Fast Forward.* And more *Fast* ASD buddies of all different *Forward* shapes sizes clothes cultures—what made Sauro so important?—and I had only a few minutes left while I watched—furniture was moved into the apartment, and Sauro gave the monitor the finger—and I couldn't have cared less about ASD and privacy and hivers and all their talk about monitors, and I just remembered that I'd wanted to watch them move into their apartment and learn the secret of their relationship, and it was too late, so why not just adios the file, when the next image was of Sauro atop Anna.

They were kissing, their clothes still on, their bodies awkwardly embracing on the too-small pale green couch in their apartment. Sauro had his hands wrapped around Anna's shoulders; Anna had her hands clasped together on the small of his back. Their eyes were shut, and the kiss lasted forever. The distant angle of the lens, the static quality of the shot, made the scene look like something out of an old porn film they had shown us during a training course on sexual history. Now, Sauro had propped himself up on his elbows and began to unbutton Anna's shirt.

"Let's go to the bedroom," Anna said. Her voice was hazy, like she was sleepy. It was the way she seemed to talk in any footage of her sexual activity. Rather than yawn, Sauro kissed her.

"Let's stay here. A couch isn't truly a couch until two lovers have used it."

Anna looked directly at the monitor. I felt like she knew I'd be watching. "I feel like there's someone spying on us."

"All that stuff gets erased."

"Hypocrite. Monitors eat our souls. So let's bare our souls in the bedroom." She kissed him while another hand reached toward his pants. "And other things, too."

"Plenty of people make love in front of monitors."

"I think you're turned on by the idea." I couldn't tell if she was excited or disgusted.

The lock in the door clicked. I almost jumped in my

seat. It was Harry. "I could count on you to find the good parts."

Whatever Sauro had said, it convinced her. The couch seemed too thin for undressing, but they managed.

"I need a little more time," I said.

"Love to give it to you, but Lang's due back soon."

"There's more I'd like to see."

"I bet."

"I want to watch," I heard Anna say. I turned to the screen. Sauro pushed himself up until his arms were straight, elbows locked. Anna raised her head, and Sauro lowered his until foreheads touched. They both seemed to be watching Sauro's penis as it slid down, rose up. "Stop," she said, and Sauro's body stiffened. His body from knees to shoulder rose at a perfect angle. For a moment I couldn't tell if the penis between Sauro and Anna belonged to either one. Anna tilted her head back, raised herself up on her elbows so her lips would meet Sauro's. He suddenly collapsed into her arms.

"Nothing like a little high drama," said Harry.

"You didn't hear all the political arguments," I said. I pointed at the screen. The date of the footage was July 2. "They've just moved into their apartment. There's a lot I haven't seen."

"I'll try to get you back in here. But it would be nice if you were gone before Lang got back. He's the only one who works here who gives two shits about outsiders looking at the files."

"I love you," said Anna.

Harry adiosed the file; the screen went dead. "I love you, too," said Harry.

The secretary winked at me when I left. I almost turned to say something, but Harry grabbed my elbow, ushered me onto the elevator. "Don't worry. Richard there thinks that everyone is lining up to fall in love with him."

"Tell him to hire a servicer," I said. "That way he'll get some positive feedback for his winks."

"Richard doesn't like make-believe. He's thinking of becoming a New Puritan."

7

ANNA AND I met for dinner every night that week, and I could feel the sexual tension build within her. In the way she would lean forward when talking about something sexy; in the greater generosity of her smiles and the reemergence of the radiance that turned heads; but also in the way she would pull away and hold her body rigid, as if rejecting everything warm she was feeling, I got the sense of one Anna, who desired everything our contract suggested, struggling with another Anna, who rejected the easy sexuality and its ten-thousand-dollar-a-day drain on her trust fund.

But you saw none of that in the dailies. The restaurants, legally defined as privately owned public spaces, were monitored, but private ownership allowed the owners to have the minimum one monitor with an out-of-date single-lens device. So when I reviewed each outing the following afternoon—after Monitoring's AI, Adolf, had transferred the preedited footage to Tricky Dick and Tricky Dick had edited and refined it for my use—all I could see of Anna, if I could see her at all, was the back of her head.

So Tricky Dick could never confirm the tension I was sure I felt building within her. Most of my touches were too casual to make any evaluations based on skin temperature and moisture or heart rate. Audio clarification let me rehear everything we said, but she controlled her voice with the skill of an actor, and never once did Tricky Dick register anxiety or desire.

Because we were docked 5 percent of our pay if we didn't go through all the dailies at least once, I went through the five-minute summaries of Anna's day, and there wasn't much there or in the accompanying footage to tell me a lot. She usually spent mornings in her apartment reading one of the bound books or listening to music. Day after day she listened to less of Sauro's jazz and to more of the music she liked: show tunes from Chicago theater; Mozart and Bach; newharp arrangements that Sauro had liked to call beautiful-woman-without-a-personality music. She had stopped reading Sauro's poetry with a glass of Scotch in hand, and by the end of the week she had stopped reading his poetry altogether.

That is, if Tricky Dick was accurately evaluating and editing the footage. Anna usually met someone for lunch, but sometimes I got footage of her lunch partner—her friend Joan from the gallery talking about her new boyfriend; her Cleveland Heights friend talking about theater—and sometimes I just got a shot of her entering the restaurant. If Anna talked about love, sex, or me, Tricky Dick hadn't saved it for the file. Tricky Dick didn't bother to tell me what she did Tuesday afternoon, but every afternoon after that she went to the cinema to see a new holofilm, including, of course, *Truest Love*.

Knowing that she was gaining control of her life, sensing the tension within her, I plotted out each evening, selecting the clothes, deciding how energetic or plain I would be, choosing in advance possible topics for discussion, evaluating when, how often, and under what conditions I should touch her hand or hold it or reach across the table to place my fingers against a cheek. And it was just as likely that Anna plotted in advance how daring or demure she wanted to be with the servicer who, unlike all the other men she'd been with, didn't have the option to reject her overtures or to refuse to speak with her the next day.

She plotted in other ways, too. Each evening she selected a small, discrete restaurant west of the Cuyahoga, away from updated monitors and her friends. Anna always made the reservations in my name, asked in advance that we be seated at a corner table or booth, and never once objected when I paid the check with my bancard. This way neither friends nor Mary Hasselbacher would know about what Anna was up to or with whom. I tried not to smile at her caution or to make jokes about it. She took her machinations as seriously as a terrorist getting around in a monitored city.

And she felt just as obvious. "Do all these arrangements seem a bit silly to you?" she asked Wednesday evening after the waitress had taken our drink order to the bar.

I shrugged. "Excessive, yes; silly, no."

"You know what a panopticon is, don't you?"

"I've heard the word."

"Probably in the file they gave you of me," she said. She must have heard the bitterness in her voice because she forced a smile. "You know, Sauro used that word so much, that you must have heard it once or twice."

"Your file's not *that* big. Remember, I did go to school."

"Okay. So you know what it means. Wouldn't you say then that monitoring turns our society into a panopticon of sorts? People can look around and see everything, make sure we're doing the right thing, keep records of us, keep tabs. It's like a big glass building, with people in the center keeping an eye on all of us."

"It's a little clumsier than that."

"Then how is it that Mary Hasselbacher found out so easily what I was up to? How did my father get his information about me?"

"Four hundred years ago," I said, "there was the town gossip. Think of everything you've done now that you wouldn't have been able to do then. Think of what they would have called you."

"Don't say that word." She sounded as if her inner ear had heard it often enough.

"I'm not in a position to."

She drank some of her beer and looked at me for a while. I smiled. She drank more of her beer.

"I must be boring you."

"No," I said.

"I must sound like a monologue in a play. I have a friend who's an actor. She was my drama teacher in college.

If she hadn't moved here to be with the Cleveland Playhouse, I might have been more hesitant about coming out here with Sauro. I talked to her last night, and I told her all about you and what I'd been saying. She said I must have been boring. Unless of course I delivered my lines perfectly."

"You weren't performing," I said. "You were talking."

"But were you performing?"

"No." What else was I supposed to say?

After several stories of the tension headaches she would get whenever she visited her family, she told me I reminded her of Sauro. When they were first getting together, he'd listen a lot, making Anna feel good about herself. "I'm worried that the more I talk about myself, the more my chatter gives me away. I feel like nothing more than a spoiled, egocentric child who talks about rebellion more than rebelling."

"You left your family and moved out here, didn't you? I'm sure your father wasn't pleased."

"Is that what it says in your file of me?"

"No, it's what you talked about the past two nights while you drank all that wine."

She blushed. "I did drink a lot of wine, didn't I?"

She wanted to talk about Sauro, but at first seemed embarrassed, as if she were a widow talking too much about her dead husband to a prospective mate. She quickly overcame her reluctance, even taking offense when I referred to him as Contini.

"His name was Sauro."

I repeated it.

"No—it's not pronounced *that* way. The *au* is a dipthong, and the tongue touched the top of the mouth with the *r*. Like this." She giggled while I tried to get it right.

She went on to talk about Sauro's commitment to ASD. His poetry became fiery—too radical really for anyone to publish it and risk losing a government grant. He worked hard on ASD rallies and political efforts. He was sincerely committed to getting rid of monitors, to closing the camps. He wasn't really good with the personal stuff— most ASDers would visit people in quarantine before they were shipped off to the camps while Sauro made only one such visit that Anna knew about. But Sauro did put a lot of energy into organizational meetings, and he liked to rewrite pamphlets so they wouldn't sound like material meant to convert the converted.

It was late, and we were finishing off a second bottle of wine, when Anna stared me down. "Your life sounds too good, Mr. Serviceman. Especially when compared to mine. Tell me something real." Rule Three: Do not let a client ever see more than just a refined image of who you are—it is easy to part with a beloved image; it is almost impossible to part with a beloved person. So I told her about my cruel grandmother, and how I felt guilty about hating her when she died. I told her plenty of jokes, though I avoided the type of ethnic jokes that would offend an ASD type.

The joke-telling must have warmed her up, because she wanted to hear more the next evening. She began to hold my hand during some of the conversation. While we ate dinner, she talked about how at first she had agreed more with her father than with Contini about monitors. "Sauro pointed out that I never had grown up with monitors. I read some Orwell and started to change my mind. I told Dad that my mind was made up; I sometimes liked to see him get infuriated. He'd grit his teeth, and his face would turn red, and he'd slam his palm against the table and say something like"—her voice deepened, a comical bass—"'I don't see how any intelligent person could buy that malarkey, not after crime has gone down and living conditions improved.'"

"Sometimes," I said, "you have to make choices."

"Between what?"

"Between whatever values you're talking about and your own safety."

"That's bullshit," she said.

"No. It isn't. If someone breaks into your apartment, Adolf recognizes that as a violent action."

"Adolf?" She giggled.

"Yeah, that's what they call the AI at Monitoring."

"Adolf?" Her smiled dropped away. "It's a telling name, you know. How do you know they call it that?"

"My roommate works at Monitoring. Anyway, Adolf—

the AI—notifies someone at Monitoring with an alarm. The monitor checks it out on a screen—you know, in order to make sure it's not kids playing, or something—and then notifies the police. No monitor, the break-in happens. Some people think the crooks are faster than the police, but in a well-monitored area, they can be followed. They probably won't attack you, and if they do, you'll have medical attention instantly."

"And I take it this attacker is Hispanic, like in the movies?" She was holding my hand while she asked the question, her eyes wide as if she were eager to hear every word of my answer.

"Most likely the guy's white."

Anna giggled and sipped her wine. "I can't tell if you argue more like Sauro or like Dad. Your politics are definitely Dad's."

"I don't have politics," I said, almost wounded by the idea.

"Everything's a political act."

"According to who?" Too late, I remembered that I should have said *whom*.

"You don't get the point. You talk about the wonders of the BEMs—"

"Bug-eyed-monsters?" I asked.

She laughed. "That's what my friend the actor calls them. Anyway, that's not the point. The whole thing with my father blew up because of monitors."

"How so?"

"You don't know? It's not in my file?"

"I don't know everything."

"Okay. Sorry. I just resent the fact that there is a file. I shouldn't hold it against you; it's part of your job."

"You were saying about how monitors wrecked things with your father."

"Okay. Here's the story. I took Sauro home for Thanksgiving because I wanted him to meet my parents. I'd never taken anyone home, and the idea was sort of thrilling. Sauro and I'd been together since March, and he'd finally decided that he loved me. My period had just ended, so we were pretty randy. Our first night there it was warm, especially for November. So we went outside to take a walk, and we ended up in the backyard." She was looking at her wineglass now. I wished I could have felt embarrassed, but I continued watching, listening. This hadn't been in either file. "Anyway, the security cameras must have picked it up. That night, my father had a nightcap with Sauro. I was sort of worried. They had talked politics during dinner, and my father turned beet red anytime Sauro refused to change his mind. Sauro's face would go stiff any time he couldn't convince my father. But still my father invited him for one more drink. Sauro told me later that Dad had gone on about how when you get older you begin to think about life, you know, question the things you've done, wonder if you've raised your kids well. Sauro told him that he had a fine daughter. I could imagine my father barking a mental 'Ha!' That's what he'd say anytime he thought anyone was full of shit. He'd bark it out, sort of like a seal. 'Ha!' Anyway, he told Sauro that I would have some decisions to make about my life. Two weeks later, right before exams—my father didn't notice things like exams except when our grades were low—he came up to college. And he told me that he saw how I was being led astray. He demanded that I break up with Sauro. He told me Sauro was never welcome in the house again. All because he saw the footage of us fucking. In the backyard."

She giggled. Then her face went dark as she remembered other feelings. "Here he was, the man who wanted me to take his place in Baxter Construction, and my so-called first sexual adventure had ruined me. You can't imagine what I wanted to tell him. I wanted to tell him about all the other guys I'd fucked. I guess I just stared at him. The words were in my head, but I couldn't get them out. When it really counted, I could never tell my father how wrong he was. So I guess he thought he was right."

"Was it worth it?"

"Was what worth it? My independence?"

"No. Screwing in the backyard. Was it worth all the trouble?"

Anna looked up, shocked. Then she saw the humor in it and smiled. "I never thought of it that way. Sauro got so excited that he came too soon. I was so nervous that I didn't want to wait and try again."

I looked for something witty to say, but nothing occurred to me. I kept thinking about Contini's file: if screwing on the couch had been in his file, why wasn't this?

"But I didn't want to make a big, long confession. This was supposed to be a monitor story. Do you get the point?"

"Sure. If there had been no monitors, your father might have walked outside instead and caught you."

"God, you're stubborn!"

On Friday night we were drinking more wine after dinner when she asked me if I wanted to hear another sex-and-monitor story.

"Only if you tell me all the details."

She didn't blush much this time. I wonder if the subject made the moment tiltillating, or if so much in her mind hinged on sex. "No. It's a monitor story."

"Oh. Another one."

"Don't the monitors affect you at all?"

"I'm used to them. When they're there, I know I'm safe."

"Is safety that important to you?"

"Isn't it to you?"

"Monitors didn't keep the UHL from blacking out Kansas."

"Okay. Point conceded. But they have prevented plenty of murders and rapes."

"But being watched has an effect on behavior."

"Like in the monitor story you wanted to tell me."

"Well, yeah." She smiled, blushed, then looked away for a moment. When she started talking, she had returned her gaze to my face. "When Sauro and I first moved to Cleveland, the only apartment we found that we liked and could afford was the one I live in now. There was one monitor in the living room. For the longest time I refused to make love anywhere but the bedroom. But one time Sauro somehow convinced me, and we made love on the couch." In one of the files, Sauro had accused Anna of a selective memory: they had made love on the couch within a few days of moving into the apartment. "At first the idea of being watched was sort of, well, exciting. But I still found it hard to get going. I had to concentrate on everything just so I wouldn't remember the camera was there."

I imagined their foreheads touching, their eyes fixed upon the source of their pleasure. I noticed that Anna's eyes were fixed on mine, as if she realized how her story was affecting me, even though she would have no idea how clearly I could see the moment. My mouth felt dry, and I drank some water.

"Do you get the point?" Her voice was a little hoarse, and she began to fiddle with her silverware to cover up the realization.

"Only if that was the last time you made love in the living room."

"No. It wasn't the last."

"So there. You forgot the camera existed."

"More or less. But what if someone watched and used the knowledge somehow?"

"I don't follow."

"Well, like if someone called us up and told us how to do it better. Or if they sent us a tape to show us how silly we looked. Sex is pretty comical if you're not participating."

"But no one called you up. And no one sent you a copy."

"But don't they do that with you?"

"What do you mean?"

"The other afternoon I saw this movie called *Truest Love*. It's about a companion who falls in love with his client."

"I've heard about it."

"Oh. Well . . . there's this scene where the supervisor watches movies of them together, just to make sure the companion isn't falling in love. Do they really watch over you like that?"

"No. And they're not really worried about us falling in love, either."

"But, you know, as my father would point out—good capitalist that he is—you're a product. Don't they monitor you to make sure that you're satisfying the customer?"

"Sure, when I was in training. And I'm sure managers at Baxter Construction monitor worker output, and your father must have someone who keeps tabs on a new executive."

"But doesn't the thought that you could be monitored modify your behavior in any way?"

"No."

"I don't believe you." She smiled; it was a taunt.

On Saturday night I made a miscalculation. I brought her a yellow carnation. During their first year together Sauro had given her yellow carnations all the time, and Anna had told him it was her favorite flower. She took the one I held out to her and looked at it distrustfully. Rule Four: Never let a client realize how much you know about her; it spoils the illusion.

Over dinner she became upset because I complimented her too often. "Look," she said, "I'm not the most beautiful woman in the world."

"I never said you were," I replied honestly. "But you are nice looking, and you do know how to wear clothes that compliment your looks. What's wrong in pointing that out?"

"Nothing, but when men start pointing things like that out, it's usually to get laid."

I shrugged. I wasn't there to get laid.

"Don't you understand? Well, how about this? Would you ever give so many compliments to your girlfriend?"

She was fishing, or she had forgotten the exclusive sexual rights she had contracted for. "I don't have a girlfriend."

"A boyfriend, then?" She didn't like that idea.

"No boyfriend, either."

"I thought all you guys had a relationship on the side."

"Some do. I don't."

"Oh." She took a sip of her vodka, kahlúa, and milk. "I thought maybe you'd have something on the side."

"I don't, and I can't. It's against our contract."

She smiled.

After dinner and wine she became wistful. "I wish we could go dancing. I want to forget about everything else."

"Why not? You seem to be a little down. It'd cheer you up."

She picked up the carnation and twirled the stem between thumb and forefinger. "You might want to file this away: my favorite flowers are yellow roses. I never told that to Sauro until we moved to Cleveland. You know, long after he'd stopped giving me the carnations. He was on scholarship. He never could have afforded roses."

"Let's go dancing," I said.

"We might be spotted," she said simply.

"If you had a good time, it'd be worth it."

She shook her head and, for a moment, looked terribly weary. "I don't want to hear anyone's opinion about what I'm doing with you." She sounded as if she'd already rehearsed for the experience.

"That's fine," I said. "We can always go someplace quiet where no one would notice. You deserve a chance to enjoy yourself."

"Sauro hated to dance."

He wasn't invited, I almost said.

She stared at her wineglass. "If I had a good time, I'd feel like I was getting back at him." She raised her head and looked me straight in the eye, her own eyes cloudy. "Can you understand that?"

"Yes. Yes, I can."

When we left the restaurant, she left the carnation on the table, some of its petals scattered like crumbs.

I walked her home that Saturday night, as I had every night that week. I kissed her good night, and her eyes held me at the door. We stood like that for a while, but she didn't invite me in; I didn't ask to be invited. "I'll see you tomorrow?" she said.

"How about on Monday?"

I expected her to try to convince me to meet her tomorrow, or to pout the way she sometimes had when Sauro wouldn't do what she wanted. Instead her face went flat, the way it had with her father. "Sure," she said. But I felt as if I could see something going on behind her eyes, a working-out of equations, a balancing of values. The unspoken thoughts made me nervous. Maybe I should apologize for the carnation. "I'll see you Monday."

She closed the door, and I found myself standing there. I considered knocking. I felt I had hurt her feelings, but, in truth, her feelings were her own business. I wasn't her analyst, though I could listen like one. The shift-janes understood that. They were paying enough money to have a good time. They knew it was a one-way relationship. I gave, and they enjoyed themselves. At the point where a real relationship could become deep, the relationship with a servicer remained superficial; that was when I would work out simple patterns to lead to termination. Personal Services couldn't afford to train people to stick with someone too long and fall in love, and, when it got right down to it, only a client intent on moral salvation would marry their servicer. As if the ways straights bought and sold things any way they could was any more moral than what we did in our profession.

I heard Anna walking about in her apartment, and I felt like I was spying, or waiting for her to discover that I was still outside her door. I descended the four flights of stairs.

The shadows of Ohio City closed in, and I fled under dim streetlights to the RTA.

There was nothing much to do on Sunday. Except for the family recreation centers, churches, and expensive restaurants that could afford the Sunday licenses, everything was closed. The datanets, the newslines, the media cables, remained open. So Harry, Kevin, Maureen from across the corridor, and I headed outside with a football. We took the fire stairs to the closed-down commercial level and walked until Slavic Village came to an end. We stepped through the flimsy air-lock doors, crossed the bridge over Interstate 77, walked through the local shackville, and headed for Washington Park. We ended up playing with some Hispanic and Arab kids dressed in clothes that made the four of us bureaucrats look rich and feel guilty. The kids played with energy that contrasted with the twisted, feeble structures of wood they lived in, the April mud they walked through, perhaps slept on. Some of their less-energetic buddies, needle marks evident on their arms, cheered rudely from the sidelines. A white kid joined the game and ended up running off with the ball.

That evening Harry, Kevin and Betsy, and I watched old movies on TV. Betsy drank mineral-added water; the rest of us drank beer and dark rum. Betsy enjoyed herself at first, talking about the possible child; she still hadn't gotten around to taking the test. Kevin seemed enthusiastic. But once Kevin had shot back enough dark rum, he started in again about building a boat to sail the Caribbean, living life as freely as the waves, the ocean currents their only guide. Helluva lot better than monitoring computers that filtered shit and sewage. Even though Betsy and the kid were included in the dream, Betsy stared off into space as if she had been left out. Before the first film had ended, Betsy left us, and we continued drinking and made fun of the movies.

That night on the news they announced a cure for some polysyllabic cancer. Experiments done on voluntary hivers in a Nevada internment camp had led to the creation of the drug. The news left me feeling depressed, and I drank enough dark rum to dream my way to the Caribbean. In spite of Harry's admonishments, I took a Hangon pill.

8

THE CLEANING ROOM is probably one of the most expensive cafeterias ever designed for low-level bureaucrats. A careful melding of smooth lines in plastic and cushion, it was designed as a place where servicers could be away from their johns and janes. The synthesizers prepare food with real meat, the liquor is not watered down, and the prices are low enough that it would become the hangout for the entire Cleveland bureaucracy were entrance not restricted solely to employees of Personal Services. Open twenty-four hours a day, except on Sunday, it is a place where most servicers can cleanse themselves with booze and bitching. Direct Services pros enjoy stretching out and relaxing in an atmosphere where their bodies are not on display; Leisure Service companions, at least the ones who haven't trotted out into the Heights, like to relax and act themselves.

For the past week I had avoided the Cleaning Room. A few choice comments at the gym foreshadowed the heckling I'd receive. I was moving into the Heights, and everybody would have something to say. I didn't want to hear it.

But Marie Archer, my supervisor, pulled me aside after the Monday-morning staff meeting and suggested that unless I wanted people to think I considered myself too good for them, I'd better show.

Marie didn't care much for the Cleaning Room herself. She'd lost a few friends when she'd put in for promotion after agreeing to marry a wealthy john she'd serviced; it was assumed she'd gotten the promotion because the john was president of one of Cleveland's biggest banks.

"I'll go tomorrow," I told her.

"Go today. Have a beer and celebrate."

"Celebrate what?"

"Another Monday, another clean blood test. That sounds like cause enough to celebrate."

I entered the Cleaning Room and tried to make it from the entranceway to the synthesizers without being noticed, but it was like trying to pretend that shit doesn't attract flies.

"It's been a while, Rod. Where you been hiding?"

"Long time, no see, Rod."

"It's about time your namesake began to rake in more cash."

I smiled and nodded at the commentary. Clustered around a nearby table were some of the people I'd trained with four years before, and I started for their table.

"Hey, CT! Get the fuck over here!"

The voice hooked my attention and reeled me in. Aggie was standing up at a crowded table in the back. I waved to her and walked over while she shooed and hushed people until they cleared a space across from her.

"How goes, CT?" She reached over the table, grabbed my shoulders, and pecked both sides of my face.

"Same as usual. Pumping away."

"And telling lies while you do it," Aggie said, as she always did. Seven years ago, when I had begun training to work in Direct Services, Agatha Jones had been a holofilm beauty, a glossy construct of legs, waist, and breasts. Her beauty had accounted for her lack of a professional name and for the well-tempered sass she used on her large and respectful clientele. Seven years later wrinkles had begun to remold the curves, and marijuana had blurred the edges. The executive director kept promising to promote her to floor supervisor, but it never happened. Aggie transferred lots of dollars from bancards to Personal Services.

"I hear you got a big one now," she said.

"You talking money or bone structure?"

Aggie looked over at a young pro I didn't recognize. The red band around his arm singled him out as a trainee.

"Henry, why don't you get a hamburger and a cup of coffee for Rod here?"

"I ain't no slave," Henry said indignantly. "And I ain't rich."

Cindy, sweet and talkative, smiled at Henry. "Don't be nasty. I'll treat with my card."

When I had trained under Aggie, she had me running all over the place. "Don't bother," I said. "I'll get it myself."

"Sit down, Rod," said Aggie. It was an order, kindly delivered. Aggie handed her card to Henry. "Rod's family. Got that?" Henry nodded defiantly and walked off. Aggie made sure he reached the synthesizers before turning back to me. "So tell me, why is everyone talking about your new one?"

"Her lover jumped off a roof."

"I saw that on the holo, I think," said Cindy. "On the news."

"A woman whose lover jumps off a roof," mused Aggie. "That's a new one. What lies have they got you telling her, CT?" Aggie called all the Leisure Services companions CT—cock tease or cunt tease, depending. Aggie liked to call me the biggest CT of them all.

"The only lies I tell her are about me."

"How does it feel to be in the big time? I miss seeing you around here."

"So far I just see her in the evenings. All she wants to do is go to dinner and talk out her feelings."

"Sounds gloomy."

I shrugged.

"So how long until you become an uppity asshole snob?"

"Hey, Aggie, you saw me after I got the file. I tried to turn the thing down. I don't want to work the Heights. I don't like what it does to people."

"Come back and work Direct, then."

"I can't do that."

Henry threw the hamburger down in front of me and placed the coffee beside it. "Satisfied?" He sat down and glared at me.

"Yeah, thanks." I looked at Aggie. "Is there something you're not telling me?"

Aggie hesitated.

"There is something, isn't there?"

"Some guy came in today and started asking questions about you."

"What kind of questions?"

"The kind of questions straights start asking when somebody comes up with bad blood."

"I'm not even fucking anyone. My blood's fine."

"That's what makes it spooky, CT. He was asking what kind of friends you had and everything."

"Did you talk with him?"

"Naw, he talked at me. Unless your blood's bad, there's no reason for me to be talking with nobody like him."

I barged into Marie's office to ask what was going on, how was it that some straight had gotten into the Cleaning Room to ask around about me.

"I've got nothing to do with it," she said. "In fact, no one wanted to hear my opinion about the whole mess."

"Who do I talk to, then?"

"There's only one person who can let straights into the Cleaning Room if they don't have a warrant. And you know who that is. In fact, I'm sure he'll be expecting you."

For ages there'd been talk that one of the executives in D.C. liked to take the sorrier cases in Personal Services and develop them into something outstanding. Fred O'Mallery was considered one of his failures. Except for the horses— who had opinions as if they belonged on the board of directors of Fortune 300 firms—most people felt that Fred was positioned where he could do the least harm. Because he was harmless, and because he usually meant well, most of us liked him.

He was a tall, gangly man who reminded you of a puppy with long legs—he didn't know how to use his body. Except for some old-timers, who'd seen it, no one could imagine him ever having been a servicer.

I found him in his office, building a pyramid with a

bunch of vid crystals. "Joseph said you were angry." Joseph was his secretary.

"I am. I heard someone was going around asking questions about me."

Fred began to dismantle the pyramid and place the crystals wherever he felt they belonged. His computer screen was off. I wanted to apologize for bothering him while he was busy, but Fred *was* the executive director. "Sit down," was all he said.

"Well, who is this guy? Straights don't get into the Cleaning Room without your okay."

"I gave him my okay."

"I figured that one out, Fred. And just in case I got it wrong, I checked in with Marie first."

"Can we talk about your client for a bit? How are things going?"

"Oh, come on."

He waved his hands in the air, as if warding off verbal demons. "Don't worry. It will all become clear. First, tell me about this client. . . ." He picked up a crystal, looked at the code number, then inserted it into the computer.

"Her name's Anna Baxter. Daughter of James Baxter. Baxter Construction. They built at least half the Construct, remember?"

"I know all that. Now, earlier this month, her lover jumped off a roof. You started seeing her on Monday. You saw her six evenings. There was no sexual contact." He faced me. "Is that pretty much it?"

I nodded.

"It's a pretty good living, isn't it? They pay for twenty-four hours, and you usually work five or six—sometimes stay the night, but then you're sleeping. And their beds are better than ours."

"It's okay."

"What about her politics?"

"What about them?"

"Well, she did spend a good amount of time talking about politics with you. Forty, fifty percent of the time, wouldn't you say?"

I wanted to know what Tricky Dick had used to define

political conversation in order to give Fred an approximate percentage.

"I guess so."

"Did she talk much about this thing in Kansas City?"

"Not really."

"I heard on the morning news that they arrested two of the ringleaders yesterday. Did you know, one of them was in the district attorney's office? Can you believe that?"

I shook my head. I had watched the news. The other arrested ringleader had been an instructor in computer literacy at the state university.

"What does your client think of things like blacking out a city?"

I shook my head. Fred talked about politics only if there was a staff party around election time. "Fred, Baxter was in Americans for Social Democracy. The Union for Human Liberation was a splinter group. They're the ones who blacked out Kansas City. Not everyone joined, you know. Especially not Anna Baxter."

"What about Sauro Contini, her lover, this Contini guy?"

"What is this, Fred? Who have you been talking to?"

I almost regretted stopping him short. He looked as if he'd been having fun. "This high mucky-muck was here. He seemed concerned about you and your client." He was searching through the crystals on his desk for something. "He wanted to know where you were last Tuesday afternoon."

"What the hell for?"

"He said that there was no record of what this Baxter woman was doing, and he was trying to complete the record."

"Doesn't he need a warrant? Who the hell was it?"

"I didn't want to rock any boat. I documented that you were at home, reviewing your client's file."

"What are you talking about?"

"On Tuesday afternoon. That's what he was so concerned about." He found what he was looking for in his coat pocket.

"Will you tell me who this guy was?"

"Here's his card." Fred handed it to me. "The address is right near the Arcade."

I looked at the card, then Fred. "What is this all about?"

"He thinks your jane might have something to do with the UHL."

The name on the card, printed above the address, was Edward Winslow Lang.

9

SOME SECTIONS OF the Construct are only three or four stories high. Preservationists had insured that certain buildings would be incorporated into the Construct with their basic features intact. So the skylights of the Arcade and its neighboring buildings were flooded with natural light (on those special days of the year when the sun decided to shine over Cleveland) and, across Superior, the library, the Treasury building, and the postal museum maintained their stone facades like buildings imported from Europe.

I walked from Prospect over to Superior, crossed one of the few car streets left in the city, and made my way to the library. The wind from the lake turned Superior into a wind tunnel, and the overhead pedestrian bridges swayed. I told myself that I should have taken the rapid, or better yet, I should have gone to the Cleaning Room and drunk my lunch. Joseph had set up a one-thirty meeting with Lang.

I decided to treat Lang like a client, find out as much as I could about him, and serve him exactly what he wanted. Then maybe this would be our only meeting. He could explain to me why I shouldn't have been watching Contini's file with a red Do Not Disturb sign lit up outside the viewing room, and he could make whatever reprimand he thought fit. I'd apologize, say the right things, and that would be that. What Anna did during her afternoons was none of my concern until she decided to spend them with me. My stomach still somersaulted.

I found the library's periodical room. I took an empty

seat, inserted my bancard into the appropriate slot, and called up a biographical search. Several paragraphs flashed on to explain the right-to-know and the right-to-privacy laws. They couldn't be keyed off, so I reread them. I was then offered an extensive choice of sources, of time limits for the search, and of prices. It was my money, so I went cheap: the *New York Times,* the Cleveland *Plain Dealer,* and *Time;* anything that could be found within a half hour on Edward Lang, antiterrorist consultant for Cuyahoga County Monitoring Services. Even with computers, money talks. I didn't get much.

Edward Windslow Lang was sixty-five. He had been born and raised in Boston; his father had been a corporate salesman, his mother a Presbyterian minister. Both his parents had converted to the Church of Christ the Scientist— his mother had died of cancer, even though a cure had been found in one of the camps, and his father had refused treatment for Alzheimer's. According to a recent *Plain Dealer* article, Lang visited his father in Boston every weekend.

Lang had gone to Harvard and became a New Puritan. He earned his master's in business administration at a school run by the same college Anna had attended. He married, was employed by Baxter Construction in their Madrid office, and had two children. When the Spanish War broke out, Lang enlisted in the army and ended up as an analyst for the American-backed government and a personal friend of Pablo Mayoral, that government's president. He had been quoted as saying the Spanish government would lose because they gave the people no cause to fight for, only a willful enemy to fight against. He was believed to have been secretly employed by the CIA, using CIA funds to bribe several guerrilla leaders. After the war Lang taught political science at Harvard.

Last December, in Cleveland, a bomb had destroyed a train car designated to carry hivers to a camp in California. The bombing convinced the mayor to bring in an antiterrorist consultant. Lang was hired on December 21. He told the *Plain Dealer* that the long night of winter belonged to the terrorists and that the long day of summer would belong to Liberty. The tide would turn, he promised, by March 21, when day and night were balanced equally.

On March 15 a computer virus blacked out Kansas City.

On March 21 a *Plain Dealer* editorial denounced the Black Out again and asked Lang about the tide. The editorial hinted that some of Lang's old army colleagues thought Lang was rather idealistic, and therefore ineffective. The *Plain Dealer* wanted to know what Lang had done to keep Cleveland safe. In response Lang convinced his employers at Monitoring to tighten security that very afternoon. That evening he assured the press that not only would Cleveland be safe, but that within months the major ringleaders of the UHL who worked in Cleveland would be in jail, awaiting the careful pace of American justice.

Whatever Lang had against me, I had enough to keep him at bay. I could tell him his war against terrorism was as successful as his father's treatment of Alzheimer's disease. I could accuse him of bribery or of being a CIA agent. Or I could ask him whose longest day it would be on June 21.

Then I discovered one more piece of juicy news. There was a reference to Lang in the article *Time* ran last year on James Baxter. Baxter and Lang, it seemed, were good friends, and some weekly called the *Nation* had suggested that Baxter used his position as an international entrepreneur to gather intelligence, which he passed on to Lang, who passed it on to the CIA.

With knowledge like that in hand, I knew I could strike as much terror into Lang's heart as he had struck into mine.

The people who lived in the Upper Stories tended to be well off; those who lived as close to Public Square as Lang did were rich or living beyond their means. I couldn't imagine a consultant's fee was adequate to pay the mortgage or the rent, and I couldn't help but wonder if there was another salary or another organization subsidizing Lang's residence.

His flat was on the fourth floor in the building right next to the Arcade: an immense two-level building of polished stone and polished brass railings, it housed expensive restaurants that served mediocre food and expensive stores that sold handcrafted goods that you could never computer-order.

The security to Lang's floor was extensive: a visual ID by the resident, bancard, thumbprint, metal-and-explosives detectors, and personal frisk. I was surprised they didn't do a body search to make sure that one of my testicles wasn't a bomb in disguise.

A Hispanic woman in a business suit IDed me and let me into Lang's apartment. The entranceway was barren of flowers in expensive vases, framed paintings, or statues that would hint at a sense of wealth. The wallpaper was faded and looked as if the corners were ready to curl away from the walls. In a virtually empty living room, there were metal shelves lined with books, notebooks, and stacked crystals. In front of the shelves was a desk with enough computer and phone gadgetry to make a personal receptionist, where they still existed, envious.

The woman led me down an equally barren hallway, past a bedroom with one bed and a bureau, to Lang's study.

Edward Lang sat behind a polished wooden desk. There were several chairs in front of the desk that looked expensive enough to have been purchased at the Arcade. Again, the walls were barren of decoration except for built in bookshelves, all filled with old-style bound books and with papers and packets stacked into haphazard piles that made the Tower of Pisa look stable.

"Mr. Lawrence," Edward Lang said, as if he were delighted to see me. "I'm glad you could make it. Pilar, will you get us some coffee?"

At first glance Lang seemed like some alternate universe counterpart for Fred O'Mallery. He was tall, and thin, and you could almost sense the gawky, socially inept teenager beneath the surface. The peach-fuzz mustache didn't help. But he carried himself with the grace of an athlete. His sleeves were rolled up past his elbows, and the muscles of his forearms had the well-sculpted look of someone who lifted. Only a soft quality to the skin and the wrinkles circling mouth and eyes gave away his age. His handshake, a surprise in itself, was firm.

"Please," he was saying, "take a seat."

I sat down. The nearby desktop was a touch neater than

his bookshelves. The only area kept clear of papers was the strip of desk where Lang had set out two family cubes. Each cube was turned at an angle to show me two faces while showing two faces to Lang whenever he sat behind his desk. About every five minutes or so the image would dissolve into a different one of the same person. On one cube his wife could be seen working in the kitchen; his son, in a picture dated fifteen years ago, was climbing a mountain. On the other, there were shots of his mother and father long before disease had hit them. The cubes were an expensive way to remind the visitor that Lang was a family man.

The woman returned with a tray. She handed me coffee cup and saucer, and I declined cream and sugar. I wasn't sure what to do with the spoon—I think it was silver—that rested precariously on the saucer. She handed Lang his cup of coffee; he didn't have a spoon to worry about. But then again, she didn't offer him cream or sugar, either. Lang took a sip before sitting down opposite me.

The woman placed the tray down on a cleared edge of the desk. She searched around the ocean of papers on the desk and salvaged from beneath them a flatscreen.

"I don't need that, Pilar," Lang said.

She gave the kind of shrug people give when they actually care. She dropped the board back on the waves of papers; miraculously, it didn't sink back to the bottom. One of the cubes now showed Lang's wife in front of a church; his son, older now, with two children on his lap.

"And, Pilar?"

"Yes?"

"This meeting's off the record. Will you see to that?"

"I'm not sure that's a good idea." She stared at me as if I didn't belong. Something about her style seemed fake.

"You may log the meeting and the complaint. But the conversation is off the record. It's the least we can do."

I sipped my coffee. Good cop, bad cop. The Cleveland Heights police had done it better.

The woman left, and Lang turned to me.

"As you heard me tell my associate, this is not an official meeting. In fact, I wish there were some way I could meet you on a more informal basis. But given the circumstances of five weeks ago, that's impossible." By five weeks ago, I assumed he meant the Kansas City Black Out. "To begin with, you're probably wondering why I made such an elaborate effort to see you today."

I nodded. It felt like a courageous act.

He sipped his coffee. "There are some concerns we have in common. Now, you probably wonder what these might be. Here you are, an employee of Personal Services, and here I am, a New Puritan. When I was an adolescent, I was a Christian Scientist. The Church had helped my father get over a drinking problem. Before that I was a Presbyterian. I've spent a good part of my life looking for the right way to believe in God. And knowing that, you probably expect a sermon."

He had caught my attention: he *couldn't* have know, not so soon, that I'd been reading about him at the library. I tried to look relaxed, slouched in my chair, the way everyone did when the social workers at Fair Haven lectured you. You listened, but you never gave the speaker the comfort of an attentive audience.

"But in this country we have a history of people with different moral views uniting when liberty itself is at stake."

He sounded sincere, quietly urgent. But I couldn't imagine what Contini's file had to do with the defense of liberty, and I began to wonder if that would be Lang's hidden stick in case I didn't leap for these carrots of kind words.

"Just out of curiosity, can I ask you what you think of your work?"

"It's a job," I said.

"You could make more mining asteroids," he said. "If you stake the right claim, you could be set up for life. Why not mine asteroids?"

"It could kill me," I said. My brother's best friend had shipped out to make it big; a suit puncture had sent him sailing toward Jupiter.

"You face some occupational risks in your current employment," he said.

"Everyone does."

"But if I recall my numbers correctly, three of your colleagues were interned at a western camp last year."

"Sure. But one was shooting up in a shackville with his lover, and another wasn't blood-testing his freebies."

Lang sat back and considered what I'd said. He drained his coffee and placed cup and saucer on his desk. On one cube Lang's wife and Anna Baxter were standing on a beach, both wearing bathing suits, both smiling, an arm wrapped around the other's waist. I looked down at my coffee, then back at Lang.

"And the third?" he asked.

"You already know this."

"Was the third colleague victimized by a bad test?"

I nodded.

"Here, let me help you with that." He reached over and removed the saucer and cup from my lap. I watched him place them on the desk within my reach. "Now, let me make sure I understand the whole thing, because all I know about Personal Services is what I read in the paper and what my minister says on Sunday. Every client takes a blood test before engaging in, um, activity with a servicer."

"Yeah."

"Did Anna Baxter take such a test?"

"No. It's different if you're working Leisure Services. The client takes the same test we take every week. It's pretty thorough; if it misses, it misses because there's a new strain of hives."

"And with Direct Services?"

"Each client takes the thirty-second test before he can go to it."

"The test looks for a few signs in the blood, correct?"

"Yeah. Then it blinks red or green."

"And it's, what, ninety-nine percent effective?"

"A little better, or at least that's what they tell us."

"And if a client tests positive?"

"The light goes red, and he's denied service. In some cities the medical authorities are called in."

"In Cleveland?"

"No. Only when a servicer tests positive. Then the train's called in."

"You don't think that's equitable?"

"No. Everyone should go or no one."

"The Americans for Social Democracy held that no one should go."

"I know."

"The Union for Human Liberation holds that anything can and should be done to be sure no one goes. It's acceptable to blow up a train or plant a bomb in a New Puritan church or black out a city and kill everybody dependent on electricity. And this, this happens to defend people who were infected by a virus they could have avoided."

I didn't know what to say.

He leaned forward, gestured toward me. "Would you go willingly to a camp?"

"If my blood was bad?"

"Yes."

"It's not like there's much choice."

"But it's always a possibility."

"A small one. More asteroid miners end up dead than servicers in a camp."

"Not if you make the comparison on a nationwide basis," he said. "Fifty American miners died last year. One hundred five American servicers died in camps. The numbers make a good argument for self-discipline, for a limitation of what we can buy, sell, or rent in a society. Or," he added with emphasis, "a good argument for servicers helping out the Union for Human Liberation."

I grimaced.

"You don't agree."

I shook my head.

"With which idea?"

"Does it matter?"

"Sure. You can be open with me."

"Neither idea is appealing. All I said was that everyone goes or no one. Maybe it wasn't true fifty years ago, but these days most people who go, go because they're careless."

"And you're not."

"No."

"Are you equally careful about your politics?"

"What do you mean? I watch the news. And I don't vote. Is that careful enough?"

He frowned when I said I didn't vote. "How about your client's politics?" he asked.

"Anna's?"

"Yes, Anna's." I couldn't help but notice that he called her by her first name. "What do you think of her politics?"

"I don't know. It's something she talks about."

"Has she talked about the Union for Human Liberation?"

"You've got this on file," I said. "You know this."

He seemed to like my response. He nodded, the same way my mother had when I had stated the obvious like it was something new. "Of course, you're right. She didn't mention it except in passing. But I would assume with all your training—your job *does* depend on your ability to read people—that you might have some intuition about her feelings toward that organization."

Nothing came to mind. I didn't understand why an antiterrorist expert cared for my opinion, intuitive or not.

"You've examined her files. On April twentieth, if I remember correctly, you specifically looked up anything in her file having to do with ASD, UHL, the Close the Camps Campaign, the camps themselves, and, the word you put in a search for, hivers. You did skim through a good portion of Sauro Contini's file the next day, and you seemed to concentrate on the politics. You must have made some evaluation—at least have a hunch, or some sort of guess."

I shook my head. This was too much. I felt as if he were toying with me, but he looked so terribly sincere, as if my opinion mattered. I knew it didn't. "Okay," I said. "I think Anna wanted to join. But Anna's about as threatening as a crystal player."

"You don't think she ever joined the Union for Human Liberation?"

"No."

"What about Contini?"

"The same."

"Now here is where our opinions differ. It's always concerned me how someone like Sauro Contini could have attached himself to Anna, turned her against her father, and pulled her into a different social and political environment."

"These things happen," I said.

"Maybe. And it's my job to find out, when certain things have happened, if they happened because of circumstance or because of advanced planning. Evidence suggests that Sauro Contini was a link between the more radical elements of Americans for Social Democracy and Anna Baxter. Her father's company had constructed over half of the internment camps. The UHL, in their January Manifesto, declared James Baxter a public enemy. A week later two Baxter Construction vice presidents were assassinated. James Baxter is well protected physically, but perhaps his daughter can somehow be used as leverage. There is the possibility that Contini was meant to be that lever. Now Contini's dead. The UHL might try another approach. It would be nice if there was somebody there to keep an eye on Anna."

"Somebody like me," I said.

"Somebody who doesn't like chaos, who likes the routine of daily life, the rule of law. Somebody who has learned to understand what's going on without there being too many explicit signals. Someone who would be willing to report back to me every week about what's going on."

"That someone can't be a servicer," I said. It came out like a whisper. I regained my voice with a stock phrase: "What transpires between a client and a companion is confidential within the Business."

He smiled. "If you were a lawyer, a psychiatrist, a priest, or even a private detective, you would have some legal rights of confidentiality. But the wording of your contract is not that binding."

"It's still not right."

"Look, Rod, I don't want to break the confidentiality between you and Anna. You might know that James and Amanda Baxter are good friends of mine. I am Susan Baxter's godfather. I don't want to intrude on Anna's private life, no matter what I personally think of it. I want you to keep an eye out for her. If her conversation suggests that she's involved with something she shouldn't be, I want to know. If she is meeting with people of questionable politics, I want to know. As a friend, I don't want her victimized. As someone with my job, I want to track down the people who might be using her and put them away."

"Adolf can do all of this. You don't need me."

"Our AI is only as reliable as the people using it. The Black Out showed us that we can by no means be one hundred percent certain that our Monitoring Services employees are one hundred percent loyal. That's why I'm asking you for your assistance."

"You don't want someone like me for this." It came out in a rush, all dignity gone.

"Oh, I very much do want you for this task. I've been through your entire file. Because she's your client, you care about Anna. You wouldn't knowingly let anything terrible happen to her. I want to help you achieve that aim.

"And if I'm wrong," he went on, "you'll have your regular fee from Personal Services, plus a little extra from the government to compensate you for the extra anxiety."

I was shaking my head, but he took care not to notice.

"It's been cleared through our legal department and your executive director. It won't be a breach of contract. You make reports to your supervisor about the ins and outs of the relationship; consider this an extra report, except you'll make it to me.

"Now, if you'd see Pilar on the way out, she'll make arrangements so that we can transfer a stipend to your bancard. She'll also hand you a crystal with some readings that I'd like you to go over before we meet again next Monday." He was already standing, his hand outstretched. The adviser had done this to Anna. I had done this to hesitant clients who were about to terminate before I'd met quota. He was acting like I'd committed myself, like I'd go out there, accept the money and the crystal, buy into his love for Anna's family and for the American way of life. I found myself standing, my hand in his. "And don't worry about the Contini file that you looked at. I'll talk with Harry Torres, but there won't be any official reprimand, or anything disastrous." I returned his smile, and I felt more comfortable knowing that he'd brought out the stick. I'd reported on enough clients to Marie, why not to Lang, if something was really going to happen? Fred had cleared it, hadn't he? "I think everything will work out fine," he said.

Pilar was waiting for me at her high-tech desk in the empty living room. She wanted all sorts of information, which she typed onto the flatscreen and had me thumbprint. She placed the flatscreen down on her desk. Beside it were four crystals in a packet with my name printed on it. Beside my file was another crystal. "These are some writings by Thomas Jefferson he'd like you to read," she said. I let her place the crystal in my hand. "I believe that Mr. O'Mallery has given you Mr. Lang's business card."

I nodded. It took at least twelve hours, usually twenty-four, to get Tricky Dick to file, classify, and evaluate footage. Pilar had the information about Fred's conversation with me within several hours, otherwise she wouldn't have known for sure that I had Lang's business card. If she had called to ask, Fred would, at best, have said, *I'm pretty sure I gave it to him.*

"Can I have it, please? We really don't want anyone beyond you and your executive director to know about this meeting."

I handed her the card.

"Now, shall we schedule the next meeting for next week, the same time?"

She was already typing it in, so I didn't respond.

"It's scheduled," she said, returning her attention to me. "Your file analysis credits you with above-average visual recall and excellent verbal recall." She listed seven numbers.

I repeated them.

"Will you remember that?"

"It's a phone number," I said. "The exchange is for the business neighborhood."

She nodded. "If the UHL should make any kind of contact, call that number. Now, if you'll hand me your bancard, I'll arrange payment of a stipend. We figured that we'd match fifty percent of the daily fee Ms. Baxter pays to Personal Services. It would be paid to you on a posttax basis after your services for us were discontinued."

The money was good enough that I had already imagined the ways I could spend it. It was so good, in fact, that I couldn't get my hand to move. Where I'd gone to school, you didn't give them anything, no matter how sweet the deal.

"Is something wrong?"

"I can't accept it."

"How much more would you like? I've been empowered to negotiate your fee. I'm not sure we can be much more generous."

"I can't take it. You're wasting your money. Sauro Contini was only a radical when his mouth moved. He was never a terrorist."

"Well, if you like, you can sign for the money at some other time. I assumed from what you're saying that Mr. Lang didn't mention March fifteenth."

I shook my head.

"On March fifteenth Sauro Contini should have been with Anna Baxter." She made it sound like a question.

"Sure. It was her birthday."

"And he loved her, right?"

"I guess so."

"On March fifteenth, Sauro Contini wasn't to be found. We still cannot track down his whereabouts. It takes a lot to get past Monitoring when a file on you has been opened. And Sauro Contini, your harmless radical, somehow got past Monitoring. He must have been somewhere. We're pretty sure he was in Kansas City."

10

ALBERT EINSTEIN WAS on, and on the screen was Anna Baxter and Sauro Contini. I finished off a beer while I watched them dancing naked, their hips trying to match the newharp music they had put on the crystal player. I freeze-framed it and stared at them while sitting in my unlit apartment. They stood chest to chest, naked, his hands on her ass, hers hooked together around his waist, her head leaned up against him. Anna's eyes were half-closed, her face glowing with a touch of red. Frozen there, they looked silly, sexless.

It was Anna who had wanted to dance, Sauro who had wanted to dance naked, Anna who had chosen the music that Sauro didn't really like. A conspiracy of desires.

Lang had made them into such simple people: Contini the Terrorist and Anna the Innocent. It sounded like something nice to believe in. Lang hadn't mentioned Anna's whereabouts last Tuesday. Why had he emphasized his concern to Fred and let the matter drop with me?

I held the empty bottle in my left hand and fought off the temptation to go get another. I wanted my head clear for when I saw Anna at eighteen hours. I was halfway tempted to call her and cancel. How could I treat her like a client when she had become someone to watch over, someone to suspect?

And here they were, buck-naked. But their desire probably kept them from thinking that they looked silly.

Besides, they probably didn't think anyone would ever be watching, not really.

Last week all that had really concerned me was the palpable tension in the air, the *would she or wouldn't she* that kept me going, calculating, considering, the anecdotes I told, the stories I listened to without comment, the ones I made fun of, the touches, the assurances.

All of that now seemed terribly unimportant, and I despised Lang for making me wonder about Anna, about Contini, about the alphabet soup of American violence. I preferred not knowing. I preferred taking care of my clients. I preferred drinking Thirty-Three beer and shots of dark rum with Harry and Kevin.

I unfroze the image, watched them dance, then make love on the rug, Sauro moving in time to some silly, bouncy music, Anna laughing at his antics. I rewound and watched again, then again, until some of the energy returned, until last week's tension, Anna's wavering between desire and rejection (which I had sensed but the monitor had missed), became important once again. Now I could feel that Anna was my client, and now I could calculate tonight's possibilities.

11

OVER THE WEEKEND Anna had resolved whatever had to be resolved and met me at her door wearing something more artistic than utilitarian. It was a long red Oriental dress, with a V-line cut that revealed cleavage but very little breast and with a slit at the calf that revealed only a thin line of skin. Somehow the dress didn't look right on her, and she didn't appear comfortable wearing it. For the first night since we'd met, she wasn't dressed as if we were just going out to dinner.

The conversation was stilted as we walked to Murmuring Brooks. The Hispanic janitor was out in front of the brownstone wall again. Someone had had spraypainted CHINGATE. Below it, as before, chiseled into the stone, was: MONITORS EAT OUR SOULS. Anna began to walk faster, and her longer strides seemed to free her leg from the long skirt's enclosure. From sandal to thigh, her bare leg stepped freely forward, the red cloth closing around it with her next step. Her thighs were too thick for such a display, but I couldn't help watching.

The evening sun at Murmuring Brooks wasn't as warm as the one outside. The bubbling of water by our table in the corner didn't do much to ease the tension within me.

"Let me order for both of us," Anna said with a glee that sounded childish. Along with one of the most expensive white wines on the list, Anna ordered trout stuffed with crabmeat for both of us, rice, and salad with the house dressing. As usual, it was all too spicy. Anna was talking about how Boston had changed once the Roxbury Construct expanded into the city, how she preferred open-air Cambridge to the Boston Construct, but all I could picture was Edward Lang, leaning back in his chair and watching me with the same care of a monitor, but this time judgment was added to video.

"Is everything okay?" Anna asked. She reached for my hand. "You seem pensive."

"Just thinking."

"I gathered that. Were you thinking about me?"

I didn't know how to answer that: either answer sounded wrong.

"Oh." She patted her lips with her napkin. "What *do* you think of me?"

"Pardon?"

"You heard me, Rod. What do you think of me?"

"I like you."

"Your pause was eloquent."

"I do like you, Anna."

Her hand found mine and pulled it to the center of the table. "Am I being insecure?"

"Yes."

She looked more unsteady than insecure. "I don't know how to explain it. It's just that I keep feeling so comfortable with you, and then I remember that I'm paying for you."

"That's okay. It doesn't mean that you should be uncomfortable or that I would lie about liking you. Let's order something sweet."

"I feel as if you're avoiding the issue."

I grasped her hand firmly and looked into her eyes. Something within their sphere of influence tugged at me, and I found myself wanting to look away. "Anna, the issue is between you and your conscience. You have hired me. I am performing a service. It doesn't belittle you or me. Right now you'd like some companionship, without all the hassles. When you want to take on those hassles again, and reap the extra reward of a two-way relationship, you terminate the contract." It was a canned speech taught to me four years ago, altered for my style of speaking. I delivered it with feeling and half believed I meant it. "And unlike a former lover, I won't feel jealous about whomever you pick up with, and I won't come back to bother you." The words were so routine that for a moment I felt free of Edward Lang.

"I don't know," she said. "That sounds too neat and simple. You know, every night I feel attracted to you. Then I remember what you are, and I begin to feel as if I have to fight to keep that feeling. It's sort of what I told you about the first time I made love in front of the monitors . . ."

Her words drifted off, and she blushed. The waitress was asking if we'd like anything else.

Anna had avoided dessert at previous meals, but I risked knowing what she liked. "How about some cheesecake, some coffee, and some brandy?"

The waitress turned to Anna for her response.

Anna looked like she was fighting back tears. She nodded, then smiled appreciatively. The smile disappeared quickly. I ordered Torres Reserva, Sauro's favorite, espresso, and a slice of cheesecake with two forks.

"I guess it's sometimes okay that you have my file," she said after the waitress had brought what I'd ordered. It was a proclamation. "This is what I like, and this is what I need." She sipped some brandy. "You know, I think I know more about this brandy than I do about you. I feel as if I spend all my time talking, but you're so easy to talk to."

"My father was that way," I heard myself say, giving away too much with the past tense. "I guess it's an inherited trait."

"Do you ever see them?"

"Sure. I'm a working person, not a slave. I get two weeks of vacation every year. I usually spend them in San Antonio." I described for her the river, the Alamo, and a few other things Harry had shown me from his trips to Texas.

"Sounds nice." She looked away, as if some stray thought had distracted her.

"It is," I said. "For a vacation. Family's still family." Most of my shift-janes had talked about their mild childhoods as if they had been pure trauma; and as if their parents were beyond forgiveness.

"How do your mom and dad feel about your work?"

"About the same way your father feels about you living in Cleveland," I said.

Her eyes returned to mine. "How did they react?"

"I don't know. I sent them a letter."

"What did you say?"

I raised my finger to my lips. "It's a secret," I whispered.

"It doesn't seem fair. You know everything from my favorite dessert to what positions I like in bed, and I know nothing about you. How am I supposed to hold up my end of the bargain?"

Just pay your bills, is what I wanted to say. "By loosening up. By enjoying yourself."

"But part of pleasure is that it's mutual."

If you have to say you're enjoying yourself, you're probably not. I had known what she had decided since she showed up at her door with the red dress on. But whatever happened had to be mutual; that was the illusion she wanted. I was paid to create illusions. "There are two things I can think of that I'd enjoy right now."

She smiled and her eyes twinkled. "What's that?"

"I'd like another snifter of brandy. Or I'd like to go to your place."

She took my hand and touched her lips to it. "Let's go to my place."

The air was cool. The streetlights cast a shadow into every niche and crevice, giving the surrounding buildings a ghostlike presence. I almost felt as if we'd been transported back in time, walking through a landscape that should no longer have existed. Anna's face was soft with wine, brandy, and something indefinable, and she leaned her head against me. I placed my arm around her shoulders. Street sounds—passing cars, a group of people barhopping, some kids shouting to each other—embellished our quiet.

I had to let go of her so we could walk up the four flights of stairs, and the moment was lost. As soon as the door to her apartment was shut, Anna reached for that moment with an urgency, as if someone looking over her shoulder could, at any moment, convince her to change her mind. The kiss was long, her arms tight around my back. I reciprocated. She stopped to gauge my reaction. I must have looked appropriately involved, because she smiled, and the glow it ignited set off a strangely sweet tension within the pit of my stomach. We kissed and touched, knocked into some furniture, and began to make our way to the bedroom . . . when she stopped.

She looked at me helplessly. "I can't do it here."

"Should I leave?"

"No. Please, no. I want you so much."

"We can go someplace else."

"Your apartment?"

I smiled slightly, thinking more of Harry's reaction than Service regulations. I shook my head. "We can go to a hotel."

"I'd prefer that it not be around here. Or—"

I nodded: she didn't want to be spotted. "We can go into the Construct."

"Yeah. I'd like that."

We descended the four flights of stairs and headed for the RTA. The long, dark shadows set me on edge. I felt the blood, almost drop by drop, flow out of my penis, leaving a strange, unfulfilled sensation dancing on the edge of my nerves. I placed my arm around her waist to make up for it.

"This feels so planned," she said as the rapid headed across the bridge.

I wanted to tell her that sex was always planned in advance. Instead I leaned over and kissed her.

The first hotel in the Construct had too many pictures of Christ hung around the lobby. I led Anna away from the reception, and we headed to another hotel several corridors east. The old couple at the desk stared at Anna and her Oriental dress while they asked for citizenship IDs that held the same family name. On our way to the next hotel, Anna asked me to register as Mr. and Mrs. Lawrence; it took her three tries to articulate the request. The desk clerk at the next hotel offered a twisted smile when she saw the names on the register. I handed her my bancard, and the smile disappeared.

The room was typical: a large double bed, a cheap moonlit landscape holo where a window should have been, some bureaus with a mirror and a holovision atop, a third-rate sensory kit beside the bed, and a bedside table lamp complete with reddish filter. In the bathroom was a coin-operated blood tester: about as reliable as a condom with a hole in it.

Anna looked around the room and got trapped into a staring contest with the monitor.

"You'll lose," I said. "The monitor doesn't blink."

She shook her head, as if trying to wake herself, and she walked over to embrace me. The smile and the kiss were contrived. Her embrace tightened for a moment, then her body seemed to relax, her kiss softened.

"There's a synthesizer down the hall. Do you want some wine?"

"No," she said, her voice hoarse. "Just you."

There was something new to her kiss. The desperate urgency now seemed like something else; there was both a hunger and a tenderness in her kiss, as if she had been waiting a long time to be generously warm to someone. My body wanted to slide into the moment, become enveloped in a world that is nothing more than a meeting of lips and tongues. But I continued to calculate each step. I was aroused. I wouldn't need any chemicals to get me going.

I found myself considering an out, a way to start the termination pattern now rather than later. Feeling like I was contemplating a bad practical joke, I considered inducing hypersensitivity. Premature ejaculation seemed like a rude joke, the equivalent of sticking your leg out in front of a blind man, but it would provide the necessary sense of disappointment, of this-wasn't-all-so-great. The rest of the sex would be good, but she'd terminate in a week or two. Then I'd be back with the shift-janes: no more head games, no more grammar and etiquette software, no more Edward Lang.

I broke from the kiss and said, "You're going to hate me."

"You're tired of kissing."

"No. Not at all. But I have to use the bathroom."

Her arms dropped to her side. "Oh," she smiled. "I wouldn't want to stop you." She ran her tongue over her lower lip. "But don't come out with your clothes on."

I closed the bathroom door behind me. The ChemKit

was in my jacket pocket. I undressed. I replenished the Construct water system. I took out the necessary air-hypo, clenched my teeth, and applied the stinger between thigh and scrotum.

The bedroom was pitch dark. I switched out the light in the bathroom and stumbled over to the bed. Anna was naked under the covers. The sheets seemed too cool, and I retreated into her embrace. We kissed as if everything we yearned for could be found in kisses. I caressed her face, found her cheeks wet, and kissed the moisture. I kissed the tips of her fingers, the palms of her hands, and she drew me back into her embrace, her kisses deeper, more insistent. I ran my fingertips across her breasts. I applied tongue to nipples. We kissed while my hand caressed, then probed, charting unfamiliar regions too well-known. She finally reached out, as if to extend the embrace into all its possibilities, and led penis into vagina, her arms and legs wrapping themselves around me. I let myself go, forgetting all about self-control and calculations; the chemistry rushed through me. I felt everything with too much clarity. For the first time in a long time ejaculation was orgasm. I heard myself groan; I felt my body shudder.

Anna's arms tightened around me. I lowered my hand to please her, and she gently drew it away. "I can wait," she said. The ferocity of her embrace revealed depths I hadn't suspected. It scared me.

"It was beautiful," she said.

Perhaps it was too beautiful.

12

"WHAT ARE YOU doing up?" she asked, her voice sultry with drowsiness.

"It's almost noon. We have to check out."

"Do you have to go to the office or anything like that today?"

I shook my head.

"Could we stay here another night?"

"Won't someone miss you?"

"Not really."

I slid in beside her, her skin soft and warm to the touch. "It's almost noon. Aren't you hungry?"

"Not for food."

13

I COULD SEE her face. Her lips were pursed, her eyes intent, her hair a backdrop for the forearm and hand that supported her head. She was lying on her side parallel to me, her hand reaching out, fingers tracing the outline of ribs. Behind her was the holo-window, which depicted beach and surf. The sun rose higher, timed to match the arc of the sun outside the Construct. But the glow of her smile, the heat of her skin, kept tugging me back to her face like some emotional undertow. It felt so relaxing and safe to lie in my own bed and remember her face.

There was a knock on the door.

I opened my eyes, and the walls of the room felt close. "Yeah," I called out.

The door slid open, and Kevin looked in. "I see that Sleeping Beauty has returned home."

"And I was sleeping."

"This afternoon maybe. But Harry tells me that if you were sleeping at all the past two nights, it wasn't here."

"I became a New Puritan." I sat up. "I was off repenting for my sins."

"You mean, at a church?"

"Where else?"

"And in what cathedral was your organ being played?"

I swung my legs out of bed, and my knees bashed into the closet door. "The New Puritans don't believe in cathedrals," I said.

"Your prayers didn't protect your knees."

I ignored him. "And you used that same joke on me two months ago."

"Well . . ." Kevin shrugged bashfully. "You want some rum?"

"God, no. I want a shower."

"How about some food?" Harry called from the kitchen. "I'll throw something into the synthesizer."

"Eggs. Unless you guys are making something else."

"Eggs?" asked Kevin.

"We just ate some sandwiches at the Admiral," said Harry.

I walked into the cubicle bathroom and set the shower for 110 degrees, even though it would only come out at a cool 95.

"It's nineteen hours," said Kevin, "and you're eating breakfast."

"You gotta eat it sometime."

"They were fixing," said Harry, "some of the snow damage in this neighborhood's solar panels. I wouldn't take . . ."

"Shit! This water is fucking *cold!*"

"That's what you get for not listening, as my mother used to say."

"You needed a cold shower, anyway," said Kevin.

"All the electricity here was on low," said Harry. "There was no television, no synthesizer. So we went to the Admiral."

"Just for the food, right?" The air-dryer wasn't working yet, so I used a towel. I slid open the closet door to find something to wear. The clothes were comfortable and synthetic.

"Your eggs are ready," said Harry. "Kevin, grab some beers."

We sat in front of the TV, I with my scrambled eggs, each of us with a beer. A scantily clad woman left Fernando Rey's lap, and another one took her place.

"What is this shit?" asked Kevin. "He just called the second woman by the same name as he called the first."

"The Obscure Object of Desire," I said.

"You've seen it before?" asked Kevin.

"It's got subtitles," said Harry. "He probably thinks it's pretty good."

"It's pretty obscure," said Kevin. "You know, it's none of my business, but I don't think you should be screwing all these women. I think you should start a movie theater. You know, for the artsy-fartsy crowd. Imagine what heights you could reach."

"Sexual, intellectual, or Shaker?" asked Harry.

"Shaker," said Kevin. "Definitely Shaker Heights. Rod's had all the sexual heights he can handle. And I can't even begin to climb the intellectual heights of this movie."

"Let's watch something else," I said. They got this way every time I turned on this kind of movie.

"How about some more of the fuck footage in your jane's file?"

I shook my head.

"I think," said Harry, "that Rod's had enough of her for a while."

Kevin finished off his beer. "Why don't we go to the Admiral, then? Or we could have our little heart-to-heart."

Harry rolled his eyes.

"A heart-to-heart about what?" I asked.

"Never mind," said Harry.

"What's wrong?"

"It's nothing."

"His new boss is pissed," said Kevin.

"He's not the boss," said Harry. "He's a consultant."

I could visualize Lang, saucer balanced on thigh, coffee cup in hand, jaw firmly set as he gazed at me. "What did Lang say?"

"He was upset that I showed you Contini's file."

"Did he do anything?"

Harry shook his head. "He should've lowered my security clearance and docked my pay. That's what he did to everyone else who showed a little more than they should have."

"Now they all think Harry's a New Puritan," Kevin said to me.

"So far," said Harry, "Lang's only promoted New Puritans."

I went to the fridge for another beer. This was when I

should be telling him that I had been to Lang's apartment. The monitor hung from the corner of the ceiling.

"Do you have any idea why this Contini's so important?" Harry called out to me.

"Kevin," I said, "do you want another?"

"Get one for Harry, too."

"Rod, when you looked at that file, did you notice where Contini spent a lot of his time?"

"Between my client's legs?" I handed them their beers and sat down. Fernando Rey was upset with the woman's resistance to his overtures.

"Is that all you ever think about?" asked Kevin.

No, I almost said. I also think about how little they held each other the past few months. "He and Anna went to a bunch of ASD meetings. And his whereabouts on March fifteenth are unknown. It said so in the Basics."

"A B-minus goes to Roderick Lawrence. Now, does this guy keep going to ASD meetings in January and February?"

"Well, yeah."

"But at this point Americans for Social Democracy is dead. The Supreme Court has said the camps are constitutional. You can't say the camps are illegal anymore, but as of January you can join the Union for Human Liberation and throw bombs."

"He went to ASD meetings, Harry. He did until he jumped off a roof. This isn't the kind of guy who helps black out cities."

"I know that," said Harry. "And you know that. But there are people who are absolutely certain that every ASD meeting this year was a front for the UHL. I'm not saying I buy that. But you were gone, and I got curious. So this morning I called up your client's file. I wanted to see if our version had more in it than yours. It turns out that Adolf has classified the file."

"You're kidding."

"I hope," Kevin said, "you're thinking a little about what this means. If they've classified her file, she must have been up to something."

"Well," said Harry, "it depends on who's doing the

classifying. But you watched the stuff with us, Kevin. Did they look like terrorists to you?"

"What's a terrorist look like? I went to a parochial school—do I look like I should be managing shit? Rod here had highly educated parents—look what he's doing. What does it matter where the two went to school or what they did in bed? They could still be terrorists."

"Are you serious?" I asked him.

"Kevin's got a point," said Harry.

"Sauro the Terrorist? He didn't have the guts to join the protesters at a camp riot. He got sick instead."

"I didn't say I agreed with Kevin. I said Kevin's got a point. We don't know for sure what the two of them were up to. And if Little Miss Baxter was up to something and Lang wants her for it, I'd sure hate to see my roommate get caught in between."

"Don't worry about it. I'll have this whole thing wrapped up in a week or two." I felt as if I were lying.

"Let's say we're all wrong about the terrorist thing," said Kevin. "And let's assume that you're right. It still means we should think a little bit about her family."

"I know you've both talked this out already. So what's the point?"

"What's eating you?" said Harry. "You didn't want this client in the first place."

"I know."

"Just listen to what Kevin has to say."

"Sure."

"You might learn something from this," Kevin said. "Now, Baxter isn't like your Rockefeller or your Detroit auto manufacturer. He does everything legal, by the book, and by the *Bible*, but when he thinks he's been wronged, he'll use any trick in any of those books to set things right. Remember that servicer who took care of this wealthy Nashville jane and how her jane went off and took too many pills? Remember what the jane's family did in response?"

"Are you saying Baxter might sue me for malpractice?" The idea was truly funny.

"You know your client better than I do, and maybe what I'm saying is dead wrong. But your client doesn't look like the stable type, you know. She runs off to Cleveland, goes into politics, gets turned off sex, drives her lover to suicide, and then cries for two weeks until she hires you."

"Kevin's not saying that hiring you was a bad idea."

"I know," I said. "It's just not something a Baxter should do."

"You were the one," said Harry, "who said that this was a woman who was getting her heart, her head, and her clit confused. And you said that had been her problem long before Mr. Italiano jumped."

"What's the point, Kevin?"

"Don't take this so personally," said Harry. "Think about what Kevin's saying. First she blamed him for everything that was going wrong. Then she blamed herself. Next thing you know, she'll blame you. And if her family blames you?"

"That sounds like a lawsuit to me," said Kevin. "A big lawsuit."

I was staring at the television. Fernando Rey's intended conquest took off her bedclothes. She was wearing a chastity belt. "I'm not liable," I said.

"Maybe not. But it's like this movie you're watching. It's more trouble than it's worth."

14

THE NEXT MORNING, after my workout in the pool, Marie called me into her tiny cubicle office to tell me how much she liked the footage she'd seen of me and Anna together.

"I'm not so sure about the premature ejaculation," she said, "but after that guy showed up here on Monday, I can understand why you'd want to push for an early termination."

"Is that okay?"

"It's up to you. The longer this client lasts, the more your name will be known among certain social circles, the more likely you'll get more janes like her in the future. There's a lot of money to be made in the Heights, plus all the fringe benefits that you don't get with the shift-janes."

She meant the gifts, and the fine dining, and the fat expense account billed back to the client, but she was also the one who had hooked up with a bank president and as good as married her way out of the Business. I felt uncomfortable with both kinds of fringe benefits.

"I know," I said. I got up to leave.

"You know, Rod," she said, giving me her inviting smile, the one with no RSVPs accepted, "you're the only one whose footage can really get me going."

"You say that to all the guys and girls."

"Just to you," she said, "and a few others."

I hesitated for a moment. She hadn't asked me about my meeting with Fred, if I'd found out anything about the straight who'd gotten into the Cleaning Room. Marie had been my trainer four years ago, and I was accustomed to her asking and me telling.

Marie smiled again, and went back to work. I left her there.

That afternoon I reviewed the dailies for Monday night and Tuesday. The written evaluation divided everything into categories: sleep, conversation, excitement, plateau, orgasm, resolution, rest, and so on. The footage could be watched, unedited. I could leapfrog through it, using Tricky Dick's file headings (first plateau, 26 April, 2347:30–2348:17), or I could watch and fast-forward over the boring parts. At any time I could flip on line commentary, and in white letters at the bottom of the screen, Tricky Dick would provide whatever estimate, facts, and figures researchers and executives had thought important to reproduce. Everything I did by touch and intuition became classification and numbers. If heartbeat rose enough above the calculated average of 75 and respiration rose above 14, Tricky Dick tried to give some number signifying a level of vascocongestion while arteries dilated and blood rushed into pelvis, a flush spreading across belly, breasts, throat, and then Tricky Dick marked this off as the time that Excitement had started, and he followed suit by keeping track of how much nipples and unsuckled breasts enlarged, reading out signs of increased muscle tension, until heart was 140 and breathing was 32, and if neck cords extended, thighs and ass went tight (and if it was all measurable, meaning I wasn't blocking the monitor's view), then Tricky Dick declared plateau, and the instant the contractions (recorded by a tiny sensor chip similar to those in my thumbs) started, orgasm was declared with heart at 180 and respiration at 41, the arms grasping, the face set in a grimace, the body gone rigid and floppy all at once with legs and feet extended, all detailed with numbers, with a final contraction count as if the ten, then twelve, then seven, then three contractions were a true measurement of someones pleasure. Resolution was the next word on-screen, and Tricky Dick followed as respiration returned to around 12, heart returned to around

75, muscles relaxed, and vascocongestion faded along with the flush.

Tricky Dick offered a final evaluation—rating the first act of the evening low due to lack of client's orgasm, exacerbated by the long resolution following that intercourse, rating highly the client's following two orgasms—and offered some good words about the weaker orgasms, which were rated high because of the amount of time I had spent with the client.

Tricky Dick didn't offer any evaluations of our discussions between intercourse when she was hungry for details of my childhood. I told her about feuds with my brother while she told me how her sisters liked to get her in trouble. She followed that with stories of their summer cottage out on Martha's Vineyard, and I matched that with our family cottage up in Michigan, even telling her how my brother and I loved to make fires on the beach and begged our father to make up more stories about the Flying Dutchman of Lake Michigan. I had once told that to Harry and Kevin when we were trading stories of childhood gullibility and laughing up a storm, but Anna thought it was endearing, so I got off the subject of childhood and to the safer, textbook discussion of sexual fantasies. That, plus the eggs and the champagne delivered by room service, got her going that afternoon.

Having seen the dailies, I wanted to refamiliarize myself with Anna's likes and dislikes. I found the first crystals in Anna's file and started to call up the fuck footage, knowing how much Anna would despise the term. Every now and then she'd looked at Sauro playfully and said, "Wanna fuck?" with the same tone you would use when saying, "Wanna play hoops?" Yet she despised the term whenever Sauro used it as a generic term for lovemaking: "I like to think of what we do as more than fucking."

There wasn't a whole lot to go on, actually. With some shift-janes I got lucky enough to have footage of a developing sexual relationship when couples tend to be most open about likes and dislikes. That era for Sauro and Anna had taken place in an unmonitored dormitory bedroom. There *was* the dalliance in the Boston friend's apartment a year and a half ago, and that was it until they moved into their Ohio City apartment last July. From July 1 until Sauro's death on April 1, Tricky Dick provided telling segments of five sexual encounters recorded in the living room, plus about ten moments of beginning foreplay before they left for the bedroom. No scene had been filed in its entirety.

In the fourth recorded sexual encounter, dated 24 November (a year after they'd made love on James Baxter's back lawn), Anna and Sauro made love on the couch. Their embrace was tight, and they held perfectly still. "This is wonderful," said Sauro. *Moaned* would be a better word. "I can feel all of your skin against mine. I can feel all of you."

"Oh, yes. See how good it is when you go slowly. You're always in so much of a hurry. See how good it is?"

"Yes." He visibly shuddered. "Oh, I love you so much."

"So much for going slow," Kevin had said when we had watched this two weeks ago. This time I was focusing in on Anna. I rewound, listened for tone of voice: *See how good it is when you go slowly.* Was that a complaint about their sex lives that she had been unwilling to articulate, or was it a new opinion, her way of struggling for what made their screwing, or their loving, less than satisfactory?

The only footage of them together this year was dated 12 January: she and Sauro were on the couch, and she was embracing him, her body passive, as if she were mentally counting the seconds until he would climax and let her get on to other things. The words *I love you*, spoken into Sauro's ear while he made his last few compulsive humps, could have rung true only in the ears of someone desperate to believe.

"I don't think I like sex," she told him 23 February. She was sitting in his reading chair, a book in her lap. He was looking through his disks for some music to play. The beginning part of the conversation was familiar—she was talking about the ASD/UHL split; he was talking about their fading love life.

"I can't believe that," he said.

"Believe what you want." She raised the book, acted as if she were reading.

He stood up. "That's a crock of shit."

"You sound like my dad."

"Is that why you picked me?"

"I didn't pick you. You're not some poor piece of fruit at the West Side Market that someone picked out from other pieces of fruit. It doesn't work that way."

"Yeah. Right. That's why you went fucking all those black guys at college. That had nothing to do with it."

"You're not making sense. And I don't want to talk about this anymore."

"You came to college, and started fooling around as soon as you picked guys Bid Daddy wouldn't accept, at least not as potential son-in-laws. Then you picked me. You thought I'd be honorable, that I wouldn't fuck you and forget you. But I wasn't good enough for your parents. So now it's time to go back home. And what would make Mr. Morality happier than a daughter who doesn't like sex anymore?"

Anna looked at Sauro the same way she had looked at her father after graduation. Whatever words there were inside, she couldn't find a way to bring them together. I tried to reconcile this Anna with the Anna I'd slept with for two nights.

I couldn't.

That night Anna wore a pair of slacks and the tight yellow shirt that Sauro had liked so much. "I rather enjoy dancing when you wear this shirt," he had said once while unbuttoning it. "This shirt really does something for me." "Then why are you taking it off?" she had said.

"I like your shirt," I told her when she came back from the kitchen with the beer.

"Oh," she said, looking down at it. "I've had it for ages." The lack of association disturbed me; selective memory, Sauro had called it.

"It looks good on you."

She smiled, then handed me a glass of beer. "You know, I couldn't remember what kind of beer you like. So

I brought some Bass Ale. I was told that was what James Joyce drank."

It was thick, somewhat bitter. "This is fine," I said. "I usually drink Thirty-Three, but this has a much fuller taste."

She didn't really seem to listen. "I was thinking we could have dinner here. I bought two steaks. And all we'll put on them is salt and pepper." My face must have given away my relief. "I noticed your reaction in some of the restaurants. You like your food plainer. Your face would look exactly like Aunt Lorena's. Her heart and liver are bad, so she has to eat bland food. You'd think she was a New Puritan like my mom."

"It's good to see you in good spirits."

She patted my cheek. "Who put me there? Let's cook some meat."

The kitchen was small and lived down to Ohio City's reputation for living in the last century. Nothing was automated. It was all white: metal, wood, and plastic, along with some chrome and some tan linoleum. A small table stood against the wall opposite the sink and stove. While Anna fried the steak in a large cast-iron pan, I moved the table into the living room and set it up with tablecloth, silverware, and candelabra.

Dinner, steak and potatoes, for once, was served the way I liked it. Anna and I chatted, and I enjoyed the way she felt at ease. We compared Cleveland history and Boston history. We compared boarding schools and public schools. It felt as if we were talking about different countries, but I didn't mind. Evening grays brightened the candles, and night's darkness settled in peacefully. I had trouble believing that wine and conversation could make a dinner last so long.

"You know," she said, after she'd brought out the coffee and brandy, "I almost canceled our . . . contract . . . after our first meeting."

"Why didn't you?"

"I was going to tell you, but I can't."

"Why not?"

"It's sort of embarrassing."

"It's shouldn't be. I'm not the judgmental type."

"I can feel myself blushing."

"I can't tell. Candlelight only highlights the best in us. So come on, tell me."

"I almost didn't call you because I felt like I would be doing it to get back at someone."

Living or dead? I wanted to ask. Instead I sat attentively and waited for more.

"It was sort of like after I . . . well, masturbated the first time. I was at boarding school, and it felt really good. And I felt free from home and everything. But this creeping guilt kept going at me; I kept feeling like I hadn't controlled myself the way I should have. The second time I did it, I did it for pleasure, but I also felt like I was getting back at somebody. I know it sounds stupid, but I felt the same way. I hate feeling bad about every time I feel good. Do you ever feel that way?"

"Not in a while. I did a lot when I was a teenager."

"Are you saying you've outgrown feeling bad?"

"No. I feel bad about different things. Never about feeling good."

"I feel like there's something wrong with me."

"There's something wrong with all of us. We're human."

"That's a cliché."

I raised my hands to surrender. "I'm sorry. But I still think it's true."

"Do you ever miss not being in love?"

Whatever I said, I knew, it would be the wrong answer. "I don't know," I said. The words didn't sound as safe as I'd hoped they would.

"Have you ever fallen in love with a client?"

"No. I had a client fall in love with me once."

"What happened?"

"The contract was terminated, and I took a pay cut."

"That's not fair."

"Yeah, it is. If I do my job right, my clients have a good time, feel better about themselves, and don't fall in love with me."

"That's a tall order." She poured herself more brandy. "What would happen if you did fall in love with a client?"

I scratched the back of my neck. "I don't know. It

would depend on the kind of person she was. Not everyone can accept the idea of having a relationship with someone who works at Personal Services."

"You'd keep working?"

"Yeah. I like what I do."

"Oh." She blinked a few times and looked away. I could tell she was fighting something within her. "I'm sorry, but maybe you better go."

If I had been Sauro Contini, I would have gone over to her and comforted her. "Do you want to talk about it?" I asked.

"Can I ask you something?" she said to Sauro's crystal player.

"Sure."

"The other night, when we went to the hotel, the first time . . . You, well, ended things so quickly. Because of your job and all, I couldn't help but think that there was something more. That you were so . . . I don't know . . . *moved*, maybe just excited, that you couldn't help yourself." She bowed her head, and a hand wiped at her cheeks. "Am I reading too much into it?"

I felt as if I were torturing her; I wanted to tell her that she'd interpreted it just right. "Anna, these things . . ."

She shook her head and forced herself up from the table. She walked over to the picture window. She seemed to stare out at the graying black that rose above the underside of trees and sides of buildings illuminated by streetlamps. "I can see my image in the glass," she said. Her voice sounded as if it belonged to a ghost. I half expected her to tell me that she could see Sauro's image, too. "It's insubstantial. Like you. I keep expecting something more."

I said her name to pull her out of the darkness, but she continued to stare at whatever reflections she saw in the window. "I think I better go. If you want a lover, someone who'll love you and fall in love with you, call in tomorrow and terminate the contract. If you want a substantial illusion, call me."

I waited for her to say something. She didn't, so I left.

I thought I'd grown used to the shadowy walk to the rapid stop, but I felt that I was being watched. I turned and saw no one. The only things around were the monitors, one attached to every other streetlamp. They shouldn't have made me feel on edge. Maybe Sauro's ghost had been whispering politics into my ear.

15

I EXPECTED TO arrive at Personal Services and have someone inform me that Anna Elizabeth Baxter was no longer one of my clients. Instead, Donna Palaez, one of Personal Services' lawyers, had someone fetch me and escort me to her office. Her office had the orderliness of someone who'd spent ten years making sure that chaos was kept out of her business life. A large holocube of Palaez with her husband and two sons was prominently displayed on the desk.

"What can I do for you?" I asked. I hadn't seen Palaez since Beatrice Knecivic wanted to marry me. The lawyers didn't stay too long at the Christmas parties.

"It's about the Baxter file. The AI brought it to my attention this morning. The content of your conversation last night with Ms. Baxter has a few of us worried."

I shrugged. I never knew what to say to her. She held her body upright as if working hard for perfect posture. Her hair was jet black, but I always remembered it as white, pulled back into a bun the way some of the New Puritan women wear their hair. Looking at her, you would never think she'd work at a place where sexual services was the active trade.

"You don't take it seriously?" she asked.

"There was a problem, as you saw, last night. Ms. Baxter has to decide if she wants a lover or a companion. Personally, I don't think she's stable enough to maintain a straight-world romance. She needs some help. She's living with too many ghosts."

"And you're the best man to be her exorcist?"

"It's what I'm paid for."

"Well, at this point there's not a whole lot I can do. I have made a recommendation to Fred O'Mallery that we should terminate this contract. The Baxter family is the type that might sue for some sort of liability if Ms. Baxter ends up in a worse state than she is in now. And you can guess that James Baxter will make it a moral issue rather than let it rest as a legal issue. As you well know, we do not need any more bad publicity after what happened in South Carolina last year." The South Carolina Supreme Court had ruled that a married woman or man must receive the spouse's permission before hiring a companion."

"I think things are fine."

"That is what you said two years ago when the Knecivic case became an issue. Even though you denied it, I still continue to believe that you were attracted to her."

"I wasn't."

"I think you're attracted to Ms. Baxter."

"I'm not."

"Well, make sure you're not. And if you are, cancel your contract. Take your vacation time, and find out whatever you need to know."

"I can't do that." To see a client within twenty-eight days after termination could mean a loss of two years worth of retirement pay.

"Well, then watch yourself and your feelings. Follow all regulations to the letter. Personal Services has taken good care of you. I'm sure you don't need a list of everything we've done for you." Two years ago she'd read me the list. "Make sure that Personal Services is your first priority, not this woman. She should be getting psychiatric help, not the kind of help you give her."

Until word got around to the real people at Fair Haven School for Learning-Disabled Children that I had charged Susie Sundai for sexual services, I had been known as the Professor. I was the only ninth-grader who liked to read books. I loved to puzzle out the stories for their hidden symbols and meanings (I was just never willing to finish an essay or complete a test). The same with the European movies: I liked to puzzle things out; not everything was there and obvious. And it's what I liked most about servicing: figuring out a client, then embellishing our fucking with an air of romance, making them feel wanted, making them feel as if they could be understood.

Aggie, of course, said I was full of shit, that it was all head games. Every time my lineup of shift-janes seemed like a parade of self-pity and sorrow, Aggie would try to talk me into going back to Direct Services: it was another parade, but one so smooth and efficient that you didn't have to worry about the stories that hid behind each marcher. A spreading of the legs, Aggie would say, a few thrusts of the hips, perhaps some feigned sighs, and it was done. Sometimes I was envious.

Like now. I took Palaez's words to heart; I didn't want bad blood between me and Personal Services. So I went over last night's dailies and thought of all the things I could have said differently, the ways I could have held myself to send out a different message. *What would happen if you did fall in love with a client?* I went through her file again, through all the dailies. The images kept piling up in my mind until I remembered things better from the monitor's point of view than my own. Her tone of voice was so well modulated that I forgot how it had sounded when we faced each other over a table, the way her eyes had taken me, the way her lips moved, the way she held her body and sometimes held my hand.

I could guess why she had been virginal in boarding school and chased after her break-heart bastards in college, why she had hooked up with Sauro, why she had left home for Cleveland. But I couldn't guess why Anna Elizabeth Baxter hired a servicer and risked everything: the opinion of the newspaper columnists, Aunt Lorena's continued support, the possible reconciliation with her father, and her own self-respect. I couldn't puzzle out her story. Something about her need seemed so deep and so desperate.

And it scared and attracted me the way Susie Sundai had ten years before. I remembered the sweetness of our first two weeks together: sneaking out of our cottages, telling the counselors (whom we all called guards) that we were visiting someone in another cottage, heading, instead, for the woods, climbing the wall surrounding Fair Haven, and making our way to a friend's apartment. There were always the real people, the ex-Havenites—living in the Coventry area (before it became a mini-Construct) or down by the University Circle mini-Construct—who would vacate a room for a while. And for the first two weeks, that's all it was: the mad dash for freedom, the borrowed apartment and the eagerness to explore, the lewd jokes made by the real people who knew, and the gossip that never made it to the unreal people—the social workers, the teachers, or the guards—because we never told them anything important, even if it was for our own good. The two, or maybe it was three, weeks were magical; and then the touch of flesh was no longer enough. Our fingers had moved in sweet ignorance over the other's body, but now, between bouts of physical discovery, came a need to probe different contours with verbal fingers that sought out a similar delight. Imitative of our guards, who had B.A.'s in psychology and who acted as if they had Ph.D.'s, we examined the other's psyche, found fault, reduced our accusations to the pointed fingers of some stock phrases, and condemned the other for being incapable of offering love beyond the contact of skin. The accusations were easy to formulate, easy to couch in sympathetic terms. Roderick Lawrence: the family that couldn't communicate, the grabbing in the night and the stranger forcing himself upon a body that didn't struggle enough, the intense shame and the too-many showers, the Free Clinic blood test that turned out (thank God) negative, the inability to confess, and the deepening failure at everything as if each parental "what's wrong with you?" was really an accusation that dirtied and sullied and made it impossible to love. Susan Sundai: the mother with a glass in one hand and a bottle in the other, the father with a belt who wanted order in a household that wouldn't hold itself together, a sister who ran away and was convinced no one could love her. We had to tear at each other to protect ourselves, and we had to help each other destroy ourselves in order to prove that we never deserved any love at all—or else the world might have cheated us out of too much.

What could Anna Elizabeth Baxter want out of someone like that? And if she knew about all that, and about the time I charged Susan Sundai for sex, the first of my free-lance tricks, and about my father's death, all the darkness beyond the illusion touched upon glass, would she caress any of those private contours with any tenderness that wasn't born of pity?

I should have terminated the contract then.

Anna called later that afternoon. She said she'd been unfair last night and wanted to make up for it. I told her I'd be at her apartment at seven.

Part 2

the client

The republican is the only form of government which is not eternally at open or secret war with the rights of mankind.
— THOMAS JEFFERSON

16

THAT FRIDAY NIGHT Anna said she'd worked up her courage. We were going to go out dancing. Somewhere between couscous and dessert she lost that courage, and instead we ended up going to a hotel in the Construct, a different one because she didn't want to see the same man behind the reception desk. She fell asleep after the first time we made love.

The next night we had dinner at Murmuring Brooks and ended up walking all around her neighborhood. Along poorly lighted streets, through darkened alleyways made creepy by the deep-lined shadows of the fire escapes, where Anna giggled at my jumpiness, we continued to walk and chat while she seemed to be gearing up to take me to the bed she'd shared with Sauro. We ended up going to a downtown hotel, the kind for well-off business people, where the help placed a mint and a tiny bottle of brandy on your pillow.

With the lights off, the window's curtains left open, a glow from the streets giving our gray bodies a silver cast, we made love once. Afterward, Anna cuddled up against me and feigned sleep. I considered all the things I could say to her to help her feel more comfortable about our being together, a client with her very substantial illusion, but I couldn't bring myself to say any of them. If she terminated the contract, then I could say *hasta la vista* to Palaez and *adios* to Lang.

The next morning we had breakfast in the hotel's restaurant, where anybody she knew who worked downtown could have come in and seen her, but she seemed cheerful in her defiance. On the rapid back out to Ohio City, she began to wonder out loud if she'd made a mistake.

At the door to her apartment, she told me I could have Sunday off.

"I had Wednesday off," I said. "We can see each other if you like."

"You're really supposed to have two days off. Maybe we should see each other on Tuesday."

"It doesn't matter. It's not like I've been spending all day with you."

"Do you want to see me on Monday?" she asked.

"Yes. I would."

"It would mean more money, wouldn't it?"

"That's one way of looking at it."

She eyed me carefully. "Is that the way you look at it?"

"Anna, you know that's not the case."

"How do I know that?"

I didn't know what to say, so I kissed her. It was a violation of everything I had been trained to do. You never leave a question unanswered: evasions can be interpreted and reinterpreted until they become an unspoken promise.

Anna's response was warm and sweet, and we stood there kissing, until a neighbor's door opened. Anna stepped away, then tugged at my arm, drawing me into her apartment. Anna closed the door behind me. We stood there and listened to the neighbor walk past the apartment, then down the stairs.

We could barely hear the door shut four flights down, and that's when Anna wrapped her arms around me and kissed me.

"I take it," I finally said, "that you'd like to spend the day together?"

She bit her lower lip, then nodded, then shook her head. "I can't afford it. Let's see each other on Tuesday."

Before I could leave, she went to the bookshelves and pulled out two books: Raymond Chandler's *The Big Sleep* and Fyodor Dostoyevski's *Crime and Punishment,* one of Sauro's favorites and one of hers. "If you can't get into pure literature, maybe you can get into the low-brow stuff," she said.

I smiled and looked at the old-style cloth bindings. Lang had given me assigned reading on crystal. "What do you think of Thomas Jefferson?" I asked.

Anna shrugged, her way of passing something off as trivial, and said, "A lot of ASD people liked to quote him. But so did an uncle of mine who didn't like ASD at all."

She thought for a moment longer, then tapped the copy of *Crime and Punishment*. "I don't think ASD types like this book. It tells you that there's no high cause that can justify murder. The people Sauro hung out with in ASD agreed with that only if you were talking about the CIA."

I took the rapid back to Slavic Village and read the first chapter of each book, then held them in my lap trying to decide which to read first. I skimmed the introduction and discovered that *Crime and Punishment* featured an angelic woman who sold her body so her impoverished family could eat. There were hidden motives behind this reading selection, just as there had been hidden motives during that first year when Sauro had given Anna book after book until, in reaction, Anna formed a strong-willed set of literary tastes of her own.

I found myself reading on in *Crime and Punishment*, trying to uncover Anna's meaning, as I walked from the rapid to Slavic Village. I hadn't read while walking since grade school. I stood outside the door to the apartment to finish a long-winded paragraph and looked up to see Maureen standing in her doorway watching me from across the corridor. I hadn't made it up to her for missing out on their anniversary. Sayeed, who lived next door to us, and who nobody liked, had shown up with a gift.

"I had to read that one in high school," Maureen said. "I sort of liked it."

I looked up from the book, a bit embarrassed. "Hi. How's Maggie?"

"At work. You wanna have a beer? Betsy and I are watching something horrible on the holo."

"Thanks. I got work to do."

Maureen likes me, but hates my job. "Suit yourself," she said.

I tried to smile at her. Then I jammed my thumb at the lock, it clicked open, and I rushed into my apartment.

After I made myself lunch, I tracked down the crystal Pilar had given me. Either she or Lang had prepared a selection of writings—the Declaration of Independence, excerpts from *Notes on the State of Virginia,* messages to Congress, and a bunch of letters. I tried to focus on the reading, but I got lost in the complex sentences: a subordinate clause would go one way, and my mind would go the other. Whatever Lang considered important had been highlighted in blue, so I just read the highlighted parts. The words all sounded thoughtful and intelligent, but terribly familiar, as if 250 years of politics had watered them down. I couldn't help but wonder if they'd been all that believable back then.

Harry came back from a shift at Monitoring just as I was finishing up with the Jefferson. About midway through I had taken a K-pill to help me concentrate, and all it had done was increase my anxiety about tomorrow's meeting with Lang. If I got lucky, I kept thinking (hoping), Anna would cancel, and then I wouldn't have to see Lang.

"What are you reading?" Harry asked.

I tried to appear as if I were concentrating. "Thomas Jefferson."

Harry whistled loudly, then laughed. "I'm impressed." He punched my shoulder. "This jane of yours has really got you going."

For the briefest of moments, I considered telling him who had prepared the crystal and why.

Harry was looking over my shoulder. "She highlighted it, and everything. I'm doubly impressed. Are you feeling more politically motivated?"

"Just bored."

"I used to teach this," he said, "a long time ago." He made it sound as if it had been as long ago as Thomas Jefferson. He scanned through it, stopping every now and then to read something. "Have you read the bit about how the tree of liberty has to be watered with patriotic blood every now and then?"

I shook my head.

"I thought an ASDer would like that kind of thing."

"I haven't read that part, but I really haven't been reading this too thoroughly."

Harry then spotted the two books and looked through each one in turn. "Maybe Kevin and I were wrong about this jane. Maybe she's good for you. If nothing else, she'll get you to be an intellectual. I guess she couldn't be satisfied with just your namesake."

"You gotta talk about something afterwards."

"I guess so. You could even say that two heads are better than one for this kind of work."

That night, after drinking several beers and watching an old movie with Harry, the beer's carbohydrates and an anxiety worse than caffeine kept the alcohol from making me sleepy. I gave up battling with my sheets and walked into the living room. The lights flashed on when my foot hit the floor, and squinting my eyes, I found the switch and shut them off. In the darkness I made my way to Albert, flipped him on, made access with Tricky Dick, and called up the dailies I hadn't looked at yet.

On Friday afternoon Anna had received a phone call that helped explain some of her behavior Friday and Saturday nights. Anna's tropical bird chirped at 1536, she flipped the phone on, and the screen lit up with Aunt Lorena Smith. Anna's great-aunt was like someone out of an old movie. She held her head up, kept her back straight, and held herself with the assurance of someone who'd been made queen for the day. Anna told her what a surprise it was and how glad she was to hear from her.

"Well, I haven't seen you since the funeral," Aunt Lorena said. "And I swung by the art gallery today, and George told me that you hadn't been to work all month."

"I'm thinking of going back next week," Anna said, and she sounded just like Kevin did when he promised to be 100 percent faithful to Betsy.

"Oh, that's fine dear, but I was beginning to worry about your financial situation. Your trust officer had lunch with me today about some real-estate concerns I had, and she let slip that you had been spending some of your capital."

"I had to buy some groceries," Anna said, "and I did go out once or twice."

"Well, I'm glad to hear you're getting out. I was worried about you keeping yourself cooped up in the dingy little apartment. Why don't you come out for dinner sometime this weekend? Rosa will make something nice, and if you want, you could spend the night. The buds are opening out here, and you could take some nice walks, like you used to last year when you stayed with me."

"That sounds like fun," said Anna.

"Good. What night?"

Anna hesitated. "Is Sunday fine?"

"If Sunday works for you, dear, that will be fine. We really look forward to seeing you. And if you'd like someone to drive you in, we can get you to work on time on Monday, and I can loan you some money so that you don't have to dig into your principal."

Anna told her that no, that was fine, and she'd look forward to seeing her Aunt on Sunday, at five?

I froze the image, then called up a billing overlay. On Monday, 26 April, Anna paid Personal Services sixty thousand dollars to cover our first six visits. I sat there for a while, letting the light from the screen bathe me with a sheen of blue. Sixty thousand dollars was almost one percent of her trust fund. Maybe her finances, or Aunt Lorena's opinion of my services, would convince Anna to give it up. I wished that the Smith house in Hunting Valley was monitored, but Aunt Lorena opposed monitoring. In fact, she had signed a petition against monitoring which one of Anna's friends had circulated sometime last year.

The next morning Anna called. She looked well rested, and her face was flushed. "Do you want to get together an hour from now?" She whispered it. Behind her was nice furniture and a real window's view of some woods. She was calling from her aunt Lorena's. "We could meet at the Coventry mini-Construct."

I felt caught up in her desire, and I almost said yes. But Lang expected to see me this afternoon.

"I can't see you until four," I said.

"Oh." Her face went blank, then she covered it with a smile. "Okay, then." She looked away, as if checking to see if the coast was clear. "How about this? I'll be registered at the Democracy Now Hotel downtown. You'll come find me at four?"

I told her that it sounded wonderful, and she clicked off.

I tried to eat scrambled eggs, but I felt, and they looked, like they'd come right back up, barely changed. The coffee only added to the acids churning up my stomach.

I took the rapid to the Prospect Corridors to find out that my blood was still clean and to sit restlessly while five different supervisors rambled on at the staff meeting. Afterward I reported in to Marie, who wasn't too happy with the weekend's footage or the kiss that I had used to evade Anna's question. "I know this one is a challenge," she said, "but it will boost your career tremendously if you rise to the occasion. You know, I'm counting on you." There was an urgency to her voice, as if her career needed the boost. I wondered if Palaez was holding her responsible, in case of lawsuit, or if this had something to do with her impending marriage outside the Business.

By now my meeting with Lang was two hours away, and I tried to get rid of my anxiety by working out in the gym with Aggie, Henry, and Eric. Aggie paired up with me and, for a while, was silent. Henry was going on about how much money he was losing during his downtime.

"This one already wants to make it big," Aggie said to me. She sounded a bit disgusted. "Just watch, he'll be servicing the whites in the Heights within two years."

"That's faster than me," I said.

"You spent a lot of time saying you didn't want to work there."

"Well, I'm in Ohio City."

"With a woman who'd be living in the Heights if it weren't for her funny politics."

"It's a democracy," I said. "Somebody's gotta have funny politics."

"Like your supervisor." Aggie had never liked Marie, and liked her even less since the announcement of her marriage and her promotion. Aggie had been working Direct Services since she was out of high school and felt her seniority should account for something.

"It takes all kinds," I said.

Eric was busy explaining how he'd gone hydraulic,

with the flood tubes in his penis replaced by balloons, and a reservoir in the pelvis that would enlarge the penis with a solution whenever a button along the hip was pressed. "It's just as hard," said Eric, "they never know the difference, and you can double your numbers."

"I don't know," said Henry. "When I hear balloon, I think *pop*, and that thing would be inside me."

"You can go metal," said Aggie.

"And set off every metal detector in town?" said Eric.

"Use chemicals," I said. "Half the johns don't mind when you're down between acts. It offers a touch of realism." I jumped for the pull-ups bar and started counting.

"If they wanted realism," Aggie said, "they'd get a date."

"Chemicals get me dizzy," said Henry.

"Besides," said Eric, "you get better tips when you're up."

"Are you sure about that?" I said between breaths and pull-ups.

"Sure he's sure," said Aggie. "Eric's got a family. He counts his tips. Henry here wants to be rich. *He* will count his."

I shook my head and tried to do five more as quickly as I could.

"What's he all pissed about?" asked Henry.

"CT here's sensitive," said Aggie. "He don't like to think like a commodity."

17

AFTER THE VISUAL ID, the bancard, the thumbprint, the metal-and-explosives detector, and the personal frisk, I was allowed into Lang's apartment and once again led down the hall by Pilar. Lang was standing, waiting for me. His sleeves were rolled up, his tie pulled down, but the energy of last week was gone. There were dark pouches under his eyes, and he looked a bit haggard, as if too many sleepless nights had caught up with him. The two family cubes offered me four new images of family members unhindered by age or disease.

"Have a seat, please," he said to me. "Pilar will bring us coffee." Pilar was already on the way out. "Now, how's the past week been between you and Anna?"

"Fine," I said. "We're screwing now, in hotels."

"Yes," he said. He shifted in his chair. "I know." He didn't sound too happy with the idea.

I wasn't too happy that he could know everything so easily, but I wasn't in much of a position to complain.

"How has the week been, otherwise?" he asked.

"Just fine."

"And you'll see her today at four?" he asked.

I nodded, impressed at how quickly Adolf had relayed him the information, how nonchalantly he dealt with it. "We'll be meeting at the Democracy Now Hotel."

He looked at his watch. "That gives us a little bit of time. I'm sure you will need time to prepare whatever it is you prepare before such an encounter."

"No. I come with all working parts included."

Pilar arrived with the coffee. She didn't offer me cream or sugar, and there wasn't a silver spoon on the saucer. Pilar nodded to Lang and left, closing the door behind her.

Lang sipped his coffee, then offered me a smile. "Now, tell me, what did you think of Mr. Jefferson?"

"It was all right. You know, I did take civics in ninth grade."

"Do you remember much?"

"Sure. I repeated ninth grade three times."

Lang looked uncomfortable. I couldn't understand why: most of his informants couldn't have been Ivy Leaguers. "You did some other reading, too, yesterday. What did you think?"

"I like the one about the detective."

"What do you think of Raskalnikov?"

"Someone smart enough to know better."

"What do you think about what Anna said, that there is no high cause to justify murder?"

"It's bullshit," I said.

He raised an eyebrow.

"Everyone does it. What's justified warfare? Or execution?" I felt as if Sauro had been doing the talking, and I wanted to take back the words.

"War and execution are sanctioned by the state; murder is carried out by an individual. In a republican democracy, the state follows the will of its people and the rule of law. Warfare and execution are two means of maintaining the rule of law, though, of course, both can and have been misused, even by our own country. But murder is one step closer to anarchy, because it's an individual acting out his impulse."

"Sure," I said.

"What do you think Jefferson's opinion would be?"

"It wasn't highlighted. I'm sure it wasn't much of an issue."

"I guess that's fair. Let's take a hypothetical situation. Let's assume Thomas Jefferson were living right now, but with the same ideas and philosophies. What would he say of the Union for Human Liberation?"

"Maybe he would talk about the tree of liberty and the blood of patriots."

"Maybe he would. But why?"

"He supported a revolution, didn't he? There are times, he said, when it's okay to abolish a government."

"Name a time."

I thought back to what I'd read. I felt as if I had to prove myself to him. "When it becomes destructive of life, liberty, and the pursuit of happiness."

"Good," he said, and I was suddenly sorry for what I'd said. I didn't want to be his star student. "Do you remember the next part?"

I did, but I shook my head.

"'Prudence, indeed, will dictate that governments long established should not be changed for light and transient causes.' In relationship to the entire population, does the UHL's desire to close the camps, no matter what the cost, fit into Jefferson's ideals?"

"They're talking about life and liberty," I said. "A hiver's life may be more transient than others, but there's nothing light about the situation."

"You could write propaganda for the UHL."

"That's not what I meant."

"But you understand the core of the problem. Our ideals tell us to close the camps, because we feel sympathy, even if the malady could have, in most cases, been avoided. Humans sin, and my own religion tells me to forgive, that it is God's duty to judge, not mine. But a complex society like ours cannot run without the bending of ideals. The same was true in Jefferson's time. When he became president, he purchased Louisiana from the French, even though the Constitution gave him no such power. When a British ship kidnapped three Americans and made them British sailors, Congress embargoed British goods. Jefferson signed the law, even though by his own thinking, such a law was unconstitutional. However, better an embargo, he felt, than a war. Do you see my point?"

"Yeah. Ideals are great, when they're convenient."

Lang sipped his coffee, then placed saucer and cup alongside the cube featuring his parents. "Perhaps there's some truth to that. So we have to choose wisely. The camps exist to keep Americans safe from Americans who were frivolous with their desires. I hope no offense is taken."

"No," I said. I wondered what made the longing for intimacy frivolous, as compared to the longing for money or a new chair. Or a career.

"Good," he said. "But we still protect the right to dissent. Members of ASD have staged protest rallies without harassment. They have published books whenever they could raise the capital and have placed texts on commercial datanets. Groups have raised money to buy the assets of someone in quarantine, so the assets wouldn't be sold at a low market value. Individuals have counseled and visited people in quarantine and seen them off at the train station. They have conducted lawsuits, and they've challenged statutes in the courts.

"You see, Rod, rule of law must be followed, or there's anarchy. A bomb here, an execution there, a city blacked out and over three hundred dead. That's not rule of law. We haven't denied anyone their rights. But you're not sure about that, are you?"

"I'm not sure how you fit hivers into the picture. Didn't Jefferson promise to protect the rights of the minority?"

"No one has taken away an inflicted person's right to vote, just certain of their liberties."

"Why can't they have a state of their own?"

"Now that's an idea. But I'm not sure the current residents of whatever state you chose would want to leave."

"Fine. Let them stay."

"Okay. But you know, as good as your idea might be, it has never been an official position of the UHL. All humans are equal and should live with one another. If I have typhoid fever, I should have freedom of the streets, the freedom to infect. If I believe in equal rights for people with typhoid fever, I should use a gun, or a bomb, or advanced computer programming to break down the rule of law."

"I didn't say anything about guns or about computer viruses."

Lang sat back and looked me over, as if he could evaluate me with a careful glance. "I think we're more or less in agreement on a few things. Would you want to see Anna involved with people who use guns or computer viruses?"

"It's her life."

"What's your job, then?"

"I'm a servicer. I take care of my client's needs."

"Can you define needs in higher terms?"

"In my job?"

"But that's what we all have to do. There are higher calls than just taking care of ourselves. Would you want to see Anna hurt, if such hurt could be avoided?"

"Of course not."

"Then keep an eye out for her, just as I've asked you to do. If she becomes involved with the UHL, I'll have to arrest her. My commitment to her family can't rise about my commitment to the law. *Unless:* there are people higher up in the UHL I can arrest in her stead. The UHL will come after her, if it hasn't already. It's important that there be someone to watch out for them, someone who cares."

I sat there and pretended to listen as he told me about his time in the Spanish War, and how he wanted to win the enemy over by presenting them with a better alternative to their leaders; how the United States, when it presented the ideals of Jefferson, won new converts to the cause of democracy. I didn't know what to think. He didn't just want someone to watch out for the UHL and inform him of their efforts, he wanted an ally, a believer.

I hadn't believed in anything in ages.

On the way Pilar set up my appointment for next Monday and asked me if I had changed my mind about the money. It wasn't much of a struggle to tell her no.

18

THE DEMOCRACY NOW HOTEL was a natural-air hotel between Euclid and Superior, with windows that opened, and plants everywhere. The giant lobby was bordered on one side by the hotel restaurant, on the other by the large entranceway to Democracy Now domestic headquarters and out-of-home shopping center. All I had was a duffel bag with some clothes and the two books Anna had lent me, so I made my way through the shopping center and ordered up a small suitcase, choosing tan artificial leather from a choice of twenty coverings, and the dimensions from a choice of five. A half hour later, at 1605, I had the suitcase, and I hoped that for the price it would impress Anna more than a duffel bag. Of course, I would charge it to expenses when I got home.

Anna was waiting for me in a room on the top floor. A skylight let in the afternoon sun to warm the room. The windows, offering a view of the wide rows of Construct corridors leading to the lake, were all open, letting in the warm May air. The room had a queen-size bed, a Democracy Now sensory kit (the model used at Personal Services), a computer terminal displaying the emblem of the Democracy Now catalog, and a liquor cabinet made of synthetic wood and stocked with enough alcohol to keep us off our feet for the next month.

Anna was sitting in an armchair wearing a frilly white robe I hadn't seen before. She smiled at my entrance and literally hopped out of the chair and skipped up to me. Her enthusiasm became my own, and I pulled myself into the energy of her embrace. She stepped back, giggled, and said, "I went shopping downstairs while waiting for you." The robe fell to the floor. She was wearing a white silk chemise, a lacy garter belt, and stockings. If Anna's body had been a little more compact, the effect would have been tremendous. But she was giggling again, most likely aware that with the broader shoulders, the slight curve of belly, the thick thighs, that this wasn't quite as sexy as it must have seemed on the display holoes. "I've been dreaming about this all day," she said. She pulled at my shirt; the velcro ripped apart, and she started to laugh. "It looked sexy in the movie I saw last night."

"It's sexy right now," I lied, and we tugged at each other's clothes and were both laughing when we ended up in bed, and the lovemaking exorcised the people we'd been worrying about when we'd each arrived.

Anna must have stopped worrying about her great-aunt's admonishments about spending principal, because we stayed at the Democracy Now hotel for three nights, leaving only for meals and once so Anna could watch me watch *Truest Love*.

The lovemaking was energetic, playful, sometimes tender, and I enjoyed the tender. Anna wanted the playful— "Let me find out how exotic you can be, Mr. Serviceman," she said—so we tried out all sorts of positions and approaches until they inspired more laughter than pleasure. Anna became frustrated that the reality wasn't matching what she must have fantasized, so she had me hook her up to the sensory kit. But before we could get going, she became embarrassed and told me to unhook her, that all she wanted was the real thing.

We talked about our childhoods, because we'd found that easy, and Anna kept telling me how amazed she was that my childhood sounded like any other, how she'd expected something tragic, like child abuse or molestation or something. We talked about our discovery of masturbation, our first caresses, our first time making love. Since my experiences of the latter two had been at the same time, when I was sixteen and with Susan Sundai, I extended the incident into a several-week story set at Heights High rather than Fair Haven. Anna reminisced about how wonderful it had been just to neck for the longest time, feeling all the juices run free, and I felt a bit envious.

She started asking me, a bit hesitantly, about the books she'd lent me, discreetly probing me for my reactions. She wanted to know why I sympathized with the guy who was "neat, clean, shaved, sober, and . . . didn't care who knew about it." After I told her about a few of the things wrong with *Truest Love,* she asked me what I thought of Sonia, the prostitute in *Crime and Punishment.* "She's too pure for my tastes," I told Anna. When Anna dozed, or during the hours when the lack of alcohol kept me awake, I took out one of the two books and read. Whenever Anna rolled over in her sleep, I dropped my hand over the edge of the bed so the book wouldn't be in sight.

As the days progressed, she became aware that I wasn't going to tell her why I had become a servicer or what I thought of my different clients, or even how many there had been. She told me that I was hiding, and I avoided the issue with some well-timed kisses. Afterwards her questions became more expansive.

What do you think should be done with the Nigerian boat people?

Should we have permitted Syria and Israel to partition New Palestine?

Should we have sided with the Spanish government during the rebellion?

What should be done with the people who couldn't afford to live in the Construct?

Were all the available pills society's way of replacing the illicit drugs used out in the shackvilles?

Rule Five: Always tell it straight to your colleagues and your supervisor. With gov officials, that's up to you. But never—never—tell anything straight to a client.

Corollary One: Whatever you tell a client, make sure it's consistent.

With my backlog of stories about my parents in San Antonio, my math major, my cruel grandmother, that had been easy. But Anna was asking questions that reached down to something within me. Each answer couldn't help but reveal the structure of the microchips, the nature of my programming, the repeating loops where nothing could get past. She acted as if what I thought and felt were vitally important. And how do you make up answers when it's already difficult to answer the same questions when you're telling the truth?

Anna began to thrive on the political talk. It was a way of being herself without having to talk about the things that hurt her most. She became more self-confident, and her conversation became lighter, less ponderous. She talked more often about going out, being more sociable, perhaps going back to work at the art gallery, like her aunt wanted.

The talk was easy, and I'd never felt so comfortable talking before.

But we never talked about Kansas City, the camps, or about hives.

By Wednesday night we were exhausted, and a new feeling overtook us. We had dinner at the hotel restaurant, and I felt as if I'd never escape the place or the constant touch of skin upon skin. Anna must have been feeling something similar because the usually talkative, socially adept woman had nothing to say. It was my job to fill up the silence; I was tired of my job. Midway through the meal Anna lowered her fork and looked at me with a steady eye. "Do you get paid well for putting up with me?"

I felt as if we'd taken a step backward into the Anna of the previous week. "It's not that hard a job," I said. "You're a delight to put up with."

"You don't get paid everything I pay Personal Services."

"No."

"But you do get paid well."

"Enough. I sometimes can eat real meat and wear nice clothes."

"But enough to pay for the nice dinners every night? For the hotel rooms last week?"

"No."

"That's part of the illusion, right?"

I hesitated. It was all down in her contract. Why spoil the illusion she had so obviously needed at first?

"Rod, who pays for this?"

"You do."

"Fees and expenses, right?"

"Yeah."

"Then I'll pay for it from now on, thank you. It'll cut down on the final bill."

She smiled, turning her nose up a bit. For a moment she looked a little like her aunt Lorena Smith.

I returned to my pot roast, but it tasted dull. I should have been happy at her newfound sense of independence, her desire to step away from illusion. All I could feel was some vague anger, and the feeling reminded me of Lang, who was a friend of Anna's father, whose name I couldn't mention to Anna because everything Anna and I did together was filed by Adolf and reviewed by Lang himself.

"Maybe," I said, "we should stop going to monitored places."

"You were the one who said it didn't make a difference."

I wondered what Lang would think about my proposition. Maybe he'd think I was a terrorist. "It just seems like a bit of a risk. There are always these leaks to the press, and half the time it's stuff that only people in Monitoring could know."

"I heard that all the time at ASD meetings."

"Well," I said. "It does happen."

"And how do you know, Mr. Serviceman?"

"My roommate works at Monitoring."

Anna finished her prime rib too fast to have enjoyed it. Knowing she was gathering her thoughts, waiting for the turbulence to build into an outburst, I took several sips of red wine. "Does your roommate have a name?"

"Harry Torres."

"You never mentioned him before."

Selective memory. "Yeah, I have. Remember when we argued about monitors? He's the guy who spotted the woman being strangled by her husband."

"You didn't tell me your friend at Monitoring was your roommate. Does he tune in at night to watch us in bed?" Her offhand anger surprised me, all her resentment overflowing.

"First, he works day shift. Second, that's not the issue. All I wanted to say was that there have been times when footage from Monitoring has mysteriously turned up in the media."

"That's my father's problem."

"But it's your name and face that gets seen. And if the gossip is good enough, all the media will pick it up. Some pretty lewd pictures have appeared on the New Puritan Network—in the name of decency, of course. It would be a great way to show Mr. Morality's immoral daughter."

"My father got rid of me. He couldn't care less."

"The slimier New Puritans would remind us all that he raised you. They can be pretty good at defining morality as if they were the only ones who had it."

"Hell of a thing for a serviceman to say."

I could feel my face heat up. "Then what do you want me to say?"

She shook her head, confused. "I don't know. I've been with you for over two weeks now, and suddenly I find out that your roommate works for Monitoring."

"We both work for the government," I said calmly, trying to placate her. "We share government housing. We even eat government food at the Cleveland Cafeteria."

"But after two weeks, after hearing so many of your stories and jokes, and I still don't even know *that*. For ten thousand dollars a day plus expenses, I could at least expect the truth."

"Fine. You're the one who's paying. And if you don't like the services you're paying for, then you can always terminate the contract." I found myself rising, then walking away. I heard her calling for the waitress, but I resisted the temptation to look back. I threw open the restaurant's heavy wood door and stormed out into the hotel lobby. I suddenly felt silly. I had the sense I was being watched, and it made me feel as if I were putting on an elaborate performance.

"Rod!" Anna called out from behind me, then she was at my side, her hand upon my arm, gently pulling me to a stop. I turned to face her, and her words spilled out in a confused rush of apologies and explanations. She had no right, she was expecting too much, she wished there was some other way. I ignored what was going on inside me, how the moroseness and anger, which shouldn't have been there in the first place, were melding into something painfully soft.

We retrieved her bancard, which she'd thrown onto the restaurant table before rushing out after me, and went back up to our hotel room. In bed she eased her body down on mine, as if it were a moment that called for the utmost in delicacy. "Don't move," she said. "This is for you." Her face was soft with desire, but she kept her eyes open and concentrated on my pleasure that same way I had concentrated on the pleasure of so many others. I recognized the look on her face, and it made me feel terribly alone.

19

WE HAD BREAKFAST in the hotel restaurant, and Anna ordered us each a printed-out *New York Times* to catch up on what we missed. We read rather than talked. The sports section was short enough that I had to read the front page to keep busy throughout breakfast. Early in the week two men held a press conference to describe how their spouses, former ASD leaders in Kansas City, had disappeared without a trace three weeks ago. They were convinced that they had been pulled in by the authorities for questioning about the Black Out and had yet to be released. The Kansas City Police Department denied the charge, and yesterday they announced that after a thorough investigation, they had concluded that the spouses, a man and a woman, were lovers and had taken off for parts unknown. The two men felt that it was pretty hard to take off to parts unknown in an unmonitored environment. On the other hand, last night three more suspected ringleaders had been arrested.

"What do you think of all this Kansas City stuff?" I asked her after the waiter had poured our fourth cup of coffee.

She shook her head. "I don't like to talk about it."

"Why not?"

"It's just too depressing."

"What did Sauro think of it all?"

"Please . . ." Her eyes implored me to change the subject. "Don't spoil what's been a really wonderful three nights."

It was the last she said until she paid the check and said she would call me this afternoon.

At work Marie was happy with the Monday- and Tuesday-night footage she had seen. She said she looked forward to the dailies for Wednesday night. "I want to see if you get any hotter." Aggie had heard about my three-day disappearance and wanted to know how much I weighed. "I wanted to know how hard to pull if you get stuck."

At lunch in the Cleveland Cafeteria, Harry, who hadn't seen me since Sunday when I was reading what he thought was Anna's compilation of Thomas Jefferson, made Aggie's point more directly:

"She's got you by the balls."

"Only literally."

It was fourteen hours, but the cafeteria was still crowded. Our voices were raised loud enough so we could hear each other.

"That's what you think," he said. "You were at it for three nights. Were you using chemicals?"

"No." I tried to hide the response with a mouthful of chicken tetrazzini.

Harry smiled his toothy grin. "She's got you by the balls."

"No. She doesn't."

"Let's watch some of the dailies together. I'll bet you she calls it making love."

I sipped some milk. "They all do."

"But I read her file, too. She's the type who would mean it."

"Come on, Harry. You're making a big deal out of nothing."

"Not nothing. Something. And I told you what something *was* last week."

"Okay, I'll give you that. One of our lawyers said the same thing. She even recommended that the contract be broken. Satisfied?"

"You mean the contract wasn't broken."

I nodded.

"You're telling me that one of your lawyers thought there might be a possible lawsuit, and no one followed up?"

"Look, she's not really ready for termination. We're screwing in hotel rooms because she can't make it in the same place where she lived with Contini. She's not talking about him anymore. She barely mentions her father. And she still can't make it to work."

"You didn't tell me you guys were screwing in hotels."

I didn't like the tone of his voice. "It's really not that big of a deal. Other shift-janes prefer hotel rooms."

"What hotels?"

I named them.

"They're all in the Construct. My boy, there are monitors in the Construct."

"And the sky's blue. I think."

"All your humping and everything you say is being recorded for posterity. It's perfect evidence for a lawsuit if something goes wrong. I'd listen to your lawyer."

"I'm going by the book. I can't get in trouble."

20

I RETURNED HOME from lunch with Harry to find a message from Anna on the computer. She requested the pleasure of my company at seven-thirty. I was to come casually, instead of dressing up, and would I please bring a bottle of white wine. Knowing it was the wrong thing to do, I put on a pair of Democracy Now blue jeans and a yellow tunic. I had the synthesizer prepare me a bottle of white wine.

The westbound rapid was virtually empty: the affluent commuters had already left for home. The eastbound rapids were full, with hired help heading back home after preparing dinner for their employers' families and with day farmers returning to the Construct after working the Parma farms.

I ascended the stairs to Ohio City, and the occasional car made West 25th Street seem desolate. The blue was bleached from the sky, and the cool of a cloudless night was already beginning to settle in.

By contrast Anna was a bundle of warm energy. There was a sparkle to her eyes, and some new electricity flowed through her body. She had dressed with a casual elegance—cotton slacks, silk blouse, and pearl earrings—and I immediately felt out of place.

The kitchen table was back in the middle of the room, but this time with an embroidered tablecloth. The candelabra was set up, and beside it was a bottle of champagne in a bucket of ice.

She brought out two bottles of Thirty-Three beer, and

we chatted while the veal finished baking. When it was ready, she escorted me to the table and told me what a treat I was in store for. She turned on the crystal player, and a mixture of strings, piano, and newharp oozed into the room: "beautiful-woman-without-a-personality music." I smiled as if I liked it. Anna turned off the lights and lit the candles. She then brought out the veal, rice, and salad. She insisted that I remain seated, as a guest should. She was being so polite, I wanted to remind her that I was only the hired help.

"I think you'll like this veal," she said. "I used a very simple recipe, no spices beyond salt and pepper."

I cut into the veal. "I'm sure it's great."

"Don't be dishonest until you've tried it."

It was good, and I told her so. She grinned and sipped some of the wine I'd brought. She grimaced, but didn't complain. I took a sip of mine; the wine didn't taste as good as it used to. I almost gagged in surprise. To cover up for my lack of finesse, I said, "What are we celebrating?"

"I called up George Mutangi at the art gallery this morning. I've decided to go back to work on Monday."

"Great," I said. "Your decision's made you look more energetic."

"And I looked horrible before now?"

"Sometimes," I said. "Especially at the beginning. Now you look fantastic."

She hesitated before saying, "I've made another decision."

I stopped eating. Maybe this would be the moment Donna Palaez was hoping for.

"No more hotels," she said. She looked down at her lap as if the decision, spoken out loud, didn't sound as profound as it had when she'd first thought it out. Softly, "We either make love here or we do without."

"It sounds like a good decision," I said, just as softly. I had more to say, but I couldn't bring myself to say it. "What's wrong?" I asked.

Anna said nothing, drank some wine and grimaced. Then, "Do you want to open the champagne?"

The bottle popped with released air, and the cork arced out of view from the candlelight. Anna drank her first glass much too quickly.

"Would you like to go out?" I asked. "We can go to the cinema. Or dancing?"

"Do you want to dance here?"

"Sure," I said.

She rose from the table and stepped closer to the crystal player. She almost looked lost, on the edge of the candlelight's glow. She held out her arms. I stood up and joined her, placing one arm behind her, the other in the palm of her right hand.

"So formal," she said.

I began to lead us around the cramped floor space. The music flowed without any recognizable rhythm, and I felt as if we were moving out of control at the slowest of paces. "I have to be," I replied. "It's to make up for the quality of my clothes."

"You look just fine," she said.

I didn't know what else to say. I had watched the two of them dancing here, and I knew it was the only place Sauro would dance willingly. The syrupy music seemed to create a chasm: with Sauro and Anna it must have overemphasized sentiment, now it gushed out with a sentiment that made our silence and our separateness seem worse.

"Anna?"

"Shhh," she whispered, "don't say anything."

Anna stepped closer and laid her head against my shoulder, and I let my cheek rest against the top of her head. I closed my eyes, but I began to run the footage of the two of them dancing naked across the backs of my eyelids. I let my eyes freeze open, and I stared at the walls of the room as we turned. I wondered if Anna was thinking about the same thing, if she wished that I were Sauro and that moment, like filed vidfootage, could be replayed, now that their dancing in this room had a specific importance, unknown at the time, and could be relived with the proper seriousness.

I imagined that Sauro was in the room, that I wasn't meant to be here at all.

"Let's go to bed," she whispered.

She let go of me to drink some more champagne. In the bedroom she pulled down the curtains and switched on the lights. Before I could touch her, she turned her back to me.

She tossed her clothes onto a chair. I undressed while she peeled back the covers. Keeping her eyes averted, she slid into bed and pulled the covers over her breasts. I slid in beside her and leaned over to kiss her. She twisted her head away, then pressed her hands against my shoulders, easing me onto my back. She maneuvered herself atop me, and the covers slid down her back. We merged easily, as if we had been imagining this moment since I first stepped into the apartment. Her hands rested on either side of me, sinking a bit into the old mattress. She rocked her hips back and forth, with the mechanical rhythm of someone in a sex-ed video. Her eyes held no pleasure; they stared down without seeing. I reached up to take hold of a nipple with thumb and forefinger, to twist with just the right tenderness the way she liked it, to see some sort of pleasure returned to her face. Almost as if understanding my need, she let the muscles in her face go soft, and she leaned down toward me. I opened my mouth to await her kiss.

She must have been holding herself the wrong way, because I slid out. The air surrounding my penis felt wet and cold.

Biting her lower lip, the expression she always had when she was determined to meet a challenge, she sat up and used her hand to slide me into her. She began rocking again, and without expression she leaned forward, lips open.

I slid out.

Her body collapsed on mine, her ribs shaken by sobs. "I can't do it. I can't get it right here!"

I whispered that it was all right, and I rubbed her back, applying pressure to some of the knotted muscles. I drew her face close to mine and kissed the wetness on her cheeks. Bit by bit, I rolled her onto her back and embraced her for the longest time before sliding penis into vagina. Her body reluctantly responded to mine, but she finally clung to me, pressing lips against ear.

"Please, tell me," she whispered, "who are you?"

The question tore at something, and I didn't know how to answer. I found myself thrusting harder in order to maintain my erection.

"Please, who are you?"

"I'm Rod."

Our skin slapped together, her body throwing itself against mine. I pumped harder, trying to rid myself of what was clinging to me.

"Please," she gasped, a sound that was at once too close and too far away from pleasure. "Who are you?"

21

I COULDN'T GET to sleep. The bedroom light was still on, and with the nighttime silence everything in the room felt as if it were frozen in time. Anna had cuddled up to me, her leg heavy across my thighs, her arm weighing upon my chest, her head resting in the crook of my arm. My hand had fallen asleep, and the tingling was spreading to my elbow. I didn't know what time it was, or how long we'd been lying there. It felt like forever. Orgasm, and a half bottle of champagne, had flushed the anxiety from her system. I still was asking myself her question: who was I? With a shift-jane, you didn't have to ask such questions. With a shift-jane you could say *Time's up* and then leave.

With the greatest of care, as if Anna were some delicate piece of plastic explosive, I extricated myself from her grasp. Her eyes opened, then blinked. "Are you going?"

Before I could stop myself, I nodded. I had planned to go only as far as the bathroom.

"Oh," she said.

Her voice was empty, and it made me want to leave even more. "I'll pick you up tomorrow at six," I said, to make it up to her. "And we'll go dancing."

"If you want." She raised her hands to me, and I bent down to accept the hug and kiss. Several days ago I couldn't have imagined anything more warm or inviting. Now my response to her warmth was perfunctory. She let go and rolled over, pulling the covers in around her chest. I dressed. Anna held her body stiff, and I knew I should be staying. I turned off the light, patted her behind, and walked carefully through the darkness until I made it to the front door.

It was two A.M., and the night had closed in with a chill. I missed the wool jacket. I walked quickly down the street, toward West 25th. I kept hoping the glow from the streetlamps would provide a bit of warmth; they looked as if they should have.

I hit West 25th, and the row of shops opposite me looked ominous. Each doorway contained a deepened shadow, and I strained my eyes to see if someone was hiding in one. I'd watched too many movies as a kid. A solitary car invaded the silence and brought me back to the real world.

I turned the corner and headed for the RTA stop. I couldn't help but walk quickly. For a moment I heard another set of steps. I turned. A breeze scattered some garbage outside the West Side Market. Paper skidded across the pavement, scratching lightly like ghosts. No one was there. Of course not.

Around the corner and down the street, delivery trucks were pulling up to the West Side Market's loading dock. I walked past. Animal carcasses were being unloaded to be butchered for Friday's buyers. The nearest truck had an emblem of a wolf's face on the side, and its eyes seemed to follow me. A chunky woman threw open the rear door of the truck. Pigs hung by hooks, their eyes open. I turned away and crossed Lorain, making my way to the rapid stop.

The RTA platform was empty. My footsteps echoed. Tracks ran either way into barely lighted emptiness. My father had told my brother and me that friendly gnomes lived in the darkness between the tracks. I had always been frightened that the gnomes would be run over by the rapids. A distant rumbling smoothed out into the steady clacking of a rapid. Paint was fading, and the rapid had a sleekness that had gone out of style ten years ago. The late trains were always the ones ready to be retired. I stepped in, but the rapid waited. It must have been ahead of schedule. The doors remained opened. Several sets of footsteps echoed across the platform.

I looked up, and through the haze of unwashed windows, I saw three men jogging to the RTA. A buzzer went off. The one in the lead, a thickset man wearing a leather jacket, shouted at the conductor sitting up front. They jumped onto the train just before the doors slid shut. They took seats at the other end of the car.

The rapid pulled away, and we chugged through a brief tunnel, then crossed a bridge above the Cuyahoga River. Each of the men sat on the edge of an aisle seat and leaned forward to talk in hushed voices. The thickset man seemed to talk the most while he zipped and unzipped the leather jacket. The jacket was cracked, mottled brown with exposed veins. The zipper, so outdated, called attention to itself. Perched across the aisle, leaning forward, one of his companions concentrated on every word. He was emaciated, and his clothes hung loosely. His blond hair was slicked back. He reminded me of footage shown from the relocation camps. I wondered how often he was stopped for mandatory blood testing. The third one sat in front of the thickset man. He continually nodded as if trying to impress the other two. His body movements were awkward, calculated. I guessed that he was underage.

The scrawny one stopped concentrating long enough to glare at me. I turned away to watch the night through the windows. I tried to imagine what the three men had been doing. Outside the Construct, on weekdays, entertainment establishments were supposed to close by midnight. I tried to imagine what sort of shift work would have ended at this hour; everything usually went eight to eight. The rapid ran hourly through the early-morning hours only as a courtesy to the many who didn't own cars.

The underage kid kept glancing at me. The scrawny one talked to the floor; the thickset man listened intently, occasionally gazing out the window as if expecting to see something. I felt as if I were being watched, as if the three men were undercover types. I hadn't felt this way since my Fair Haven years, when Coventry had been unmonitored and infamous for various illicit activities. Two uniforms hung around to keep order and drink free coffee. No one knew how many undercover cops there were. None of them ever stopped anything important from happening; they just went after hustlers and gays. After the first arrest and suspended sentence, you learned the look of the undercover cops. You only got caught if you were stupid or, deep down, wanted to be caught.

The rapid stopped at the Terminal Tower. Two men and two women got on. The three men at the other end of the car continued talking in hushed voices. The kid stopped looking at me. I thought of getting up and moving to another car, but it seemed a silly idea. I stared out the window and watched for gnomes.

I got off the rapid at Broadway and Harvard and headed for the gates. I was trying to decide if I should tell Harry and Kevin about my brief bout with paranoia when I heard several sets of footsteps. I turned. It was the three men: they were so busy not looking at me, that they had to have been watching my every move. The platform had several monitors; if there was any violence, the police would be notified instantly. I decided to stand still, see what would happen. The three men walked up to me, then passed by. The exit gates beeped three times, almost simultaneously, as they passed between electric eyes.

The platform was empty.

I left and made my way home. I had to walk several corridors of a business sector before I reached the entrance to Slavic Village. Everything was shut down and blacked out. The corridors were nightlit. Behind me and before me darkness, each section lighting up when I entered it, display holoes activated by my presence, gesturing in quick vision-bytes, speaking the necessary slogans before I hit the next section and light was drawn out of their presences, returning them to the dark. This area of the Construct was all new; the corridor went on forever. I was surrounded by black, walking on a floating island of light and noise. Some innate sense in me didn't trust the blackness, didn't trust other areas to light up when other humans, who might just be out there, stepped into them, didn't confide in the infrared monitors. It wouldn't be dignified to run, so I increased my pace.

I crossed an intersection, then stepped onto a new section. I had taken two steps before I realized that the lights hadn't come on. I turned to head back, when the lights that had been behind me shut off.

The darkness was blinding; the silence without ads deafening. Even the red lights of the monitors had switched off. The floor's pressure against my feet was the only reality, and my head began to spin. My digestive tract felt like watery spaghetti sauce. I wondered how you died a dignified death.

The lights shot back on, and I closed my eyes against the sudden brightness. Then, sensing someone there, I let them snap open. Standing in front of me was one of the three men, the thickset one, who wore the leather jacket. I could only stare at him. Section ads surrounded us. The makers of Hangon had developed a pill that tranquilized while it fought tension headaches. Democracy Now provided clothes laser-cut to your idea of comfort. Personal Services Sensory Chairs would let you live a selection of over one thousand moments. The thickset man stood there casually, hands in his pockets. He didn't pull out a gun or a knife. The stubble of a several-day-old beard was black. His eyes were green. "My name's Papa," he said.

I looked off in the opposite direction, toward the impossible-to-see entranceway to Slavic Village. Standing several meters away was the scrawny one. He leaned against the glass pane of a store as if for support.

"That's Mama," said Papa.

I considered knocking Papa down and making a break for the intersection. Standing by the corner was the kid.

"And that's Baby."

"And I'm Goldilocks," I said. My voice was hoarse.

"You sound a little upset," he said. "And, you know, I can't blame you. They call us terrorists." He grinned. The grin was mischievous, not sardonic. "Have we terrorized you?"

"I didn't wet my pants." The remark sounded more puerile than defiant.

"You do know what I mean by terrorists?"

"UHL," I said.

"Good. An educated man. And you can probably tell me the main goal of the UHL."

"To close down the relocation camps. Because a

society that oppresses one group of people no longer can consider itself democratic or just."

"I'm impressed. But you don't sound very sympathetic."

I shrugged.

"It makes sense . . . that you aren't . . . sympathetic. You like things to be nice and orderly. You like routine."

"Do you want to read my palm and tell me my fortune?"

He smiled this time. "You won't believe this, but I can imagine what it's like: standing in this corridor, listening to these ads, and surrounded by three people the media calls terrorists. Maybe we *should* tell you your fortune. Maybe you can tell us why the Union for Human Liberation blacked out Kansas City."

"What?"

"Why black out Kansas City?" he said. "Pretend it's a test question."

"Multiple choice?" I couldn't help myself. As I said it, I expected him to pull out a gun from the pocket of his leather jacket.

"No. Not multiple choice. Or true and false. Short answer. Ten points."

I hesitated; the words didn't come at first. "To give Americans a taste of what it's like to live in a world controlled by others."

"Again, little sympathy. Fair's fair, I guess. Can you make an educated guess as to how we managed to inject a computer virus that would infect an entire city for twenty-four hours?"

"Friends in high places. And it wasn't a guess. Some of them were arrested."

"Yes. Five have been arrested. And one was hung. And two disappeared." The mischievous quality had vanished from his face, drained from his voice. "Would you care to guess what happened to them?"

I shook my head. It took some effort. My neck muscles had become very stiff.

"Do you think those who disappeared, who were probably drugged, maybe even tortured, for information, do you think they got what they deserved?"

I couldn't say anything.

"People died in the Black Out. Babies. Old people. Maybe even people who wanted to close the camps. Maybe some terrorists deserved a little torture. If they were the right ones, that is."

I looked over at his cohorts. The scrawny one looked bored, or perhaps he was just tired. The kid forced back a yawn; he was too far away to hear us clearly.

"It would seem to me," he said, "that a person in your profession should harbor a natural sympathy for our cause. Could you explain to me why you should think about that?"

I remained silent: he would tell me anyway.

"To start with," he said, "you should think about the thirty-second test. Nine-nine point nine percent efficiency. That means, on the average, that one out of a thousand clients could have a false reading. That's a big risk, day after day, doing what a servicer does. But then, you work in Leisure Services. You and your client get complete testing. But what are there, twenty-one kinds of hives right now? What if number twenty-two—or even twenty-three—comes along in the form of one of your clients? Then what? You're fine for a while, until you get the symptoms, or they develop a blood test to detect the new hives. Then what?"

"I guess I go to a camp."

"And what have you done wrong?" he said.

"It probably won't happen."

"Maybe. Maybe not. But you can never be sure what a client is up to. A test not taken. A test forged. You might be at less risk then your colleagues in Direct Services, but you're at risk. How would you like to be relocated?" He pronounced *relocated* like it was three different words. *Re. Lo. Cated.*

"It won't happen."

"We want the person who built the camps."

"He's probably in the phone book," I said. "Call him up."

"Shouldn't you be a little more terrorized?"

I was, but I couldn't admit that.

"You see, we need to arrange a meeting. A meeting without government forces joining in. We think there might be some way to use his daughter as leverage. His daughter is your client; you could be of great help to us and to the Cause."

I found myself shaking my head.

"We weren't asking. You see, Mama, Baby, and I, we're walking a thin line between those of our family who want all-out revolution and those who want strategic attacks against cities. I want a propaganda victory; I want us as the good guys in the media. I want James Baxter, in front of me, for a little dialogue. And we will need your help to make that happen."

I was still shaking my head.

"We're not asking for a whole lot right now. We just want you to go to Personal Services tomorrow or Saturday. Go to the Sensor Arcades, to the Sensory Chairs. Ask for the Relocation Experience. I'm sure you've heard of it. It took an ASD lawsuit and a court order to get Personal Services to provide it."

I nodded weakly.

"That's all we ask right now. And the four of us can chat sometime afterwards."

"Okay," I said. I just mouthed it. The sound didn't come out.

"And, if I were you, I wouldn't mention this to anyone. Since the UHL was formed, we haven't been sure where Anna Baxter has stood. Sauro was a little queasy about violence, but he considered helping. But with Anna we were never quite sure. Mama over there has reason to suspect she's CIA. Her family's a good friend of Edward Lang. So be careful. The CIA has very specific techniques for taking care of people suspected of being in the UHL."

I didn't believe anything he was saying about Anna, Lang, the CIA. It must have shown in my face.

"You don't have to believe me. You can think about this instead: I stand here threatening you, and no police have shown up. From that you can probably draw certain conclusions as to how we can move about in a monitored city. We have friends in Monitoring. So we hear the same rumors they hear. Rumor has it that certain people at Monitoring suspected that Sauro Contini was one of us. Rumor also has it that Sauro Contini didn't jump off that roof. Someone lent him a hand."

22

I KEPT ON waking up all that early morning. Feeling trapped, like on a lost ship, I floated in and out of darkness. Sleep came for brief moments, which seemed briefer than they probably were, and the rest was a voyage of sounds, strung together like a long, impossible river: my head rolling against the pillow, the rustle of moving sheets, the occasional voice outside in the corridor, the sliding of processed ingredients up to apartment synthesizers, the sliding of trash down chutes to points of separation for recycling, dumping, or cremation, Harry putzing around outside, watching TV, getting ready for work, more voices in the corridor, on and on, so that each blank space of sleep was welcome and far too short. After I heard Harry leave, I imagined getting out of bed and greeting the new day as if Anna Baxter and the Three Bears didn't exist. I went back to sleep.

When I finally got out of bed, I was surprised to find that it was only one o'clock. I thought of Anna, Lang, the UHL, and my stomach dropped down into my bowels. I asked Albert to plan my diet for the day. Albert wanted to know what I'd had for dinner the past four nights so he could properly select the right balance. I programmed the synthesizer for eggs. It asked if I wanted hard-boiled or scrambled. I chose scrambled; it fit. Once they were on the plate, I could only stare at them. Some coffee turned my stomach into a trapeze artist, so I opened the bottle of dark rum that Kevin had left us. After several shots my stomach was still doing triple flips, but the rest of my body couldn't have cared less.

I kept thinking of what to do, who could help me. I couldn't help but glance up at the monitor. I didn't feel much like toasting it today. Whoever I told, someone else would know. How long would it be before Lang found out that the UHL had contacted me? How long would it be before the Three Bears found that I'd seen Lang? Why did they both tell me that Anna was on the other side? I very briefly considered playing one off the other, promising to play double agent for both sides. At the end all I could see was a guaranteed trip to jail or the crematorium.

I called Donna Palaez. Her secretary put me on hold for ten minutes. I squeezed some lemon juice into a glass of dark rum and added ice. I finished it off just before the lawyer came on-screen.

"What can I do for you, Mr. Lawrence?" she asked.

"Have you seen a tape of last night's encounter?"

"You mean with Ms. Baxter?"

"Yes." I became anxious. Had the other encounter been recorded and filed? "What other kind of encounter would I have?"

She shrugged. "As long as you get blood-tested, I am not concerned about any kind of encounter you have."

"What did you think of the footage you saw?"

"Are you referring to anything specific?"

The previous evening with Anna had been eclipsed by my dark encounter with the Three Bears. I couldn't remember exactly what had happened. She had drunk champagne, we had danced, and it had been awful. There was no monitor in Anna's bedroom, so Palaez hadn't seen Anna demand to know just who I was. I shook my head. "Just the general tone, of the evening, I guess."

"My evaluation remains the same, I am sorry to say." She didn't sound too sorry. "I don't think it's legally wise for you to retain Ms. Baxter as a client."

"I don't either."

"Our executive director does, however." She sounded bitter. "He has told me that you are quite capable of handling everything. He has told me that unless she proposes marriage and you accept, that I shouldn't worry. Now, is there any other way I can help you?"

I called Fred next. I had two more glasses of rum with ice and lemon juice while I waited on hold.

"Sorry I took so long to get back to you." Fred paused and looked carefully at his screen. "You look horrible. Are you okay?"

"I don't feel too well."

"You're up-to-date on your vaccines, aren't you?"

"Of course I am. Look, Fred, I called because I'm getting in over my head in this Baxter thing."

"Don't worry. I've gone over everything with Marie, and we both think you're doing great."

"What about a lawsuit?"

He hesitated. "We're not worried." He sounded worried. "On top of that, Rod, I can guarantee you that this kind of work, if done right, will lead to a big promotion."

"This is bigger than I can handle." I hated to sound so desperate. The rum had made it easy to be honest.

All I could do was stare at him; one job in the Heights didn't get anybody a promotion—the job itself had been a promotion.

"You're just getting cold feet," Fred went on. "You'll do fine. I've had Tricky Dick get hold of some texts and simulations on bereavement, sexual adjustment, and some other things that might help with this Baxter woman. He's simplifying some of the language; the materials should be ready for you this afternoon. It's going on her account, so you won't have an access charge. How does all that sound?"

"Great."

I called Anna next. She didn't put me on hold. "Rod!" she said. "You look awful." She sounded genuinely concerned.

"I feel awful. I'm coming down with something."

She was silent for a moment. "Like an aversion to me?"

"Of course not."

"You sound like you've had half a bottle of Scotch."

"Three-quarters," I said. "And it was rum."

"I'm sorry about last night. I said some things I shouldn't have said. I promise you I'll be on better behavior."

"I can't take you dancing tonight."

"We can see a holofilm. How about a dirty one?" She smiled. A week ago that particular smile would have seemed very enticing. The trapeze artist spun in the air before grasping the second bar; my stomach did the same.

"Let's go dancing on Monday."

"What about tonight?"

"I can't make it. I'll see you Monday."

"I won't get so serious. I promise."

"It's not you. I've got some personal problems. I'll have them cleared up by Monday." I flicked the switch; she vanished into the gray screen. If I got lucky, she'd fire me.

I didn't think I'd get lucky. I didn't think I'd get my problems cleared up. I finished the bottle of rum and went to bed.

I struggled with sleep. The darkness behind my eyes wavered. I was trapped aboard the same ship, floating. I heard strange voices, stranger sounds. Nightmares kept waking me up. I couldn't remember any of them.

A dog was barking. Hound of the Baskervilles. Everyone else had thought it was sort of boring, so I had to read it while no one was in the cabin. In class I had told the teacher that I hadn't read past the first chapter. The dog stopped barking. I realized that I was damp with sweat. My head ached. The hound went at it again. Who would be his next victim?

I forced open my eyes, but the darkness didn't leave. I reached for the light switch. The dog stopped, but he was followed by a distant hammering. Who could be building something? The dog barked, but this time I recognized the voice of Fido, our doorbell.

"I'm coming," I shouted.

I somehow made it out of bed and into the living room. The light flipped on with my entrance, and I found the door. Anna stood in the corridor. She was wearing the same slacks and tight yellow shirt she'd worn the other night. It took her a moment to recognize me. Then her eyes grew large, and her preprogrammed smile disappeared. "Is this how you always answer the door?"

Sayeed was standing in his doorway, staring. At first I

thought he was looking at the picnic basket Anna was carrying, but the air chilling the sweat on my body revealed the cause of their surprise. I was naked.

"Nothing you haven't seen before," I said.

Anna said nothing. She seemed to watch me, as if matching the tone of my voice to whatever internal condition I was suffering. A couple walked by. "I wish you'd meet me at the door like that," one said to the other.

"Are you going to invite me in?" she asked.

It was against regulations, and it broke a specific clause in our contract. I waved to Sayeed before stepping back into the apartment, gesturing for Anna to follow.

She walked in and raised the basket to my attention. "I thought I'd play Little Red Riding Hood to your sick grandmother."

"Watch out for the wolves," I said, not very kindly, as I headed for my bedroom to get something to wear.

"If you're going to be that way, I can go."

I didn't say anything. The monitor was picking up everything. Palaez, Fred, Lang, and Papa Bear would all be checking this one out. A client never visits her servicer at home, even if he's sick and drunk. Knowing my performance was for everyone, I slid open the closet door and reached for a pair of pants. They were jeans, cut exactly to my measurements by Democracy Now lasers. The jeans slipped out of my hands and fell to the floor. I bent over to reach for them. The trapeze artist in my belly was joined by a ballerina in my head. She started to do the most wonderful pirouettes. I stood upright so she'd stop.

"Do you want me to stay?"

I tried again for the pants. The trapeze artist and the ballerina somehow met in midair.

"Rod?"

I tried to look up and focus on her face. She looked concerned. The trapeze artist and ballerina embraced. I kissed the floor.

I woke up for a moment to feel the floor under me, a blanket atop and to watch Anna change the sheets on the bed. I woke again to help Anna walk me to the bed. I woke once or twice while she washed my body with a damp washcloth. I slept comfortably for a while. I felt safe.

Anna had eggs, sausage, juice, and coffee, all nicely laid out on a tray for me before she shook me until my eyes opened. She helped me sit up, then handed me two Hangon pills. The first bite of eggs was the most difficult. I expected the trapeze artist to come out of hiding, but he and the ballerina were too busy elsewhere to bother me. The second bite made me realize how hungry I was. I sucked up the food like a vacuum hose while Anna related her adventures with the synthesizer. She'd brought some Chinese food to heat up, but she felt that I needed something a little blander. She said the synthesizer food fit the bill; I was too hungry to care. Besides, I wasn't a snob. It had all the vitamins and minerals I'd ever need injected into it.

"What time is it?" I asked.

"About six."

"Has Harry shown up?"

"Harry who?"

"My roommate."

She shook her head, but after that she kept glancing out my bedroom door as if he might show up at any minute.

"He's probably at the Admiral of the Port downstairs."

"A port?"

"The Admiral of the Port. It's a bar. Harry, a buddy, and I drink too much there. Then we usually come back to the TV room to watch old movies."

"Where's this TV room at?"

I pointed out the bedroom door. From where she was sitting, on the edge of the bed, her hip against mine, divided by a thermal blanket, she could turn and see several armchairs and the TV set. "You can see the lap of luxury I'm living in."

"I always thought you guys did better."

"No. It's our work that keeps the government's budget balanced."

She was supposed to smile at that one, but she didn't. She looked at me for a while; I could almost see the thinking going on behind her eyes. "Was it last night?" she said.

"Last night?"

"Yeah. Was it what happened last night that made you drink a whole bottle of rum?"

"I didn't get much sleep, that's why I'm sick. The rum didn't help."

"But why?"

Her eyes met mine and waited. I could tell her about my three A.M. meeting, about how working for her now scared me, almost literally, to death. Or I could make up something.

"You have to be honest with me. I feel like I've been using you. Before you say anything, I know that's what you're paid for. But you're not being paid to be treated the way I've been treating you. I didn't sleep much last night, either. I kept thinking about why you left. I reread the contract. I knew something must have been going on inside you for you to leave like that. It's against the agreement."

So's being here, I wanted to say. But it'd been a long time since anyone had cleaned me up and brought me breakfast in bed at six o'clock at night.

"Will you tell me why?"

"A friend at work. She tested bad."

"You mean . . . ?"

"Yeah. She's in quarantine until she can take care of her money and stuff. Then it's off to the camps." This was a lie. No one had been sent off to the camps since last December. The media had covered it thoroughly, and business dropped for a week. For a moment I didn't think Anna would believe me.

"Did you sleep with her?"

The inference hurt. Anna thought I was upset because I was at risk. "No. She's a colleague, a friend. And they're going to ship her off."

"I'm sorry." Her voice was barely audible. She had seemed stung when I pointed out that a whore was a friend. "What happened?"

"She was screwing on the side, or someone got through the test."

"How can that be?" She was probably worrying about herself, about anything I might have getting through the tests.

"She's in Direct Services. The clients are given the thirty-second special. If they pass that and look healthy, they're asked to pay the price and enjoy the occasion. The thirty-second test is for shit. They're calling everyone who had contact with her since her last full battery of tests. To warn them, of course, not to find the one responsible. But you never know. Some of the hives don't surface for years."

"Did you ever work in Direct Services?"

"Years ago."

She hesitated; she didn't want to ask, or she didn't want to know the answers, to the obvious questions.

"Look, Anna, you have an exclusive contract with me. I'm not screwing on the side. I get blood-tested every Friday. I haven't had a male client since Direct Services. I'm safer and better documented than any possible pickup or boyfriend."

"You don't have to patronize me. I was just asking. I know you're safe, or as safe as they might come. But do you know how safe I am? Don't you worry about the camps?"

"Not much."

"You sound smug."

"I'm just not that worried. If you play it safe, it doesn't happen that often. It's not like everyone is going to the camps."

"Maybe you should find out what the camps are like."

"Give me a book. I'll read it."

"You haven't even finished the other two."

I had, but I was never one for making a big deal about how much I'd read.

"The place where you work has those sensory chairs. When I was in ASD, we got them to put in a tape on the camps. So people could see what it's like. You should try it out. Maybe you wouldn't be so smug about the whole thing. Go tomorrow, I'll take you out to dinner afterwards, and you can talk all about it with Little Red Riding Hood."

I felt as if she'd gotten the roles mixed up. I was the sick grandmother. I didn't know who Little Red Riding Hood was. Anna was the wolf, who just happened to break our contract when I was sick, who just happened to ask me to do the same thing I'd been asked to do very early this morning. Go to the sensory chairs, see what it's like, and then we'll talk.

23

"What's wrong?" Anna said.

I shook my head; the thought didn't come lose. I considered asking her straight out if she was UHL.

"Do you want me to change the subject?"

I found myself staring at the monitor, which in turn was staring at me from above the bathroom door. A battle of wits with a bug-eyed lens. I was losing.

"If you promise to go to the Sensory Arcades, I'll change the subject," Anna was saying.

I was trying to remember how many angles the monitor lens caught, the mechanics of how Adolf or Tricky Dick filtered all that data into the best flatscreen images possible for human viewing.

"Will you go?" Anna asked.

"Yeah. I'll go."

"When?"

"Tomorrow. Will that make you happy?"

She had been leaning forward to kiss me, and the tone of my voice knocked her back. She examined my face for a while, then turned her head to see what I was staring at.

"What's wrong, Mr. Serviceman?"

"Nothing."

"Something about that monitor bothers you. I can't see why monitors should start bothering you now. We've done all sorts of things in front of them." She smiled mischievously. I imagined watching those moments on a screen, and blood sank out of my belly and converged at a lower level.

"You know," I said. "I could be penalized for letting you stay here. It's against our contract."

"What would they penalize? Your pay?"

The way she said it made my whole concern seem petty. Only someone who'd grown up wealthy—who had heard the ritualistic *sorry dear, time is money, I have to work* and had known the words were essentially untrue, or that the need for that money wasn't vital—could feel that a monetary penalty was a petty reason for concern. I could only nod. It wasn't the real reason I wanted her gone.

"You could always charge it to my expense account." The words were forced. I began to sense the hurt of the other night; I didn't want to abandon her again.

"I could do that."

There was the faint glimmer of a smile. My words had encouraged her. Her hand slid across the thermal blanket, found my erect penis, began tracing the visible curve of the glans. "Some men, you know, like to make love when they're not feeling well. One guy told me it helped to relieve internal tensions. Couldn't you tell your bosses that I had to come for medicinal purposes?" Her smile was enticing. I was almost surprised at how quickly the hurt had disappeared, how quickly she could bury whatever was tormenting her.

"It's not very convincing." I began to unbutton her shirt.

"Or you could tell them that we like to do fantasy stuff. You know, role-playing. In my bedroom, where there aren't any monitors. So they can't know if we're making it up or not. You say that one night I had too much to drink and said that I wanted to fantasize that I was in love with you. And the only place we could fulfill that fantasy was here, because everyone has to make love once in their lover's bed. So once, just this once, I came over, to keep you warm while you're sick and to fulfill that fantasy so it's over and done with."

She was naked, by then. She took another sip of wine, and I hit the light switch while she replaced the glass on the bedside table. I lifted up the covers so she could try to slip in beside me, but after finding too little room in my very single bed, she placed her body atop mine, supporting her weight on elbows and on knees pressed tight against my thighs. While she planted kisses all over my face, I reached down to lead penis into vagina. I didn't want to repeat last night's fiasco. One of her hands found mine, pulled it away. "I just want to kiss," she said. "Lovers kiss more than anything else." Her kisses became slower, warmer. "Don't pay attention to anything else. Just feel my lips, my tongue, my teeth, my mouth." We kissed, on and on, and I felt warm and safe and wanted to bury everything the way Anna had, as if it would go away if I didn't think about it, enjoy the moment for what it was, for that's what I was being paid to do.

The more we kissed, the sweeter the tension. I couldn't remember feeling this wonderfully on edge since Susie Sundai and I first made it together. The prolongation, the deferment, the buried anxieties built within me, and I felt something so strong that I wanted to give it a name.

We told each other how wonderful it felt, and my words rang true this time. Anna told me how great her desire was, and we struggled with the blanket as we rolled over, found the right embrace, and my penis didn't feel like some distant extension. I was sensitized, and I could feel cheek against cheek, smell the scent of shampooed hair, sense the outline of her breasts against my chest, feel the wetness of belly against belly, the warmth of her thighs wrapped around mine, her heels touching the back of my knees. My arms were curled behind her back, hands wrapped up around shoulders; her arms slid across my back, hands firmly grabbing buttocks. The sense of touch overwhelmed me, and I forgot about the observer in my head who made sure I did everything just right. The monitor could watch for both of us. With that parting thought I just let go, embraced, enjoyed, but still hoping, way in the back of my mind, that I didn't become so overwhelmed that I would come before Anna did.

"Can we come watch," Kevin called out, "or is this just for our listening pleasure?"

I looked up. The bedroom's darkness had gone gray. A white rectangle of light from the main room was cast onto the closet door. Anna's body went into suspended animation.

"Oh, shit," I said. I couldn't help but continue pumping, ever so slowly.

"Who's that?" Anna whispered, as if they would hear her.

"Are you alone?" asked Kevin.

"No." I rolled off Anna. At the sound of approaching footsteps, she pulled the blanket over her head.

Kevin looked in, his face a dark oval against the light. "Are you trying to break the Curse of the Apartment?" He said it with capital letters, like we all did.

"I thought I'd give it a shot," I said, not knowing what else to say.

"I thought you had an exclusive contract."

"I do."

"Are you breaking it now?" He was looking at the outline of the extra body under the blanket.

"No."

"Oh, shit," said Kevin. He sounded disappointed. "Well, I brought Betsy with me. The three of us were going to have some dark rum, if you two care to join us."

I reached over Anna's head and flicked out the light. "We'll be out in a bit."

Kevin disappeared and was replaced by Betsy. She had her blond hair tied back in a ponytail. "We shouldn't embarrass you like this. Do you want us to go back downstairs to the Admiral?"

I shook my head.

"Come out and celebrate with us." She lowered her voice to a whisper. "This is my last drink. I took the test. I'm pregnant."

I couldn't help but smile. "That sounds great."

"Come on out. I'll close the door so you can have some privacy."

Betsy closed the door. I pulled the blanket off Anna's head. I leaned over and kissed her. "Do you want to go meet them?"

"Do you want me to?"

"We haven't much of a choice, do we?"

"You don't sound too enthusiastic."

I shrugged.

"I don't see how you can be this way."

"What way?"

"One moment you are intensely making love to me, almost like the fantasy was . . . well, and then your friends show up and you act as if you wish I'd dematerialize."

I gave her my best smile and my warmest kiss. "Anna, I want you to meet my friends."

Anna came out of the bedroom with hair mussed, cheeks flushed, and the biggest chipmunk smile in the world. You never would have thought she was anxious about meeting Harry, Kevin, and Betsy or that she'd started to complain about a tension headache while she'd buttoned up her shirt. "Hi, guys," she said, loudly, cheerfully, covering up all the awkward silence emanating from the small dining-room table.

I grinned foolishly and blushed as I made introductions. Kevin was immediately charmed and offered Anna some dark rum. Betsy smiled politely at Anna, warmly at me. Harry shook hands, nodded, and sat down. Harry, more than Kevin and Betsy, knew what this meeting could mean for my career.

Harry went into the kitchen and came back with glasses filled with ice. Kevin picked up the open bottle of dark rum. "It's lucky I bought another one of these," he said as he poured. "The one we had expected to find in the liquor cabinet wasn't there. But we did find an empty bottle by the phone."

Betsy cut two slices from the lime, handed me one, and asked Anna if she wanted the other. "Squeeze it; it adds to the flavor."

"Mysterious things happen," I said. I became aware of how tired I still was. The glass of rum in front of me unsettled my stomach. I forced the glass to my lips.

"I gave Rod a bad evening," Anna said. "He drank it all."

"What happened?" Betsy asked, concerned. Betsy felt that if you talked out a problem, it would go away. Since

Kevin never talked about problems, her theory seemed to be reinforced rather than refuted.

"I was attacked by terrorists," I said.

"No," said Anna. "It's my fault."

"If Rod's involved," said Harry, "I wouldn't take all the blame."

"Well," said Anna, and she glanced at me first before continuing, "a colleague of Rod's tested positive for hives."

I tried to look innocent, as if I'd never said it. Harry poured himself more rum. "Dumb move," he said to me. The minute Anna realized she was the only one who'd heard about it, Harry would be proved right.

"Oh, no," said Betsy. "We hadn't heard anything about that. How horrible."

"Who was it?" asked Kevin.

It was the wrong thing to ask, because it reminded Betsy of all the things they hadn't talked about. She glared at Kevin and asked him to pour her more rum.

"We're getting gloomy," said Harry. "Let's change the subject."

By now Anna's smile had disappeared. She reached over to take my free hand; I let her. Harry frowned.

"We haven't done much to make a good impression for Anna," said Betsy.

"That's okay. I'm something of a surprise guest."

Kevin poured her a bit more rum. "Well, your presence is a lot more delightful than Rod and Harry's."

"I've always thought," Betsy said to Anna, "that Rod had one of the most romantic jobs. He works to make people happy." She tried hard not to look at Kevin. "It's nice to have romance every now and then."

Anna nodded. "Rod's the best thing that's happened to me in quite a while."

"I'm not sure that's saying much," said Kevin.

Betsy slapped his arm. "Kevin!"

"Oh," Anna said, "but it is. I thought I had friends and family I could count on when the worst happened. And the person who was there, who'd let me blabber, who put no pressure on me, who said all the necessary little things— that person was Rod."

Kevin shook his head. "I didn't know you had it in you."

"Yes, you did," said Betsy, who believed that nothing good came out of sarcasm.

"I'm even going back to work on Monday," said Anna.

"Where do you work?" said Kevin. "If I'm not prying, or anything."

"Oh, no. I work at Mutangi's Art Gallery. It's in the Coventry mini-Construct."

"Rod's old stomping grounds," said Harry.

Anna looked at me.

"I hung out there when I was in high school. It was just when they started to build the mini-Construct there."

"What kind of work do you do there?" asked Betsy, who knew all about Coventry and why it was the last place we should be talking about.

"I'm a gopher with a title. I feel sort of guilty because my aunt got me the job."

"Is that the kind of work you'd want to do?" asked Kevin.

Anna nodded. "I'd like to run my own art gallery someday. Before, um, Sauro, my boyfriend, died, I was thinking of taking a licensing course so I could qualify for business ownership."

"I didn't know that," I said. The surprise must have registered in my voice.

"Didn't I tell you?"

I shook my head.

"Guess I've got some secrets of my own." She sounded childish, and fiercely independent.

An hour and several shots of rum later, we all were laughing. Anna focused on Harry, asked him questions, told him jokes, and Harry warmed up to her until everybody was friendly and everybody had forgotten that Anna was my client. When Anna said it was time for her to go, Betsy said she hoped they'd be seeing Anna again.

Anna protested that I should stay home and rest, but I escorted her home anyway. In the RTA she kept looking at her fingernails, as if she were trying to decide if she wanted to grow them long or not.

At the Terminal Tower stop, she looked up at me. "Do you think your friends liked me?"

"You were a big hit, especially with Betsy."

"But Harry didn't like me at first."

"Harry knows what will happen."

"What?"

"We broke the contract. On Monday my boss will probably terminate it, and I'll probably take a cut in pay." The idea should have made me happy.

"Why didn't you tell me that?"

"I fainted, remember?"

"I think you wanted this to happen. I think you're afraid of this whole thing."

"Please, Anna, don't read too much into this. Remember what Betsy said. My job is to give you some romance. It's a one-way deal."

"Is it?"

I walked her home and kissed her. She withdrew from my embrace. "Do you want to go home?" she asked.

I did, but I knew that was the wrong answer. "We have some unfinished business."

"Oh?"

"Some folk remedy you were practicing for my hangover?"

"There was a fantasy along with that, remember?"

I nodded.

"Do I get the fantasy?" she asked.

I shook my head. "Sorry."

The neighbor down the hall opened her apartment door, saw us, and closed the door again.

"Then, let's see each other tomorrow, after you go to the Sensory Arcades."

I kissed her good night.

"Rod?" she said. "What's the Curse of the Apartment?"

"You don't want to know," I said.

"I don't want to know, or you don't want to tell me?"

"It's sort of silly. It just seems that every time that

Harry or I bring a woman to the apartment to stay the night, things soon end up for the worse. That's the Curse."

"Do you bring women home often?"

"Occasionally, but I haven't in a while."

She held the door open with one hand and looked down at her feet. She was thinking all sorts of things that she didn't want to say.

"Anna?"

"If we, well, you know . . ."

"If we what?"

"This is sort of embarrassing."

"With me?"

"Yeah. I shouldn't be embarrassed with you, should I?" She said it with a smile, but there was an edge to her voice.

"Well?"

"If we stuck with the fantasy, you know the one I mentioned, if we stuck with that, well, in the fantasy, do you think we broke the curse?"

"Of course we broke it. But only in the fantasy."

That night I dreamed I wasn't a servicer. I dreamed Anna and I were making love, just as we had earlier in my bed. All the same sensations built up in me, and I wanted to give the strength of feeling a name. I told her I loved her, and semen stained the sheets.

24

IN MY SEVEN YEARS with Personal Services, I had taken advantage of my 50 percent discount at Direct Services only a handful of times, when Kevin had wanted to go drinking and whoring. I had never made use of any of the other services, though I had worked a while on the phones. The Sensory Arcades was the last place I had expected to turn up. I felt awkward going: we made fun of people who went to the chairs, the same as we made fun of those who rented holoporn for viewing alone. I hoped no one would recognize me. I spent a lot of time looking at holographic displays of promised experiences and tried to think of all sorts of reasons not to go through with this. I could skip the Relocation Experience. Instead I could be the centerpiece of an elaborate orgy, or the focus of one woman's, or man's, desire; I could pilot the Quintana starship to New Spain, or I could mine asteroids, risking life and limb in the new frontier; or I could be someone who looked like the Deerslayer on the old frontier. In all the promising holoes, the protagonist began to subtly change, first hair color, then size, then facial features, until someone who looked like me was featured in each anticipatory scene. I looked up. A monitor looked down, catching my image, feeding it to Tricky Dick, who, in turn, transformed the generic image into me, all in order to suggest that all these experiences could be mine.

I either had had them or didn't want them anymore. I

walked over to the counter. Above the counter, hanging from the ceiling, was a monitor.

"How can I help you, sir?" the man behind the counter asked. He was fat and balding and didn't look very happy. He either had a hangover or had been doing jobs like this, earning minimum scale, for a long time. There was a nameplate pinned to his breast pocket. His name was Julius.

"I'd like a chair."

"I figured that. Any specific sensation or experience?"

"You got one on the relocation camps, don't you?"

There are only one or two other things I might have mentioned that could have earned such a look of distaste. "Yes, but it's rarely used. Most people want something pleasant."

I almost started to defend my choice. "I'll take the camps. Maybe it'll frighten me into behaving."

He didn't like the joke, either. He clicked his teeth, twice, in rapid succession. "One, for Relocation." He typed something on his computer, then looked at the screen. "Program number Z765." He must have been working minimum scale for a while; a communication mike had been implanted in his head. Someone must have replied, for he said out loud, "Let me charge him first, get his uniform fit, and then he'll be all yours."

I handed him my bancard.

"Are the clothing measurements filed on the card accurate?"

"Yes."

"Has the medical data been updated within the last year?"

I responded with a stare.

"Just in case anything happens. Is it updated?"

I nodded, and he inserted the card in the slot by his vidscreen. All sorts of information flashed on. One line was highlighted.

He looked back up at me. "I take it you want your discount?"

"Earning a commission?"

He grunted. "No."

"Then I want my discount."

"It was a rhetorical question," he said.

"Sorry." I felt like a snob: class warfare within the service sector.

A woman wearing a white lab coat came for me. She was broad-shouldered and had red hair twirled together in a high spiral. Her nameplate read Dorothy. She smiled at me, almost as if in recognition.

"Everything's set up for room fifty-five," said the man behind the counter.

She offered him a smile of appreciation. "Thanks, Julius." She nodded in my direction. "Follow me."

The sensory chair looked like a hyped-up dentist's chair. It was located in the center of a room that was no larger than a junior exec's office. The thin white partitions that separated us from all the other sensory chairs looked just as cheap as the walls found anywhere in low-rent neighborhoods of the Construct. These just looked newer, cleaner. In one corner was a small terminal, in the other the door to a closet.

"Your clothes should be ready in a minute." She booted the computer. "Let's go through some quick questions, to program the variables in this scenario. Okay?"

"Sure."

"Which hives do you contract?"

I shrugged. "Pick your favorite number," I said. "I'll take that strain."

"Five," she said, and typed it in. "How did you contract it?"

"I'm a servicer. It happens every now and then." Saying it out loud made the possibility that much more imminent. I considered getting up and leaving.

"I don't think a servicer has ever requested this tape. In fact, we don't see many servicers."

"I'm doing it to keep a client happy."

The woman paused for a moment, as if thinking about what my response meant. "Well, I hope she's paying you enough. It's not an easy experience."

"Easier than living through it." I didn't sound, or feel, all that sympathetic.

"Of course." Her voice was curt, all friendliness gone. "Now, would you like any sexual experiences at the camp?

We have a penis sheath that provides sensation and collects semen. We also have, for anal intercourse, a . . ."

"I'll go celibate."

"Now, there are several variations to the scenario. All of them, of course, will be influenced by your own psychology. You can be the type who gets along, or you can fight the bureaucracy, or you can volunteer to help organize the place. Also, do you want to participate in the medical testing, or no?"

"I'll be part of the medical testing. But I don't want to have anything to do with any of the other politics."

She typed for a while, then turned to me. "I am required to warn you that the United States Bureau of Artistic Licensing has determined that this is not an accurate perspective of life in the internment camps; rather, it is a piece of propaganda that reflects the values of the Americans for Social Democracy and is only included due to the First Amendment rights as established in the case of Munroe versus Personal Services of Cuyahoga County."

"Do they have a disclaimer like that for all the experiences?"

"No. Just this one." She walked over to the closet. A light above it had blinked on. "Your clothes should be ready. You can take off the ones you have on."

I removed my clothes, folded them, placed them on the chair she had vacated. She handed me a pair of rubber-coated underwear. "Diapers?" I asked.

"Some of this is vivid." She handed me a white jumpsuit next. "This is totally recycled material. No one else has worn it." Then she handed me a pair of white slippers. The clothes were light fitting. Straps were sewn in several places along the arms, legs, and torso. Each strap had a metal snap.

She set me up in the chair, attached me to it, little snaps where each band connected, then softer, padded straps to hold me in place. She told me it was to prevent sleepwalking; the perfunctory humor didn't help my mood. Her fingertips massaged my scalp; I let myself relax. The sensation went as far as my neck; everything else remained tense. She snapped on a rubber skull cap. "Now remember," she said, "this experience lasts roughly as long as a sleep cycle, less than ninety minutes. The experience flashes images on your retina, provides occasional sensations or smells to the proper parts of the brain, and the rest is provided by your imagination. This will seem like a very vivid dream. It will have the logic of a dream, the jumps a dream has. Only at rare moments, like in a dream, will you experience a table-and-chair reality. The sensory chair will induce a sleep state, then the experience will begin. Heart and breathing are monitored, and if there are any irregularities, the experience will be interrupted. If we cannot continue, you may choose an alternative." She smiled; it was as perfunctory as her humor.

"Don't worry. This is all I'm interested in."

"I know," she said and patted my arm. "Lie still and relax." I did, and I waited to sleep. It took me by surprise.

It should have been vivid, but I can't remember who told me my blood was bad, what he looked like, or where we were. I remember being escorted by two men who wore white coveralls and white latex gloves and who walked with their faces straight forward as if a ghost they couldn't see walked between them. They loaded me in the back of a van. I don't remember the van ride; maybe it wasn't included in the experience. The van stopped in front of a concrete building next to train tracks. Across the tracks was the railroad station and the Construct.

The quarantine room was small, painted white, and smelled of disinfectant. There was a vidscreen, a computer terminal, and a series of slots above a counter. The door was sealed shut. The walls had all sorts of dents, as if someone had taken a hammer to them. Someone came to tell me all sorts of stuff. I think it was supposed to be a man, but I pictured her more as Anna's adviser at Personal Services, the one who'd explained the contract to her. Here, in the room (but it really must have been over the vidscreen), she told me why relocation would be good for me. I wouldn't have to worry about infecting others. I would be safe from crackpots who might try to kill me. I would be treated by specialists, by men and women who'd dedicated their lives to finding some sort of cure. Sometimes people with hives one and four returned home. But I was half listening. Hives five, that's what I'd chosen—or had it chosen me?—and this whole thing was beginning to feel a bit more substantial, a little less like lying down in a chair, wearing paper, hooked up into a dream. The adviser was telling me they'd provide all sorts of counseling to help me through the trauma. I'd be living and working with people who shared my plight. There was no way my assets could pay for the cost of room and board, for the tremendous costs of the medicine. I would be given work, and paid union wages, for as long as I could work, and the government, in its wisdom and generosity, would cover the rest. Every month I would be provided with an allowance of ten thousand dollars; all other earnings would defray medical costs. They needed my thumbprint on the lighted square where a document shone on the vidscreen. If I signed a living will, I wouldn't have to prolong the agony when the worst happened, if it did happen. Again, my thumbprint. If I showed up once a week for routine testing, I would be provided with extra rations of bottled water and nutritional supplements. If I participated in the testing of experimental drugs, my monthly allowance would be doubled. Always agreeable, I thumbprinted every square she asked me to.

She told me when my train would leave, and the vidscreen went blank. My train. My father had liked an old song about a train that carried the souls of the dead. My train. The souls of the dead. Hives five. I'm gonna die. I kept saying it over and over—hives five; I'm gonna die—until I heard myself wailing, sounding like movies I'd seen of twentieth-century Muslim women at funerals, but I wasn't just wailing, I was pounding at the walls, as if I could pound my way out. I started screaming. Who did this to me? What kind of God could let this happen? I had played it by the rules, and now this? I wailed and yelled and pounded, adding to the dents in the wall, so the next person here could wonder for a while what had caused the dents and then find out for himself.

Counselors came on the vidscreen to ask how I was feeling. I was able to flip them off. Doctors came on to take my HPI, my history of present illness, and I couldn't flip them off. One right after the other, asking about heart, lungs, stomach, kidneys and blood, then about surgery, and medication, and so on: how many beers a day would you estimate? and wine? any illegal substances? (and don't worry, this is all confidential) any sexually transmitted diseases (other than this one, that is)? what kind of work did your father do? your mother?

The slots opened and out came the waldoes, colored gray or white. I laid my arm in a curved, metal tray, and various devices came down to take blood pressure, blood, and heart rate. I took my shirt off, and a white cylinder came out to listen to heart and lungs, to tap my abdomen lightly. Then came other devices to collect urine. I stood on a sensitized pad, which registered my weight. Waldoes delivered dinner (it looked like meat and potatoes), and the vidscreen delivered my test results.

More counselors tried to talk with me, but I flipped them off. I couldn't flip off the woman who looked like Donna Palaez and who had some long official title and wanted a list of all my sexual partners of the previous three years. I couldn't stop from laughing. I couldn't flip off an older man who came on to tell me that my life insurance had been terminated and that I would be paid some kind of equity. To help defray medical expenses. And I couldn't flip off the court-appointed real-estate agent who looked too much like Henry, Aggie's new trainee. He informed me that I owned a house, and that I had received three offers to buy it. It was a buyer's market. All three prices were ridiculously low. I chose the highest bid; the money would help defray medical costs.

A man and a woman, dressed in white overalls and latex gloves, escorted me from the unsealed quarantine room, out of the building, through a tunnel beneath the tracks, and to the rear of a train, to the car that bore the relocation symbol. They handed me three rolls of quarters to use for the food machines: everything took one or two quarters, twenty-five or fifty dollars. I was the only one in a car that could seat forty. The machines ate my quarters; sometimes they gave me food in exchange.

At Chicago two people boarded. Three more in St. Louis. By Nevada there were ten of us, and we still had to make it to California. Each had one suitcase. I had one, too. One of us, a woman, ran a continual fever. She used up her quarters just buying water to replace what she had lost in sweat. We took turns buying her water.

A teenage boy boarded in Alburquerque and sat next to me. He was always in tears. This wasn't supposed to happen to him. His mom was dying; if she didn't have the money, the hospital wouldn't take her in; how else was he supposed to raise it? "Sure I bought morphine, but so did you. But the rest of the money went right into the hospital. All of it. My ass was all I had, and I rented it out to the highest bidder. So did you. Why did you get to live longer than me? You never did it for anything good, did you? Well, did you? Why do I have to die with you?"

But I didn't have to die. I wanted out, and I could get out. I forced my eyes open.

"*Do you want* to go through with this?" the woman in the white coat asked me. The red hair spiraling above her head was nightmarish.

I sipped water from a cup. The water hadn't cost anything. I nodded. It took an effort to nod. It would have taken a greater effort to say, *No. I'm getting dressed and leaving.*

The train station was unmarked. People dressed as if they were working outside an orbital factory escorted us to a bus. The road to the camp was solitary and long, and like a tour guide the driver droned on: Death Valley was past the Inyos to the east, those were the Sierra Nevadas on our right, the brown hills down south were infested with rattlesnakes, a group of Japanese had lived here last century, but he wasn't supposed to tell us that.

The camp was so unimpressive, it was daunting: take army barracks and, like a kid with building blocks, stack them up in an effort to make an imitation Construct, and there you have Camp Five. If it had a name, it wasn't posted anywhere. Alongside the barracks were squared-off areas lined by irrigation ditches and populated by apple orchards, crops, hogs in pens, and cattle; the rest was sand and tumbleweed. The camp was surrounded by electrified wire, and beyond that, barbed wire and sentry posts with machine guns on top. I guess the machine guns were to protect us from the crackpots. Beyond the wire and sentry posts stood a six-story structure of concrete and glass.

The bus drove past the cemetery, also surrounded by barbed wire. Two gaunt men wearing gray tunics were digging a grave. Their movements were slow and jerky, as if the shovels were too heavy. Whoever rested in the pine casket wasn't in a hurry. At the far end of the cemetery was a white obelisk; farther off were mountains. They were the loveliest mountains in the world.

The bus pulled up in front of the main building. Three children were playing with a ball, two of them running and laughing, the largest, a pudgy Hispanic boy, mostly watching. Two women in gray tunics sat nearby, one, a black woman watching the children, the second, a white woman resting her head on the black woman's shoulder, her mouth open, her eyes shut, her skin pale and marred: dark lesions spread across her face, reminding me of all the documentaries they'd shown us at Fair Haven to scare us into behaving properly. The movies hadn't done any of us any good.

The camp was maintained by its members; administrators, doctors, technicians, and guards resided in the concrete-and-glass structure across the way. Five organizers, dressed in their suitcase clothes, came to greet us before they separated us and led us to the conference cubicles just inside the doorway.

The plasterboard walls inside my cubicle were smudged and dented. I sat down in front of a vidscreen, and on came my own personal counselor, who told me everything I needed to know about the camp. My ID card slipped out of one slot. Its light blue plastic had my photo in one corner, my name printed in the opposite corner, and across the middle, in raised gold print, my ten-digit ID number: the first six, the date of my arrival; the second four, the last four numbers of my social-security number. My ID card was also my bancard and my medical card, and he told me how to use the conference booth to conduct private transactions with other camp members. He didn't use the word *inmate*. Through another slot I received my twenty-one meal tickets for this week. I'd receive my special-ration cards when I showed up at the infirmary. He pointed out that my ID card was coded blue rather than white because I had volunteered for medical testing, which could double my monthly allowance. I would receive job counseling tomorrow. Through the third slot came a watch with a black plastic band. "This is being supplied to you to help you take your medicines on time. The watch can be programmed to beep at the appropriate hours."

"I'm not taking any medicine."

"You will."

I was assigned to quarters located in the far corner of the farthest barracks. The room had two bureaus and two bunk beds and enough floor space for one person to walk between all four pieces of furniture. Two of my roommates weren't in. The third was lying in a lower bunk, the sheets drenched with sweat. He forced a smile and shook my hand and told me I was missing the last shift for lunch. He said he was going to skip eating, but I insisted that he join me. He was so weak, he could barely get out of bed. His clothes hung loosely on his body. He threw his arm around my shoulders for support, and I could feel his bones against my neck. "I don't want a wheelchair. You have to go to the vampires first, before they'll give you one of those." Sand crunched under our feet as we walked down the corridors to the lunchroom. I told myself that whatever he had wasn't catching, at least not this way.

The mess room looked like the cafeteria in a school that had gone bankrupt. Even though the lunch shift was to end in ten minutes, we stood half-an-hour at the end of a long line while my roommate's weight pulled on me more and more. Finally we were served: greasy hamburgers, french fries, iceburg lettuce, milk, and coffee. I handed over my meal ticket. The man at the register also wanted my ID card so he could register an approximate calorie count into my file. "You do test once a week, don't you?" he asked. I handed him my blue ID card, and my roommate stared at the card in dismay. "You're not one of those," he whispered. "Oh, fuck you." He pulled his arm away from me as if I were the one who was wasted and diseased. He collapsed with the third step.

People at the nearby tables looked up from their food, then returned to eating. My far-too-thin roommate made a few vain efforts to push himself up off the floor.

"Let me help you." I got his arm around my shoulders again and was pulling him up.

"You probably want something for helping me."

I shook my head.

"But I can't pay you," he said. "My allowance ran out a week ago. I don't even have enough to buy extra water."

The infirmary was underground and climate controlled. The doctors and nurses here were, like everywhere else, camp members, all in various stages of health. A row of beds rested along the walls where almost all the work could be done by waldoes, and that's where you'd have to lie down to be checked out by a specialist in the concrete-and-glass building. Or to be given a routine checkup. For me it was routine, and a nurse curtly directed me to a set of waldoes and a vidscreen. A healthy doctor came on the vidscreen and asked the usual questions. HPI: heart, lungs, stomach, nerves, and blood; surgery, medications, beer-wine-and-drugs; sexually transmitted diseases and social background. Then the waldoes reached out and did their work. First the CBC—complete blood count—and the number of T helper cells and red blood cells were low; then weight, urine, and stool. Everything was as fine as it could be for now, but the doctor on the vid wanted fine to last awhile. I received my first prescription. Once every eight hours. A nurse first gave me cards to buy extra water and nutritional supplements. She then handed me a medicine belt, helped me load one of the pouches with the green tablets, and reminded me I'd be fined if I came in for a refill before the two-week supply was used up. She wouldn't let me leave until the beeper on my watch was set.

I signed up to work in the fields. I was issued two gray tunics and a pair of work pants, and I was assigned to work with a tall, thin Pakistani woman with dark, serious eyes and a shy smile. While we weeded by hand, she talked about the woman she lived with, referring to her as her wife when the stories were kind and as her husband when they weren't. The Pakistani woman didn't have hives; her wife did. Two bouts with pneumonia so far, but her wife was getting better. After her wife died, she'd be allowed to leave the camp if she tested negative.

It was too hot to play in the sun, so kids ran up and down the cooling corridors that led underground to the infirmary. I was watching them when a man came up to me and warned me about the Pakistani woman. "She's a troublemaker. We pay her for her work, but she won't work with us. She won't let her roommate go to the infirmary, and she's buying all her medication on the black market. You don't want to associate with the likes of her." The man's dark hair was styled so that every curl was right in place. I recognized him as one of the organizers who'd met us when we'd gotten off the bus. His suitcase clothes looked as good as new, as if he'd gone shopping just before they came for him.

I wanted to take a shower, but the water didn't go on until dinnertime. We were in the desert, there was plenty of solar energy, so the water was as warm as you wanted it. The tap was set to turn off in five minutes.

I woke once to the sound of rain, the too-thin mattress hard, my back stiff, but the rain made me nostalgic for home. It turned out to be a sandstorm, but it sounded just like rain.

There are all the other sounds. New kids trying to jump on mattresses until they realize there are no springs. Children laughing. Feet running across the sand. Balls bouncing against walls, the surface of the thick Sheetrock cracking with repeated blows. The silence of people sitting with nothing to say. The long monologues of people reminiscing—the overheated laughter at something vaguely funny. The crying—no, more like sobbing. The silence. The beepers. On the hour. All the beepers. The children tell beeper jokes; the adults have been here too long.

One night I woke to the sound of machine-gun fire.

The next morning a group of us stood outside in the main compound and listened to the soft, sharp sound of shovels sliding into the sand.

I helped my roommate to the toilet, and I helped him finish his shower in time, and he kept telling me that if you didn't have a lover, most people expected to be paid for this kind of help. But I didn't charge him or ask for any other kinds of favors, so he started to call me his brother. And he started to gain back some weight. He always sniped at our other two roommates, and it was easy to see why in a camp full of dying people, no one took much interest in him. It was a new month, he had one hundred bills again, and he could afford the nutritional supplements and extra bottles of water he needed when the fevers left him dehydrated: weary, lethargic, unresponsive.

Sometimes the trucks that bring our food and our bottled water break down on the road, and they give us half-rations. For those who are slimming, who've lost all interest in food, it doesn't matter much. They sell their meals in exchange for liquids or make a transfer of credit at the conference booths.

What passes for air-conditioning goes out some days, and we all sweat like we're fevered. Other days the refrigeration goes out, and we all have the runs.

At lunch I sit with my brother and with the others who have blue ID cards. Every now and then I strike up a conversation while waiting in line. Almost everyone who has a white ID card goes silent when they see my blue one. They usually don't say anything; they just walk away.

Brother woke with night sweats. His sheets were drenched. He wouldn't let me change them, didn't want to go to breakfast. I ended up sitting with a blue-carded woman who told me how prominent a lawyer she had been. She found out how I'd earned my wages, and she left for better company.

The Pakistani woman I work with tells me she's volunteered to help with the oral-history project. She calls the people who don't live in the camps the truly sick. She asked me what I did in my previous life. I told her. "Don't be embarrassed," she said. "You didn't work for the camps." I made excuses never to eat lunch at the same shift; I don't want her to see my blue ID card.

It was getting harder and harder to talk with people. Barbed wire and sentry posts, and beyond: mountains capped with snow like something out of a postcard. I dreamed about climbing those mountains, my dream within a dream, even though I hate to hike.

Brother's fevers returned. His allowance had already been used up. My extra food and water rations lasted a little over a week. Keeping his clothes clean, his sheets clean, buying him bottles of water, packets of nutritional supplement, I used up my double allowance more quickly than I could have imagined. I walked down to the conference booth after hours, when the organizers had long departed. A gaunt man, who had two healthy teenage boys as bodyguards, bought three of my meal tickets. We inserted our cards into the appropriate slots, and he made the credit transfer. The next morning I bought more water. It was a medicine now, but they wouldn't prescribe it, not enough, not out here, not with waters that had long ago been diverted to the cities. When farming, I watched water drain into the parched ground so there'd be apples this fall.

A man as thin as my brother told me he needed a loan to get some drugs from a black marketeer. I told him I didn't have anything. Before I knew what was happening, he had kicked me in the groin, punched me in the head, and had grabbed five meal tickets from my pockets before I could fend him off.

Along the covered concourse, where children play when the sun is too volatile or when the wind blows the sand too hard, are a series of convenience stores to purchase water, accessories, and cosmetics. We get to test-market new brand names, paying reduced prices if we want to hide the lesions on our skin, give color to the pallor we carry months before our burials.

My dying brother: thrush, a childhood sickness, was next, dotting his tongue and mouth all white, followed by bleeding lesions. Then it was a violent red rash across his torso, and calamine lotion was out of stock, on order, and he itched until tiny rivulets of blood rolled down his body like beads of sweat.

I am hungry all the time. The calorie readouts per meal are always between five hundred and seven hundred calories, so maybe it has less to do with calories and more to do with nutrition. An hour before the next meal, you are hungry; by suppertime you are tired. I felt it worse. I sold off too many breakfasts to make sure my brother had enough water. The black marketeer, continually wiping sweat from his face, said it was a shame that I was slimming down when I was still hungry: "You know, I've heard you had some skills that could earn us both some extra cash."

The postal service charges extra for out-of-the-way places like the camps, but the care packages keep coming. The Pakistani woman brought me a brownie from hers this morning. My fourth roommate hid his; occasionally you'll catch someone sneaking in to steal a hoarded morsel. A teenage girl down the hall told us how much she hates her parents and sold off every item. The next day two teenagers pummeled her until her arms and face were black-and-blue, her nose broken. She had undersold the black marketeers.

His eyes went next. Cytomegalovirus. He refused to stay in the infirmary for the IV hookups, and the oral antibiotics weren't effective. The operation to save the retina wasn't mandatory; my brother didn't have enough cash to pay for the operation. So first there were the complaints that there wasn't enough light. Then he could make out only the outline of things. I'd hold my hand up in front of him so he could count my fingers. Soon he couldn't count those. After a while he stopped complaining. I just led him around when he had the strength to get up. Someone, a man, who wasn't in much better condition than my brother, called me a regular guide dog. I went for the man, punching him in the head and belly, thrilling with each blow, until my hands hurt. Nobody stopped me. A few cheered me on.

The Pakistani woman broke down in tears. She'd tried to break up a fight and no one had helped her. She said the good ones had all died or were in the infirmary dying. People used to break up fights. People used to help each other without charging. "I don't charge my brother anything," I said.

You could see my brother's skull beneath the skin, the hollow temples. It was hard to believe he could still be alive. I told him he should try the experimental drugs, double his income. "And prolong this?"

My fever lasted several days. It had started. I was glad.

My brother slipped into a coma. I had to rent a wheelchair to get him to the infirmary he always refused to go to. They said he was too far gone, that he'd thumbprinted a living will. I sat next to his bed and waited it out. Several beds down, some patients were comparing their ID numbers, talking about how long they'd lasted. One called out to us, asked our numbers. I shook my head. I didn't like to talk much anymore. I just watched my brother's labored breathing. I wanted to tell him I love him, but I couldn't. He died. I kissed his eyelids and cried because I hadn't done that while he was still living.

Like everyone else who still ate three square meals, I fasted for a day in his memory. During the same day I arranged a grave plot. A woman who had crosses dangling from her ears slapped me when she learned I wasn't waiting three days until I buried him. Four people quoted four different prices to help bury him. The Pakistani woman and her wife, a withdrawn Navaho woman, helped me dig the grave.

The fourth bed in their room was empty. I had to sign over two months of my allowance to an organizer in order to arrange a reassignment. But it wasn't a difficult move. Most of my suitcase clothes were worn out; all I had to move were my camp grays and some toiletries. I shave only every now and then.

———

"*Don't call me sister.* Too many brothers sleep with their sisters. Call me brother."

"Does that mean," her wife asked, "that he should call me brother-in-law?"

"No, brother will do. Won't it?"

I nodded.

———

The air started to chill, too late to help my first brother's sweat. Low-grade fevers all the time. Then the fever rose; my whole body shook. I went down to the infirmary, and they gave me something that took care of it right away. Then, came the pneumonia. They took me in at the infirmary. By the end of my stay, some new wonder drug had rid me of the pneumonia—and of all the equity from the sale of my house and my life insurance.

———

Someone asked me where I was from. Cleveland, I said. Oh, was the reply, I knew a Susan Sundai. She was here last year. She died so quickly.

It seemed too much of a coincidence, and I didn't want to believe her dead, not Susie, someone from that whole time had to emerge unscathed, and it all overwhelmed me, not Susie, I should have dreamed it had been someone else, and I forced my eyes open, to put an end to it all.

The old woman, the one who just told me about Susan Sundai, is still sitting in front of me, every wrinkle on her face so vivid, I can count them. "Are you okay?" she asks. "You just went blank for a second. Maybe you should get some neurological testing, or something? I'll walk down there with you."

The old woman is very real, and she won't go away.

———

It is December, cool, and time to slaughter the hogs. As with everything else involving our work, there is no automation. Our work would take no time at all if there were machines to help us. We work in pairs. My brother and I hold the pig, a third worker applies the knife to the throat. It surprises me how quickly the blood drains, how soon the pig gives up on life.

I go down to the infirmary at least once a week. Blood, weight, urine, stool. They ask me about coughing, night sweats, shortness of breath, dry heaving coughs, diarrhea, appetite, strength, pain on swallowing. I always say yes to several of them.

The purplish blotches on my skin have surprised me. An ointment and three different pills seem to take care of it, but my two brothers say that I am acting short-tempered. They ask what drugs I'm on. I'm not thinking straight, or I wouldn't have been eating with them, but there in line I hand over my blue card so the number of calories can be registered.

I'm getting better, but now my brothers won't talk with me. "It's not like I'm collaborating or anything," I keep saying. "Look," my brother, the Pakistani woman says one day, after days of silence, "they're learning to cure your symptoms, that's all. It gives them all kinds of drugs they can market to the truly sick."

"You'd do it," I say.

"If I was at home."

Her wife, my brother, nods, then adds, "Same goes for me. If I was at home, I'd want to live as long as I could to be with the people I love. But not here. I'm not going to let science benefit one bit if I have to die in a place like this."

Next comes something with too many syllables: the skin numb to the touch; inside, sharp jabs of pain. They give me something that just makes me dizzy. They can't take blood this week because it's coming out with my shit. They advise me to wear a surgical mask so I won't pick up any loose bugs. I laugh. No one wears them. Not here.

My brother's wife is doing fine. Why am I getting so sick? I don't want to be so sick. I don't want this pain. I force open my eyes, and my head falls onto the mess-hall table. My brothers help me down to the infirmary, and a rotund doctor—must be new to the place—piles on the demands: repeat these numbers after me, who are these pictures of, how many fingers am I holding up, what's your birthday, what's the date? I guess my answers aren't that good, but I really should not be here, I am trying to tell them, I should be able to open my eyes and be gone. But here I am.

Everything else must have been the dream.

In the infirmary, on my stomach, swabbing my hip with iodine, off-green sterile drapes around the bare skin. First injection, lidocaine, and it stings, grating against the bone, then a large bore needle, handle like a corkscrew's. Sharp deep, going for bone marrow. The throbbing afterward. I like to lie down on my back, but can't anymore. Whatever they found out didn't help cure me. Pneumonia again.

I go to sleep and wake up in the apple orchard. A guard had been watching me step closer to the barbed wire. I don't remember walking out there. I peed in the sink and don't remember doing it. I shit on the middle of the floor. Maybe I'm saying crazy things.

The doctor on the vidscreen shakes his head and prescribes something new, so new that they'll triple my allowance if I take it. I wake up twisted in bed, pain running along every nerve. My brothers hold me back, tell me my testing days are through. I flop like a fish on the bed, trying hard to hate them and hate myself, but finding out that I couldn't care less.

They halve my allowance money, then deduct the cards I have for extra water and nutritional supplements from that. The organizers say I still owe a hundred bills for my room reassignment, so they take ten of my meal tickets. It doesn't matter much; I'm not very hungry. I sometimes work. I sometimes shave. I sometimes shower. I stare at barbed wire and the mountains. I'm not going anywhere. I open my eyes and I am here.

I am too weak to really do anything, but I must smell bad because my two brothers take me to the showers and help me in. I can't steady my hands to hold the soap, and one brother supports me while the other washes me down.

A child turned five. He didn't have the disease, though his mother had. They were going to send him to his grandmother. There was a big party today. But it felt like a funeral: he was crossing over into a better world. I tried to be happy. I couldn't have cared less.

My brothers—and now others since I'm not testing—try to help me eat. It is hard to swallow. I feel as if there are golf balls in my throat, under my arms, in my groin.

I babble on, telling them all sorts of things, I guess, about the rape, the despair, Fair Haven, the free-lance tricks, my father's death, the morphine, the jails, the cleaning up, the new job. I think they tell me stories, too. I sometimes wake up screaming.

My brother reads me my mail, from my mother, from my brother Art. I can't understand why my father doesn't write.

My brother is called Papa now and her wife is Mama—they change my sheets and wipe my bottom enough. Someone else, a man, who isn't sick yet, who is waiting, has started to help them. He is thin, blond, with a beard. He looks like Mama Bear must have looked when he was healthy, but Mama Bear is part of a different dream that I've given up on. But this man comforts me, tells me everything will soon be better even though the pain is worse. There are things I can do, once I die and cross over to the other world.

Maybe these are my last rites. I sweat and shake and cough and breathe air that feels thick as concrete, and I hate my existence, my faithless body, myself. So badly, I want to die gracefully, my body as fresh as it was in all the advertising footage from Personal Services. My family hovers around me at the edge of some soft darkness that I remember craving once before. The failure of flesh calls for surrender, the grieving of Papa and Mama and the friend who comforted me calls for surrender. But I'm holding out.

I have to say one last good-bye to someone important. But I can't remember anymore who it might be.

I awoke when I died, crying out. The woman with the lab coat was unsnapping everything in an efficient hurry, then pulling me to her. I huddled in her embrace, and I let her hold my head awkwardly against her breasts. I cried, my back heaving with loud sobs. She offered me water. My paper suit was soaked with sweat and had torn easily. I felt as if I were back in the quarantine room, waiting for it all to start over again, but this time they'd hired someone to comfort me for a while. "I don't want to go back," I heard myself sob. "I don't want to go."

She professionally rubbed my back and murmured maternally, "There, there, now, there are things you can do about it." The last words didn't ring true, and I looked up at her face. I remembered her now, how she'd set me up in the chair, that the chair was in the Sensory Arcades, that I'd requested the Relocation Experience. I let her comfort me, and I gained control of my breathing. I wondered why she told me I could do something about it. I half expected her to hand me New Puritan literature on my way out, remind me of how degrading my line of work was.

Her breasts started to feel more like breasts, but I liked their comfort too much to let go. I looked up and smiled shyly, still childish in my need.

"My friends call me Goldilocks," she said.

Her nameplate said Dorothy. Her hair, set in a spiral, was very red. I knew who her friends were. I'd met three of them.

25

I WENT TO THE Personal Services pool and tried to swim myself to exhaustion, but I remembered too much. Lang would send me there if I tested bad. I would send me there if I tested bad. Papa Bear said no one should go. Lang had warned me that the UHL would show up. All I had to do was press out the seven-digit number Pilar had given me. All Papa Bear had to know was that I had contacted Lang. And on and on, except with each thought I watched someone I knew in a dream die again.

I dried off, dressed in shorts, and played hoops with some off-duty pros. I missed too many easy shots. So I showered, dressed, and walked home.

I walked on autopilot; I didn't see people, I didn't hear displays, I didn't smell any attractions. I was sure the makers of Hangon had something for my mood, but I didn't know what it could be. Since I hadn't gone to work on Friday, I'd missed the weekly battery of blood tests. I felt like I'd walked under a ladder or dropped a mirror on a black cat. I headed back to Personal Services and watched a machine draw blood from my arm. I kept thinking again and again that I shouldn't have requested the Relocation Experience, that it was a bad omen, no servicer worth his salt would have done it.

Once home, I discovered that we were out of rum and beer. I ended up watching last century's movies; their problems seemed distant and pleasantly contrived.

I must have fallen asleep. The cold, sweating glass of

a beer bottle woke up my cheek, the rest of my body following in turn. Harry stood above me. He placed the open bottle in my hand.

"Some hair of the dog that bit you," Harry said.

"The dog that bit me had rabies." I sipped the beer while Harry sat down. He'd changed the station on the TV. They were showing one of the spate of movies made several years ago about families who moved from the Constructs into surrounding, unmonitored neighborhoods and found themselves caught up in the machinations of thieves, rapists, and old-fashioned drug dealers. Most of the violence was done by Hispanos, most of the drug-dealing by homosexuals: the movies were popular, and the ASD, still in its heyday, had protested the hell out of them. "Trying to bring me back to reality?" I asked.

"You're the one who said it."

We sat there like that for a while. A hood busted a monitor, then raped a blond passerby. Her father responded to her cries for help; he got there too late to save her from the rape, but just in time to save her from the stabbing.

"Looks just like Ohio City," I said. "You see this on the streets all the time."

"You know," said Harry between sips of beer, "it's none of my business what goes on between you and your clients."

I couldn't think of any response.

Harry said nothing while I showered and dressed. I wore the best clothes I'd purchased for the job: nothing synthetic, a light jacket, and the Beijing tie. I stared at the mirror forever, making sure all the looks were right. I looked as if I still had a hangover from yesterday's rum. I told Harry I'd see him tomorrow and made for the door.

"Rod," he said.

I turned.

He had some lecture planned. I could see it in the way he was leaning forward, in the way he tried to look formal. I could imagine all his warnings, and I'd know that each one of them was right. "Never mind," he said.

"If you say so. Have a good evening." I left him there.

26

"You're overdressed," said Anna, "and you look awful." She wore jeans, a white blouse, and pearl earrings.

"It's getting to be a habit," I said, as she stepped aside and let me in. "But this time, it *is* your fault."

"My fault?"

"Yeah. I went on your errand this morning."

"Errand?" Then her eyes widened, and she almost looked pleased with herself. "Oh, my, you really did go. Here, sit down. You know, Sauro would have waited several weeks so it wouldn't look like it was my idea. Can I get you a beer?"

"Please." I almost collapsed onto the couch, then thought better of it. I sat down, casual and controlled.

She returned with two long-neck green bottles: Thirty-Threes. Yesterday with the picnic basket, now with my favorite beer; I felt as if she were doing my job. I thanked her and then drank more than half the bottle.

Still standing, she raised her bottle, smiled, then proceeded to drink it all. "I learned how to drink beer in college. It's a skill my father wouldn't appreciate."

"Maybe he did it in college, too."

"Did what?" She was already walking back to the kitchen.

"Drank beer in one long gulp."

She returned with two more beers. "I'll take it easy with this one. You look like maybe I should have bought more than I did."

"I'm okay."

"Do you want to talk about it?" She sat down next to me and placed her hand on my knee.

I shook my head.

She was silent for a moment.

I didn't know what to say, either. I hadn't been trained to live through my death and make pleasant conversation all in the same day.

She said, "You look like a nice hot bath would do you some good."

"Then I'd be underdressed," I said.

"No. I mean it. Let me play Little Red Riding Hood one more time." She patted my thigh and stood up. "I'll do a better job of it than I did yesterday. Come along."

Her *come along* was imperious. I half expected her to start using the royal *we*. Rule Six: If the client isn't breaking the law or breaking the contract, the client is always right.

I followed Anna to the bathroom and leaned against the doorjamb while she made all the preparations. She turned on the water, tested its temperature with her wrist, and adjusted the faucets until the water was to her liking. She left and returned with more beer, and a giant, soft towel, which she hung from a peg. She laid out soap, shampoo, and washcloth. Amidst all the activity, I found myself marveling at the flow of water, the luxury of time that a bath implied. I hadn't lived in a place with a bathtub since I had left my parents' home.

"Most people take off their clothes before taking a bath," Anna said. She smiled. She enjoyed playing Little Red Riding Hood.

I wasn't too keen on playing the ailing grandmother, but I tried to look pleasantly exhausted as I took off my clothes, folded them neatly, and piled them in the hallway. If Anna hadn't been a client, I would have just dropped them there.

The water was almost too hot, and the heat slipped between strands of muscle, relaxing calves, thighs, lower back. The air above the waterline felt cool. I bent my knees and slid down into the tub until water touched my chin. "I think I could stay here forever," I said. Muscles unwound; a knot of memory remained.

Anna sat on the toilet seat, suddenly uncertain of what to do. "Let me wash your hair," she said.

"Sure."

I slid down and submerged my head underwater and rose up, water dripping from my hair. Anna had already poured the shampoo into her hands and began to rub it into my hair. Her fingertips massaged my scalp.

"I guess," she said, "I should have given you one of Sauro's books, instead."

"You've already lent me two."

"Which you haven't read. I meant his books on the camps. Sauro subscribed to the ASD publications from the camps."

"It would have been an easier experience."

"I guess it wasn't very fair of me. I never could work up the courage to go."

"Nice of you to send me in your place." I had meant to sound pleasantly sarcastic.

"Sorry," she whispered. "I sometimes ask people to do things without thinking. It's a family trait."

"This scalp massage feels good," I said.

"I'm glad you like it." She dipped her hands in the bath; soapsuds floated away. She began to massage my forehead, my temples. "Can I ask you a question?"

"Sure."

"Do you ever worry about the camps?"

I almost said *no*, but that had never really been the truth. "In the back of my mind, yeah. But I probably thought of it the same way you did when you were sleeping around before you met Sauro."

"I wouldn't say that," she said. "Let me rinse your hair."

"Why not?" I asked, happy to change the subject.

She dunked a cup in the bath, then poured its water over my head. "I'm not sure I slept around with all those guys for the sex, though it was sort of fun. And there was a kind of romance to it. Like driving recklessly." She poured more water; suds and water cascaded down skin, spread out across the surface. "I never took a single blood test. I was scared to death my family would find out, but I think I kept hoping they would. Like it would prove a point, or something." More water, fewer suds. I resented how easily she talked about herself. "My friend Sophie told me I was fucking in exchange for hugs and kisses. I think I was tired of being the oldest daughter, you know: the role model for my two younger sisters. You get the point."

"You left out the camps."

She smiled. "There's no talking circles around you." She ran her fingertips across my hair; it squeaked. "I guess the point is that in the back of my mind I was scared of getting hives, but deep down I was hoping for them."

"Why?" I asked, even though I half knew the answer.

She absentmindedly picked up the washcloth and shook it in the bathwater. "Because I deserved them for what I was doing. And I'd end up in one of the camps my father had built, and he'd get what he deserved for what he was doing." She rubbed soap into the washcloth.

"Self-destructive."

"I don't know. I was trying to do the things I wanted to do, but I wasn't doing the things I was supposed to do. (Lean over, and I'll scrub your back.) I don't like talking about it a whole lot. I forget things, and I'm not sure really what I felt."

"There's nothing wrong with being confused." The pat line was meant for clients who wanted to terminate their contract after only a day or two of service.

"No, there isn't." The rough edge of the washcloth and the lubrication of soap felt good against my back. "But there is something wrong with the way I resolved my confusion. I joined Americans for Social Democracy. There were people, you know, in ASD who said my father was like the businessmen who built concentration camps for the Nazis last century. Those businessmen got slave labor; there's no slave labor in the relocation camps."

"Why did you join, then?"

"I finally read one of those books of Sauro's. It was an oral history of one of the camps. The internees had compiled it. I had refused to read it for the longest time because it was known that those books were propaganda. But Sophie, my drama prof, was directing a play about the camps, and I was auditioning for the lead. The lead was a woman who ends up in the camps. So I read Sauro's book for background. And that's when I felt the recognition. Part of me felt I belonged there. Part of me felt that any of those people could have been me."

"Was your sex life really that sad?" I asked, wondering how much of her history she was rewriting. "Didn't you have any fun screwing around?"

The washcloth stopped. "I don't know." She blushed and looked away. "I had a good time with the guys who liked to dance. The sex was okay, I guess. But the first orgasm I ever had that wasn't self-inflicted was with Sauro."

"God, it sounds like the twentieth century."

She didn't hear me. "Anyway, that's when I decided to join ASD."

"What about the Union for Human Liberation?"

"What about them? They have a silly name."

"You were in ASD when the whole thing split. Did you think of joining them?"

"You sound like a friendly version of the FBI." She leaned over and kissed my nose. "And you look a little less morose."

"Than the FBI?"

"Than before. Let's get you rinsed off, dried off, and I'll give you a nice back rub."

I unplugged the bath, and the water rushed down the drain, more slowly than the sound implied. I turned on the shower, soaped down what Anna missed, rinsed off my back and everything else. Anna watched, and I found her gaze disconcerting.

Afterwards she held the towel open and began to pat the wetness away from my body: face, arms, chest, belly. She stopped for a moment, tenderly lifted up my penis, and placed a kiss upon its singular eye. She smiled up at me. "Tempting, isn't it?" she said. "Turn around, and I'll dry your back."

She lingered on back, buttocks, back of thighs. I wanted to release myself to sensation, but I was busy deciphering her actions.

"Your files on me must not be very good," she said.

"Why not?" I turned around, but she didn't hand me the towel.

"My period started this morning, and you didn't know it."

"Such is life," I said.

"Sauro would have acted like I'd done this on purpose. Just so we couldn't have sex."

"Well, since you enjoy fine food, conversation, and dancing, there's plenty we can do. We still haven't gone dancing yet."

"I don't want to make love," she said firmly.

"That's fine. We don't have to."

"Do back rubs make you horny? Sauro used them as an excuse to make love."

"A good back rub puts me to sleep."

She took my hand and led me out of the bathroom and to her bed. I began to feel that I was with several Annas at once: one who enjoyed the sensual, the other who wanted to exert some control over it. I felt as if this were a test of my own control: how long could I enjoy all this sensuality without corrupting the tenderness into sexuality? If the client wasn't always right, I would have left.

Anna, still wearing her jeans, white blouse, and earrings, set the oil on the bedside table and positioned me in the center of the bed. The drops of oil were cool on my skin until her hands spread them out over the surface of my back. Her fingers began to knead around my shoulder blades.

"I'm really enjoying this," I said, "but I feel like you're doing my work."

"Haven't other women done this for you?"

"Other clients? At times, but not so emphatically."

"Consider it an act of contrition. If you make me feel guilty enough, I'll do just about anything."

"Guilty for what?"

"The Relocation Experience."

"Are you feeling guilty because I went or because you didn't?"

"You've got a knot here," she said, and applied pressure to a spot on my lower back. "Both, I guess. I really didn't have the right to make you go, especially since I never went. I think I was the only person in ASD never to undergo the experience. I used to tell Sauro that I was too embarrassed to go to a Sensory Arcade."

"Did Sauro go?"

"Oh, yeah. Twice."

"Two times?"

"Sauro loved to take things seriously. He went the first time just before he joined ASD. He took the interurban down to Boston. That was just before the guys you work for pulled it from all the Arcades."

"They only had it in four or five cities." I said. "It wasn't like it was a big money-maker."

She squeezed my buttocks a few times and went to work on my left thigh. "Well, after we won the lawsuit, almost all the ASD people in college went to Boston and lined up for it. I couldn't bear to go near Personal Services. I was more conservative than I had thought. It's funny to think that a year later I'd end up roaming their corridors. You know, I almost went to have a Sexual Experience rather than to hire a companion."

"So you were in ASD when they sued Personal Services?"

"We sued the U.S. government, remember, and yes, I was a member. But we were in New Hampshire, and the lawsuit was initiated in Cleveland."

"I know."

"But I did meet the head lawyer for the case." She shifted to my right thigh. "He grew up out in Parma before everybody was Eminent Domained into the Construct."

"What was he like?"

"Nice enough, I guess. He wasn't very happy. He was working on the case against the Relocation Camps. Stuart was excited that it was going before the Supreme Court, but he was being edged out of the suit. The ACLU had initiated the case. They were arguing Bill of Rights, due process and all that, and they didn't want to be associated with the more radical elements of ASD."

"That's too bad," I said. The ACLU had lost the case; the Supreme Court had declared the camps constitutional.

"Plus," Anna said, while her hands shifted down to my calves, "Stuart had been in love with this guy Luis whom he had imported from Hollywood to testify in the lawsuit about the Experience. Luis had helped program the images. After the trial he'd gotten some other kind of job to stay out here with Stuart."

"There's a lot of past tense there. What happened to him?"

"The tense is called past perfect. Luis suffered from past imperfect. He tested positive. He got shipped off last June, just after we got here. He got shipped to Camp Seven, where all the rioting happened. I heard he'd gotten killed when the National Guard opened fire. So, I guess, Stuart didn't have much cause to be happy last summer."

"That's an understatement. Didn't Stuart end up testing positive?"

"They dragged him in and tested him every week until the end of the summer. His cousin told me that Luis had probably been sick before coming out here and that Stuart had been careful."

"Do you still see him?"

"It's been a long time." Anna raised my right foot into the air, began rubbing it absentmindedly. "I think the last time I saw him was in November. We had these emergency meetings after the court declared the camps constitutional. He looked horrible." She started to apply pressure, beginning with the heel, moving out toward the toes. "He'd come to the meetings wearing this old leather jacket straight out of the twentieth century. We'd be talking about the American Holocaust, and he'd just sit there zipping and unzipping his leather jacket."

Anna dropped the first foot and was picking up the second. Her touch repelled me. I forced myself to hold still.

"You're tensing up," she said.

"Sorry."

"Do you want to change the subject?"

I twisted my foot around, an imitation of relaxed behavior.

"Do you think he joined UHL?" I asked.

"Who?"

"Stuart."

"He could have. A lot of us could have. It wasn't a good time. First there had been the riots out in Camp Seven, and the National Guard shot down all those who fled the camp. Then the march in Washington, and the police showed up with tear gas. Then someone bombed a New Puritan church in Boston, and so on.

"We'd protested, we'd demonstrated, and we'd sued.

We did everything legal, and the camps were still there. We backed losing candidates, we sent out petitions, we published books. And the Supreme Court says camps are constitutional. We'd done everything, or almost everything, by the book. And got nowhere. We were talking morality; they were talking self-protection. And we lost. Whatever we did never seemed to be enough. Their people were quoted more often in the datanets, on the holo; their people were in power. It was like the law was always against us if we played it their way."

"Why didn't you join the UHL then?"

"I don't know. I didn't believe in violence, or I was scared of violence, who knows? Those were the worst days of my life. I wasn't in love with Sauro anymore." She returned to my shoulder blades.

"Did Sauro think of joining?"

Anna laughed; it sounded more like a bark. "I think he wanted to. We both wanted to."

"Were you guys out somewhere when they blacked out Kansas City?"

"Out? Why would we be out?"

"It happened on your birthday."

Her hands stopped for a moment, then resumed stretching out the muscles of my back. "Yeah. I guess. I don't remember. Sauro and I didn't do much of anything."

"Why not?"

"I just don't like birthdays."

"What did Sauro think of what happened in Kansas City?"

"He didn't like it. But he kept talking tough about it. He kept saying how it'd show how much strength the UHL really had, that it wasn't some powerless little organization of incompetent fanatics."

"Did he mean it?"

"How could he? Every night we'd watch the news and hear the horror stories. The ventilation in an old folks' home had no back up, and thirty died. Premature babies in a county hospital didn't make it because the back up systems had been hooked up into the computer system and went down with it. People on the subway got trampled in the dark when people rushed out into the tunnels. Half the time Sauro looked like he was going to cry. I couldn't make up my mind if I thought he was really sensitive or really weak."

I didn't know what to say. I knew Sauro hadn't been with her on her birthday. I'd seen footage of her reading a book, pacing, taking sips of Scotch, trying to act as if it weren't affecting her.

"That's enough for your back," she said. "Roll over, okay?"

I didn't like the edge in her voice. "It's my turn," I said. "Let me give you a back rub."

"No. Just be quiet. Let me finish what I started."

I rolled onto my back, and she poured a thin stream of oil up each leg. Her hands started with my right ankle, forefingers pressing down, pivoting upon thumbs, then moved up slowly, up calf, along thigh, back of hand brushing against scrotum, against glans. "Spread your legs," she said. She worked the muscle inside the thigh, the incidental brushing continuing. Penis rose and flopped against belly. She eyed it for a moment, then went to work on my left ankle, applying pressure, hand inching up along calf, then thigh. Her fingers held my scrotum, applying pressure along the skin, lightly fingering testicles, turning them between fingertips. Fingers then reached forward, pulled glans from belly into air for examination. Oiled fingers traced a lovely path, but Anna looked more determined than tender.

"Anna?"

"Let me finish," she whispered.

Fingertip brushed along cleft while a hand grasped farther below and tugged skin downward, delightfully; I sighed. The oil coating her hands, coating my penis, heightened the light touches, sent out lines of pleasure with each tug of the closed hand. I watched Anna watch her hands, and some of the delight left me. There was a depth of concentration, as if she were measuring her sense of control over me. The sensuality of contrast, one naked and the other clothed, had disappeared, and there seemed more a condescension to the needs of the penis she was now servicing. I wanted to pull away, tell her to stop, but I was mesmerized by her intensity. Release built within me, but Anna let go, and the sensation subsided. She grasped my penis with both hands, began pulling up and down. I closed my eyes, tried to concentrate on sensation, but oil was absorbed by skin and soon there was only the friction of skin upon skin. Soon I could almost feel skin flushed red. The soreness added to the sensation, and I felt my body go stiff with pressure. I let myself thrust at her, feeling my lack of control measured against her control, nothing balanced by pleasure given or received, just the mechanics of thrust, the pressure of closed eyes, the desire for release, and finally, mechanically, release.

Anna withdrew her hands and laid them in her lap. She looked down at them, staring at her hands as if it were a way to avoid looking at me. I sat up and slid over to her. With forefinger and thumb lightly touching each wrist, I raised her hands to my lips. She didn't pull her hands away; she just watched me. I tenderly kissed her hands. "You don't have to," she said. I continued kissing as if her fingers, her palms, her wrists were the only things that mattered.

"Would you like a back rub, now?" I whispered.

She shook her head.

"Wash up and get undressed, and I'll give you one."

She was naked except for white bikini briefs when she walked back into the bedroom. Nudity had no mystique; her familiar body seemed ugly. Before she could speak, I ushered her onto the bed, got her to relax, then began to work. I reached around, massaged forehead and neck before I began work on the back.

"Can I ask you something?"

"Sure." I had started to spread oil in long strokes from buttocks to shoulder blade.

"I don't understand something."

"What?"

"How you became aroused."

I began to knead around her shoulder. "Take it as a compliment."

"But after what you'd experienced this morning, after everything I'd talked about, how could you respond that way?"

"It's the nature of the machinery."

"You could have pulled away," she said.

The client's always right, even when she's wrong. "I'm not a mind reader," I said, and I heard the petulance in my voice. It was unprofessional.

"Every man I've ever known has been like that. Something about that disgusts me."

I didn't know how to respond. I began to roll my thumb along the base of her neck. I pressed deeply, trying to work away at the tensions. The true ones went much deeper than her muscles.

"You really think they'll cancel our contract on Monday?"

"Probably."

"Just because I went to your place?"

"And because I let you in. It wasn't very professional."

"Is this still a professional relationship?"

I found myself hesitating. "Yes."

"Maybe it's for the best, then. Everything's getting so mixed up."

I didn't really want to know what *everything* was, not if *everything*, as far as I was concerned, would be over on Monday. So I progressed along her back, going from shoulder blades to upper back, moving to lower back and buttocks. I had barely finished with her lower back when I found she was asleep.

I spread the covers over her and considered leaving. I didn't know if I wanted her to wake up alone. Palaez, the lawyer, was right, too much was wrong with her; I wasn't the one to rescue her.

I dressed and walked back to the living room. I found Sauro's books on the camps and pulled out several volumes. I looked through the pictures and read the long-winded commentary until I fell asleep on the couch.

I awoke with a start. The lights were off, and I didn't know where I was. Streetlight glow gave shape to a few things, and I felt, for the barest of moments, that I was in the attic in my parents' old home. I fumbled for a light and almost knocked the lamp over. I could feel my heart in my chest. The antique chairs, the couch, the coffee table, the crystalplayer, the one-eyed lens: I was in Anna's living room, not back at home, in the attic. There were no hooks around which you could fasten a tie before fastening it around your neck. My father had been dead for years. Why should I think about him now?

27

THAT SUNDAY MORNING I woke up in Anna's bed with Anna cuddled up to me. Her warmth, my comfort, turned the previous night into a falsehood, something I must have dreamed in my perversity. We showered and dressed. Anna made eggs. The silence of the morning made last night and everything else very real. I had never allowed this to happen with any other client; I had always found friendly words for any unnecessary silence. But I couldn't bring myself to say anything. We finished breakfast, and I cleared the plates from the table.

"I want to be alone for a while," she said to my back.

"Do you want to get together tonight?"

"Our last night together?"

"Only if they cancel the contract." I tried to sound as if it wouldn't happen.

"I'll call you," she said.

On my way out she handed me a book called *Jude the Obscure*, by Thomas Hardy. Having nothing better to do when I got home, I started to read it. Jude, the mason who wanted to go to Oxford, reminded me a bit of my father, who had lost faith in his thesis, lost out on his Ph.D., and lost tenure at his important eastern college. The only thing my father had kept was a tie that bore the college colors.

By 16 hours Anna hadn't called. I had no idea why this book had been so important to her, and I was fed up with all of Jude's suffering in the name of love and marriage. Harry returned home from a Sunday-afternoon shift at Monitoring that he'd taken on for a friend. Kevin, who'd visited first his mother then Betsy's for Mother's Day, showed up about an hour later. We drank beer, talked politics, and watched baseball. On the news that night they announced the discovery of a possible vaccine for hives two and six. I had taken the vaccine for hives three when it came out several years ago: it had cost me three months of my salary, paid off in twelve painful installments.

On Monday morning, after I found out that my blood was still good, I went to my mailbox at Personal Services expecting to find a message concerning my contract with Anna Baxter. There was none. Instead there was a message to see Donna Palaez.

I sat down in her very ordered office, and she sat up straight on her side of the desk and glared at me. Maybe it was her job to cancel the contract. Maybe she'd demote me, and I'd get shift-janes again.

"I called you in so I could get your thumbprint on a document."

"Sure," I said.

She pushed the lit flatscreen across her desk. I picked it up. It didn't look like a contract-release form.

"Do you want to know what the document says?"

I shrugged.

"It states that if there is a lawsuit initiated by anyone holding Personal Services responsible for your conduct with Ms. Anna Baxter, Personal Services can be held responsible only where its contract with Ms. Baxter has been violated by a Personal Services' representative—you, in this case—who has followed all rules and regulations that Personal Services set forth for its employees."

"Meaning?"

"That I'm trying to make you liable for whatever is going on between you and Ms. Baxter. You let her into your apartment, which violates her contract and our regulations. Not only were you drunk, you permitted Ms. Baxter to suggest that your relationship was less than professional."

"Maybe the contract should be terminated, then."

"Not maybe, Mr. Lawrence. It should be. But Fred O'Mallery will not let me terminate this contract."

I couldn't look her in the eyes.

"Can you tell me why?"

I shook my head.

"I thought not," she said. "Will you thumbprint the statement I've handed you?"

"You're making me liable?" I said.

"For any time you don't follow our regulations. If you follow regulations; if you start watching the dailies again; if you take your blood tests on time; if you see Ms. Baxter five days out of seven, and if you reassure her and us that this is only a professional relationship, then, no, you are not liable."

"Oh."

"There's something else you should know. If Personal Services is sued, we will sue Roderick Lawrence for breach of contract. We have done a lot for him since the courts turned him over to our care."

"I know," I said.

"Psychiatric counseling, drug rehab, job training, sure and steady promotions—you really don't want to endanger your relationship with us. For all its drawbacks and risks, working for Personal Services is much more rewarding than working minimum scale or mining asteroids."

I couldn't disagree. I thumbprinted the document.

I called Anna at home hoping that she would have had second thoughts and decided to terminate. There was no answer. I remembered that this was her first day back at work. I found the number of the art gallery in the Coventry mini-Construct and called her there. She was embarrassed to have me calling and got angry when I used the word *contract*. She told me to pick her up at her place at five o'clock.

I was still employed by Anna Baxter.

So I still had to see Edward Lang.

28

LANG LOOKED HAPPY to see me. I tried to return the favor.

"I've been cramped up here all day," he said after some pleasantries. "Let's take a walk."

Pilar didn't look too happy with the idea, but she never looked happy about anything Lang did. Maybe he'd made her read Thomas Jefferson, too.

Lang took hold of my elbow and led me out of his apartment to the elevator. "A walk will be nicer. We can stop somewhere, and I'll buy you lunch."

We took the elevator down to the commercial-level walkway, and Lang, hand still on elbow, led me through the business district. Clerks and processors—young people and older women—were already stepping out of elevators, heading for restaurants, stopping at kiosks, running errands. Light flooded through the skylights. Plants wound their way up poles and columns. Water sounded in a nearby fountain. Men and women were brightly drab in their gray and navy blue suits adorned by colorful scarves and ties. In jeans and a shirt I was underdressed. Lang, in slacks, shirt, and tie, looked as if he'd left some of his plumage behind.

"You know," Lang said, "I had a nice, but rather urgent, conversation with your supervisor this morning."

"With Marie?"

Lang shook his head. "I'm sorry. I mean with your director. Fred O'Mallery."

"Fred called you?"

"Yes. And he was rather concerned. He wanted to

continue helping me, as he had, but he didn't want to put a branch of the government at risk. I personally find it interesting that the courts hold that you cannot sue Human Services, but that you can sue Personal Services. It does put you in a legal bind. It's too bad that sometimes our circumstances encourage us to consider the legal binds first and the moral binds much later."

"I think the contract should be terminated." I had intended to remain quiet, let him do all the talking.

"Oh." He stopped for a moment to face me. We were at the entranceway to Saks. People went in and out, around us, almost as if we weren't even there. "Can you tell me why?"

I wanted to keep walking; he didn't budge. "She's hired me as a companion, and she's expecting more from me than is professional."

"So," he said, stretching the word out, "you would agree with your legal counsel, Ms. Palaez." He said her name carefully, as if it were important that he pronounce it correctly.

I shrugged. I liked the gesture. He could read into it what he wanted.

Lang took my elbow again, and we resumed walking. "Do you want to terminate your commitment to her because of legal reasons, or has something made you anxious?" He didn't even stress the word *something*, yet, for the briefest of moments, I felt as if he'd known about my early-morning meeting with the Three Bears.

I wanted the emphasis on Anna and me. I said, "Life would be easier for both of us."

"Easier." He said it with disdain.

We ended up at a Spanish restaurant. The interior was all white stucco, and little iron odds and ends hung from the wall. The maître d' called him Señor Lang and led us to a table. I glanced up at the nearby monitor. Lang refused a menu and ordered for us. "I hope you don't mind," he said.

"It's a free lunch," I said. "What can I say?"

"There are some things," he said after a while, "that maybe you don't understand. Or rather, things that I haven't made clear. Things look pretty big and important when you find out that Monitoring has classified its file on Sauro

Contini and Anna Baxter. We even have a file on Roderick Lawrence. It, too, is a big packet, and it is highly classified. It would be enough to make you feel that you and Anna are the center of our investigation. But you're not.

"Our job at Monitoring is to insure that the UHL does not repeat in Cleveland what it did in Kansas City. Now, there *was* a crime committed last December. Somebody bombed a westbound train that was taking five quarantined individuals to a camp. The bombers were caught, and they will come to trial in about a month. But we're investigating who put them up to it. If we do anything that is even vaguely illegal, we risk a mistrial.

"So we have to use other methods to track down their coconspirators. If we want to bring them to justice, we have to do everything by the book. We have to obey the right-to-know laws. We have to have the proper warrants, and so on. But we also want to make sure that the law doesn't protect the UHL long enough for them to do something else. So we consider other means. We monitor the hell out of certain people. We set up surveillance to verify the footage. We tap phones. We plant bugs. A lot of former ASD members live in private establishments that could legally go unmonitored. We convince the state to rescind job licenses. We convince insurance companies that a particular client is high risk. We get the IRS to perform a thorough tax audit. We get Health Services to haul someone in for weekly blood testing for as long as the law allows."

"I get the point."

"No, Rod, you don't. We have all this pressure, but to whom do we apply it? If it's the wrong person, and we apply too much, the UHL has another, very dedicated member. If it's the right person, none of what we found out can be used as evidence in court.

"There are people with whom I work who think that my methods are too slow. But right now we spend most of our time keeping an eye on what's going on. We find gaps that we can't account for." He watched me for a moment, as if perhaps he'd found a gap last Friday around two in the morning. "If we discover there's a shipment of guns, we follow it. If we find teenagers breaking security codes, we check it out. If some footage that was supposed to be there isn't, we follow that up. If someone is sending around an antimonitoring petition, we find out who's organized the campaign." He paused for a moment, as if I might react. "We do what we can given the manpower in Monitoring, the willingness of other agencies to help, and the distinct possibility that a very complex AI, is already being used by UHL infiltrators." He sipped his red wine. "Another resource is people like you."

"I feel moved," I said.

"It would be nice if you actually were. Does anything ever move you?"

"Sometimes."

I expected him to say *like what*, but he asked something else entirely.

"Pardon?" I said.

"I just asked if a client's request could move you . . . perhaps, to do something you hadn't done before."

He ate some of his tortilla and watched me. I finished off mine, and the waiter brought us paella.

"I just couldn't help but notice," he said, "that Anna asked you to try out the Relocation Experience."

I ate some of the yellow rice and seafood.

"It's an odd request."

"Yes," I said, "and very unpleasant."

"I know. I suffered through it, too. About a year ago. It's a stunning piece of propaganda—accurate, complete, and horrifying. James Baxter himself has repeatedly requested that Congress double its internment camp budget so the places could be made more livable. But you don't learn about that from the Experience. You see the children suffer, but there's no mention of the sins of their fathers and mothers."

"I guess so."

"Did Anna tell you that almost everyone who joined ASD went through the Experience?"

"Yeah."

"Probably everyone in UHL has gone through it," he said. "But, I'd say ninety-five percent of ASD members went through it before joining, and they always chatted about it with someone afterward. Sort of the way you and Anna most likely talked about it."

I wondered if he could extend the hearing range of the monitor in Anna's living room, if he'd heard the conversation during the bath and massage.

"I also think it's interesting that you convinced Anna that it wasn't a good idea to sleep together in monitored hotels."

"Well, it gets a little difficult to do your job when you think about all these investigators checking up on your performance the next morning."

That stopped him, fork in midair, and I wondered if he had watched a little more footage than he might have liked. "I can assure you," he said, "our interests are not prurient. I suggest we change the subject."

"Sure. We can talk about how politics make strange bedfellows."

"I take it that Anna has not told you whether she joined UHL or not."

I sipped the wine. If the hearing range of Anna's monitor extended into the bedroom, then he already knew. "She's not UHL," I said. "She's not much of anything right now. Except back at work."

"Well, work is a step forward. Did Anna tell you flat-out she wasn't UHL?"

"I didn't ask," I said.

"I just hope she isn't in over her head," he said to himself, but clearly enough for me to hear it.

I expected him to say more, but he'd made his points. I ate as if eating were important, but the food seemed tasteless. Lang told me all sorts of stories about the Spanish War. His last one was about a resistance group in the south of Spain. They had a charismatic leader who had been effective at winning popular support among the poor country people. So Lang had key informants send word out that the guerrilla leader had dreams about lizards. He had so many dreams about lizards that his *compañeros* in the leadership were, in private, calling him *El Lagarto*, the lizard. "Lizards are a symbol of bad luck in southern Spain!" Lang exclaimed.

I tried to smile while he laughed.

The smile must have derailed his routine, because he stopped talking for a moment. I guess most people must have laughed with him on his bit of manipulation. I was wondering how he could talk about Thomas Jefferson one moment and tell this story the next. "Ben Franklin said that those who gave up liberty for temporary safety didn't deserve liberty or safety. Sometimes one must wonder what he meant by temporary." He finished off his wine and asked me if I'd been to the shackville near Slavic Village.

"I've been there several times."

"To visit?"

"No. I don't know anyone there. You have to cross through it to get to the only park nearby."

"What do you think of it?"

"It's horrible."

"You know, Harold Baxter, Senior, when he started building the Roxbury Construct, felt that one day everyone in the U.S. would be given shelter. He thought his Constructs would create the kind of compact architecture that could make it economically feasible. You may not have known this, but he retired a week after the first major exposé about how second-generation Construct families could no longer afford services and were now living in shacks. He was heartbroken." The coffee arrived, and he asked that a little brandy be added. After he tasted the mixture, he returned his attention to me. "How many ASD programs do you think deal with the camps?"

I shrugged.

"Seven," he said. "How many do you think deal with people in the shackvilles?"

"I don't know. Five?"

"One. And the UHL has none. Plus, in the January Manifesto they refer to shackville residents four times, and camp internees twenty-seven times."

"But the camps are their issue."

"And that's their most tragic flaw. Or maybe it's the tragic flaw of our society. You give sexual pleasure for your trade. I track down terrorists for mine. The terrorists are trying to free people who already made a decision that affected their lives. Meanwhile none of us is doing anything for those living without shelter. There's not enough medicine, there's not enough money. And it's rarely their fault. Those are the ones we should be held responsible for."

I knew he meant it, and I knew that neither of us would do anything about it. For a tremendous moment I liked him and the things he wanted to stand for. But after he had paid the check, he looked me straight in the eye and said, "The minute anyone drops a hint to you that they're UHL, I want you to call that number Pilar gave you." The moment was over.

29

HARRY CAME HOME while I was getting ready to see Anna. He found himself a beer, positioned himself at Albert Einstein's vidscreen, and watched me every time I came out of the room to get something.

"What's wrong, Harry?" I finally asked.

"You saw Lang today."

I found I couldn't leave my room and face him. I took off my shirt and looked for a new one.

"I could be in deep shit for telling you what I saw in Monitoring."

I put the second shirt away and looked at a third. "You want to know why I didn't tell you?"

"I want to know how long this has been going on. Lang doesn't have lunch with people just for the hell of it, you know."

"Nothing horrible is happening. I don't want to get you in trouble again." I was looking at my fourth shirt.

"What are friends for?"

I didn't like any of my shirts. "How did you find out?"

"A friend was doing random monitoring at lunchtime. She recognized Lang, went back to the image out of curiosity, and saw you. She remembered you from the times I'd brought you to the office."

"You probably want to know why he wanted to see me."

"Yeah." Harry was standing in the doorway, beer in hand. "I did. And my friend was going to play it for me. But Adolf had already erased it from the central files. We did a program check, and a half hour later we found out that the footage had been stored in your file."

"Oh."

"Adolf shouldn't be erasing stuff like that so quickly, you know. So I decided to check up on my roommate and buddy's file. There was barely enough in it for a crystal. So I went through it. The footage of you and Lang at lunch isn't there. I tell my friend. She does more searching. An hour later she finds that there's a second file for Roderick David Lawrence, and it's classified so high that neither one of us can get into it."

Harry watched me while the information sank in.

"You know, Rod, we liked her when we met her, so I can't tell you we told you so. But it's not like Kevin and I are stupid. We warned you about terrorists, we warned you about lawsuits, and now you've got Lang. Why can't you just dump her?"

"They won't let me," I said. "I tried this morning."

"Then you didn't try hard enough." I watched him finish off the beer. "Is Lang paying you anything?"

I shook my head.

"I don't know what to say. You're not religious. You're not patriotic. And you never say no. I have no idea what Lang's getting you into, but it can't be any good. Is she really that special? It would make sense if she was special."

"She's a client," I said.

"Not anymore. Not if you're working for Lang. Now she's a cause." With that pronouncement Harry headed for the kitchen. "Do you want a beer before you leave?" I didn't answer, and he came back with one for me, anyway. "You look like you need a transfusion," he said, and handed me the bottle.

I twisted off the cap and raised the bottle to my lips. The beer barely tasted like anything: just carbonation running down my throat.

"Need another?" he asked.

I shook my head.

"Tell me the truth, now. Do you love her?"

"No," I said.

"Then dump her."

30

I DECIDED THAT I wanted to erase everything between Anna and me as neatly as Adolf had erased my lunchtime meeting with Lang.

She greeted me at the door, wearing her bright yellow shirt and a pair of tan slacks. Tiny diamonds hung from her earlobes. She kissed me on the lips. "Now," she said, "was that kiss professional or was it professional?"

"Professional, I guess."

"You guess?" She hooked her arm in mine and led me into her apartment.

Sitting on the couch was a thickset man, one sturdy leg crossed over the other. He held a bottle of Thirty-Three in his hand. He had shaved rather carelessly, and there was a blot of blood on his right cheek. He wore Democracy Now jeans that fit him perfectly, and a white shirt. Draped over the arm of a nearby chair was an old, lined leather jacket.

"Rod, this is Stuart Greenspan, my friend Sophie's cousin." He rose from the couch as Anna said, "Stuart, this is my companion, Rod Lawrence."

Papa Bear and I shook hands.

He smiled wryly. "It's good to meet you."

"Anna's said nice things about you," I said. I looked to Anna, and she probably read my anxiety as confusion.

"I got fed up with hiding out," Anna said. "There's a lecture at Case, then my friend Sophie's having a reception, and she insisted I bring you along." I got the sense that

Anna had been planning otherwise. "She sent Stuart here to make sure we showed up."

"Great," I said. I excused myself and headed for the bathroom. I kneeled by the toilet, my head bowed over, but nothing came up.

There was a knock at the door. "Are you okay?" asked Anna, her voice coming through the closed door.

I stood up, closed the toilet seat, and sat down. I was sweating. "I'm not feeling okay," I said. "Maybe you better go without me."

Anna's voice lowered. "Not on your life. Sophie will make a big deal about it if I come without you. I've finally gotten up the courage to take you out into the big wide world and to hell with Mary Hasselbacher. Please, don't be the one to back down on me."

I washed up and emerged. I was so pale that Anna reconsidered. But Stuart said the change of scenery would do me good. He had on his leather jacket, and he was already zipping it up and down. "Sorry to show up unexpectedly," he said. "I went to Sophie's to help her prepare for the party, and she ordered me over here."

"Let me get some aspirin," said Anna, "and we'll go."

Stuart's car was a solar/gas model. The sun had been out today, so the air conditioner was on. The car had bucket seats; I sat in the back. Anna didn't argue the point. Stuart drove us across the Hope Memorial Bridge and along Carnegie. We passed under the pedestrian bridges that connected the Prospect Corridors with the Carnegie Corridors. Anna chatted away. You'd never think that either of them had ever been in ASD. I stared out the window and watched for gnomes.

The Construct ended with the Cleveland Clinic, and there was a short stretch of residential shops and homes before we reached the University Circle mini-Construct. Stuart turned the car down a road that would take us to underground parking beneath Case Western Reserve University.

The lecture was in an auditorium built to hold at least several hundred, but there couldn't have been more than one hundred in the audience, maybe half of them students. Anna looked depressed the minute she saw the rows and rows of empty seats and insisted we sit in the back row, away from things. Stuart wanted to chat a bit with the speaker, and he promised to pick us up at the end of the show.

The speaker was a slim Vietnamese man with graying hair. A grandchild of refugees who'd lived in Thailand, he had emigrated to the U.S. in his teens. He had been one of the ACLU lawyers to take to the Supreme Court the lawsuit that charged that the camps were unconstitutional. Anna whispered that he was also the one who had removed Stuart from the legal team. From a distance, the two chatting men looked like good friends who hadn't seen each other in years.

Speaking with a faint accent, the ACLU lawyer informed the audience about the prison conditions of the five suspected leaders of the Kansas City Black Out. First, he spent a half hour describing their backgrounds, the evidence the state had against them, and so on. Now the five were kept in high-security confinement in a specially built basement section. There were no windows. There were no doors. There weren't any doors on the toilet stalls or curtains for the showers. The walls were painted white. The linoleum was white speckled with black dots. The ceilings were white. The food was bland. The water was always lukewarm. The guards were instructed not to speak with them.

The ACLU was suing the state on several grounds. First, the prisoners had been convicted of no crime. Second, the prisoners were being given worse treatment than the two serial killers that had operated in unmonitored shackvilles. Third, this was sensory deprivation, which all European countries had banished as a form of torture. He spent another half hour talking about precedents and ramifications. I yawned only once.

Afterwards Anna looked despondent. "We used to fill this place up when he spoke," she said.

"What an asshole," Stuart said as he took Anna's arm. "No wonder he lost it before the Supreme Court. He probably bored the justices to death."

"You looked chummy enough," Anna said.

"I gotta be nice to him," he said. "He's one of my cousin's best friends."

Sophie Greenspan's house was one of the monster houses on Fairmount, and it seemed ironic that two doors down stood a church that wasn't much larger.

Once upon a time, Stuart explained during the drive, Euclid Avenue was called Millionaires' Row and was lined with houses that would make Sophie's look like a bungalow and the church a chapel. They had ballrooms and large dining rooms and dozens of bedrooms. Then, once upon a time a little bit later, out in the country (soon to be the suburbs) the country clubs were established, so wealthy families now could have homes better suited for their families and do their entertaining at the clubs. Once upon a time, a little bit sadder, blacks and immigrants of all sorts of colors and languages and menus filled the vacuum left by wealth, but without wealth's money. Large homes crumbled and crime rose, and wealth came back to demolish their former homes and build a hospital, a university, and anything else that looked better than poverty, until it was safe to follow gravity back to the center of the city. Blacks and immigrants and working whites now had the Construct. The suburbs became more rural. Houses that couldn't be sold were sold to the city and became lots. It's a happy story. Everybody who keeps up their housing payments gets their zoological rights: enough food, enough water, enough shelter. That is, if they don't fuck the wrong person at the wrong time or if they don't have the wrong parents or if they don't use the wrong needle when nobody in Monitoring is paying attention.

Anna asked him to calm down.

I noticed that he really hadn't mentioned the shackvilles. I reconsidered what Lang had said.

Fairmount Boulevard was a long, pleasant road divided by a median where long before a trolley once had run. Most of the houses in the area were still there. If you squinted, you could see monitors attached to the streetlamps. Cars of all makes, models, and states of repair were parked along the side of the street. Stuart drove his car into an already-crowded oval driveway.

Sophie's stone house exhibited French windows and lots of ivy. A hedge in front was perfectly clipped, and nearby trees, small ornamental things, were fleshed out with leaves and a hint of sprouting color. The wooden front door, which looked as thick as my arm, was open, and people were in the front hall, drinks in hand, chatting. They seemed to spread out from there. A winding staircase toward the rear of the hall curved its way up to the second floor.

The people milling about in the front hallway were like the cars out front—of all makes, models, and states of repair. They greeted Anna and Stuart with enthusiasm, and I found myself lost among the diversity. We're delighted to see you again, you're looking so much better, it's nice to meet your companion, it's so long since we've seen you. I heard one woman whisper to Stuart a bit too loudly, "I hadn't seen you in so long that I thought you'd gone underground." I found myself examining the lines where wall met ceiling: the plaster molding was intricate and bare of monitors.

"Don't look so shocked, beloved. Remember, internal monitoring is the option of the private owner."

I turned around and met Sophie Greenspan.

Sophie was, as my mother would say politely, large boned. She had breasts like a ship's figurehead. She wore a dark green dress, belted around a waist a touch smaller than her hips. She had olive skin and thick black hair tied behind her head. She wore no makeup. And everything about her was energized, from the way she held herself, to the way her dark eyes held my gaze, to the way she let her face liven and darken as she spoke, while she listened. She was an actress who never left the stage. Looking at her home, I decided I'd gone into the wrong branch of the entertainment profession.

"Hi," I said.

"A man of many words. I'm Sophie Greenspan, and I'm just thrilled that Anna consented to bring you here. Now I see why she kept you to herself. She can't share you, can she?"

I was surprised to find myself blushing. Anna seemed to have overheard, because now she was at my side, both her arms wrapped around one of mine. "I can't share him," she said. "It's in the contract. Though I guess I could renegotiate."

Anna and Sophie laughed.

"Don't look so upset," said Sophie. "Anna and I have some friends for whom threesomes and foursomes are the rage. You'd think that there weren't any hives."

"Well," said a nearby man, "when you cart people out of sight, you can believe that there isn't any."

"It's the American Toilet Syndrome," someone else said. "Just flush what you don't like right out of sight."

"Out of sight, out of mind."

"You can tell," said Sophie, "that most of the folks at this party are dedicated members of Americans for Social Democracy."

"They'd have to be," said Stuart, "to sit through the speech we just heard."

"They're former members," Anna said. The tone of her voice contrasted with Sophie's gaiety, Stuart's cheerful cynicism. "There is no ASD anymore."

"Well," said Sophie, "Rod seems to be the brightest person I troubled to invite. He doesn't spout silly nonsense any chance he gets." She was looking at Stuart, who grinned sheepishly. Did Sophie know that Stuart did more than just talk? "Anyway, I better take care of my other guests before I steal you away, Rod. Anna will introduce you to everyone. Don't worry about threesomes and foursomes; ASDers like to talk about sexual freedom but they're about as staid as New Puritans."

"We just drink more," Stuart said.

Sophie departed, and Anna led me to the kitchen, where there was beer in the fridge and wine on the counter. I was impressed at how old-fashioned the kitchen was: no synthesizer, no computer, no dishwasher. For beer Sophie had chosen Thirty-Three—Anna seemed a bit put off by that—and some Brazilian beer. The wine was all pressed in Ohio on a farm owned by my life insurance company.

Anna led me out of the kitchen, through a long pantry, into a dining room with a table arrayed with all sorts of food, through that, across a hall, and into a small library. I felt lost. The TV—not a holovision—was off. The ACLU lawyer was listening carefully while a well-dressed Arab woman talked about the death rate due to hives being lower in France because there weren't camps, and how they spent more money on research than on internment. A pudgy man who looked Hispanic and dressed in a business suit countered that there were unofficial neighborhoods for hivers. A younger black man, wearing synthetics, argued that that was a whole lot better than a camp. On the other side of the room, a white woman in denim was tearing down Democracy Now's plan to set up a plant at Camp Three. Anna and I stood there, listening to these fragments, while my eyes wandered. The library was full of books, all neatly arrayed, many bound in what looked like leather. On the table sat a phone and a blank vidscreen.

Anna apologized for breaking into all these wonderful conversations and then introduced me as her companion. Everyone was friendly as they shook my hand, but a few offered me knowing looks, making it clear that they didn't approve. One joked about testing me to see if I could remember all their names. He was a little surprised when I did; my training came in handy.

Sally Kim, who had a faint accent that she'd brought with her from Korea, wanted to know how much of the film *Truest Love* was accurate. I told her that I hadn't liked it. Sally wanted to know about the part where he took out lenses that gave him the ability to see her body heat and turned off the sensors in his—there she got embarrassed and Emma White took over, describing the rest of the scene, in which the servicer became a more natural lover without his high-tech equipment.

Anna whispered that she had to talk with Sophie, and before I could do anything, she was gone. Someone got me a fresh beer as I tried to dispel the myths about Personal Services, sounding like a PR man on why Personal Services wasn't just another sign of American decline. Norman White, Emma's husband and a parole officer, started asking me about the class makeup of Personal Services. He'd already decided that we were all poor people who worked Personal Services to make more money than minimum scale.

"I grew up within a mile of here," I said. "My father

taught junior-high math. My mother was a bank manager. I wasn't poor."

"Anna said you have a degree in math," Sally Kim said. "At Cleveland State, right?"

For some reason I hated the lie becoming public knowledge. "Yeah."

"How did *you* end up in Personal Services, then?"

"Don't be so abrasive, Norman," said Emma.

"I was just curious," Norman said.

"That's not the issue," said Timothy Molina, the pudgy businessman.

"Timothy," said Bill O'Brien, a well-muscled white man who had recently slipped his arm around Timothy's. They wore gold rings on their wedding fingers.

"He's a guest," said Emma. "Let's not play ASD ideology games."

The ACLU lawyer nodded his head in agreement.

"You haven't heard what I have to say, yet," said Timothy Molina, "so let me say it. If this gentleman here feels the topic is inappropriate for this kind of party, he can tell me."

Stuart Greenspan stood at the edge of the group, smiling at me in sympathy. I didn't want his smile.

"I think your organization is part of society's problem," said Timothy. "Not because sex is bad, but because like everything else in life—except for food, shelter, and work—sex shouldn't be guaranteed."

"But different cultures are different," I said.

The pat line didn't phase him. "Right. But look at it this way. My compañero"—he gestured to Bill, his spouse—"and I have this emblem on our licenses. You know what it means. If we were a heterosexual couple, we wouldn't have it. Because of that emblem our blood is tested every three months. There are eight states with safe-sex laws that won't let us visit together, unless we both have valid commercial reasons to be there. And the minute we complain, we're reminded that our questionable desires can be taken care of by you folks, because everything you offer is contained, tested, and safe. Everyone acts as if homosexual was just sexual, as if there was no tenderness, no love in the whole ordeal, as if men and women were only fit for each other when it comes to love."

"Timothy," said Norman, "what do you want him to do?"

"I want to know why he couldn't care less about what I'm saying. He's the one on the line. He's more likely to end up in a camp than any married homosexual is. I want to know why he lets all of this go on and does nothing."

"I just do my job," I said. I looked away from Molina and caught Stuart's eye. "I don't hurt anyone."

"Great," Timothy said. "Do you even vote?"

"No, I don't." Timothy smiled as if that were the expected answer. I felt as if I had to defend myself. "It never seemed to make a bit of difference who won an election."

Molina looked disgusted. I think he would have been happier if he had stepped back and punched me, or, better, spit in my eye. "People like you . . . ," he started to say.

"Timothy," said Bill. It sounded like a reprimand.

Timothy ignored him. "No wonder some people take to guns, or kidnapping, or blacking out cities, killing preemies and old folks hooked up to machines. People like you leave them no choice, and they make the rest of us who care look like murderous clowns."

Stuart was nodding in agreement. Others were looking away. Bill took hold of Timothy's arm, and Emma said, "That's taking it a bit too far, Timothy. You're making it sound as if all the fault belongs to Rod here. You're blaming the victim . . . again."

Timothy let his spouse calm him down. Stuart had disappeared. Amongst all these people committed to voicing their beliefs, I wanted to find some way to counter Timothy's argument but my mind was blank, and somebody was gently tugging at my elbow.

I expected it to be Anna, or maybe Sophie or Stuart. It was Beatrice Knecivic who led me to the dining room. She looked much healthier since the last time we'd met. Her cheeks were flushed; the dark circles under her eyes had faded; the whites of her brown eyes were no longer cracked with red. Once far too trim, and probably even anorexic, she now was pleasantly plump. "Boy, do you look surprised," she said.

"You look wonderful," I said.

"Do you mean it?" She looked down at herself, then patted her belly.

"A little weight looks good on you," I said.

"How are you doing?"

"I'm healthy," I said.

"What brings you to this kind of party?"

"An invitation."

"Are you still working at, you know . . . ?"

"Personal Services? Yes."

"I take it you have a client here."

"Yeah." I half wanted to say I was invited on my own merits. "How have you been doing? It's been a while."

She thought for a moment. "Three years," she said. "I can't believe it was that long ago. Three years ago this past January. God, what a horrible winter. You were about the only good thing about it. Do you want to get something to eat?"

I glanced over at the food spread out on the dining-room table. There were three kinds of bread, four kinds of meat, potato salad, macaroni salad, and pâté.

"Rod, is something wrong? I'm sorry if I'm embarrassing you. I just wanted to say hello." She kept her voice low. Several people glanced over, probably wondering how Beatrice knew me.

"No, that's okay. It's good to see you."

"You say the nicest things. I hate to ask, but who are you working for?"

"Anna Baxter."

"Oh." She put three large spoonfuls of potato salad on her plate; three years ago she wouldn't have touched it. "That must be a tough one. I heard about what happened to her boyfriend. No one told me she'd taken up with someone else."

"You don't know her?"

"I know her from a distance. I was the type who'd sit in the back of the room during ASD meetings and then sign up for all the volunteer programs. Anna and her boyfriend were always up front. I think they did a lot more talking then doing, but you never know. You hear rumors sometimes."

"About what?"

She thought better of what she was saying.

"Oh, nothing. You know, I joined ASD after you called it quits."

"My bosses terminated the contract," I said.

"Whatever." She hesitated. "Maybe this was a bad idea."

"No. I'm just a bit uncomfortable, that's all. You know, I don't usually run into former clients. Especially ones who wanted to marry me."

I had managed to say it nicely. She smiled and blushed.

"So what did you think of ASD?" I asked.

"It was the best thing that ever happened to me. I got involved. I went back to school, finished my degree, and now I'm studying medicine. I'm working at the free clinic Graham Plar has set up just west of Ohio City."

"You sound happy."

"I am. It took me a long time, but I realized that what I truly needed wasn't a lover or a husband. It was like I was busy with the mayonnaise, and I hadn't even put any ham or cheese on the sandwich." She wrinkled her nose, then laughed. "Not a great metaphor, huh?"

"I get your point," I said.

"But you don't agree. I know you really like your work, and boy, I still have some nice memories, but I think you'd be a happier person if you did something else."

"Today someone told me to get a job mining asteroids."

"If you discover the right metals, you could make it rich."

"I could cut my life span in half, too. I'll stick with what I do."

"Don't take what I say as an attack, but do you ever think about what your job does? You create an image of sexual happiness. It seduces people, it misleads them, makes them want things they can't have."

"Ads do that," I said. "All Personal Services is, is a place where people can go to safely explore their needs and feelings. You know, we live in a free society."

"But it's not a free society. Your job exploits people's needs, and, in turn, someone else exploits yours."

"Are all you ASD people like this?"

She grabbed my arm and laughed. Several people turned to watch her, to listen to what we were saying. "You got me there. I'm sorry, Rod. It's not fair for me to pick on you."

"Especially after saving me from Timothy Molina."

"*Especially* after saving you from Timothy Molina. But I can't help it. I go on these rounds, dispensing medicines, going into these shacks that are like something out of twentieth-century Brazil, and I get so fed up with this country. I think this would be the greatest country on Earth if everyone just went celibate for two or three generations."

Beatrice and I talked a while longer. Then she saw some friends and we said good-bye. I ate another ham sandwich and looked around. Norman emerged from the pantry with two beers and handed me one. "You looked a little lonely without a bottle," he said. It was the Brazilian beer; its taste was too thick.

"This is good," I said. "I've never tried it before."

"It looks like Anna's trying you out for some of those society parties she and Sophie go to."

"Oh."

"I get invited to them when they're fund-raisers. All these rich, divorced people bring their younger companions and leave them by the bar while they go off and mingle. How does it feel to be a status symbol?"

Anna looked into the dining room and saw me with Norman. Among this crowd, I'm sure I lowered Anna's status.

"How are you doing, Norman?" Anna asked loudly, with this big huge smile that Norman thought was for real. He gave her a kiss. "Your friend here and I were just talking. He's a nice guy."

I tried to look bashful.

Anna hugged my arm. "I think so," she said to Norman. To me: "Feeling better?"

"The beer helped."

"Are you enjoying yourself?"

"Immensely," I said.

"Great. I'm going to take some more aspirin. I'll be right back."

She headed for the kitchen. Norman told me he'd talk to me later. I finished my ham sandwich and sipped my beer. The library, from where I stood, looked empty of people. On a table sat a small phone with a compact screen; I could press out Lang's seven-digit number and tell them Papa Bear was here. Laughter from the kitchen was loud enough to hear in the dining room. A couple walked out of the pantry, and more laughter followed them. The couple stepped in front of me as if I weren't there. They made sandwiches. "It's amazing," one said to the other, "to watch them get along. You'd never think that Anna was mad for what Sophie did." The couple left the dining room with their sandwiches.

Stuart Greenspan walked in, holding a bottle of Brazilian beer. His thumbnail was scratching away at the table. "You look like you're feeling better than you did this afternoon," he said. "You also look like you've been deserted."

"No. Anna's out having a good time with Sophie."

"How about we step outside, get some fresh air?"

"I should be getting back to Anna."

"Anna can wait. I'd like to get to know you a little better."

The dining room's French windows were open, and we pushed the long, thin screen doors open. Evening spread across the yard, darkening the green of the grass, of the sculpted bushes, transforming trees into extended shadows. We walked toward the back of the yard and came upon a clay tennis court. Stuart gestured to a bench, and we both sat. We were silent. I was surprised that Papa Bear had nothing to say. The party came to us as a low murmur. Everything out here seemed so still.

"I heard you tell Norman that you're from around here," he finally said.

"Yeah."

"Where did you grow up?"

"I don't care much for small talk," I said.

"I can't imagine why else we'd be out here. You're

contracted to Anna, and I'm committed to someone, so I can't see why else we'd be here together if it weren't for some friendly chitchat."

I looked at him for a moment. In the grays of the evening, he was a curve of skin, a glint of eyes, and all the rest shadow. Maybe this wasn't Papa Bear at all, just someone who looked like him. "Anna told me about Luis," I said.

Stuart nodded.

"She even showed me a picture," I lied. "Funny thing is, I met a guy who looked a lot like him the other night. He didn't look too healthy, though."

"How does it feel to be in an unmonitored environment?" he asked.

"No different," I said.

"You know, people get hyper about ASD types. Sometimes they bug unmonitored houses. Ever since I represented ASD in some cases, I kept finding bugs in my unmonitored apartment. I purchased this device that can detect them. I've always told Sophie to buy one, but she believes her First Amendment rights protect her. The problem with bugs, though, is that they aren't official, therefore you never know who's listening, or what they'll do with it. If they don't have a warrant, they just can't take it to court, that's all."

"Do you want to go back in and get another beer?"

"No," he said. "I like being away from the crowd. I get tired of all the political conversations. In a way the Supreme Court decision was a relief. We knew where we stood, and we could go on to other things. I'm going through relicensing so I can work in the public defender's office. They like hiring ASD types—we work hard for little pay, and they don't have to worry about big law firms buying a lot of us off. Plus, the State of Ohio has just bought all this software so we can do research in half the time and double our caseloads. You ever think of doing something different?"

"No."

"Someone told me you went to have the Relocation Experience. That didn't make you consider, just for a moment or two, a career change?"

"Not at all."

"You think it's fair that if you catch something from a client, you get sent off?"

"It's a risk I take. I signed up for it."

"But why should the risk be a death sentence?"

"Ask a doctor," I said.

"You heard Timothy Molina back there. In France you aren't quarantined. You live out your life carefully. They brand a sign into your wrist, but that's just to make sure no one sucks up your blood. Your chances for survival can be as good as fifty-fifty. Eighty-twenty in your favor with hives one and four. At the camps, it's different; it's a death sentence. The Supreme Court didn't listen to that part of the argument."

"I thought you were tired of political conversation."

"It's the lawyer in me. I like to disagree with people. So, tell me if you got sent to a camp, do you think it would feel like a punishment?"

"For what?"

"For the sinful life you're leading."

He said it seriously, and I couldn't help but laugh.

"I don't mean to be funny. I personally don't think what you do is sinful, but I think you do."

That stopped me. I looked at him, found it hard to breathe.

"I've read all sorts of stuff. I have yet to read about a servicer who joined because his career goal was to deepen the erotic experiences of others. There are doctors who become doctors to get rich, but many of them believe in the ideal of health. There are plenty of lawyers who become lawyers to get rich, but many of them believe first in the ideal of justice. Not many Americans feel comfortable about the ideal of pleasure. It's supposed to be a by-product, a reward, not the goal itself. So I don't see how, in our culture, you ended up giving pleasure as the pursuit of an ideal. Something else got you there. Perhaps something you're secretly ashamed of."

I didn't like the way he was probing. If he truly had friends in Monitoring, then someone had seen my file, someone had told him the chain of cause and effect that several therapists had come up with years ago. I said, "I thought we were out here for small talk."

"You said you didn't like small talk."

"I don't like this kind of talk, either."

He raised his hands, as if surrendering. "You're right. I'm not being fair. I was in ASD. We had all sorts of positions on hives and Personal Services, but it's not like we did a very good job of including the servicers. If there was still an ASD, that's something I'd want to change."

I stared off across the yard. Everything had become shades of black. If there was a bug somewhere, I could just say *I know you're UHL* and let Lang take care of the rest.

"You don't care much for this political stuff, do you?"

"Not really," I said.

"You like law and order, I take it."

"I guess so."

"Enforce a law, then, even if it's unjust. Obey a law that's unjust."

"You know," I said, "there are courts, and there are elections."

Stuart Greenspan nodded. "In 1776 it was declared that all men were created equal, but until 1865 slavery was legal. In many states blacks were prevented from voting, by law or contrivance, until the end of the twentieth century. Almost all of this was done legally, with the permission of the courts. Should people who opposed such injustice have done nothing?"

I didn't know enough history to respond: U.S. History had been taught in eleventh grade.

"You know, the president who signed the law that started construction of the camps campaigned on an anticamps ticket. He won the election with fifty-five percent of the popular vote, but within three years the camps were started."

"I get your point. If another anticamps person runs for election, I'll register to vote. What else do you want me to do? Join the Union for Human Liberation?"

"No," he said, "not at all. I'm just talking for the sake of talking. I became a lawyer because I like arguments. I like to convince people."

"Do you want to convince me that blacking out Kansas City was right?"

"No. Because I think it was wrong. I think the UHL showed that it was more powerful than people thought, but it also alienated a lot of sympathizers. In fact, if we're being bugged right now, then anything we say that sympathized with people in the camps would launch a file at Monitoring and an investigation. Isn't democracy great?"

I felt defensive. I said, "It's done okay by me," but I was ticking off in my mind each tactic Lang employed to track down or harass suspected members of the UHL. I was thinking about what was in my short file, and what was in my longer, classified file.

"Maybe it has," he said. "It's getting a bit chilly. Shall we head back in?"

"Sure."

"You know," he said as we stood up, "I was downtown today. I saw you in one of the plazas. Of course, I didn't know who you were at the time, but I recognized the guy you were with. I'd seen interviews with him on the holo."

"Oh," I said. I wanted to sit back down again.

I forced myself to walk with Stuart back toward the house.

"Sophie's told me he's a friend of Anna's family. Did Anna introduce the two of you?"

"No." Too late I realized I should have lied.

"Oh. Then it's sort of an odd acquaintanceship, isn't it?"

I couldn't find any words.

"You know, I used to read these articles about him in the *Nation* when he was a major figure in the Spanish War. The Army said he was Army, but everybody knew he was CIA. After that he lectured at Harvard for a bit, but I guess that didn't work out. Cleveland's his big comeback. If you could call Cleveland a place to make a comeback. Some people say he's still CIA. Anna's probably told you stories of what CIA people did to the enemy in Spain. I wonder if they'd do that to their own people."

"We only had lunch," I said.

"Did he talk about Jefferson?"

"No. We just had lunch."

"I saw him on an interview when he came to Cleveland last—what was it?—December? He loved to talk about Jeffersonian democracy. I thought it was sort of funny. When I was a law student, I couldn't get enough of Jefferson. I was able to forgive him his slaves and the Indians he'd rather see dead. I loved his ideals, the way he wrote about democracy. I thought it was funny to see this man who disagrees with everything I stand for quote the same man, and admit to the slaves and the Indians. It's too bad the people Lang works for don't believe in Jefferson. You might want to think about that next time you have lunch with him."

I was struggling with Stuart Greenspan's words, trying to decode his actual meaning, when we walked back into the dining room. Sophie and Anna were there. Anna came up and gave me a hug. "So that's where you disappeared to," she said.

"We just stepped out for a chat," Stuart said. "Rod's a nice guy. Politically unaware, but a nice guy."

"Don't worry about what he says," Sophie said to me. "Stuart places too much emphasis on political awareness."

I couldn't help but look at Stuart. He smiled at me as if we shared some secret joke. I tried to smile back.

"I've gotta go," he said. "But I'll see you sometime soon. You can count on that."

"Looks like you've made a friend," said Anna.

31

EVERYTHING ELSE AT the party passed in a stomach-clenched daze. The ACLU lawyer was in one of the living rooms talking about how the Constitution had once been an inclusive rather than exclusive document. By the dining-room table someone was arguing that the UHL wasn't powerful enough to have blacked out all of Kansas City, that the UHL was just taking the blame for all the systems that shouldn't have failed while his buddy argued that it didn't matter how responsible the UHL was, the government would use it as an excuse to clamp down whenever they could

Every once in a while, Anna would come in to squeeze my arm and introduce me to one or two people before returning to other conversations with other people. Each time I stood alone, I reconsidered her smiles and tried to connect her to Lang or to Papa Bear. I wondered if reading Thomas Jefferson would help.

Bill O'Brien drove us home. Pudgy Timothy Molina wanted to stay with the dwindling numbers of the party and begin organizing a Memorial Day rally. On the way back to Ohio City, Bill apologized to me for his compañero's behavior at the party, and he apologized again at least three or four times before letting us off.

Once we were at her apartment, Anna poured two snifters of brandy and took her fourth (at least) dosage of aspirin. She asked me my impressions of various people we'd met at the party, and even though I had been trained to remember faces, names, and behavior, I had to brush through the jungle of other thoughts to come up with even some vague, polite observations. Anna didn't seem to notice my trouble; rather she bubbled with social energy as she painted in my colorless recollections. "So, Mr. Serviceman," she finally asked me, "what did you think of the party?"

Sometime, while standing in the dining room at Sophie's, between the third ham sandwich and the fourth beer, I had decided that I'd be 100 percent professional this evening and keep everybody who was monitoring us happy. So I didn't mention my abandonment to people I didn't know. I didn't describe how everyone seemed comfortable talking ideology and my job but no one seemed comfortable talking with me. I didn't ask her why she kept flitting about and taking more aspirin than the bottle could possibly recommend. I remained professional: "I had a pretty good time," I said.

"What did you think of Sophie?"

"I only talked with her two or three times, but I liked her."

"Really?"

"You never talked about Sophie that much until today," I said, and began to wonder why. "What did Sauro think of her?"

"He thought she was one big image. That was when we were at college. He'd met the professors who'd joined ASD, or at least helped out at rallies, organize seminars, that sort of thing. Sophie wouldn't help out, besides direct that play. That really upset him."

"Did Sauro change his mind?"

"You bet. The only people who dislike Sophie are theater people who are in competition with her. As soon as we got to Cleveland, he fell under her spell." Sauro's change of heart toward Sophie didn't please Anna, so she changed the subject. "How about a little more brandy?"

I accepted even though it would only upset my stomach more.

She brought the bottle to the table. There was a moment of silence, and I somehow knew I'd misread the source of her energy. "How do you know Beatrice Knecivic?" she asked.

"I met her several years back," I said. Rule Seven: Don't mention other clients; stick to the terms of the contract and focus on the personalized relationship. Easier said than done.

"Was she a client of yours?"

I considered lying. "Yeah."

"Is it okay if I ask how long you worked for her? I wouldn't want to be unprofessional."

"It's okay. About three months. I was doing shift work then. I saw her five days a week for four hours a day. We'd get together in the evenings."

I thought she'd ask me questions about shift work. Instead she asked, "How long ago was this?"

"A year or two ago. I don't really remember."

"Someone overheard you guys say three years."

"Maybe it was three."

"Were you only working one shift, then?"

For some reason—I'm not sure it was a good one—I didn't want to lie. "No. I was working two."

She became silent. I had lied to her—I hadn't gone to college—and now anything else I said would sound also like a lie. I could tell her the truth. But she hadn't purchased the rights to any of it.

She sipped her brandy. I imagined that she was waiting for me to follow Sauro's script. I'd ask her what was wrong. She'd say nothing. I'd insist something was wrong. She'd insist there was nothing wrong. If there was something wrong, it would be my fault. I would be defensive, invalidating the honesty of my desire to know. I geared my next lines so they came out evenly, without a hint of underlying meaning.

"It was a long party," I said. "I'm getting tired." I smiled to suggest that tired shouldn't be interpreted as bored.

"Do you want to sleep here?"

The answer should have been a well-delivered *If you want me to*. "Yes," I said.

"I mean *sleep*."

"That's what I had in mind."

"You don't have any pajamas here. Maybe you should bring some stuff tomorrow."

"I'd like that," I said. It was a routine line.

"And you could stay here Monday through Friday, you know, like the five days the contract says."

I nodded.

"And if I take you to parties, I won't desert you."

Anna was uncomfortable with the idea of me sleeping naked, so I wore my underpants and T-shirt to bed. Anna wore a nightgown that must have been designed by a New Puritan: the fabric was thick, white, and voluminous. We said good night, kissed, and tried to sleep. Anna cuddled up to me after a while, and we lay there in the darkness, which turned to a gray outlined by the black forms of furniture. The fire escape outside had become bands of darkness against the bedroom window.

Anna's hand, which had been draped across my chest, slid down across my stomach. I should have stopped her, but I felt so incredibly distant that it didn't even feel as if it were my penis that her hand grasped, my glans that her thumb slid over. It might as well have been someone else's because nothing happened.

The routine was for me to apologize and for her to tell me it was all right, that these things happened, and then I would discreetly get hold of my ChemKit and pump in the necessary VC in the bathroom. But my ChemKit was at home.

She let go of my penis and rolled away and said nothing. We both held our bodies still. I stared at the ceiling. She faced the window. I reached over to touch her face; her cheek was wet.

"Anna?"

She started crying.

"Anna?"

"You can leave," she said between sobs, "if you want. I can't do anything right."

I said all sorts of reassuring things, and she kept crying. I wished I had my ChemKit so that I could have given her the illusion of desire. But it wasn't lack of desire, I told myself, but all these things I knew but wasn't supposed to know. And none of them I could tell her, not here, not where she might just tell me she was UHL and where Edward Lang might just overhear.

Later, toward an early morning that felt as gray as it looked, I awoke, if I'd ever really slept. I stared forever at the bold lines of the fire escape outside the bedroom window.

"Anna?" I said.

"Yeah?" Her voice was groggy, but I hadn't awakened her. I wondered how long she'd been staring at the fire escape.

"Did you tell Stuart that I'd had the Relocation Experience?"

"No." Her voice was bitter. It had been the wrong question. "Why would I?"

I didn't answer. I couldn't imagine why she would, but I wanted her to be innocent of everything. Besides, it was more than obvious that Goldilocks, whose nameplate had said Dorothy, had told Papa Bear.

32

LATER THAT MORNING I awoke feeling exhausted and drained: a hangover without the headache. Anna looked a bit more rested, and she encouraged an erection that had been initiated more by a full bladder than desire. She took off her nightgown, spread a towel across the bed, and we made love. After an hour and on our second towel, we were both sweaty, she'd come twice, and I hadn't come at all. "I guess you just feel differently," she whispered to herself, but she said the words clearly enough for me to hear them.

"Things will be better tonight," I said.

"Will they?"

She took a long shower while I lay in bed wishing I had brought my ChemKit. The hot water of the shower did not rinse away the malaise I was feeling, but it seemed to cheer Anna. Over breakfast she said, "I still want you to move in."

I smiled, leaned over the table, and kissed her.

"I'll go into Personal Services today and change the contract. We'll set my lock to your thumbprint, and you can pack up that new suitcase of yours and move some stuff over here. Starting tonight I'm going to take you around with me everywhere. I won't care who knows about it, not Mary Hasselbacher, not my parents, not anybody. I'm going to be independent and happy."

There was an edge to her voice that worried me, so I said, "And we'll keep it professional."

She kissed me. "You bet we will. We'll eat, we'll drink, we'll dance, we'll screw, and I'll have the time of my life." I should have felt happy not to be included.

The dailies I viewed later showed that while I went to Personal Services to work off the beer and ham sandwiches of the previous night, Anna had called in sick at the gallery. She crossed the Hope Memorial Bridge on foot, as she had three weeks before, sweating easily in the late April heat. The controlled environment of the Construct at seventy degrees made her shiver. She cut across several walkways and plazas until she arrived at the heart of the commercial neighborhoods and one of Cleveland's more prestigious banks. She asked to check on the status of her trust fund, and her aunt Lorena's trust officer left whatever business meeting she was in to go over it with Anna. The officer was a conservatively dressed woman who was at least as old as Aunt Lorena. She had grown up in a time when prostitution was illegal, hives was a rumor, and the dollar hadn't been devalued five times. To her the one hundred thousand dollars that Anna's account had already paid out for ten days of personal service seemed larger and more immoral than it was; worse yet, Anna was committing the cardinal sin of spending principal. The officer tried to express this very discreetly to an increasingly distraught Anna. Anna kept her cool: it was *her* account, and she thanked the trust officer for her concern.

While I had been sitting in a sauna, sweating out my anxieties, telling a delighted Cindy that my jane wanted me to move in, Anna was walking to the edge of the business neighborhoods and to Personal Services, where she demanded to see Roderick Lawrence's supervisor. The adviser, who'd handled Anna almost three weeks before, offered to assist her. "I will see his supervisor, thank you," said Anna. Something about her manner set the adviser off to a different cubicle where she called Marie, who referred the matter to Fred.

The adviser led Anna along a series of thin corridors that had been designed for visiting straights, taking them the long way around the Cleaning Room, the medical offices, the auxiliary services, and to a receptionist's waiting room.

Anna avoided looking at Joseph, Fred's secretary. The adviser immediately ushered Anna into Fred's office and abandoned her there. Fred was wearing synthetics, but he wore them as if he were dressed for a party in the Heights. He didn't act as if he'd just been pulled out of a conference call with his superiors in D.C. or that he had sent out a message that he wanted to see me exactly one hour later.

"How can I be of service, Ms. Baxter?" Fred asked.

"I have some questions about Personal Services."

"I'm sure your personal adviser could have answered them quite well. She's been with us for a number of years." His voice was condescending, even though Fred would never admit to, or even be aware of, his disdain for the higher-paying customers.

Anna sat up straight to gain some dignity against his tone of voice. "I don't want salespeople-type answers. I want things straight."

"Okay, shoot."

Anna asked about the payment schedule and about what happened to her money.

Fred gave an elaborate explanation, using all the big, impressive words he'd learned over the years from self-help software and in-house training sessions. He explained, more or less, that Personal Services was a not-for-profit organization formed by the U.S. government to regulate an industry that has existed in every civilized society. It was designed to meet the needs of certain citizens while at the same time eliminating associative crime and regulating sexually transmitted disease. A certain part of the fee is a government luxury tax that goes to the U.S. Treasury. Other monies were used to maintain offices, recreation areas, training centers, cafeterias, residual employees, and all related materials, plus some R and D.

"How much does Mr. Lawrence get paid?" Anna tried to sound disinterested.

Fred explained to her that a personal companion—he almost slipped and said servicer—was paid expenses and 50 percent of his daily fee. However, after taxes; health, dental, and life insurance; union dues; and licensing fees, it came to about 30 percent of the fee, which wasn't all that much considering that a trained companion could sometimes go for up to ten weeks without work, getting paid only a minimal fee for being on call if a client should select him, or her. "We keep on so many companions," he said, "because variety is a necessity, plus we need a surplus in case a companion moves in with a client indefinitely."

"What does that mean?"

Seeing what she was leading up to, Fred became a bit less defensive. "Well, most companions aim at limiting the terms of a contract. However, for those who would like a live-in companion, we do charge fifty percent more—that would be fifteen thousand dollars a day—and it would mean that the companion would move in indefinitely with the client, up to six days a week, and take care of the client's needs until she terminates the contract."

"It's sort of like leasing his contract," said Anna.

"You could look at it that way, I guess. But he is still employed by Personal Services and subject to all its regulations."

Anna leaned forward. "Could I *buy* his contract?"

Fred had been rubbing two crystals together, and he stopped. Anna looked horrified at what she'd just said. Her face contorted. Fred began to explain to her that by law all paid services that include sexual services must be conducted through a government-approved agency. He was trying to explain why, but Anna only watched his face and turned pale. Then she told him she was kidding, that she'd never been much good at humor, that she had the information she wanted. Fred tried to talk her into staying, but before he could say much, Anna was out the door and fleeing through the tiny corridors that went around the heart of our business.

After the workout, sauna, and shower, Cindy and I went to the Cleaning Room for some lunch. We made up all sorts of reasons why Fred might have asked to see me so urgently. Maybe he wanted to congratulate me on the new money I'd be bringing into Personal Services. Eric joined us and started talking down Hispano johns. Cindy reminded him her husband was from Mexico, and Eric said that her husband wasn't a john. Eric and I started talking about what made for the worst johns and janes, and Cindy, who kept her soul sweet, dreamed up reasons why those we complained about had turned up so sour. We were having a good time when Aggie and Henry showed up. Henry, who usually carried his body with an athlete's grace, slumped over the table with a beer in his hand. "He just came off an all-nighter with Sherry and Larry," said Aggie. She sat down next to me and handed me a glass of beer. "I got this for you."

"Sure you don't want it?" I asked. Eric was telling Henry how Sherry and Larry only showed up for those in training because of the 50 percent discount.

"I think you'll need it." Aggie placed the beer in my hand.

"Everyone here," said Eric, "except maybe for Aggie, has had Sherry and Larry during training."

"Larry was in college," said Aggie, "when I was in training. He used to show up with some guy back then. They liked sandwiches."

"Yuck," said Cindy. "I hate doing that."

I sipped the beer and wondered if Anna had already upped her payments. Word spread fast; Aggie wouldn't be too impressed that I had my other foot in the Heights. "What am I celebrating with this beer?" I asked her.

"You're not celebrating," she said, her voice almost a whisper. I couldn't help but listen carefully. "You're relaxing."

"You're just upset because they're saddling me up."

Aggie patted my hand. "Tell me about this Baxter woman."

She'd done the same thing when word got out that Beatrice Knecivic had wanted to marry me. She had patted my hand and said, *Tell me about this Knecivic woman*.

"Aggie, what have you heard that I haven't?"

Henry glared at me from across the table. "Why don't you tell him?"

"Tell me what?"

"Hush," Aggie said to Henry. To me: "You got a strange one, CT. But you better let Fred tell you. You'll hear it straight, then."

"Come on, if you know, you have to tell me."

Henry leaned forward. Aggie grabbed at him, but he ignored her. "Your jane wants to buy you out."

I immediately made my way to Fred's office, but Joseph told me to wait for a while. Joseph looked a bit upset about something. Palaez showed up a bit later, refusing to look at me, and Joseph let her right in. I picked up a flatscreen, called up an article on baseball, but I couldn't focus my attention on the words.

"You can go in now," Joseph said twice before I heard him.

Fred and Palaez were awaiting me. Fred was sitting behind his desk, twisting at his mustache with one hand, twirling a crystal between his fingers with the other. Palaez sat upright in a chair, a flatscreen in her lap. Fred gestured to the only empty chair near his desk. I sat down. We all said nothing for a while; Fred didn't know how to begin.

"Do you want to know why I came to see you before I was supposed to?" I asked.

"We know why," said Palaez. Her voice was hard. Fred faced her, tilted his head toward me, signaling her to go easy.

"Then will you tell me what started the rumors?"

"What rumors were you told?" Fred asked. His voice was kind and false.

"My client wanted to buy me out. I'm not quite sure what that means. I don't have any stock."

"Ms. Baxter," said Fred, "came here to ask me some questions. In the end, she wanted to purchase your contract from us. I guess she wanted you to work exclusively for her."

Even knowing in advance, I couldn't help but react. I felt like I'd been betrayed.

"Why?" I asked.

Fred held up the crystal. "You can look at this later and see if you can come up with an explanation. I'm a bit disappointed how things have gotten out of control."

Palaez said nothing. She didn't need to.

"Donna here," Fred explained, "has presented to me a case for termination. I know she's had you sign all sorts of documents to try to reduce our liability if you mismanaged things. However, at this point I can't see continuing. Both Ms. Palaez and I have been in contact with Mr. Lang at

Monitoring. We knew he felt it important that Ms. Baxter have a companion, but we feel that Ms. Baxter is too much of a risk. Lang's people and our people in Washington just got back to me, and they're in agreement. In fact, it's sort of embarrassing, but the government people I talked to didn't seem too happy with Lang's idea in the first place."

Then why had Lang been doing it? I wondered.

"Do you understand what I've said?" Fred asked.

"You're asking me to terminate the contract."

"Fred's not asking," said Palaez.

"I don't think she's ready to be on her own," I said.

Fred looked at me as if for the first time. "I don't get it. You've been trying to terminate this thing for a week."

Palaez watched me.

The monitor above recorded everything.

"We've got things under control," I said. "I think a professional relationship with a companion can help. She's cut back on her drinking. She's no longer morose. She's gone back to work. She's regaining control of her life."

"Are you that good in bed?" asked Palaez.

"There's more to being a companion than sex," I said.

"Yes. There is. And Ms. Baxter is misinterpreting this *more than*. If you'd been more professional, if you had left less to interpretation, this situation could have been avoided."

Fred waited until he was sure Palaez had finished. "Look, Rod," he said, "we don't mean to get on your back. You're twenty-five, and we all know what it means to be twenty-five. She's twenty-three, young, vibrant, and attractive in her own way. If you're attracted to her, that's fine. It happens. We're just asking you to terminate the contract. If there is something between the two of you, you can see her nonprofessionally in twenty-eight days."

"And you can't have it both ways," said Palaez. "If you don't terminate the contract, we'll have to ask you to resign."

"I don't think you'll have to do that." I could hear a hint of desperation in my voice. "I like working here."

Fred smiled. It was time to be conciliatory. "You've been with us for six or seven years now. You had an excellent turnover in the local beds. You did a great job with the shift-janes. You're beginning to move up. It's always tough to go full-shift, but the pay and the fringe benefits are exceedingly good. If you handle this right, you could probably go anywhere you wanted in Personal Services."

I offered a professional smile. "I'll do my best."

"Good."

Palaez provided the closure. "We expect that you'll terminate the contract tonight. I'll have a flatscreen programmed, that you can take with you. Get it thumbed."

I nodded.

"And you'll come back tomorrow, ready for reassignment."

So I didn't have to pack up anything to take to Anna's after all, except for a flatscreen. It dawned on me as I walked home that I wouldn't have to see Lang anymore, and if I saw Stuart Greenspan again, it would only be socially.

I almost felt relieved. Almost.

33

To AVOID THINKING about Anna that afternoon, I read how Jude, the obscure, returned to his wife, for the sake of what was proper and correct, even though he truly loved Sue Bridehead. I tried to understand why he set out in a storm to see Sue, why he died of sickness later. It all seemed so absurd.

Afterward I watched the footage of Anna asking for my contract. Three times I watched her go through the motions; three times I listened to her questions. All our time together for the past three weeks had been recorded and studied, and I couldn't make sense of it. I found it easier to understand Jude, and I didn't understand him at all.

Avoiding Harry, I went back to Personal Services, to the pool, and swam away the faces that were resurfacing in my consciousness. I had brought a change of clothes and dressed in the locker room. I had the flatscreen with me, and I considered bringing it along to Anna's. But I didn't know how to walk into her apartment, holding a flatscreen inconspicuously at my side. I could always gift wrap it, I thought. I angled the flatscreen into my locker and closed the door on it.

On the rapid to Ohio City, and on the walk from the rapid stop to her apartment building, I rehearsed everything I would say. I knew what I'd say if she asked me why. I knew what I'd say if she asked me how I truly felt about her. I knew Palaez would review the footage, so I reworked the words in my head, then whispered the words to refine the delivery, insuring that everything came out as professional, judicious, and sensitive.

I buzzed at the building's entranceway and knocked on Anna's door. She opened it and smiled. Lack of sleep had drained her face of color. The skin blusher and eyeliner only made her pale skin look whiter. I had expected her to ask me why I hadn't just pressed open the lock, but she didn't. Instead she led me to the kitchen, handed me a Thirty-Three, and started searing two steaks. She talked about this, that, and the other while bustling from the frying pan to the table she'd set up in the living room. She told me that in several weeks Sophie was opening in a new production of *Romeo and Juliet;* we'd have to go. She didn't ask me why I hadn't brought along my new suitcase.

We sat down to eat. Timothy Molina was organizing an upcoming rally in Public Square; maybe we should go. She uncorked the wine and filled our glasses. Bill O'Brien was such a saint to put up with Timothy's political activeness, still fighting for a cause that was dead. Norman and Emma White, by the way, slept in separate bedrooms, and what did I think of Sophie's cousin, the lawyer she had told me about? Anna poured her words into each moment of silence as insistently as she filled our wineglasses.

"Why did you want to buy my contract?" I asked the question calmly, just as she was reaching over to pour more wine into my glass. The wine almost ended up in my lap.

She avoided my eyes. "Isn't there anything confidential in your business?"

"Confidentiality has nothing to do with the Business."

She placed the bottle on the table. "How many people know?"

I shrugged. "You made a strange request."

"How many?"

"Anyone who was around this afternoon who cares."

She looked me in the eyes. "That's not why I went in."

"All I know is what I was told."

"Which was . . . ?"

"I was told that you wanted to buy my contract."

She didn't say anything.

"Can you tell me why?"

"I don't know. After what happened last night, I felt . . . I don't know. I was being stupid. I never should have gone in. Okay? Are you happy?"

"My superiors," I said, "feel our . . ." I found I couldn't say *relationship*, or any of the other things I'd practiced on my way here. "They want our contract terminated."

Anna said nothing. She looked straight into my eyes and held herself still, as if, if she looked hard and long enough, she'd be able to read my mind.

"If you want, you could hire a new companion."

"I don't want another."

"It's for the best."

"Whose best?"

"Yours."

"What's best for you?"

What's best for the Business, I wanted to say.

"Rod," she said, "what do *you* want?"

There was a touch of desperation in her voice. Over my shoulder was the one-eyed lens of the monitor. For the monitor my answer should be impersonal, professional, sensitive to her needs, but still accomplishing the objective laid out for me by Palaez.

"Rod?"

A drop of perspiration rolled down my side. The monitor recorded my hesitation.

"This has to be our last night?" she asked.

I nodded.

"Let's skip the rest of dinner," she said. "Okay?"

"Sure."

We walked into the bedroom and closed the door on the camera. I reached for the top button of her shirt, and she said she wanted just to kiss, for now. We embraced on the bed and kissed and drew out the tension. With some clumsiness and some shy smiles, she undressed me, then I her. We caressed and kissed and looked each other in the eyes.

"I'll be right back," she said. Anna left the bedroom for the bathroom, then returned with a towel.

We made love, and the tension within me found its release. Her embrace was strong, like our first night in the motel. We held each other, said nothing, and the reds, then browns, of sunset through curtain became the grays of twilight. We made love again, our arms locked around the other. Her palms connected with my chest, and she pushed me up. "I want to look," she said. She sounded shy, as if this were the most intimate thing one could ask. I raised myself up, my hands sinking into the old mattress, and we found our foreheads meeting as we looked across a landscape of chest and belly to the stem that connected us, that no longer seemed wholly mine. Anna smiled, and there was something tender and familiar about the smile, something untouched by desire. The slow motion of our bodies, the focus of our vision, overwhelmed me with a sense of how we were enjoined. I wanted to be her and her to be me, to feel what the other was feeling, to transform the act into something truly mutual. And in the frustration of our closeness, we reached our separate moments.

In the quiet gray we lay there, one leg across my thighs, her head leaning against my shoulder. I tried to imagine what this would be like if there had been no Sauro, no ASD, no UHL. But there was still my job, and there was still Aunt Lorena, James Baxter, a house in Framingham, a summer home on Martha's Vineyard.

"Rod?"

"Hmmmm?"

"How do you feel about me?"

Rule Eight: Turn a client's personal questions upon herself. "Well, what are your feelings toward me?"

"I don't know. They're warm. My feelings toward you are warm."

"Why?"

She raised her head upon her hand, supporting herself with elbow and palm, her other hand absentmindedly tracing patterns across the hair of my chest. "Selfish reasons, I suppose. Most men seem to do it for themselves first. You're the first one who responded so quickly to *me*."

That's my job, but I didn't say that.

"Can a companion see a client after a contract's been terminated?"

"Regulations say that a companion may not be socially active for at least twenty-eight days after services are terminated."

"Four weeks?"

"Yeah."

"And after that?"

"Our lives are our own."

"With cameras watching," she said, automatically.

"Everyone has cameras watching them."

"There are no cameras here," she said. "You and I are the only two who saw us make love . . . who saw your penis hold our two bodies together . . . who hear us talking."

I didn't know that.

"Doesn't that make a difference?"

"Who knows? Maybe."

"Rod, do you care for me at all?"

"I like you, Anna."

"That's not what I'm asking."

I held myself stiffly, as if I didn't want to give myself away. The fingers tracing patterns on my chest became hesitant. Each touch was different now. Each one measured out the time it took me to respond. Each one added weight to each word I would say.

"What do *you* think?" I asked.

"I'm not sure," she said. "Sometimes I feel a real warmth in your touch. Other times I feel as if you're someone going through the motions. You know, like someone who's pushing buttons. And you push the buttons I like having pushed. But I'm not stupid, Rod. I've spent this whole afternoon thinking about what happened this morning and the last three weeks. I know that for whatever reasons I hired you, there was a part of me that wanted you to fall in love with me so I'd know how special I was. So I'd know it wasn't my fault that Sauro jumped. And ever since I started forcing things last week, it's gotten worse. I'm tired of trying to force the issue. I just want to know what you truly feel."

"I don't know," I said, and I was surprised by how truly honest the words sounded.

I had expected her to ask me more, but she continued tracing patterns on my chest and said nothing. I liked the feeling of fingertips against skin. I wanted her to say something more. "If I terminated your contract," she said, and her fingers stopped, "would you see me again in twenty-eight days?"

"Yeah," I said. "I think I would."

Part 3

the contract

*Pay attention:
a solitary heart
is not a heart.*
—Antonio Machado

34

THE LAST FOOTAGE on Anna's file showed her walking into Personal Services, asking to terminate the contract between herself and Roderick Lawrence, and thumbing the flat-screen bearing the image of the appropriate document. The adviser, who must have been kept oblivious of the situation, started a sales pitch on other offerings provided by Personal Services. Anna told her thank you, no, and left.

Marie was relieved the whole ordeal was over. "It would have reflected poorly on both of us," she said. Our meeting lasted all of two minutes, ending with the suggestion that maybe I use my three weeks of accumulated vacation time to visit my family in Traverse City.

Fred was equally distracted, barely stopping in the hallway to promise me a juicy client to make up for things.

Aggie feigned disappointment. "Fuck, man, I wanted to spend at least an hour telling you why you shouldn't go into the Heights." Four years ago she had spent three hours telling me not to transfer from Direct to Leisure Services. "Once you start kissing them," she had said, "it all gets confused."

But the talk around the Cleaning Room had to do with a woman who had been tortured to death in an abandoned home in unmonitored Pepper Pike. Her body had been found on Monday. For twenty-four hours the media had kept it hushed up, but last night a woman running for state rep on a prosafety campaign released the news to one of the more self-righteous New Puritan networks. By morning everyone had heard of it. I half wanted to call up Anna and make one last argument in favor of monitoring. I had some blood drawn so I'd be declared clean and ready for the next client, then I worked out in the gym and took a shower. At lunch I sat down with some of the companions I had trained with. Word was going around that a woman in Noncontract Services hadn't shown up for work on Monday. Brenda said she was certain the woman had worked in Media. Ray had heard the Sensory Arcades. William thought it was the phones. Peter and Carol were sure she'd been a marriage broker.

At home I put together all the crystals of Anna's file—the original two plus all the recorded dailies—in order to turn them in tomorrow. On impulse I made a copy of each crystal and placed them in a drawer. I sealed the originals in a carrying case and found myself staring at the case.

I tried to distract myself by calling up another Chandler novel, then I tried a movie, but in the end I found myself sitting in front of Albert Einstein, my hand on the drawer containing the copied crystals. After I had heard her voice, listened to her talk about her childhood and her family and Sauro, I could turn down the sound and just watch the animation of her face, her body. I slammed the drawer shut, breaking the reverie. I would destroy the file, write Anna a note, tell her the whole thing was off. Instead I left the carrying case on top of Albert so I'd see it in the morning.

At the Admiral of the Port, Harry was surprised that Anna had terminated the contract. "You know, I was getting worried that we might lose you there." Kevin said, "Well, back from the Land of the Unlaid Who Need Laying. Let me buy you a beer." We ended up talking about the dead woman and monitors and all the other things in the news. The New Puritan Dirty Linen Campaign had already achieved the resignation of several Personal Services supervisors in Kentucky and the impeachment of the lieutenant governor in Georgia. *Why would they want to torture someone?* We argued if it was greed or incompetence that had led to the poor workmanship on the Buckeye and Kinsman Construct Extensions. *They're going to show pictures of her on the news at eleven.* We took three different sides on the President's Retraining Program to educate and retrain refugee Hispanos in order to return them to their natal countries. *How did they get her to go into that abandoned house?*

The baseball season was in its second month, and the Cleveland Indians had gotten over their April winning streak: they hadn't been in a World Series since the turn of the century. Kevin kept drinking beer. While Harry talked with Bernardo, the bartender, about the team, Kevin talked about the expected child: "We could always move out of Slavic Village, you know, and find a place in the oxygen forests. But I'm not sure that's safe anymore. Not without monitors. And, hell, you're not safe with monitors anymore. Kansas City proves that. When you think of having a kid, it means along with buying a mitt and a bat and a soccer ball and a puppy, now you also gotta go out and get an emergency generator and some oxygen masks. It's like an investment in your future." Later in the evening Kevin dodged fly balls that looked as if they would shoot out of the holovision and bonk someone on the head. With each dodge Kevin turned to us and smiled bashfully.

We didn't wait to see the dead woman on the holo; Harry and I had to help Kevin home. Kevin told Betsy I'd jilted my client. "That's too bad," she said. "I really liked her." I almost told her that Anna and I were planning to meet in a month.

The next morning I had a message from Marie that I had a client for the weekend. There was also an urgent message: all servicers free at ten hours were expected for a special staff meeting in the holo theater.

The theater, which seated four hundred, was crowded. Seats in the front were the only ones available. An anxious edge to the murmur of conversation. Up front Fred, Marie, and two other supervisors were standing with three people. A man and a woman were in police uniform. The third person was a tall, balding man in a beige overcoat with a belt around the waist. Fred gestured toward me as I walked toward the front, and the man watched me as I took a seat in the fourth row. Close up, the man's wrinkles, the pouches under the eyes, became visible. His shoulders were slouched, his movements slow.

Marie introduced Detective Ohls and the two officers while Fred looked on, rubbing two crystals together in his hand. Ohls did all the talking. Dorothy Souto, he said, had reported for work on Saturday May 8 and had left work at 1400. There were some discrepencies in the record about what happened next. He told us each one. The coroner had estimated her time of death between midnight and two hours on Sunday, May 9. "We've asked you to this special meeting to ask if anyone here saw Dorothy Souto on Saturday, May 8." Ohls looked directly at me before continuing. "We'd also like you to ask any of your colleagues who couldn't make it to this meeting. I realize that Personal Services is a big place, so let me show you what she looks like in case you didn't see her on TV last night or in the *Plain Dealer* this morning." A face flashed up on the wall screen. Dorothy Souto had red hair twirled together in a high spiral.

As everybody filed out of the theater, I made my way up to Ohls. "I saw her that Saturday," I said.

He nodded. "Your name's Lawrence, right?"

Marie and several others had stopped to listen.

Ohls turned to Fred. "Is there someplace where I can talk to this guy in private?"

We ended up in a small cubicle used for counseling. Fred wondered if he should sit in, and Marie suggested that Fred should call in one of the lawyers. Ohls reassured them that was unnecessary.

Once we were alone, Ohls behind the desk, me in front, he pulled out a palm-size flatscreen and called up his notes. He told me what time I'd seen Dorothy Souto and what Experience I had requested. "That seems kind of a funny choice," he said.

"A client asked me to go through it."

"I didn't know clients could ask you to do stuff like that. Who was your client?"

"That's privileged information."

"It would take me an hour to find out who it is."

"Anna Baxter."

He nodded, obviously impressed. "Moving up in the world, I see. Now, I went through the file on your visit.

And everything looks fine, from the point of view of my investigation. But then, at the very end, Souto tells you her friends call her Goldilocks."

"I don't really remember."

"Come on, all that red hair, and she calls herself Goldilocks? We talked to some of her friends yesterday"— he read a list of five names; two of them worked phones— "and all of them called her Dorothy."

"I barely remember. The Experience was a bit traumatic."

"I'll bet," he said. He pressed several buttons on the flatscreen, then handed it to me. I saw what he wanted me to see, and I pushed it back his way. "Just look at it."

I shook my head.

"You've dealt with the Cleveland Heights cops, and you know what they could do to cause you all sorts of trouble. Do you want to find out what a Cleveland cop investigating a murder can do?"

I picked up the flatscreen.

"Press return after you've given each image a good look-see."

It was Dorothy Souto in close-up, every spot where she'd been bruised, burned, pierced, and cut. There were five angles on her throat, where a knife had divided skin, muscles, and arteries. At last was an autopsy report, listing all the damage done that hadn't been visible. If there had been only two shots, I would have vomited, but by the end I felt as if I had been drugged. "Satisfied?" I said and handed it back.

"Nice work, don't you think?"

"Depends on your standards," I said.

"I fought in Spain, in the battle of Granada. I was a career officer at the time. There were a lot of enemy sympathizers in the area. It made for a very difficult battle. We held Granada—the city and the province—for ten days. During that time, some of those sympathizers turned up in the countryside looking a lot like Dorothy Souto in those pictures. We were told two stories. Some of them had been tortured and executed by guerrillas for being government informants. Others were tortured and executed by members of rival guerrilla groups. We always had thought it funny that all these different guerrillas were following the same m.o."

"I don't know anything about that war. I just watched it on the news when I was in school."

He held up the flatscreen and offered me another glimpse of Dorothy Souto. "It takes a while to do work like this," said Ohls. "You can torture people for information. But if you just want information, there are at least five different chemicals you can try. The CIA probably has five more the media doesn't know about. Why torture someone then? Unless you want to scare some other people. Remember, it took a while to do this job on her."

He waited, as if what he said would have some effect on me.

Ohls consulted something else on his flatscreen. "Yesterday afternoon we interviewed Julius Douglas. Julius works as a receptionist at the Sensory Arcades. He was on duty when you signed up for the Relocation Experience. Remember him?"

"Yeah."

"He remembers you, too. Not many people ask for that experience, you know. In fact, Julius said that every time someone has asked for it, Monitoring has conducted a follow-up interview with him. It took all night for two of my officers to track it down, but it's on file. Two guys show up. They have ID that says they're with Monitoring. They want to verify the names of the person administering and the person receiving the Experience. Funny thing number one is: they don't actually work for Monitoring. Funny thing number two is: they *didn't* do a follow-up on your visit. Funny thing number three is: the night after she administers the Experience to you, Dorothy Souto gets tortured and murdered." He gave it time to sink in.

"At five this morning we got a judge to issue a warrant so we could look at the footage of you getting the Experience. We couldn't help but notice that this woman with red hair called herself Goldilocks, though no one else did. It makes me wonder about the Three Bears. Have you met any bears lately?"

"I haven't been in the woods."

"We're going to crack wise, are we? Won't adolescence ever end? How about this: are you a bear?"

"No."

"That's one way of answering both questions truthfully. Are the bears UHL?"

"I have no idea."

"I think they're UHL. You keep reading about how people in the camps make up new families to be part of. I guess if I was a faggot, I'd make up a family, too. Mama, Papa, and Baby. Sounds like family, to me. We got another warrant. Your phone bill to Traverse City is less than what I spend on a glass of beer. Maybe you needed a new family."

"I've got a life right here."

He looked around the cubicle as if he could measure my life by its physical dimensions. "Nice life," he said.

"I'm not UHL, and I didn't murder Dorothy Souto."

"I don't think you did. But I think you know something about what happened to her."

"I don't know anything."

"You know I could take you in. I think there are enough inconsistencies in what you've said that I could convince some judge to let me use chemicals."

He may have been tougher than the Cleveland Heights cops, but his threats weren't any more convincing.

He shook his head and slipped his flatscreen into his jacket pocket. He tightened his tie. "You're good," he said. "I hope you're as good as the big boys." He reached into his other jacket pocket, pulled out a card. It had his name and all sorts of phone numbers. "Consider calling me. They left more than one body in Spain. Now it looks like they've brought the war home. I'd sure hate for the next body to be yours."

Ohls got out of the chair slowly. His age showed in the way he walked out of the room, taking each step with a certain deliberation. For the briefest moment I wondered why he hadn't retired, and I wanted to answer some of his questions. But once outside the cubicle, he avoided me in the hallway like my blood was bad, and I had nothing left to say.

It wasn't long afterward that I found myself sitting in Fred's office along with Marie and Palaez. Palaez wanted to know exactly what Detective Ohls had questioned me about. Fred seemed only to want to listen, and he was expertly twirling two crystals between his fingers. Marie sat still and looked professional.

"Just why were you at the Sensory Arcades?" Palaez had to ask for a third time.

"I had the Relocation Experience," I said, for the third time.

"But why?"

"My client asked me to."

For the third time she flashed Fred an *I told you so* look and waited in vain for Fred to pick up on the situation.

"Rod," said Marie, "will be working with another client now. Anna Baxter is a thing of the past."

Palaez finally had to accept that, and she let me go. Marie followed me out of the office. "That woman is out for our ass," she said. "Do this new client the way I trained you, and everything will be fine." She handed me a packet containing one crystal. "And Rod?"

"What?"

"Don't let too many people know about your Experience at the Arcades."

Aggie, Cindy, and Henry were still in the Cleaning Room when I got there. I tossed back a beer before I made it to their table.

"Are you okay?" Aggie asked me. "I heard the cops had a talk with you."

"Yeah. The woman who got tortured and killed. I saw her last Saturday."

"We heard," said Henry.

"Word travels fast," I said.

Aggie looked disappointed. "Why were you seeing such stuff?"

"My client asked me to."

"Why didn't you tell her to stuff it?" asked Henry.

Cindy told Henry to hush.

Aggie said, "You getting scared of bad blood, aren't you?"

"Not really."

"Because I should be more scared of it than you are. I see anywhere from five to twenty a day, and no one gives them the complete battery of tests. They get the thirty-seconder, then they get me. And you don't see me talking about no camps, or running off to the Arcades, do you?"

"My client asked me to," I said.

"What right she got to ask you to do something like that? Was this the last one?"

"Yeah."

"She probably trying to scare you into marrying her. Just like I told you would happen. You know better, CT, than to do stuff like that."

"Our shift started five minutes ago," said Henry.

Cindy smiled sweetly and stood up. "I guess we gotta go."

Henry passed me his trash before standing.

Aggie remained seated. "Transfer back to Direct," she said. "If you got cops talking to you, you ain't long for this business."

The three of them left me there.

I read the afternoon updated edition of the *PD* when I got home. There was a picture of dead Dorothy Souto lying in her own blood. It said that Dorothy Souto was a suspected member of the terrorist Union for Human Liberation. Antiterrorist consultant for Monitoring Services, Edward Lang, said that Dorothy Souto had been in contact with federal agents about turning state's evidence in return for immunity. Obviously her cohorts had discovered that and tortured her as an example to others.

I tried to take my mind off things by reading, by watching some TV, but I couldn't concentrate on anything. Goldilocks was dead. But she had known what risks she was taking. She worked for the group that had blacked out Kansas City. But if she hadn't called herself Goldilocks, would they have abducted her? What if someone else had administered the Experience, would they have abducted him instead?

What would happen if they ever thought I was UHL? Would I too, be taken in a car out to some abandoned house? Would Adolf be programmed to erase the pickup, the transport, because once I was out in the country, there were no monitors to follow the rest? And after I told them about Stuart Greenspan's desire to meet James Baxter, about how Luis, presumed dead in the riots at Camp Seven, was now out, would they let me go, or would the same knife that had found Dorothy's throat find mine? I didn't want to die that way.

35

THE CLIENT WAS second-generation Indian, the kind Columbus had gone searching for. She lived in one of the giant houses on Shaker Boulevard. Her husband was away for the weekend at a medical convention, and she was sure he was going some hands-on research with a female gynecologist from Akron. I wore some of the nice clothes I'd purchased to work for Anna and took the RTA out to Shaker and Warransville, where she picked me up in a car big enough to be from the twentieth century. A slim woman, she wore an elegant sari and some jewelry that could rival Anna's trust fund in its value. She drove the car to her house without looking at me once.

The car was parked in the garage behind the house, and there was a garage entrance; no one saw me enter. Without saying a word the client led me up to the master bedroom. We took off our clothes and spent most of the weekend there.

Every now and then she went downstairs to warm up prepackaged Indian cuisine for us to eat or left the house to run an errand while I remained on the second floor and kept away from the windows. By the end of the weekend I'd run out of positions that didn't require gymnastics training, and I felt the kind of weariness that prisoners feel.

When we weren't making love or eating bland curried chicken, we watched the holovision. I once asked her what the political situation was like in India, and she said, "If you want to talk about that, I'll give you my Dad's phone number. I haven't been to India since my grandparents died."

Sunday afternoon she dropped me off at an RTA stop and then drove off to the airport to pick up her husband.

I expected to get home and find a message of reproach from Anna. Of course, there wasn't one. There was a message from Pilar. Due to the death of Edward Lang's father, there would be no meeting this Monday.

On Monday morning I had my blood drawn again and sat through a long staff meeting. Afterward Marie met with me in her office, told me how excited she was by the sensory feedback info from my weekend encounter, and to file a report with Tricky Dick on what had happened, since there was no matching footage. "It's too bad we couldn't see you in action. Heartbeat and everything else tell me it was a hot weekend. You're making us both look good." She picked up a small packet. "I got a twenty-four-hour job, if you want it. This businesswoman from Boston would rather pay extra than stay overnight with a temp in one of our rooms. How about it?"

I got to spend another night at the Democracy Now Hotel. The woman was about my height, but she had the shoulders of a halfback and the moves of a professional wrestler. Between long monologues on the ins and outs of the shipping industry, we acted out some of her more elaborate fantasies. She said she felt free, away from Boston and people who knew her. She loved not having to spell out everything she liked. She was amazed at my training, how much, for instance I knew about Boston without ever having visited. After lunch the next day she bought me a cut-to-size shirt at the Democracy Now store to replace the one she'd ripped. Just before leaving she asked for directions to Ohio City so she could visit a friend from grade school who lived there. I told myself it was just a coincidence that she had a friend from Boston who lived in Ohio City and didn't ask the friend's name.

The next day Marie was ecstatic about the footage and Tricky Dick's evaluation. "A few more like this, and they'll forget the name Anna Baxter."

The next client requested me by name, which thrilled Marie to no end. Cheryl Jussi, with the *j* pronounced like a *y*, was a compact blond woman who worked as a teacher at a school for the developmentally handicapped and lived in a house in Chagrin Falls. Cheryl had come in on Tuesday, so her blood was already declared clean, her file ready. She wanted to see me this evening.

Her file contained one crystal. With the adviser who'd handled the selection and contract, Cheryl had sat with her arms crossed, her shoulders hunched forward as if trying to hide herself. She sometimes spoke too softly to be heard and blushed at every mention of sex. She didn't look like she was dying for a servicer, but she told the adviser if she liked me, she'd want to keep me on indefinitely. Along with that footage there was the *PD* coverage of some charity fund-raisers, a few other documents, and ten minutes of her teaching. That was it: Chagrin Falls, like nearby Pepper Pike, was unmonitored.

I signed out one of Personal Services' cars and headed out Carnegie to Cedar, catching Fairmount and driving past Sophie's house. I wondered if I really wanted to see Cheryl Jussi. She had requested me by name, but she wouldn't say who'd made the recommendation, just a friend, she'd said. Now Fairmount was a two-lane road going past Pepper Pike homes, many of them expensive at one time, most of them deserted now, just like the home where Dorothy Souto had died. I wondered if someone had invited Dorothy Souto out here, someone she knew.

Cheryl Jussi met me at the door wearing a plain white dress. We sat down together on a sofa in a living room that looked as if it had been decorated twenty years ago by someone with money. It had been her parents' house, she explained. The rest of the house felt terribly empty, and the silence of the place was unnerving. She opened some champagne, but it wasn't until the second bottle that she was able to relax and meet my eyes without instantly glancing away.

She invited me up to her bedroom during the third bottle of champagne and pointedly ignored my suggestion that maybe we could go out for supper or eat something here. In bed she stretched out under me, asking me to hold her by the wrists, and proceeded to writhe beneath me as if struggling to get free. Twenty minutes later she came, and I felt relieved. She looked relieved, and terribly embarrassed. "Why don't you take a shower and get dressed," she said. I caressed her cheek. "Please," she said.

The shower was refreshing, cleansing me of the sweat, but not of the draggy feeling left by the champagne, the not-so-pleasant exhaustion from the sex. I stepped out of the bathroom almost as presentable as when I first appeared at her front door. The bed was made; the room was empty.

Cheryl Jussi was not in the living room, but Stuart Greenspan was. He was wearing a gray suit with a maroon-and-black tie. Standing by the sofa, he held a bottle of the Brazilian beer we'd been drinking at Sophie's in each hand, his left hand extended toward me. I took the beer. I didn't know if I was supposed to shake his hand or not. Is this how Dorothy Souto had been greeted last Saturday night?

"Sorry for all the elaborate tricks, but I needed to talk with you without anyone knowing that we've talked."

What was I supposed to say?

"We need to talk about you and Anna." He gestured for me to sit down.

"There's nothing to talk about."

"There isn't? You two are going to be seeing each other in three weeks."

"No, we're not."

"You're not?" He looked down at his beer, then returned his gaze to me. His fingers were picking the label off the bottle. "You've changed your mind, I take it."

"Changed?"

"You did promise to see her in twenty-eight days. I planted the bug myself.

"Oh."

"Several of us even went to a lot of trouble to make sure that Lang's record of your conversation—the one where you said you'd get together—got sort of lost between recording and storage. You probably didn't know that Lang got a warrant to extend the monitor's hearing range in Anna's apartment after the Kansas City Black Out."

Then Lang had heard Anna tell me she hadn't joined the UHL.

"In fact, Lang might suspect that you were talking about something a little more important than a get-together, so don't be surprised if he puts some pressure on you."

"I don't follow."

"Look, Rod, we know you're in Lang's pay."

"He hasn't paid me a dollar," I said. "Not one."

Stuart nodded thoughtfully. "Okay, but we know you've seen him at least once. We also know that he sent a message canceling a meeting two days ago because of his father's funeral. Have you told him about our meetings?"

"No."

"Does he know I'm UHL?"

"No."

"Does he know I want to have a face-to-face meeting with James Baxter?"

"No."

"Why am I supposed to believe you?" he asked.

"We're both here, aren't we?"

"Yeah. And Dorothy Souto's not. And that's the other reason we're having this meeting." He reached into his coat pocket and pulled out his wallet. He sorted through some cards until his fingers located and plucked out a flatcard photo. He rubbed the corner until he got the picture he wanted and passed it to me. "This is Angel."

Angel was a young black woman. She was very tall and very thin, with her hair cut short. Her eyes, even for a photo, were intense, but her smile was faint, almost as if embarrassed by her own seriousness. "Is Angel really her name?"

"It's not the name her parents gave her, if that's what you mean. And that picture is ten years old—we were at graduate school together. We were making a last-ditch effort to lead a straight life together."

It was odd to hear the word *straight* in a different context. "Am I supposed to know her?" I said.

"Not directly. Angel ended up being an expert in computer design. She flies all over the country as a consultant. She never had any official ASD ties, and she never subscribed to enough left wing journals to make the FBI suspicious. But she and two other people designed the computer virus that shut down Kansas City."

I looked again at the flatcard, the faint smile on her lips. It had been a cliché by ninth grade that bomber pilots never really feel the impact of their bombs.

"Before that she had ordered the assassination of at least two Baxter Construction VPs. When asked if any should be avoided, she said get the first two that are accessible. One of the first two happened to be her uncle."

"Nice person," I said. The photo, the smile, didn't suggest that kind of heartlessness.

"The word *angel* can be misleading—it doesn't always mean good and sweet. Angel, the one in the picture, wants to be Justice. Justice without a human face. Equal treatment under God, that sort of thing. You don't make exceptions for friends. You don't make exceptions for family. Baxter Construction builds concentration camps; everyone at Baxter Construction is implicated. Everyone who doesn't take necessary action, in fact, is implicated. The three hundred who died March fifteenth were casualties of war. Innocents always die in wars. It's too bad, but it's true."

"Is this you or Angel who believes that?"

"Oh, I agree with her. In theory. But my parents had been very devout and moralistic Jews. I wasn't there, I was against the entire endeavor, but I, too, am responsible for those three hundred deaths." He placed the beer on the table and leaned forward, resting his elbows on his knees, pointing both index fingers at me. "In Kansas City the authorities disappeared two people, hung one, and arrested five more. Of those eight, four were UHL, and only two had any part in the Black Out. Does that bother their conscience even a little bit?"

I found myself shaking my head, not because I disagreed, but because it was all too much.

"Angel considers Kansas City a success. I think it was a failure. People who sympathize with those who are dying in the concentration camps don't want to have anything to do with a UHL that kills off babies and old people. I want a different kind of victory."

"You want to meet with James Baxter."

"Yeah. I want something to happen to bring him here. I want a situation that we can control."

"And you want Anna and me back together."

"Yes. But not in three weeks. I don't know who killed Dorothy Souto. Angel thinks I'm on the wrong track, and she might be trying to sabotage my plans. Her people could have killed Dorothy. Lang could have ordered it, but that doesn't seem his style. But it is the style of the people he works for. They're the ones who want results faster than the justice system will allow. Both your buddy Lang and I are under a lot of pressure to produce results fast. I can't afford to wait three weeks. Tell Anna that after one week you couldn't wait any longer. You can invite her out here. Cheryl will get an indefinite contract so you're safe as far as your work is concerned. After three weeks you get together officially, declare your love for each other, and we call Big Daddy. He'll catch the first plane to town to meet you."

"Is that what Sauro was supposed to do?"

"We expected Anna to be one of us. Sauro was just her lover."

"Until when? You say Anna's not UHL. Anna says she's not UHL. Even if Anna was UHL, she wouldn't risk her father's life."

"After Kansas City we put pressure on Sauro to try to get Baxter to come to Cleveland."

"He wouldn't do it?"

"He couldn't. He was too busy losing Anna to betray her father."

"And you were hoping for something different, weren't you?"

Stuart shook his head. "Remember, Sauro didn't make it out of this one alive."

"Because he wouldn't do what you asked?"

"No. Because somehow Lang found out."

I didn't know what to say. The beer tasted warm and awful.

"We need your help. I've tried to set up a situation that protects you more than we've ever been able to protect anyone. And it's like your fantasy come true. We're giving you an unmonitored house and three weeks to do what you wanted to do all along."

"And you guys handle the betrayal."

"If that makes it easier."

"If I say no, do I walk out of here alive?"

"Yeah."

"How do I know I don't get my throat cut like Dorothy Souto?"

"I don't cut throats." He took a sip of his beer, then gauged me with his eyes. "But I might get my throat cut if I don't time this thing right."

I shook my head.

"Look, Lawrence, you've already died once. In the camps. Doesn't that give you any kind of courage?"

Cheryl let me out the front door the next morning, and I drove the Personal Services' car back to the parking garage under the Prospect Corridors. I had spent the night there and walked out the next morning, still saying no. I wanted to believe that took a kind of courage.

36

I SAW MARIE that afternoon after lunch. She wasn't too happy that one sexual encounter had produced a canceled contract, even though Cheryl Jussi had been very apologetic and told her adviser that it had been quite good, just not her style, a mistake from the start. "You were trained to help them decide it's never a mistake."

"I told you from the word go this one didn't look any good."

"Well, it doesn't matter. This very morning someone came in, requested you by name, and took out an indefinite contract, with one week paid in advance. She met you at a party she gave and was sure you'd be perfect for her." Marie held up the packet. There were two crystals. The name printed on the packet's tag was Sophie Greenspan.

Had Anna put her up to this, to keep me from seeing other janes? At the party I had gotten the impression that Sophie had screwed Sauro once or twice. Maybe Sophie was continuing the tradition. Or maybe Sophie had received a call from her cousin late last night, after he'd driven home from Cheryl Jussi's place in unmonitored Chagrin Falls, and maybe he suggested that Sophie carry out the same plot a little more inconspicuously.

I tried to bury the thought. I was an expert at burying thoughts, but this one kept coming back. I was beginning to think like Lang, and I didn't want to think like him. There had to be something to say for holding someone's hand, looking them in the eye, and knowing *who* they were.

I spent the rest of the afternoon and the next day going through Sophie's file, but there wasn't much to find. The Basics. Sophia Rachel Greenspan, born thirty-four years ago on August 19; a social-security number; a draft-registration number; a B.A. and a Ph.D. in theater arts from Yale; current employment, the Cleveland Playhouse.

Then came Tricky Dick's usual idiosyncratic Life Summary. Sophie had lived the first years of her life in Parma, where her parents had grown up. Her father had been an air-force pilot; when Sophie was five, he was shot down over the infamous Fire Zone Emerald during the Latin Wars. Sophie's mother didn't qualify for veteran's benefits—she made too much money as a waitress, the only job she could get—and mother and daughter moved to Slavic Village, which was then a run-down neighborhood of clapboard houses, over-priced convenience stores, and bars. Sophie gained a half-sister, fathered by a mechanic who didn't want to get married. Sophie went to the local public school and did extremely well. She received scholarships to Yale, where she finally received her Ph.D. in dramatic arts. She taught at the same college Anna attended, and she was denied tenure after six years there, after directing a play on the relocation camps. Her father's grandfather had left her a nice little nest egg, which she had invested wisely, along with all of her savings.

The second crystal contained footage. There was plenty of recorded material from her performances. I felt as if I knew her better from her performances than from the rest of the footage in her file. She was more likely to be on a stage than in front of a monitor.

There were, however, several rich people who had monitored homes and who held fund-raisers for the Playhouse. There was footage of Sophie chatting at the parties, being as delightful as an extra zero before the decimal point on a donation, sometimes later migrating to a bedroom with someone.

Friday night, following tradition, Harry, Kevin, and I watched the fuck footage. There were five segments. Adolf or Tricky Dick had blanked out the names of the home owners and of Sophie's partner. Sophie was always on top, and she made her orgasms sound so delicious that I couldn't believe she was enjoying herself that much. Harry and Kevin were both amazed at how well she carried her size. "This new client," said Kevin, "has nipple erections bigger than my wife's breasts. I don't think your hands are big enough to handle her. I don't think anyone's are.

On Friday both our bloods had been declared clean, and the adviser reconfirmed our meeting at five o'clock Saturday afternoon at Shaker Square. At 1630 I found myself on a rapid to the Heights, carrying me through the darkness that lies beneath the Construct, the transit's electric hum and metallic clicking lulling me away from my thoughts. I remembered coming back from downtown, my father sitting next to me. Arthur should have been there, too. The vinyl of the seats was ripped, foam rubber bulging up through the tears. We watched giant cranes swing steel beams into place, assembling the Construct around us. I couldn't remember why we'd gone downtown.

The rapid emerged from the tunnel, and sunlight filled the car. I squinted and lost the memory. I looked around at my fellow passengers. The well-dressed were mostly white, a few black, even fewer Hispanic; a few parents managed children and shopping bags. Other passengers, dressed in some sort of service uniform, were usually black and Hispanic; the uniformed whites were mostly women. I was dressed as if I might live in the Heights—a yellow cotton shirt, khaki slacks, brown leather shoes—but I lacked the children and the shopping.

Sophie was waiting on the platform. She wore a reliable smile, and her eyes searched the tinted windows for my face. Her black hair was tied back, and her clothes hung loosely, failing to disguise the size of her breasts.

I stepped down from the transit car, ready to greet her. Before I could tell her how nice it was to see her again, her arms had pulled me into a tight embrace. Her lips were against mine, and my tongue feigned interest. I placed my hands on her hips to insure some distance; I didn't want her to discover that only my tongue could pretend such eagerness. It looked as if I'd be using chemicals again.

"Oh, Rod," she gasped, when she finally released me. "I've been waiting for this moment for days. I feel a bit guilty, but Anna told me she was done with you. I haven't been able to get you out of my mind since the party. I have steaks marinating in the fridge and silk sheets on the bed."

Before I could respond, she grabbed my hand and dragged me across Shaker Boulevard and past the first set of shops. "I've got my car parked over by the Inn," she was saying, "but I have to buy a few things quickly. If you don't mind, that is."

"No. Not at all. I have all the time in the world. And all my attention for you."

She seemed to blush. "Oh, how nice! You must have been practicing that line for weeks." She dragged me across a road divided by a median, the cars stopping for us, or better said, for her. She wasn't stopping for any of them.

"You know," she went on, "you keep hearing that there are fewer and fewer cars every year. With the RTA and the Construct and all that . . . but this place still fills up at noontime like a glass of sherry during cocktail hour. With everyone going around and around the Square looking for parking spaces, you'd begin to think that we had more cars than we did before the Construct." She looked at me as she pulled me along. "You did eat, didn't you?" She stopped outside a bookstore and awaited my reply.

"Yes," I said. "I ate before heading out here."

"Good," she said, abruptly jerking my arm and tugging me after her into the bookstore. "They say that one is not good for anything on an empty stomach. And I want you good for a lot of things."

I watched her look at books, all of which were hardcovers, all of which were spread out, with no pattern to their arrangement, on heavy wood tables. Audio and vid crystals were kept downstairs, as well as the paperbacks "for the frugal customer who still does not want to strain his eyes with the light of a computer screen," said the fine print of an engraved wood placard. Sophie found herself a large Shakespeare anthology full of "darling little photographs. Oh, how I love pictures. So much more artistic than holoes, don't you think, Rod, dear?" and a large tome on the Construct ("You keep hearing so many things about the Construct these days, and I just don't know what to think anymore about it").

After Lang and Anna I was disappointed that she didn't pick out a book for me to read.

She carried the two heavy books up to the register. "I thought I would get myself several things to read," she said to me as the saleswoman ran her bancard through the computer and flashed a readout pen over the books' spines, "but I do hope you won't give me the opportunity to even touch them."

She then introduced me to Elaine, the saleswoman, announcing proudly that I was straight from Personal Services, one of their best. In the clothing store, where she bought a dress, and in the Crystal Store, where she purchased a jazz anthology, she also introduced me to the people behind the counters. Most took it naturally; one of the older women looked at me as if wondering—*would I want the same style, or perhaps something slightly taller? Perhaps with a distinguishing limp*.

Sophie finally put me in her car, and, as she maneuvered her American version of a European model out of its parking space, she told me about her father and how important a role he had played in keeping the Cleveland Playhouse alive (which I knew wasn't true) and how an actor, who spent all her time being other people, needed someone for company. I almost told her to get a dog, but she was already talking about the parties she would take me to, the important Clevelanders I would meet, the wonderful times we would have. Sophie confirmed every fear I'd had about working the Heights.

We drove along wide streets divided by grassy medians. Large homes, protected by manicured bushes and tall trees, glided by. There were empty lots and vacant, crumbling homes and I couldn't help but think of Dorothy Souto.

"A real shame," Sophie said. "It just seems as if there aren't enough people who can afford homes like these. I once thought of dividing a home like that up into apartments, but my investment counselor advised me that most of the potential renters would prefer to live in the Construct.

And there's something probably politically wrong with being a landlord."

I nodded. The bushes in the vacant lots spread out in search of sunlight. Tall grasses and wildflowers competed with them. The wealth of color seemed spontaneous, alive.

"Do you ever talk, Rod?" Sophie asked.

"Huh?"

"I'll bet you thought that I was going to do *all* the talking. Anyway, we'll have plenty of time for talking once we pull out the sherry and hop into bed. I do hope you are secure enough to be on the bottom. So many men don't like doing it that way."

She smiled at me. I pictured myself staring at her heavy, naked breasts, her face peering over them and smiling down at me. The guys in the footage had liked it well enough.

"I wonder," she went on, "do I have to pay extra to share you with my friends?"

My stomach turned. The car slowed to a halt. The red stop sign had a hastily painted graffiti *immigration*, dripping below the stark white lines of the four official letters.

"We're here," she called out.

The car crossed Fairmount and took us into the circular drive. In the late-afternoon sun, the house loomed above us like a gray dinosaur curled up after its midday meal.

Sophie flipped through her keys as we walked to the heavy wooden door.

"Have you ever thought of getting a printlock?" I said, having almost nothing else to say, not knowing why Sophie had hired me. "They're almost impossible to pick."

She shrugged. "I like the sensation of inserting something into something else." She thrust the key into the lock. "It satisfies my latent desire to be a man."

She turned the key, something clicked, and the heavy door swung open. We stepped in, and I felt as if I were seeing the front hallway for the first time. A curving wood stairway led to the second floor. Paintings decorated the walls. Lights shone from wall fixtures. A deep red Oriental carpet covered most of the polished wood floor.

"We're home," Sophie called out as she slammed the door behind us. I tried to remember if the file had said anything about pets; she had shouted as if she were calling out to someone else in the house.

But of course, it was Anna. Her face was set aglow by her smile, and she practically skipped into my arms. She pressed herself against me, her tongue finding its way to mine. I felt more betrayed than surprised: *if anyone found out* . . . I tried to return her embrace with equal warmth, but everything in me tightened: *whose idea was this?* She must have felt the tension, because she pulled herself away from me, slowly, by degrees. She stepped back, her smile now forced, like the first time we'd met. I glanced over to Sophie.

"I think he's still confused, the poor boy," Sophie said to Anna.

Anna watched me carefully. "I'm sorry, sweetheart. But I couldn't wait a month."

37

ANNA HAD NOTHING more to say to me. After all these elaborate arrangements she had made with Sophie, I had backed away. She looked as if she had resolved never to trust me again.

Sophie put on her Domineering Hostess mask and talked up a storm, obscuring everything in a cloud of words. In the kitchen she poured wine for Anna and herself and brought me a Thirty-Three from the refrigerator. She led us to a small library and directed Anna and me to sit on the same couch. She met our discomfort with energy, vividly describing preparations for *Romeo and Juliet*, how it was scheduled to go to Chicago, how if she was kept in the lead role, this production could be her big break. She asked me to pick out a crystal from her collection—mostly classical, jazz and some pan-cultural stuff—and put it on her tiny stereo. Sophie also owned one of Anna's favorite pieces; I wondered if it had been a gift. I put on the Beautiful-Woman-Without-a-Personality crystal. Anna recognized the music with the first chord and patted my hand.

For dinner Anna and I ate a casserole she had made while Sophie told me how Anna would come over before they went to a party and how she'd read from Ibsen or Shakespeare while Sophie finished getting dressed. "I'd hope you'd take advantage of the same library," and she listed the writers in her collection. I nodded attentively, and Anna tried to give me a smile of camaraderie. I couldn't help but look away.

"Well," Sophie said, "I want to lose a few pounds before the play opens. So there's no dessert tonight. What would the two of you like to do?"

Anna waited for me to answer.

"Well," I said, "there's not a whole lot we can do. We really can't go out. If a monitor picked us up together, I'm sure my boss would know about it by Monday."

"There are no monitors here," Anna said.

"What would happen," said Sophie, "if you broke that one little rule about not seeing each other for a month?"

"I'd get fired."

"That's silly," said Sophie. "They'd fire you for falling in love?"

"The people I work for don't like to make up regulations just for people to break them. Anna and I have already broken a few."

"Well, there are plenty of rooms here. In fact, there are four bedrooms, not to mention the ones in the old servants' quarters. You can share, or you can use different rooms." Sophie offered me her Most Beautiful Woman in the World mask. "And I know how badly you were looking forward to sleeping with this voluptuous body, but we'll just have to wait. I conserve all my energies for a play. So my bedroom is out of bounds, I'm afraid to say."

I smiled and thought and barely heard Sophie ask me if I'd stay with Anna. That *had* been the plan, that I'd stay with her, but there was supposed to have been seventeen more days for me to think it through, to reconsider everything.

"I'd like you to stay," Anna said, "but not if you don't want to."

Sophie sat still, and I didn't know what to say in front of her that could be completely honest.

"I'd like to stay," I said. I listened for the honesty in my voice, and I didn't hear it. Anna looked as if she didn't either.

"Well," Sophie said, "I have lines to review. Are you two going to head upstairs or not?"

Anna whispered, "You don't have to be so blunt."

"I guess you two could stay down here and play chess."

Anna nodded, then looked at me, and I gave her the

kind of smile that gets presidents elected. After we finished the dinner wine, Anna led me up the curving stairs and to the guest bedroom, where she'd already unpacked her things. I closed the bedroom door behind us and embraced her; thumbs rubbed along the tips of index, middle, ring, small fingers, activating the sensors, providing evidence that I was keeping Sophie satisfied. Anna planted kisses on my cheeks, across my forehead, upon each eyelid, before returning her lips to mine. I hesitated for a moment, despising what I'd just done. "What's wrong?" Anna asked. I substituted kisses for explanations, caresses to erase doubts. One thing led to another, and the touching of flesh left us momentarily satisfied while the wine left us tired. Anna fell asleep, and I stared out the windows. The shades weren't drawn; there was no nearby streetlight to brighten the room's darkness with gray.

Even with my eyes closed, barely awake and sleep returning, I felt as if I were being watched, that being watched had brought me this far awake. I imagined I was in a nondescript room, a monitor hanging from each corner of the ceiling, each one focused on me.

I opened my eyes.

I was in Sophie's guest bedroom, in one of the twin beds. Anna sat atop the opposite bed, hands at her sides. She was wearing a red silk robe that was too big for her, but the fabric draped over her body in a wonderfully suggestive way. I wondered how long she had watched me breathe. She realized my eyes were open, and she smiled.

"I brought you breakfast," she said.

She helped pile up pillows behind my back and then placed the tray on my lap. Steak and eggs and fries and good, plain juice that turned out to have champagne in it. "Sophie's gone for the day," she said. "I thought we could celebrate our reunion."

"There's more champagne?"

"And plenty of juice."

After a quick trip to the bathroom, I ate my breakfast to an audience of one. She watched each of my gestures, the way I held myself, the way I chewed.

I was impressed by how much Anna had already made

the guest room her own. Her clock-radio/crystal player was on the table between the two beds. On top of the bureau she had arranged her cosmetics. She had arrayed a number of books on the radiator cover. I couldn't help but wonder how many of her clothes she had packed, if Adolf had saved that moment for her file, if Lang would notice that we'd both packed our bags and headed for the same address.

"Rod? Can I ask you a question?"

"You can ask me two."

"What happened to the files and stuff you were given on me?"

"I turned them back in."

"So you can't go back home and look up something about me or watch me make love with Sauro, or anything like that?"

"No. And don't be upset about that. It was my job. I needed that information to do my job well."

"You did do your job well." She reached over and took a sip of my doctored juice. "But there's so much other stuff you know about me, and I hardly know you at all."

"We have plenty of time," I said, appreciating how the vague words sounded so promising.

"But you have an unfair advantage," she said. "I don't even know what you really like in bed. I just did the things that guys in general seemed to like."

"That's a pretty good starting point."

"But I want to know what you really like. I want to start from the beginning. I want to make whatever time we have together something new. I want it to be a back-and-forth, a give-and-take, like with a real couple."

"You want to start from scratch?"

"Yeah." She sipped more of the juice.

"Okay." I smiled. "Take off that robe."

Anna hesitated, her hands resting on the belt's knot.

Still naked from last night, I rose from the bed and folded the bedclothes over until they took up a small portion of the space at the end of the bed. I sat back down against the pillows.

"Well, I guess it's only fair that since you're naked . . ." Anna took off the robe and folded it, placed it on her bed. "What next?"

"Sit down with your back to me." Her skin against my chest was warm. We adjusted our bodies until we were comfortable, her right leg draped over my right, her left leg pressed against the inside of my left. I placed fingertips upon temples. "Now, I'm going to start here and touch and caress. If something feels particularly pleasing, tell me, and I'll do it until you want me to go on. I'm not going to touch your breasts or your vagina. We're not going to make love."

"But isn't making love the point?"

"Yes. But not this morning. This morning we're starting over. We're just going to touch."

"This is like something I saw in a sex-therapy book. Was this part of your training?"

I said it was and caressed her temples, brushed my hands across her forehead, then down along her cheeks.

"I don't think I want to do this."

"Why not?"

"It's part of your job."

"Well, pretend we're a married couple."

"Right."

"Just pretend. And we're not sleeping together anymore. It's not working out, and we blame each other for the bad sex. We go to a therapist. This is one of the things she tells us to do. It's a way of getting to know the other's body."

"Have you done this with other clients?"

"You're not another client anymore. And yes, I have."

"And they did it to you?"

"Sometimes."

"Why?"

"Sometimes for fun. And with three clients, it was because they thought they didn't like sex."

The muscles in her back became tense. She had told Sauro, during their last months together, that she didn't like sex.

"Honey," I said, trying out the word I'd never used before, "it really cuts down on our options if you don't want to do things that I did as part of my job. But if you prefer, we could always go celibate."

She said nothing, then, whispering, "I like that."

"This?" I said, and once again brushed fingertips across collarbone. "Or the idea of going celibate."

She patted my hand. "This. Now, how about a little lower, getting the skin right under the bone."

"You're a sensualist in disguise."

"Will you want me to do this to you?"

"If we're starting over, yes."

"What will be different about me doing this with you now and me doing this with you a week ago?"

"A week ago I would have made sure that I liked about every other new touch."

"Would you really know which ones you liked, which ones you didn't?"

"A touch is a touch," I said. "If you expect your clients to be sensitive to your needs, then you're expecting too much."

"Are you expecting me to be sensitive to your needs?"

"I don't know. The lower your expectations, the less room for disappointment."

"I like that," she said and guided my hand over her thigh. "But I don't like what you just said. Hope is what drives us forward, what makes it possible for us to work for something better."

I wanted to remind her what sort of things happened when hopes were dashed. "My being here is a sign of hope, isn't it?"

"Yes." She sounded pleased with the idea. "Yes. It is."

I caressed her knees, and it tickled her.

"Rod? When I do this with you, will you be honest?"

"Yes," I said.

"Are you really learning anything by doing this with me?"

"Yes. I'm touching you for the first time. I'm not seducing you. I'm getting to know what you like when you're touched, when we're not touching just to arouse."

"But arousal can be nice." She placed my hand in an appropriate spot.

"Later," I said, and moved my hands to her ribs. "For now, touching is the thing."

The morning passed in touching. Outside the window, sunlight brought out the best of colors: the brown grays of the tree trunks, the greens of new leaves. We switched positions, and Anna found it easier if I lay down and she sat between my legs, our splayed legs crossing over each other. I closed my eyes and felt her touches carefully, letting touches go by without comment rather than preferring almost every other one, informing her which touches I liked, which ones were nice when done once or twice and became tickles if done too often, which ones could go on forever. I opened my eyes several times, and Anna looked as if she were concentrating, trying hard to remember what I liked, what I didn't.

After lunch we made love. My skin was so sensitized that the touching was almost painful. We napped afterwards for the longest time, the champagne working its way through our bloodstreams. We woke and touched, and each brought the other to a climax.

We showered together, enjoyed the play of soap against skin, giggled, dried each other off, and came downstairs with cheeks flushed red. Sophie was home, and the way she carried her solitary figure made me feel guilty.

We stood in the kitchen, Anna and Sophie with wine, me with beer, while Sophie grilled some sort of crab-and-chicken dish. At the dinner table, all of us drinking wine, Anna and I both high from our day's consumption of alcohol, we became silly, and Anna had me repeat all sorts of jokes that I'd told her and Anna kept asking Sophie what sort of impression she thought I'd make on Anna's father if James Baxter were to meet me without knowing my choice of trade, and she told Sophie how if every day was as good as today, we'd probably skip the trip to Boston, but we'd be sure to visit Rod's parents, plural and happy, in San Antonio.

It would have been easy to go with the flow of Anna's energy and Sophie's mannered, delighted responses, to do everything possible to maintain the flushed look on Anna's cheeks, the brilliance in her eyes. But then we wouldn't have really started over.

"My parents don't live in San Antonio," I said.

Anna's face went blank. The good feeling couldn't have lasted an entire day. "What?"

"My mother and my brother live near Traverse City, up in Michigan."

Sophie eyed me carefully.

"What about your father?" Anna asked. Her voice was so soft that I barely heard her.

"He's dead."

"How?" she asked, as if it had just happened.

"He killed himself. When I was still in high school."

Anna said nothing. She stared toward me, but didn't see me.

"Anna?" Sophie said.

"I'm sorry," I said. "I thought we were starting over."

"And your grandmother?" she asked, remembering the story I'd told her.

"My mother's parents died in a shuttle crash. My other grandfather died of cancer. My grandmother won't have anything to do with me. She lives in California and sends my mother and my brother a Christmas card every year."

"Is there anything you told me that was true?"

"Maybe the jokes," I said.

"Today was the joke." She said to Sophie, "I'm going to excuse myself before I say something really nasty."

I stared at my plate of food. I had seen footage of Sauro calling after her; I knew the gesture was useless. I listened to her dramatically loud footsteps as they curved up the stairs, lost them as they walked down the hallway, heard them again as they paced across the floor above the dining room.

I waited for Sophie to offer some sort of commentary. She sipped her wine and gauged my reactions.

"She's not my client anymore," I said, as if that would explain everything.

"I take it Anna thought your parents lived in San Antonio, that they were happily married, and that they had finally accepted your career choice."

"Something like that."

"Sounds like something from the holovision. Maybe you missed your calling, my sweet little prick. Maybe you should have been a scriptwriter."

"She didn't hire me to tell her the truth." I said, then said nothing for a while. "Do you think I should leave?"

"That's your decision."

I looked at her. She hired me the morning after I'd turned down her cousin's offer. "Why are you doing this?"

"Anna heard about you through a friend of hers. The friend liked your performance, so to speak. Anna called me in tears. She was certain that if you were given a month to think about it, you'd take the easy way out."

"You mean, not see her."

Sophie nodded. "Anna's only dumb or naive when she wants to be. She's spent a lot of time with you. Something special had to shine through your performance. No actor plays a role without presenting a true aspect of themselves to the world. You feel something for Anna, but you haven't made a key decision."

"I'm here. Isn't that a decision?"

"It's not the key decision. You have to decide if Anna's worth the risk. Or if there's another reason you're here."

I thought about her cousin, about Lang. "What do you mean?"

"If you stay with Anna, there are going to be people that say you did it for yourself, that you were attracted by her money, that you were tired of risking hives. I'm not one of those people, mind you. I feel like I can pick up on someone's character pretty quickly, and I think your intent is sincere and that you're as confused as Anna is. I'd really like to help the two of you out and—" She patted my hand, and offered me her Most Beautiful Woman in the World mask—"if that doesn't work out, you could always chase after me."

I headed upstairs after the wine was finished. Sophie said she had to review her lines alone, no distractions or temptations. The guest room was dark, and I fumbled my way over to the guest beds. I waited until my eyes adjusted to the dark. I could make out Anna's body in one of the beds. She was breathing quietly. I touched her cheek, and she didn't respond. I considered leaving and found that I didn't want to. I considered sliding into bed next to her, but I assumed that she wanted the space to herself, that she didn't want me that close, not right now. It was as if all our words and touches today had been for nothing. I undressed and got into the other bed. The sheets were cool to the touch.

38

THE SHARP PULSES from Anna's tiny clock–crystal player almost shot me out of bed. It had been right next to my ear. I reached over, shut it off, turned back to curl up with an edge-of-sleep dream of Anna, and found, of course, that she wasn't there. The vague, almost unfamiliar, sound of rain falling and lightly tapping the ground, and the muted gray light that slipped in around the edges of the drawn shades, brought back old memories. I heard the rustle of bedclothes. I turned over to watch Anna, naked, rise from the other bed. Except for the movement of hip, the curve of breast, the softened features of the face, Anna had been built all wrong: the shoulders a touch too wide, the torso too straight, the thighs too thick. But the face, the curve, the movement, and something indefinable were more than enough, and I wanted her to fill in the blanks of my edge-of-sleep dream. She walked over to the bureau and searched through the drawers for underwear and bra.

"Where are you going?" I asked, still drowsy.

"To work."

"Why don't you come here for a little bit?"

"You weren't so interested in me last night."

"I thought you were asleep."

"It took you long enough to get up here. I felt that the message was pretty clear."

"Let me make it up to you."

"I'll be late for work."

"It's not as if they'll fire you."

"I like to carry my own weight. I don't like to act as if my aunt got me that job." She walked over to the closet and searched through it for a choice of clothes. She pulled a gray skirt from a hanger and set it down on a nearby armchair.

"How about a kiss, at least?"

She walked over and touched closed lips to mine, then stepped back to the bureau to slip into underpants, skirt, bra. She brushed her hair. "I'll be back around six," she said.

I measured out my words, knowing that she would record them, interpret them, prepare them for reediting and replay. "I'll be here," I said.

"And if we sleep in separate beds?"

It had been her test for Sauro, in the months before he died: do you still want me without the sex? Maybe now it was delivered with a different emphasis. "I want to be with you," I said.

She slipped on a white blouse and laced her shepherd shoes. She went into the bathroom to brush her teeth and came back to rub moisturizer into her skin. "What are you going to do today?" she asked as she removed from the bureau and placed in a purse—which I'd never seen before—her wallet, Chap Stick, a tiny bottle of moisturizer, a small bottle of aspirin, various papers, a brush, pens and pencils.

"I don't know. Work out. Have lunch with Harry."

"You can read the book I gave you."

"I finished it. It was okay."

"Are you going to read Sophie's file?"

"Yeah," I said. "They'll want a progress report. I'll have to make up something."

She held her body stiff and looked away from me and at the drawn shades. "You can fuck her if you want. I'd hate to see you lose your job."

Knowing a good exit line when she heard one, Anna headed for the guest-room door. I threw back the covers, tried to reach her in a few long strides, but ended up hopping after stubbing my toe on the bedpost. Anna couldn't help but smile.

It deflated the seriousness of my words: "Anna, I'm here, aren't I?"

"Yes, you are." She tried to say it playfully, but there was a formality in the way she stood distant from me. "And if you're not going to sleep with Sophie, you better take a shower and get dressed." She heard the coolness in her voice and tried to soften it. She lightly touched my penis. "Anyway, Sophie was imagining something impossibly large."

With her second exit line, she was gone.

The bathroom was porcelain, tile, and peeling wallpaper. It looked as if someone might have considered modernizing it two decades before and had settled on just replacing the shower head. The water was hot, and I liked the way it pounded my back, easing out the tensions. I wanted to stay in there forever, but knew I couldn't. There were no solar panels on the roof.

I stood in the dining room. The large window offered a view of the backyard; I could see the bench where Stuart and I had talked two weeks ago. Water glistened, and everything seemed greener against the morning's gray. There were no monitors here. I could ask Sophie anything I wanted, and she could tell me exactly what I wanted to hear in such a way that I'd believe her, even if it was only a performance and she really was connected with her cousin's schemes.

Sophie was in the kitchen, frying eggs on the electric stove. She was wearing a skirt and a loose-fitting blouse. Her hair was tied back in a ponytail. "How do you want them, dear heart?"

"I don't know. I haven't had fried eggs in a long time."

"Well, then, you get them sunny side up. The yoke always breaks when I flip them over." She turned the stove off, tilted the frying pan, and the eggs slid onto a plate. "Get yourself some juice or some milk out of the fridge. Just bring the bottle to the breakfast table."

The refrigerator was packed solid with food. Eggs, bottles of milk, bottles of juice, packages of meat, fruit, bread, sticks of butter. I wondered what it all had cost.

There was enough to feed the entire Cleaning Room at lunch hour.

"Is there some sort of animal in there?" asked Sophie.

I grabbed a bottle of juice and closed the door. "No," I replied. "There's just more food than I've seen in a while."

"Wouldn't want you and Anna to go hungry. Now come sit down and eat your breakfast."

I brought the juice with me to the wooden breakfast table. Sophie had set my plate atop a cloth place mat. Alongside was a cloth napkin and silver knife and fork. The salt and pepper shakers were carved wood figures of, I discovered later, Don Quixote and Sancho Panza. Through the breakfast-room window I could see the driveway, still stained with mulch that hadn't been raked up the previous fall. Rain made brief crystalline kisses upon the puddles.

Sophie sat down in the chair closest to mine. She opened the bottle, leaned over, her breasts pressing against the table, and poured the juice into a glass. I took a sip. The juice was bitter. "What sort of juice is this?"

"Oh, Rod," she said, raising her hands to her lips to hide a slight smile. "I'm so sorry. Anna told me you only liked plain juice, but I only got one bottle. You must have consumed it all yesterday."

"What's this, then?"

"Orange juice," she said. "Drink it. You'll get used to it."

"Maybe."

"There's a lot of maybe's in this house. Like maybe did you make up for your slip of the tongue last night?"

"I told the truth," I said.

"I know. A slip of the tongue. So, did you guys work things out?"

At Personal Services I fed Tricky Dick the sensory information from the implants, logging in Saturday night's one sexual encounter and Sunday afternoon's two at different hours to correspond with times I knew Sophie had been in the house. I hadn't recorded my Sunday-morning session with Anna.

Marie was happy with the data, told me to keep up the

good work. The staff meeting was short. Fred told us he'd talked to the police and there was nothing new on the Dorothy Souto murder.

Before lunch I worked out in the gym with Cindy, Aggie, and Henry. Aggie was cool. "You didn't tell me you got an indefinite."

"Must have been embarrassed," said Cindy.

"Real embarrassed," said Aggie. "He used to tell us he'd never work the Heights."

"Hey," said Henry, "I'd go."

"Someone's gotta take you first," said Aggie.

"Do you like her?" asked Cindy.

"She's nice enough. And works all day. It's less work than doing shifts."

"Work less, get paid more," said Aggie. "It don't seem honest. But mark my words, CT, someday one of these indefinites is going to have a reforming streak in her, and you'll be married off before you know it."

After lunch I almost made it out of the Cleaning Room before I remembered. Even though Anna Baxter and I, officially, no longer saw each other, Edward Lang still expected to see me this afternoon.

Lang was exhausted. The pouches under his eyes were dark, his cheeks sagged like an old man's, and his movements, when he got up from behind the desk to shake my hand, were slow. I wondered if it was due to his father's death. When Pilar was out of earshot, he offered to pour a little Spanish brandy into my coffee. He poured some into his, then mine.

"I've asked you in today for a debriefing. First, I'd like to go over the ASD event you attended on May tenth.

"I'm afraid," he said, "that I have to ask you to look at some pictures. Fortunately, they're a little less grisly than the ones Detective Ohls showed you last week." I must have looked relieved because he said, "I knew you'd appreciate that. We even have hardcopies."

He handed me a bound set of photos. Each one had a number in the corner. I flipped through them.

"Do you recognize any of them?"

"I've seen a bunch of these people in Anna's file."

"How about at the party?"

I hesitated. So far I had done a good job of telling both Lang and Stuart Greenspan absolutely nothing.

"We know," said Lang, "that roughly half of those people were there, just from monitors on Fairmount. What we need to know is who spoke with you."

I had never given Pilar my bancard; they had never paid me one red dollar. To refuse would imply that I had taken some political stand. And what if it was the UHL who had tortured Dorothy Souto?

The photos was monitor-angle views of various faces. The photos were numbered. I read off the number, stated the name given to me at the party, and listed the subject of our conversation. He was particularly interested in pudgy Timothy Molina's tirade against my voting habits.

"You know, Molina has applied for a permit to hold an evening rally in Public Square on May thirty-first. It will be a Memorial Day commemoration for those who have died in the camps."

"No one told me," I said.

"Back to the tirade: what was the reaction of Molina's—spouse?"

"Bill O'Brien tried to calm him down, that's all."

The second-to-last picture was of Sophie Greenspan. Lang wanted to know what Sophie Greenspan had talked about, and he seemed surprised when I told him that she didn't seem all that political.

"That's interesting. Sophie Greenspan is someone I'd like to keep an eye on."

I didn't say anything.

"She's admirable in that she's a one-woman paper reduction act; there's very little documentation on her, except for her work in the theater. She directed a controversial play in New Hampshire. It had been written by a Close the Camps activist. Anna played the lead. Sophie never paid any personal money to ASD, but Sauro Contini paid for her membership. She did volunteer work for ASD causes that weren't camp related. Last June she circulated an antimonitoring petition."

"She sounds dangerous," I said.

Lang shook his head like he had heard the joke before. "Not dangerous. Just suspicious. Her cousin is a lawyer and has done a lot of ASD work for minimal remuneration. And that petition could have been an ingenuous way to set up contacts. Five young signatories had no previous political connection, and they ended up joining ASD. Two of them joined the support groups that aided the rioters at Camp Seven."

I shrugged. "I don't know anything about a petition."

"Interesting," he said, and let me sit for a while with the word. "Now," he said, and flipped to the last photo, "how about her cousin, Stuart Greenspan?"

I don't think I gave him the benefit of a reaction. "He drove us to the lecture, and we talked once or twice at the party."

"About what?"

I told him about how Euclid used to be called Millionaires' Row and how people there had moved out to big houses on Shaker Boulevard and Fairmount when the country club had developed.

"Interesting," said Lang in a tone that implied it wasn't. "Did he talk much about politics?"

I tried to look as if I were recalling Greenspan's exact words, but I was considering what to say. If Lang had an informer there, he knew that I had taken a stroll outside with Greenspan. If the place had been bugged, then Lang had heard what we said. "Nothing special," I said. "Just the usual crap about my high-risk profession."

"Did he mention the UHL or the Black Out?"

"He said he thought the Black Out was a mistake."

"A mistake. Why?"

"He thought it did too much damage and turned people against the UHL."

"Interesting. I wonder what he thought of the riots at Camp Seven. That did too much damage, and it turned people against the ASD, but he led a group of one hundred Clevelanders there."

I remembered watching the National Guard shoot down people running from the camp, the clouds of old-style tear gas enveloping protesters. I couldn't remember anyone thinking it was ASD's fault.

"Okay," he said, taking the book of photos from me, "I think that's all for now. You have a good memory. You know, the FBI could use people with a talent like that. Anyway, you can have your Monday afternoons back. You're off the hook for a while. But we'd appreciate it if you'd keep an eye out for us. I'm sure you'll see Anna every now and then, and maybe Sophie Greenspan's cousin. Just listen, see if you overhear anything. If you do, give a call. We'll keep paying you the same stipend, for your trouble, until our investigation's closed."

"What should I say if Detective Ohls asks me anything about your investigation?"

"Detective Ohls has been assured that you're not a material witness, so I don't think you'll be hearing from him. The police are pretty good at laying off when they're told that national security is at stake." That and the money were two wonderful carrots; I began to wonder where the stick was.

He stood up, took my hand, and smiled. "Pilar will call you if we need to see you again."

"Fine."

"And when you figure out why this Souto woman called herself Goldilocks, give us a call."

"Of course," I said.

Back in the apartment I sat in front of Albert Einstein. The crystals I'd copied from Anna's file were arrayed in front of me in an orderly row. I could pick up any one, insert it, and take a look at whatever footage I wanted. I could look at it again and again until maybe I would know for sure whether Anna was CIA or UHL. Or both. But I wanted her to be innocent.

Every crystal from Anna's file reminded me of the crystals that Lang must have, the amount of footage he had to have trusted Adolf to analyze or other people to examine because there would be just too much of it. All afternoon I kept thinking and rethinking: how much did Lang really know? and what was he expecting me to do?

39

I MET SOPHIE where she'd dropped me off that morning, at the playhouse. She gave me a tour of the theater: the back rooms, the stages, the offices. She introduced me to actors and techs who were still around and to her director, and I tried to look energetic and dedicated. This was the wrong crowd, and no one was too impressed. The techs did a better job than the actors of hiding their first impressions.

Afterward Sophie drove us to the Cedar-Fairmount shopping center and led me to the florists. "Pick out something nice for me," she told me and the monitors. Sophie hugged my arm and looked enamored of me while the salesclerk showed me around, my mind trying to connect the names of different flowers with the kind that Anna said she preferred to the yellow carnations that Sauro had bought her when they first fell in love. Sophie touched my elbow. "I'd just love a small bouquet of those yellow roses over there."

Yellow roses: what Sauro should have given her, if he could have afforded them.

———

Anna wasn't home to receive the flowers, even though the gallery had closed at five. At seven Sophie started dinner and lectured me on Shakespeare while I kept my eye on the kitchen's old-fashioned clock, watching the second hand twirl much too slowly. Had somebody kept an eye on the clock three Saturday nights ago, anxious for Dorothy Souto to return home? I called Anna's apartment twice, and there was no answer.

"Don't worry," said Sophie. "She's just testing your resolve."

After dinner Anna bounded in, cheeks flushed, shouting out an enthusiastic, "Hi, guys!" as if this was when we were expecting her.

"You shouldn't come home so late," Sophie said after giving her a hug. "Lover boy here's been worried."

"You have?" Anna gave me her delighted chipmunk smile. Her eyes lit up. And she gave me a hug, and a kiss. She gave me another when she saw the yellow roses.

Sophie and I drank brandy while Anna ate a warmed-over supper. I listened to the rhythms of Sophie and Anna's back and forth, the natural understanding they had for each other, and I wondered: if sex wasn't a need, would I have been needed here at all?

Nothing was mentioned about the previous night; Anna and I went up to the guest bedroom arm in arm. She came out of the bathroom wearing the same skirt and blouse. I was sitting on the edge of the bed I'd slept on last night; she sat down on the other.

"Can I ask you something?"

"Sure."

She said nothing.

I considered letting it go at that. "You want to ask me about my father."

"Sort of. I wanted to ask why you didn't tell me. Why you told me all that stuff about San Antonio."

"It sounds nicer. After Sauro's death you didn't want to hear about my father's."

"Maybe I did."

"No one wants to hear sob stories from their companion."

"I didn't expect you to be perfect."

"Okay. But I've told you now. I've wiped the slate clean."

"There were a lot of stories."

"I haven't talked to anybody about it in years. I've put

it behind me. We're here together," I said. "Isn't that enough?"

"Sometimes I wonder."

"Wonder what?"

The internal battle went on behind her eyes, as if she were struggling to decide which of many questions she was going to ask. "If being together is enough. I thought I knew you."

"You do know me. You know how I act. You know what political opinions I have. You know what kind of jokes I tell." I threw my hands up in the air. "You've seen me drunk, sick, and depressed."

"I started a file on you." She was looking at her fingernails. She was picking at the cuticles of her index nail and soon ripped it away from the rest. "I went to the library and spent a lot of money putting out a name search, looking for all the info that was considered public knowledge."

"Okay. So you know my dad was a math teacher at Heights High and he was survived by wife Lisa and sons Roderick and Arthur. You know I was arrested twice for private soliciting."

"Four times," she whispered. She must have looked it up. Juvenile offenses are not recorded as public knowledge until the third repeat offense.

"You know the third time I had all the privileges at Fair Haven School for Troubled Children taken away, and the fourth time I was eighteen and sentenced to thirty days in drug rehab and given over to Personal Services for training."

"I also went through Personal Services' public catalog for all the years you were there. I even called up some of the ad footage. I even looked at some of the specialty stuff." She made specialty sound like a euphemism for disgusting.

"So, now you know."

"Do you tell this stuff to anyone?"

"Some friends at Fair Haven knew. The psych people at Personal Services—they handled my rehab. My first trainer, I told her a lot of it."

She wrinkled her nose. "Your trainer. You mean the person who taught you how to fuck?"

"Oh, I knew how to fuck. Just not well enough to charge for it."

She looked away, as if ignoring the whole issue. "And your friends who I met, they don't know?"

I shook my head.

"You're still not telling me stuff. You got some awards as a student at Roxboro Junior High. You were top of your class in eighth grade. I know what sort of kid ends up at Fair Haven."

"Sort? What sort?"

"I didn't mean it that way."

"You're still your daddy's girl. There's the sort of people who sell their bodies. There's the sort of people who end up at Fair Haven. There's the sort of people who go after women with trust funds."

"Are there not?"

"No. There are not. My father was a teacher, just like yours. If your father hadn't gone on to make it big, you'd have grown up in a house just like mine."

"But my father wasn't the type of person . . ."

"I know. Your father had character. *Time* magazine called him Mr. Morality. I sell myself. I act nice for money. I fuck nice for money. But I don't build camps with government money and then tell people how to go about being moral. I don't tell people it's their fault that some virus got hold of them. Viruses don't think. They don't have morals."

"Some people don't, either."

"Am I one of them?"

Anna didn't answer.

"If you want," I said, "I can leave."

"I didn't want this kind of conversation."

"What kind did you want, then?"

"I want to know who you are. So when you and I are going out together and people talk about us behind our backs, I'll know there's nothing they can say that I don't already know because you've already told it to me."

"You think we'll last that long?"

"Not at this rate."

"Why be with me?" My voice came out as a whisper.

"Because you're not selfish. Because you're thoughtful. Because you seem decent and honorable and you don't make a big deal about being decent and honorable. I always figured some . . . things . . . had happened in your life."

"Why do you want to know those things?"

"Because they're real."

"I'm not seeking salvation. I'm not here for you to make me into a better person."

"I know." That's all she said for the longest while. Then, "My father liked to censor things, too, you know."

I shook my head; I didn't understand.

"He paid someone a lot to program our computer so we wouldn't be able to read any newspaper articles or see any holo coverage of something violent or horrible. Coverage about his business was also unavailable. He and Mom had these passwords so they could watch or read what they wanted once we were in bed. He didn't want us to know how horrible the world could be; he wanted us to feel safe. At the same time Mom always told us not to talk to strangers. If we knew anything at all, it was because at school they didn't protect you as much. At sixteen my father gave me the passwords in exchange for my promise that I wouldn't watch the news in front of my sisters. I grew up pretty naive and trusting. In college I was always surprised at how cruel people could be."

"I don't get the point."

"You're censoring, too. You are protecting yourself and you're protecting me. Either way, it's not much of a compliment."

"Will you go down and get me something to drink?"

"Dark rum?"

I nodded.

She came back with two glasses with ice and poured the rum. She didn't bring the lime. She sat down on the edge of her bed, reached out her arm, and held my hand. She kept her eyes on mine while I sipped the rum. I kept drinking, forming words in my mind, and felt the warmth of her hand. I drank until her hand on mine seemed sort of silly. It shouldn't have been that big a deal to tell her. They had told me over and over that it could have happened to anyone.

So I told her. I stared out the windows while watching

her out of the corner of my eye, and I told her. She never once took her eyes off me.

I was fifteen. I walked a few blocks from home to the grocery to get some milk for dinner. All around the store on Coventry were new foundations, pylons, metal girders for the mini-Construct that was going up in fits and starts. On my way home a white guy grabbed me by the arm and pulled me into the hollow of a construction site. He put a knife to my throat, so I let him. I went home. I could smell him, and I could smell the lubricant he'd used, but no one else did. They yelled at me for being late and missing dinner and not having the milk. I locked myself in the bathroom and took the longest shower of my life. I had expected them to figure it out. There was no way I could tell them that I didn't fight or scream. There had to have been something wrong with me, or else that guy would have chosen somebody else.

No one figured it out.

Everything fell apart after that.

Anna took the drink out of my hand and placed it on the bedside table. She tried to sit next to me, but I didn't move. She placed her arm around my shoulder. I let my head lean against hers.

"There's more," I said.

"Later."

We sat like that for I don't know how long. I don't remember getting undressed and getting into bed.

The next morning's brightness flooded in around the drawn shades, separating us from last night's confession. Anna's body was warm against mine, her fingertips tracing lines across my body. She smiled, revealing smooth, white, perfected teeth. Eyes sparkled. I was afraid to speak. I touched her cheek, and she tilted her head foward to kiss my hand. My palm slid past her cheek, along her hair, and with easy pressure brought her head closer to mine.

Very slowly, following the ritual prescribed by films and holovision, she lowered her half-open lips onto mine. Her hand squeezed my penis with the same gentle firmness that she had squeezed my hand last night. We kissed, and she closed her eyes. She looked shy, demure. I traced my own lines across her cheeks and her chin. We rearranged our bodies, kissed more, and my fingers adorned her face, then her breasts. From some other reality my penis stretched forward and demanded attention, release. The ritual continued, and we shifted bodies, shifted sheets, blankets, bedspread.

Anna opened her mouth several times to say something. I could see the need in her face, her desire to say the words and name the moment. She bit her lower lip, almost spoke, then kissed me to hide the intent. She looked at me then, as if waiting for some response to the silence.

I heard the words in my own head. But she had been the first to feel them, and she should be the first to say them. Instead I did, my voice hoarse, the words without cadence: "I think I'm in love with you."

"You are?" My mind was so clouded that I barely heard what must have been doubt in her voice. "Oh, God . . ."

Her arms tightened around my back, and she embraced me as if she were trying to pull my entire body into hers. Frightened by her intensity, I pushed myself onto my elbows and caressed her cheek. It was damp.

"You're crying," I said.

"I haven't felt this warm in so long."

"I love you," I said.

"I love you, too. Oh, God, how I love you."

Her arms drew me back to her, and I kissed her tears, knowing from previous footage how the gesture would move her. Sensing the moment, I repositioned legs and hips, and we held each other in the measured silence. She let hips slide downward, then up, and I pressed forward, matching rhythm. Thighs wrapped around thighs anchored motion into place, chest pressed against breasts, lips and tongues touched. Each back and forth, each rub of skin against skin, foreshadowing the slap of loin against loin, carried us toward our separate moments. She cried out for me to come with her as she thrust harder against me, and when her orgasm shuddered through her along with my release, she gripped me tightly.

"We're one," she whispered loudly. "We're together. We're one."

And in that one quick instant, when I was part of her and she not part of me, I felt lonelier than I ever had in my life.

40

THE NEXT MORNING Anna wrapped herself tightly around me and said she didn't want to get up. I suggested she call in sick, and she hesitated before smiling, then nodding. The windows were open, and we could hear the sounds of the landscapers at work: the whir of rotary blades, the snip of shears, the rustling of canvas dragged across the grass, the calling of voices. The smell of cut grass enveloped the room, and we made love.

"Tell me about your dad."

"I thought we were having a good time."

"What was he like? Until . . . you know . . . was he a pretty good father?"

"Yeah. Of course."

"Well, what made him a good father?"

If the therapists had ever asked me that, I couldn't remember. It took a long time to describe him; I had to remember him first.

"I don't see how you could have stood it in ASD. Your father was one of their prime enemies."

"No. My father's business was."

"And everybody there kept the two separate, right?"

"Well, not exactly. They kept them separate when I was around. But, you know, every now and then I'd walk into a room and people would stop talking."

"Did that make you feel like you had to prove yourself?"

"Sure. I wanted to all the time."

"You could have joined the terrorists."

She shook her head. "Let's talk about something else. Or do something else." Her eyes brightened.

"*Does that* feel good?"

"_____"

"I'll take that for a yes. What if I do this?"

"Mmmm."

"That last one sounded feigned. Now keep quiet. No more prepackaged sounds. We're going to get to the real you. How about that little twist?"

"Ow."

"*Oh, God,* that feels good. Oh, God, how I love you."

We ate lunch—a cheese-and-garlic omelet—on the back patio. The landscapers were gone, and the yard had a certain elegance to it. The buds—blue, pink, white outlined by brown—spread out and laced the bushes.

"Do you think we can say it out here?" she asked.

"What do you mean?"

"We only seem to say it when we're coming."

"It's a nice time to say it."

"But it's like we say it to make things more exciting."

"You're the second person I've ever said it to. Outside of family that is."

"Can't you say it here?"

"Can you?"

"That's not fair."

"I love you, Anna."

"I love you, too."

"Easy for you to say."

"*Do you want* to be on top or bottom?"

"What about the neighbors?"

"You're the last person I'd expect to see embarrassed."

"I'm just naturally shy."

"There's lots of bushes. No one will see us."
She was wrong; Sophie came home early.

"*How did you* end up going from Heights High to Fair Haven?"

"It's a long story."

"I'm not going anywhere."

I told her about the failing grades. I saw a whole batch of sympathetic teachers, even more sympathetic counselors. They all asked what happened: it was like I'd gone from an A student to a D student overnight. They all asked if everything was okay at home. They all asked if it would easier if I studied in a school different from the one where my father taught. They all asked the same questions; I gave them all different answers. A second fight, when I broke a kid's arm, got me suspended indefinitely. I didn't tell Anna about the petty thefts or the vandalism they never caught me for.

I had recorded two of the sexual encounters. Wednesday morning I logged one at 8 hours, before Sophie had left the house, and the other at 22 hours, the hour she'd told friends that she stopped going over lines in order to relax before bed.

Anna left work early that afternoon. "I can't do this too often. Joan asked me who was responsible for the bags under my eyes."

"You can take a nap."

"You kidding? I haven't had this much fun losing sleep in ages."

"It's not like we haven't done this before."

"We weren't in love before."

"*Do you tell* Joan that you're sleeping with someone?"

"Why?"

"Just curious."

"I'll bet you you're just scared because the gallery is monitored."

"That's not it," I lied.

"Well, just to make you happy, I tell her that I'm not

with anyone. But she thinks my cheeks are too flushed in the morning for that to be true."

"Has Joan always taken a personal interest in your sex life?"

"Only in a gossipy sort of way."

"Sounds fun."

"Well, you should be thankful."

"Huh?"

"When I was really down, Joan sort of hinted that hiring one of you guys might be a fun way to get over my blues."

"Seriously?"

"Well, partly. I don't think she ever thought I'd actually take her advice."

Over dinner Sophie suggested that I stick around in the morning and we could go over *Romeo and Juliet* together. "That way you'll appreciate my stunning performance," she said. Anna looked away when I agreed to stay.

"*What do you* tell your bosses about you and Sophie?"

"I tell them things are going well."

"Do they ask you what you do with her? With Sophie, I mean."

"Sure. I log in what Sophie and I do."

"Do you say you sleep with her?"

"Yeah. I log in how many sexual encounters we have. The numbers are a bit exaggerated."

"I'd hope so. But about these numbers . . . do you and Sophie make love as often as you and I do?"

"No. She's too busy."

After Sophie and I spent hours going over the play, I took the RTA downtown and logged in two sexual encounters for the morning. Marie was happy with the results. She told me there was a late-night party after next Thursday's preview of the play and that she'd be attending it with her fiancé; she looked forward to seeing me there. "A party like this will be a test of all your social skills. I'm sure you'll come through with flying colors."

I told her I was sure I would. I didn't tell her that

Sophie had promised to take Anna to the party and that I'd have the evening off.

"Now," I said at dinner, "why is it necessary that they die?"

"They love each other," said Anna. "They don't want to be with anyone else."

"It's been just a few days. They could be *wrong*."

"They're fourteen years old," said Sophie. "They're carried away."

"You mean," said Anna, "it can't happen after you're fourteen?"

"Maybe," said Sophie.

"People fall in love more than once," I said.

"Not true love," said Anna. "That's only once."

"Do you kill yourself for true love?" I asked.

"That's not love," said Sophie. "That's honor."

"And aren't the two related?" asked Anna.

"No. They're different. Very different."

"What's true love, Anna?"

"I don't know."

"What do you think it is?"

"I really don't know. I guess it's like an ideal, something you aim for."

"If I was your true love, what would you do?"

"I'm not sure that's a fair question."

"Am I the person you love until you find your true love?"

"No."

"Is it possible that I'm your true love?"

"Can I ask you the same question?"

"Yeah. It is very possible that you're my true love. I fell in love once before when I was sixteen and didn't know any better. I don't use the word lightly."

Her hand touched my cheek. "If you were my true love, I'd stop hiding parts of myself away from you. I'd take you around everywhere with me and never be ashamed of your career. I'd reconcile myself with my parents. I'd find something I want to do with my life so we could afford, well, you know . . ." Her lips were soft against mine. "And, Rod dearest, if you were my true love, you'd stop hiding too. You'd reconcile yourself with your family. And you'd find yourself a new career."

"You make them sound like wedding vows."

"I'm not talking about marriage. I'm talking about purifying the heart. About giving up things so you can be with someone. If this is really true love, if it really is, then I'd give up anything to stay with you."

Friday morning my blood was tested. In my mailbox was a message from Harry and Kevin asking if I was lost. They included a map to the Admiral of the Port.

"*Love is context,* not content."

"You sound like Sauro. What does that mean?"

"I don't know. It's just the things we talk about, the things we do seem to mean more."

"I'd hope so."

"I'm not making myself clear. There's so much we don't do. Sexually, I mean. And it's not important. It's just gymnastics. The pleasure's different."

"You mean that things feel better when you care about the person you're screwing?"

"I guess. I thought it was a little more profound than that. There's something selfish about sex, but at the same time, you're being incredibly altruistic, you enjoy giving pleasure, even thought there's a part of you worrying about yourself."

"Maybe we should try that theory out with some of the gymnastics."

"*Did you do* a lot of experimentation with Susie Sundai?"

"Sure. Some. Mostly the obvious stuff."

"What happened to her?"

"I don't know. I guess she made it out of Fair Haven."

"What about the two of you, you know, during Fair Haven?"

"Fair Haven wasn't a good place for things like that to happen. The guards—the social workers who lived with us—read other peoples' books about what Freud said. One guard told a friend of mine that he kept trying to commit suicide because of his toilet training. We all learned, if we didn't know already, how to be pretty self-destructive. I guess that was their cure: force us to the bottom so we had to come up."

"Is that why you charged someone for sex?"

"Yeah. It was a middle-aged woman. She had looked pretty lonely. She was a cop."

"There were other women that you charged?"

"Yeah. And other cops. At the end, there was always a cop."

"And that's how you ended up at Personal Services?"

"Yeah." I didn't tell her the first person I ever charged was Susie Sundai. She didn't notice—or she didn't mention—the scar on my left wrist, so I didn't tell her about the razor blade and passing out because I'd done it wrong. And how one of the guards had heard me keel over.

"You know, Stuart told me about your family's friendship with Edward Lang."

"Stuart would. Ed Lang and his wife are the kind of friends you call aunt and uncle—everybody in ASD hated that I called this guy Uncle Ed."

"Why?"

"He was in the army in Spain. He became a personal friend of the Spanish president, so everybody thought he was CIA. You know, like the evil CIA that murders and tortures the Enemies of Democracy. It gets sort of silly."

"Do you see him much now that he's in Cleveland?"

"Some."

"Do politics come between you two?"

"No. Uncle Ed's not like that at all. He talks to you like you have a right to your opinion, but he'd sure like to change your mind. It was exciting when I was a girl—he'd tell all these war stories about the people he knew and stuff. It sounds sort of silly now."

"You sound disappointed."

"Maybe I am. I tend to be really idealistic, and then I get disappointed, because nothing is what you hoped for. Your loving father turns out to be a builder of concentration camps. Your lover is a poet but hardly spends anytime writing poetry. You get the picture."

"Did ASD disappoint you the same way?"

"Yeah, I guess."
"Will I disappoint you . . . one of these days?"
"Not if I can help it."

"*Do you know* why your dad did what he did?"
"Do *you* know why yours did?"
"Be fair."
"I'm sorry. My father died of too much failure."
"I don't get what you mean."
"Well, he graduated magna suma rexus whateverelseus cum laude from grad school, got hired Ivy League and was never able to turn his dissertation into a book. . . ." I tried to explain the best I could—because I heard it second-hand, from my father's best friend who had had one too many at the reception following the funeral—about how my father was working on number theory and social history and how he lost faith in numbers and how lack of publication meant lack of tenure, and how he ended up first at a bank, then, hating those kind of numbers, teaching mathmatics at a high school, where years later his very proper son would lose control. The failure of his career, the failure of his son, the news of my first arrest . . . I didn't tell her the sense of failure that my mother, too, had carried around the house, along with green bottles of red wine, how she'd been a promising art student who'd given it all up at twenty to raise two children, while Dennis Lawrence went from very promising to unpromising while my mother took the material of all our failures, building her own house of failure, with resentment and regret, until my father hung himself from one of the rafters.
"It sounds like you feel about your dad's death the way I feel about Sauro's . . . sort of responsible."
"They made their own choices."
"That's nice to say, but do you believe it?"

While Anna was out picking flowers in the backyard, Sophie played one of her favorite jazz crystals, talking me through the music, its anarchy, the improvisation growing wildly from set themes: a piano, as Sophie would point out while I strained with untrained ears, picking up the musical idea from the bass, playing with it until the trumpet burst forth with its own variation.

Later that evening Anna and I sat alone on the back patio, both of us drinking white wine. The sky was a darkening blue, the sun casting hints of orange into far corners of the yard. I felt as if it all made sense. The colors intertwined with the trimmed green bushes; the spontaneous music burst forth from a prewritten score. I wanted to tell her about how love, and landscaping, and jazz were all related, but in the open, between sips of white wine, I couldn't get the words to sound right. So I told her that I loved her, and she said she felt the same way, too.

41

PERSONAL SERVICES WAS closed on Memorial Day. The art gallery was permitted to be open as long as it made no sales, but Anna wished she had called her aunt: Lorena Smith visited her husband's grave every Memorial Day, and Anna felt she should have joined her. The theater was dark; Sophie went to visit her father's grave and then drove out with her half-sister to visit their mother, who now lived with a retired nurse in Pittsburgh. I headed to my apartment, relieved to be alone for a while. I was reading *The Lady in the Lake* and drinking a Thirty-Three when Cheetah, our phone, screeched. Aggie's image lit up the screen. Aggie only called with one kind of news.

"It's Cindy," she said.

"It can't be." I was shaking my head.

"The final test came in today. She called me from quarantine."

"But I saw her on Friday. She looked great."

"That's the way it goes, CT. We're going over to see her tomorrow morning. Meet us at nine, in the Cleaning Room, if you want to come along."

That evening Anna complained about a tension headache, and claimed that nothing was wrong. She kept looking at me as if she had something to say and didn't quite know how to say it. Sophie insisted that both of us join her this evening at the Memorial Day rally that Timothy Molina had organized. Anna was already smiling at the idea, Sophie assuring me that it wouldn't look right if any of us didn't attend.

Several hundred people turned out in Public Square, many of them underdressed for late May's chilly air. A platform and a PA system had been set up, and Timothy—obviously made nervous in front of an audience of more than five—spoke in halting words about those who had died, who were dying in a country *"where we keep saying we believe in democracy and justice."* He asked us to stand in solidarity with those who were now in quarantine and those who had recently left Northeast Ohio for a new, precarious future out west.

Then Sally Kim, who at the party wanted to know how true *Truest Love* had been, walked up to the mike and spoke forcefully. *"My name is Cindy Molero. I was born twenty years ago in Cleveland and grew up in the Hough corridors. My name then had been Cindy Wahid. I lived with my mother and my two sisters. I married Esteban Molero a year ago, and I have a ten month old daughter. I have worked for Personal Services since I turned eighteen. I am now in quarantine. I will leave for a camp next Monday."*

Norman White walked to the mike. *"My name is Leonard Scott. . . ."*

I found myself looking away. Sophie had her arm wrapped around mine for the benefit of the monitors. Anna stood beside me, gazing at her fingernails. "Was this Cindy a friend of yours?"

"Yeah."

"Did you know her as well as the last one?" Her voice was bitter.

"I lived in a shackville with my son."

"Cindy's a friend."

"I thought the last one was, too. I mentioned something about it to my friend Joan, and she told me we'd've read about in the *PD* if it had happened. Timothy told me the last whore to be shipped out was in March." The use of the word whore was forced.

"I was shipped to Camp Seven in Nevada last Monday."

"Is that what's been bugging you all evening?"

"Nothing's bugging me. I just thought we'd started over."

In the commotion of the rally I wondered if anyone would pick up on that.

Aggie, Henry, Eric, and I were joined by four others to visit Cindy. We could only talk to her by phone, however, so we might as well have stayed at Personal Services. She cried the whole time, swearing she'd done everything by the book, that even her husband had taken weekly blood testing. They were going to ship her off next Monday, and she asked us to see her off. Even Aggie hesitated. I promised to be there. She told us that someone who didn't know that she was married had offered to buy her flat at half the going rate. She thought it was funny, and we tried to laugh. She said two women—one of them had been Oriental—had come by yesterday to see if she needed help arranging daytime care for her daughter. "Wasn't that nice?" she said.

"Sure," said Aggie. "But they wouldn't have given you the time of day if your blood hadn't tested bad."

At the Monday-morning staff meeting, Fred went over our earnings projections for the week and told us how much Tricky Dick estimated we'd lose until business returned to normal in Direct Services. Ten Leisure Service clients had already canceled their contracts. Two had demanded exclusive sexual rights without a fee increase, and Fred, going against union contract, had given in.

Afterwards Fred waved me over. "Could we rendezvous in my office in about fifteen minutes? We have to talk about Anna Baxter."

He must have heard that we were starting over.

Without Donna Palaez to get him going, Fred rambled and stalled. He talked about how the Sensory Arcades were a failure in huge parts of Africa and how he didn't understand how blacks in one place could act so differently from blacks in another.

"Well," he said at last, reaching for several crystals, "enough of that. When's the last time you've seen Anna Baxter?"

I hesitated, then decided he knew something. "This morning."

Fred stammered. I'd caught him off guard. "Where, where was this?"

"In my client's house. At breakfast. The two are good friends."

"Have you seen her other times?"

The house wasn't monitored. "She's visited a few times."

"That's fine." He inserted a crystal into the computer recess, and the vidscreen lit up. He turned the screen at an angle so I could see it. The image was of the Mutangi Gallery. Adolf—I couldn't imagine why Tricky Dick would have prepared this footage—provided an angle on the counter. Standing behind the counter was Joan, Anna's co-worker. In front of it was Lorena Smith, who stood there very calm and poised. They exchanged a few niceties, and George Mutangi joined in. Then Aunt Lorena called Anna over. Anna kissed her wrinkled cheek.

"I've been trying to call you, dear, for the past two weeks. I haven't heard from you in a while, and I became worried. I was on my way to visit your Uncle Richard's grave, so I decided to stop in."

"I'm sorry I haven't kept in touch."

"Is everything all right?"

"Yes, Aunt Lorena. I just became tired of the apartment, so I've been staying with my friend Sophie."

I couldn't tell, not on a screen this size, but I got the impression that the old woman was hurt, upset that Anna had chosen to stay with Sophie rather than her.

I watched Fred, who was watching me. I expected him to stop the footage, but it went on. Anna was explaining how Sophie was getting ready for opening *Romeo and Juliet*, that the preview would be Thursday, the opening on Friday.

"Well," said Aunt Lorena, "could I tempt you to my house for dinner tonight? It is Memorial Day. Your friend Sophie could come. I'd be delighted to have her."

Anna hesitated. "I've got a date," she said.

"Oh, I wouldn't want to intrude. Just call me when you have a free evening."

There was more chit and chat, and then Aunt Lorena told George to give her a call sometime, that she'd love to help support the Krieger exhibition in July. George was all restrained smiles, and Aunt Lorena left for the cemetery.

Joan walked over and nudged Anna, and the sound picked up to capture Joan's whisper. "You still haven't told me if we're going to meet this guy who's putting the bloom on your cheeks every morning."

Fred hit the off button. The screen went gray. Fred waited for me to say something. I tried to figure how he'd gotten this footage. Palaez, knowing the ins and outs of public right-to-know laws, just maybe could have gotten it. Or:

"Lang gave this to you," I said. I couldn't figure out why, unless he still thought Anna was UHL, that Sophie was UHL, that I'd turned UHL, and that we spent our time away from monitors plotting something monstrous. Or maybe he just wanted me away from Anna. "You couldn't have gotten this any other way. Lang wants you to think something's going on."

"Isn't there?"

I was going to deny it, but I couldn't.

"Look, Rod, Donna Palaez doesn't know about this."

"She doesn't?"

"If she did know, what would she want?"

"My head."

"Maybe."

"I've logged in the sensory data."

"You have. And maybe Donna would have Tricky Dick graph things out, compare heartbeat patterns this past week with heartbeat patterns when you were servicing the Baxter woman. Tricky Dick might corroborate a similarity between the two patterns."

"What do you want me to do?"

"I want to be able to prove, if necessary, that Roderick Lawrence is abiding by the terms of his contract with Personal Services."

"So what should happen?"

"Ms. Baxter should go back to her apartment. Or move in with that old aunt of hers. But I want proof, in your file, in Ms. Greenspan's file, that you're doing your job the way it's supposed to be done."

"*Fred knows,*" I told Anna while she changed out of her Art Gallery clothes and into some jeans.

"Knows what?"

"That you and I are sleeping together, that Sophie hired me for cover."

"He can't know. He must just suspect it."

"He *knows*. He got hold of some footage from the gallery when you told your Aunt Lorena that you're living with Sophie."

"That doesn't mean I'm sleeping with you. You got those sensory things. Couldn't you just record a few of our times together and say that's you and Sophie, all hot and heavy?"

"I've already done that."

"You never told me that."

"They don't believe I'm sleeping with Sophie."

"You didn't tell me you were recording what we were doing. You goddamned liar. You didn't tell me. How could you do that to me?"

"*I'm moving out,*" she said to Sophie at dinner. "I'll leave you two alone, and you can do whatever you want to save Rod's job."

"Isn't that taking it a little too far?" asked Sophie. "Wouldn't it be enough if I just took Rod with me everywhere? I'll take him on errands. I'll take him to the dress rehearsal tomorrow, the preview the next day. We'll go to Herbert Milanes's reception. Everyone will know Rod and I are together."

Anna looked down at her plate: originally the two of them were going to the reception.

"Would that be enough?" Sophie asked me.

"Yeah. I guess."

"No." Anna was shaking her head. "I'm moving back to the apartment." She looked up, caught me with her eyes. "Do you want to get together again?"

I considered the timing. "Sophie could terminate the

contract on Monday or Tuesday. We could see each other two or three days later."

"Why do you have to be so damn calculating? This is not a business venture, you know."

I said nothing. Sophie held her body still, trying to look impossibly invisible.

"You and your goddamned job."

"Look," I said, "my job wouldn't be so important if I believed in forevers."

"What's wrong with forevers?"

"I've never seen one in my life."

"*Do you love* me?"

"You know I do."

"Then tell me."

"I love you," I said. The words came out a little too easily. They had meant so much more two weeks ago when they had been harder words to say.

So I tried to prove my words with actions. She started to say no, then kissed me. We embraced, made love, our bodies lacking interest, but there was a certain safety in the rhythm of hips, in the substitute for passion, the ritual releasing of juices, the whispered *I love you*s.

That night I dreamed I married Cindy and traveled with her to the camps.

The morning light was a muted gray. The sound of the rain was lulling; the chill that fell with it gave a soft quality to the warmth in the bed. Anna was lying close to me, her leg over my leg, her hand upon my chest, her head resting against my shoulder. "Rod, what if our relationship does last?"

"What do you mean?"

"I mean you and your job. If what we have lasts, will you leave your job?"

"I don't know."

"Aren't you willing to risk anything?"

"It's easier to risk your career if you have a trust fund."

"There are all kinds of risks, Rod."

"So far I've done everything the way you've wanted it."

She looked at me as if that couldn't be true.

She packed some of her stuff in a bag, saying she'd get the rest later. Sophie ran out in the rain to start the car and drive Anna to the gallery. Both of us stood in the hall, as awkward as people who have just been introduced.

"I'll see you next week," she said. "If you still want to see me."

I found myself reconsidering everything.

"You know, Sophie has seats for us together on Friday. Can we manage that?"

"I guess."

"Do you really want to see me?"

"Anna, if what we have lasts . . ." I hesitated, but felt I had to say it. "Then I'll give up the work." I heard the words, appreciating the delivery, not feeling as if I'd been the one to say them. But Anna's smile was glorious, and she embraced me as if she didn't want to let go, making me glad to promise her everything. It was wonderful, delightfully scary, to entrust everything to her feelings.

"I'm so happy," she said. There was the sound of victory in her voice, and I didn't feel so trusting anymore.

42

AFTER SOPHIE DROVE off with Anna, I made my way to the East Room, where Sophie kept her computer and called up today's *Plain Dealer*. The Indians had won their fifth game in a row. A section of the Hough neighborhood had collapsed, killing five and injuring thirty. Monitoring had picked up on a wife-beating, but the police arrived too late to save the woman's life; the husband was in custody; the two children were in a private shelter. Police investigations on the murder of Dorothy Souto continued. Sergeant Bernard Ohls, the Cleveland Police detective in charge of the investigation, said there was substantial evidence that Souto was a UHL member who had used her position in the Sensory Arcades to recruit members for UHL by administering the Relocation Experience. The Experience had been declared propaganda by the U.S. government's Historical Review Board. Edward Lang, antiterrorist consultant for Cuyahoga County Monitoring Services, officially revealed that Ms. Souto recently had been recuited as an informant and was most likely tortured and executed as an example.

There was a nice color picture of Dorothy Souto, in her white lab coat, her red hair piled high. Adolf must have done some retouching to give her such a nice, generous smile. They had never shown her so lovely until they had pinned the blame on terrorists.

Sophie walked in while I was reading the article a second time. "What are we challenging our minds with today?" she asked, and closed the heavy door behind her.

I had my hand on the keyboard, and I almost dumped the info.

Sophie was behind me now, leaning forward to get a look. Her breasts pressed up against my back. "Who's she?" Today's picture of her was on the screen.

"She's the woman who got tortured."

"Oooh, so we're going to be gruesome today?"

The warmth of her breasts had made its way through her shirt and mine. "Did you ever see her?" I asked. "She worked at the Sensory Arcades. It says here that she liked to administer the Relocation Experience."

"I went through that ordeal in Boston," she said. "But she does look familiar."

I jumped to another section of the article. "They say she's UHL. Maybe you saw her at an ASD meeting?"

Sophie reached forward, ran fingers along keyboard, and called up an arts program. She rearranged Dorothy Souto's hair, added a touch of makeup. "I never saw her at a meeting, but then again, I didn't go to that many."

"I thought you were a member."

"Sauro paid my annual dues. I joined when he and Anna moved here. You know, ASD people make good, down-to-earth friends, but I still like my snobby socialite friends. The sincere ASDers don't like you to live a life more complex than your ideology."

"What about Dorothy here?"

"I think she came once to one of the parties I threw last summer. It was like the party you came to, the political crowd. She and another woman came with Stuart."

"Your cousin?"

"Yes." She barked a laugh. "He always brings women to parties. It's a holdover from the old days."

"Did you talk to her?"

"Why the interrogation?"

"She worked in Personal Services," I said. "She's the one who administered the Relocation Experience for me."

"Why in God's name would you want to go through that?"

"Anna asked me to."

Sophie stepped to my side, and I missed her warmth. I couldn't understand why my thoughts were betraying

Anna so readily. Sophie scanned through the info, passing over the photos of the tortured body as quickly as they appeared. "I never thought Anna could be that political without Sauro," Sophie said to herself. "I shouldn't be looking at this. This is gruesome enough to interest anybody."

"Sauro was tortured the night after she gave me the Experience."

Sophie stepped back and looked at me. Her expression was serious, as if perhaps I had done the deed, then she put on her maternal mask and patted my cheek. "Poor boy. You think you caused this."

"No," I lied. "It's just a coincidence. But things like this bother me."

They bothered her, too, and she had to mask the expression. "It's too bad you're in love with Anna." She delivered the line as if she meant it. "Because I can think of all sorts of delicious ways to take your mind off the screen. But I have a play to get ready for. And you have your morning workout."

When I got to Personal Services, I called Cindy. She was pale; her face was puffy; she said all she did was cry. I went for a solitary workout in the pool, but I couldn't shake loose the feeling that I'd made a mistake: I shouldn't have sent Anna away. The Cleaning Room at lunchtime was usually overcrowded and noisy. Today half the tables were empty, and there was a subdued hush. Aggie and Henry waved to me from a table, but I waved back and left.

At the apartment I felt lost. I paced back and forth, and nothing occurred to me. I went to the Admiral late in the afternoon to drink some Thirty-Threes with Harry and Kevin, and I had no idea what to say to them.

Sophie made a quick meal and left for dress rehearsal. She said little at the table. I tried to read *Romeo and Juliet* while she was gone. I was overwhelmed by the house's immensity. Night came, and darkness cloaked the house. I went to bed before Sophie came home, but I couldn't sleep. I imagined them drawing lines of blood along Dorothy Souto's body, the way I had once traced imaginary lines along Anna's cheeks, over the curve of her breast. Dorothy became Anna, and I held the knife. I heard Sophie come home, and I listened to her walk back and forth. I felt as if I were listening to pacings of a ghost through a haunted house.

The next morning, during breakfast, I asked Sophie for a list of people I could expect to meet at the party and that afternoon, at home, I popped a K-pill, called for beyond-subscription access and called up ten names, all of them belonging to some of the most prominent families in the Cleveland area. The list didn't include the mayor of Cleveland or the head of city council. I got bored and frustrated. I had never known people like this. So I called up the etiquette manual and started memorizing stock phrases for the occasion.

I was rehearsing introductions when the Cheetah started to screech. By the tenth screech, I decided to answer. It was my brother Arthur. It had been two years since we'd spoken to each other. Every December I sent Arthur and our mother a nice holiday card.

"Hi, Artie!" I said, brimming over with enthusiasm. He hated to be called that.

His face still had that hard, determined look, the grim, forward looking eyes that our father had said, would take him to Princeton. Artie held himself like our father, cut his hair just as short, and wore clothes at least ten years out of date. He had inherited our mother's self-righteousness. Two years ago, when I had visited them in Michigan, he had made it clear what was expected of me to be a moral person and a true member of the family.

"Rod!" he said, as if that moment had never happened. "How are you? I've been trying to get hold of you."

I was taken aback. He honestly seemed happy to talk with me. "I'm fine, Artie. How are you?"

"Good. The phone company just transferred me to the zoo neighborhood of Traverse. The Construct is about to extend itself there, and I've been put in charge of sales."

"I'm impressed."

"I suppose you have a client right now," he said. "I tried to get you all weekend."

"That's the first time you've called them anything as nice as clients."

"Come on, Rod. Don't hassle me. I'm trying to be nice. I'm really feeling good these days." A shy grin was forming on his face.

"You found yourself a woman," I said.

"Do you always think like that?"

"Answer the question, Artie. You're in love, aren't you?"

He laughed. "Yeah. I guess I am."

"How's Mom taking it?"

"You know Mom. She thinks I'm getting too serious too quick."

"What's her name?"

"Miram."

"Miriam?"

"No. Miram. She's from New Palestine—well, what used to be New Palestine."

"Are you guys making any plans?"

"Sort of. I'd like you to come up this weekend and meet her."

"I can't. My client is an actress, and her play opens this Friday."

"Then come up Saturday. I can help with the airfare, if that's the problem."

"That's not the problem."

"Mom would really like you to."

"I know." The words were heavy and dead.

"Then why don't you come up? I don't see what's bothering you."

"You know damn well what's bothering me."

"Rod, it won't be that way this time."

I grimaced.

"That was two years ago, remember. Mom and I have lived and learned." He paused. "You could spend the afternoons with Mom *before* she hits the *vino tinto*. Then you and I can go out for the evening. You and I can go to Joe's, or we can find you a date and go out with Miram. I really want you to meet her. We're family, you know."

"I just can't make it this weekend."

"Will you think about it for some other weekend? We

really want to see you. Please, just think about it. I assure you, things have changed."

"Okay," I said. "I'll think about it."

I sat there for I don't know how long, the gray screen barely reflecting my image, just the hints of color in my shirt, several lines that established a face, a shadow of hair, and two dark spots where my eyes must have been. I had wanted to tell Arthur about Anna.

43

THE THEATER WAS full on Thursday for the preview. The men wore suits; the women wore dresses; and I was reminded that I was among people who bought synthetics only when it was part of the style. I wanted to be with Anna, who didn't care what I wore.

None of the play made sense, even in the scenes that Sophie and I had gone over. I shouldn't have taken that K-pill—I hadn't taken any in quite a while, and I found that I was coming off this one with a thud. It had been a mistake to let Anna leave.

"Yond light is not daylight," Sophie was saying, her eyes closed. The stage seemed distant, like an unrealistic holofilm. The actor playing Romeo stood beside a railing, which I guess represented a balcony. Sophie lay on a pallet, a lavish quilt pulled up to her naked breasts. "It is some meteor that the sun exhales to be to thee this night a torchbearer and light thee on thy way to Mantau. Therefore stay yet; thou need'st not to be gone."

It was dawn, though, not a false light, and Romeo had to leave. The lighting around the stage brightened from pinks to yellows to white. Juliet jumped out of the bed, as if in shock, and ran for a robe. Anna didn't have to leave, not really. But then I knew, watching Romeo descend the balcony and depart, how it all would end, even if Anna didn't. She had too much upbringing to fight against. Even without an Edward Lang or a Stuart Greenspan to complicate things, the ending remained the same. I tried and failed to follow the play, so instead I waited eagerly for Sophie to stab herself, so it would all be over.

Sophie had been given a private dressing room to impress the representatives from Chicago on opening night; usually her director preferred to have all the cast dress together. I found myself sitting by the makeup mirror while people congratulated her, embraced her or kissed her on the cheek, almost all of them asking if they'd see her at Milanes's party. The men wore overcoats that had been out of style when I was a kid, and the women wore furs from the beaver and mink farms. Several ignored me; some stared; some asked to be introduced.

In the parking lot the air seemed strangely crisp for early June. I wished I owned a fancy overcoat myself. "What did you think of the play?" she asked cheerfully, as if the question weren't really important.

"I couldn't concentrate."

"We'll just have to go over the lines tomorrow. You're too intelligent not to enjoy Shakespeare."

"I'm not fourteen, either."

"But just as sensitive."

We got into the car, and the front windshield fogged up immediately. She turned the ignition and cursed Cleveland weather. The hot air from the defroster began to erase the vapor that clung to the glass. "Now tell me the truth, my love. The real reason you couldn't concentrate was because it was the first time you've seen my beautiful and gorgeous body without clothes."

"Not really. I've seen you naked."

"Oh, you must have been spying, you naughty boy."

"Sort of."

"You're supposed to be smiling," she said. "No one is allowed to be unhappy when they're with me. Now, I know you've seen tapes of me fucking other people. Anna wishes you hadn't."

"It comes with the job."

"Oh, please, don't be like this all evening. We're going to a fancy party, and we should have a good time."

I shrugged. Anna had wanted to go to this party.

"Look, my sweet professional member, there are only

two reasons that I'm going to this party the night before opening night. One, Milanes, as creepy as he is, gives a lot of money to the Playhouse, and we're under orders to treat him nicely. Two, you told me you wanted to keep your job, so I'm taking you out in public to show you off as my sweet, tempting status symbol."

"Sophie . . ."

"Never interrupt an actress during a performance, especially when she's on a roll. Now, if I'm going to be a metaphorical whore for the Playhouse and act like you're my literal whore for your boss, and if no one's going to appreciate it, I'd just as soon not go to this party. I'd really rather take you home, put the silk sheets on my bed, and see if you live up to the advertising footage they showed me of you. In glorious action."

I didn't know what to say.

Sophie clicked on the interior light and looked at me. "Oh, my, I'd never have believed it! You're blushing! That must mean that deep in your heart you are intrigued by my voluptuous curves and my articulate sensitivity. But seeing how my best friend in the whole wide world is Anna, it's probably best that we go to the party."

44

HERBERT MILANES, PRESIDENT of Democracy Now, was one of Cleveland's few civic leaders with a national reputation. I had spent over half-an-hour this afternoon, over-stimulated by the K-pill, reading about him.

His aristocratic grandparents had fled the Cuban Revolution. His father, married to the daughter of paternal friends, moved here and made his initial money investing in Cleveland's Japanese-owned steel firms, making his first big killing after orbital factories were built, making his second big killing by pulling out of earthside steel just before asteroid mining and space factories killed the industry. Making use of new-style lasers and computer programming, he developed Democracy Now, which his son had taken over. It was the first major company to take advantage of the new technology to offer cheaply a tremendous variety of clothing styles, produced to specific measurements and ordered from the individual home (*IN THE NEW AGE OF DEMOCRACY*, the ad reads, *WE CREATE OUR OWN CLOTHES*). His computerized factories made him the enemy of the labor unions. His support of the Mail Order Limitation Laws earned him the friendship of the service unions. His open support of the Construct made him a sometime host of James Baxter, and his voluntary installation of monitors throughout his home and offices gained him a civic reputation and an invitation to dine at the White House. His wild parties, rumored as the place to be for some discreet orgying, made him a continual subject of New Puritan attacks on moral hypocrisy.

I had recognized his picture instantly. He was one of the five men Sophie had screwed in upstairs bedrooms.

His house captured his personality. Bulky and square, it looked like a miniature castle, its urine yellow facade huge and cumbersome enough to look like it had been stolen from some art museum. Two lion statues crouched on either side of the glass-door entranceway. Huge spotlights, erasing the shadows upon the house and imbuing the grounds with a ghostly aura, made the house a Hollywood spectacle. The Cuban who made conspicuous claims to America's immigrant heritage as a home for refugees stocked the well-lit interior of his home with art that appeared to be Pan-Cultural but was most likely, according to Sophie, little more than American versions of African and Asian styles. Befitting his belief in the service sector, the party moved in time to the careful gestures of valets who ushered drivers and passengers out of cars, then parked the cars on Fairmount Blvd; bartenders who, behind the podium of three makeshift bars that were merely tables covered ceremoniously with thick white tablecloths, conducted people in and out of an amorphous line, recognizing gender and seniority as they brought people to the front of the bar, served a variety of drinks from an array of bottles and aided by a few mixing machines for the most popular drinks; and waitresses who passed around trays of hors d'oeuvres and collected crumbled napkins to be tossed and empty glasses to be washed in the kitchen and reused. All of these—the valets, the bartenders, and the waitresses—were dressed in identical white and black uniforms. So many white faces amongst the partiers contrasted with the darker ones of the servants, most of whom were Black, Hispano, or Arab. Their boss, who wore the same uniform but who walked back and forth between them all and never seemed to mix a drink or carry a tray, looked Vietnamese. On the holovision, there wouldn't be such an obvious separation of color; the producers would have been sued by the actors' union as racist.

After Sophie capably parked her own car on Fairmount, she led me, her arm tucked through mine, past the cars sliding down the driveway and out onto the street, taking me into the subtly organized anarchy inside: Young college students wearing faddish keffiyahs wrapped about their shoulders chatted with young business-people in three piece suits; middle-aged people wore at least jacket and tie and listened to retired folk who dressed in a variety of styles, befitting their good ol' days when Pan-Culturalism had been considered the trend to bring world peace and unity and prosperity. One woman was explaining to a younger woman why she preferred sex with women. A daughter was explaining to her father why she, unlike him, would never make use of Personal Services. A college student mused to several others about the possibility of contacting God in the Sensory Arcades. As we orbited past groups, faces turned to Sophie, male hands shook hers, female arms offered slight embraces, all of them congratulating her on her performance. Other cast members were there and equally celebratory, offering me the same embrace they all gave Sophie. But the director, who was already saying her good nights, gave Sophie a warm embrace and me a cold glare.

Sophie finally came to a halt in a room full of French windows and decorated with shiny wood furniture that somehow looked too old to sit upon. A chandelier—truncated rainbows caught in all its crystal and light—hung down and branched out like an upside-down glass tree. Embedded in the plaster molding that rooted the chandelier to ceiling, barely visible unless you were looking for it, was the monitor. Sophie flirtatiously, and quickly, kissed me on the lips and pointed at the bar. "Would you get me a Scotch on the rocks, dear?" she asked. "And get yourself something nice." She turned, her eyes wide and her smile artificial, to talk with a nearby group of people—several of its members had waved to her when we had entered the room. After a long wait at the bar—the bartender seemingly noticing almost everyone before eyeing me, addressing each as sir or ma'am, even if they were much younger—I returned to Sophie, who now was talking with only one person, and handed her the Scotch. I held a beer. She took a sip of scotch. "Oh, how lovely," she said. The delivery was perfect; there wasn't even a faint hint of the self-parody she usually employed when she donned this role. I felt disappointed. "Now, Rod," she said, gesturing to the olive-skinned man in a three-piece suit. "This is Herbert Milanes." She accented the last syllable, an accent his father had dropped while living in Miami. "Herbert, this is my companion, Roderick Lawrence."

Milanes's smile became a knowing one when he heard the word *companion*. She might as well have called me her horse.

I shook his solid, thick hand. "A pleasure to meet you," I said, straight out of the etiquette book.

"I'd say the pleasure is mine, but Sophie employed you, not me."

Sophie laughed. I was impressed that such a civic leader made Harry and Kevin look sophisticated. I tried to understand why Sophie had slept with him.

"Oh, Sophie dear, I hope Herbert has told you how wonderful we thought your performance was." A thin and delicate woman embraced Sophie. After a moment she stepped back and looked at me curiously. If her brown eyes had not been so dark and clear, I would have thought she was albino. "And, Sophie, who might this be?"

"This is my companion, Roderick Lawrence."

"Martha Milanes," she said firmly, her delight in the gesture of holding out her hand to mine spontaneous. There was a simplicity to her that made her seem incapable of any artificial gesturing. I wondered if she knew that Sophie and Milanes had once gone upstairs together. I took her hand as she said, "Pleased to meet you."

Knowing no other response, I said, "The pleasure is mine."

"You can say that to Sophie, Roderick," said Milanes, "but please, not to my wife."

Martha Milanes slapped playfully at her husband's bicep. "Oh, Herbert! You're so terrible."

"And original, too," I said under my breath.

Sophie abruptly grabbed my arm. "If you both will pardon us, I would like to introduce Rod around. We have to head home soon. I'm exhausted and want to get to bed."

Milanes's knowing smile turned almost obscene. Such a smile reduced everything, and the envy in it somehow made me envious of what neither Milanes nor I had in Sophie.

"I can imagine," Martha was saying. "Especially with tomorrow night being the big night. How will the play be?"

"It's written by one of the best," I said.

Sophie smiled sweetly at me, but something about the way she narrowed her eyes told me to keep quiet. "It's Dolores's best work of direction so far. In fact, there's supposed to be two women coming from Chicago to see if they want to move the production there in the fall."

"Oh, I heard," said Martha. "That must be so exciting."

"And nervewracking," said Sophie.

"Well," said Milanes, "it's about time that Dolores moved on to Chicago or New York. Some place worthy of her talents."

"And Sophie, too," said Martha. "Sophie's the best Cleveland has to offer." She shook her head. "But it's too bad that Cleveland always has to lose its best talent."

"She's the best thing in the play," I said.

Sophie hugged my arm. The gesture felt sincere, and a vague warmth slid through me.

Milanes laughed. "It seems, Sophie, that you've invested in a fan club, more than anything else."

Sophie looked up at me as I prepared to respond. She firmly took hold of my hand and squeezed. "The four of us will have to get together later," she said, her voice drowning out my first tentative words to Milanes. "I really want Rod to meet some more people."

They told me how nice it was to meet me as Sophie dragged me off.

"Now," Sophie said sternly, her voice so soft that I was compelled to tilt my ear to her lips, "my fine love machine, we will, as Lady Macbeth said, 'make our faces masks to our hearts, disguising what they are.' You *were* trained for this kind of performance?"

I nodded.

"Then let's see that training in action."

"I'll be on my best behavior. As long as everyone is nice to you."

She giggled, a soft, luscious bubble of sounds that

should have sounded childish. "Oh, you do adore me." Abruptly her mouth was against my ear, her tongue softly tracing ridges. I just as abruptly pulled away. Sophie smiled at me, her lips loosely pursed as if she were tempted to kiss me. "You're blushing again."

I shrugged.

She exhaled loudly, returning to her lady of society role. "Well, just watch yourself. Too bad I didn't have you read *The Little Foxes*."

"Huh?"

"Never mind, my well-educated honeypot, let's just meet and impress a few people before we leave for the silk sheets at home." She leaned forward and kissed me, her lips open. I met her lips, keeping my tongue to myself, and quickly stepped back, patting her behind. I thought of the monitor, embedded in the curlicues of plaster between ceiling and chandelier. Would they believe that as a gesture of our sexual relationship? Is that why she nibbled at my ear, talked of silk sheets, held me close? "Don't you like to kiss in public places?" she asked.

I thought of Susie Sundai and I sneaking off into the Fair Haven woods. "Only when there's no one else around."

She smiled, took hold of my arm. "Let's meet a few more people."

We became proton and neutron on an erratic trajectory, picking up electrons, casting them off, finding new ones. Sophie's positive energy kept attracting people, pulling them into our orbit. I wanted to fly by some heavy particle, make use of it for a slingshot effect, and fly back home, where I wouldn't have to worry about Sophie's motivations or mine.

She told how Dolores directed plays. She explained how she prepared for the role. She told jokes she had learned while growing up in Slavic Village and compared them to jokes she'd learned in New England. She'd told about departmental warfare when she was a professor of drama at the college in New England. She explained why she preferred acting to teaching. She joked—when we were in a library that rivaled her own for the number of leather-bound books that seemed to be fresh and unopened—about how she and Dolores had put together her present performance of Juliet. By now she had gained about fifteen listeners, including Martha Milanes, who joined because she just loved this one story. The problem, Sophie explained was how to develop a "fair Juliet" who was beautiful in the soul but not, by present cultural standards, in body.

"You're beautiful on the stage," I said, truthfully.

"And sexy," said Martha.

"Even with her clothes on," said her husband, who had just joined her, a tall drink in his hand.

"But the problem," said Sophie, "was how to run naked across the stage without everyone laughing. With this belly and especially with these big bouncy breasts of mine."

Everyone laughed along with Sophie.

One man, wearing a sports coat and khaki slacks, appearing slightly rumpled and out of place, shook his head. "I don't see why nudity and sex can't at least be kept out of Shakespeare. If there has to be eroticism in theater, it shouldn't be at the Playhouse." He smiled shyly, as if he might have said the wrong thing for this crowd.

"Here, here," said a middle-aged woman, raising her glass. Her hand was smooth and plastic.

Someone patted the young man jovially on the back. "I see we have a New Puritan here."

"Who is *he?*" a woman whispered to the man beside her.

"Did you invite him, Martha?" her husband asked.

"I'm not a New Puritan," said the young man. "I just feel that there's a time and a place for everything."

"I couldn't agree with you more, young man," said the middle-aged woman with the prosthetic arm. Her voice sounded older than her looks. The Cleveland Clinic was doing all sorts of expensive work with skin-tissue regeneration. They could sometimes improve the tone of your skin, but not your vocal chords.

Another young man, also wearing khaki pants and a blue sports jacket, although wearing it all like it had been dry cleaned on him, cut through the clutter of people, and took the first young man by the arm. "New Puritan or not, Ken, you are making a nuisance of yourself."

"There's nothing wrong with a little controversy," said a young woman.

The "middle-aged" woman glanced at her. "There's no need to get anyone upset."

"But you agreed with him," said the college student.

Milanes turned to his wife after the two young men had disappeared. "Darling, if they weren't invited, shouldn't we have Nguyen ask them to leave?"

"They're not causing any trouble, honey."

"But it would be nice to know who they are."

"If you want to know, you can always introduce yourself. I'm sure they'll tell you what a wonderful party it is and offer you their names."

"I just might do that."

Sophie continued talking, launched on a new story that seemed overly familiar. If they kept listening, she probably would start teaching them Shakespeare. I let myself drift out of the room and be drawn to the bar. After an interminable wait, the bartender addressed me as "sir" and offered me a beer in a fresh glass, automatically handing the old glass, smudged with the mist of fingerprints, to a passing waitress.

"Hi, Rod." The delivery was so matter-of-fact that I didn't recognize the voice at first.

It was Anna. She was wearing an elaborate blue dress fashioned with white scallops. Standing next the her, wearing a gray suit, was Edward Lang.

"Uncle Ed, this is my former companion, Rod Lawrence, and Rod, this is Edward Lang."

We shook hands.

"It's a pleasure to meet you," said Lang.

"The pleasure's mine," I said.

"Uncle Ed," said Anna, "and Aunt Thea have been friends of the family for ages. Uncle Ed taught international affairs at Harvard Business School when my father was a student."

"How nice," I said.

"I told Uncle Ed how you brought me back into the real world after Sauro died," Anna said to me, her voice making everything sound past tense. "He had a tough time believing me."

"Now she's going to tell you how being a New Puritan clouds my judgment," said Lang.

"So I thought it would be great if he could meet a personal companion in the flesh," said Anna. "Uncle Ed and I have our disagreements about what happened in the Spanish War, but I must say, he did go around, talked to all sorts of people, and found out why people on the other side were fighting."

"Are you doing the same thing here in Cleveland?" I asked.

"You sound a bit like the political types Anna hangs out with."

"Rod?" said Anna, in disbelief. "Rod's perfectly apolitical."

"Really?" said Lang.

"I had to force him to go get the Relocation Experience," said Anna. "He acted like none of that could ever happen to him."

I didn't like how Anna was discussing me in the third person, but I didn't know what to say, not in front of Lang, not in front of the monitors.

"What did you think of the Experience?" Lang asked me.

"I'll leave you two here to talk," said Anna. She patted both of us on the back. "I want to go find Sophie."

Lang and I said nothing for a while. I stared down at my beer. He didn't have a drink.

"Do you come to these kinds of parties often?" I asked.

"If I'm invited, but I don't often come to parties like these. With what goes on upstairs, I really can't condone them."

"You should try an ASD party. They talk politics more than anything else."

"Oh, I went to a few, until people found out who I was. Anna's not distorting the truth. I do like to know why people do what they do. Once we know that, we can offer a better alternative. That's the only way to truly win a war. No one wanted to listen to my opinion on that issue in Spain. So we used brute force to win that one."

We stood there for a bit, a beer in my hand, Lang's hands empty.

"Truth to tell, I didn't realize I'd see you here," he said. "Anna seemed at loose ends, and she really wanted to come to this party. I hadn't seen her in a while, so I decided to come along. You know, she told me that you two planned to get together some time next week."

"I can keep an eye out for you again."

"To tell you the truth, I was a little happier when I thought it was a fling. I'm sure her father will feel the same way."

"Are you going to tell her father?"

"I don't know. His family just left on a tour of India and Pakistan. I saw them at my father's funeral. They told me that Anna had been invited on the trip. I had hoped she would go."

Anna hadn't mentioned any such trip.

"The truth is: I don't think I'll have to tell her father. I think things will have worked their natural course by the time he returns to the States."

"You didn't find it too difficult to tell Fred O'Mallery."

"Pardon?" He asked, but he stepped into a corner, letting me follow.

"You know what I'm talking about. You're the only person who could care who would have access to Adolf. Adolf would have told you that Anna wasn't in her apartment, who would have spotted her leaving Sophie's house to walk to work and coming back there at night, and who would have picked up on her telling her Aunt Lorena where she was spending her time."

Lang nodded. "I guess I would be one of the few people who could have done that."

"You're also the one who told the *PD* that Dorothy Souto was a terrorist and an informer."

"And she wasn't?" asked Lang.

I had said one thing too many. "She didn't try to recruit me when she administered the Experience."

"But she did call herself Goldilocks," said Lang. "I kept wondering when you'd call me up and explain it to me better than you had to Detective Ohls."

"I really don't remember her saying it."

"You did look upset at the time, and maybe you didn't hear her say it. But then I remember how good your memory is. And I remember Detective Ohls' thoughts. You know, about bears."

I looked at him as if he was crazy.

"Maybe it was nothing," he said. "But it struck a chord with me. It made me a little more uncomfortable with another moment, where things didn't quite jibe. So I had some of the top people in Monitoring go over everything with the AI. On the morning of May 7, around 2 a.m., you left Anna's home, you took the RTA, got off at the Broadway and Harvard exit, and walked home. There was randomized footage that the AI had saved for later review. Everything looks perfect, even the timing is right, but all that can be tinkered with if you have a topnotch programmer play with things. The thing that looks odd, is that when you get on the rapid, your cheeks are flushed. When you get home, you are very pale. You look like you're very sick, and the next day you are sick."

"I didn't feel well when I left Anna's," I said.

"Fine. So then my men go through the transit car's footage. We get people in all the seats, and you're the only one who gets off at your exit. But the toll count read four people exiting."

He waited for me to say something before going on.

"The toll reading could have been an error. We don't think so. We look for other evidence. We want to verify if you were alone or not when you left the RTA stop. We find that at Fleet and Spafford, merchants had reported their clocks as being several minutes behind. Worse, various simulation devices that need continual electricity were found off at store opening the next morning. CEI has no record of a power shortage, so we checked output averages—the average output for that time of evening had dropped just a bit, to confirm what the merchants had complained about. It took days of work, brainstorming, looking for any anomaly possible, but we found three very strange things. A personal companion leaves his client in the middle of the night. He gets off the transit car with three other people—who are never seen on any footage. Then a short power outage. And a very sick man comes home."

"That's four things," I said.

"Fine. Four strange occurrences, and I'm not going to ask for explanations, not here, not during this wonderful party, where everyone is having a good time. But three people—Papa Bear, Mama Bear, and Baby Bear, perhaps—and I never heard about it from you."

"Because it didn't happen." I didn't sound very convincing.

"I'll expect you on Monday, at our usual time. And, I'd be careful now. You *are* an informer. They could end up doing to you what they did to Dorothy Souto.

"Why don't you just tell Anna what's going on, and then tell her to leave me alone. I don't want to be any part of this."

"Because Anna may be one of them. It was Stuart Greenspan who suggested that Anna hire a servicer. And it was Anna—wasn't it?—who suggested you get the Relocation Experience, where you just happened to meet Goldilocks. Sounds to me like someone's looking for a new recruit."

"I'm not UHL," I said.

"Oh, I figured that. You're trying to stay in the middle, and keep out of the whole thing. It's time now to make a commitment."

"And you're going to influence my decision."

"I hate to say it, because it's a bad tactic. But in this case, I am going to use a bad tactic." He sounded angry, as if I'd betrayed him in some more personal way. "If you turn out to be UHL, you can already guess what will happen to you."

"And it's not the same thing that would happen in Jefferson's America?"

"No," he said, his voice still low, but his expression belonging to someone having an intense conversation about something socially acceptable. "I'm afraid not. Now, if Sophie Greenspan does something faintly suspicious, I want to know about it. If you can find out anything about her, that will help me, I want to know about it. If she or some other member of UHL makes contact with you, I want to know about it. If you fail as an informer, I'll make sure you're working minimum scale somewhere, and I'll make sure you never get any kind of retraining license. I'll put you back in the gutter you crawled out of."

I forced one of Sophie's grand, artificial smiles. "It's nice to feel like a cockroach."

"Cockroaches don't live by moral choices. People do." He held out his hand, smiled as if this conversation had never really happened, and said louder, more cheerfully, "It was nice chatting with you. I better go find Anna."

I glared at his hand, and he let it fall to his side. He walked away. Stuart had advised Anna to hire a companion, Lang had said. Anna had told me that her friend Joan had suggested it in jest. The answer hadn't been in my file. Why would Anna lie? I finished my beer, then got another. I started to drink that one quickly, and remembered where I was.

I wandered out of the dining room and ran into Chauncey Blassingame. A terribly skinny man with a light brown complexion, he was popular among his janes because he was a talented piano player. He was less popular among his colleagues because he was so pompous back at the Cleaning Room. Alongside him was a woman who was as thick as he was thin. She wasn't thick the way Sophie was. In Sophie there was coordination and grace and a sense of being alive. Here there was a dowdy woman with a friendly smile that quivered. "Rod," said Chauncey, "this is my sponsor, Mrs. Patricia McBeadle. Patricia, this is Sophie Greenspan's companion, Mr. Roderick Lawrence."

"Oh, don't be so formal," she said as she offered me her hand. It fell limply into mine.

"Pleased to meet you." I said automatically. I looked away and saw Lang chatting amicably with Martha Milanes. He was fitting in rather nicely at this party he didn't approve of.

"I have heard a lot about you," Mrs. McBeadle was saying.

"I hope what you heard was positive."

"Oh, I assure you, it was. Now, you were with Anna Baxter before you were with Sophie, weren't you?"

"Yes. I was." Lang was telling some sort of story, and he had several other listeners.

"Poor dear. She's been through a lot. You see, I'm a friend of Lorena Smith, so I know how this whole thing happened. It was such a shame about her young man. So nice. Never did fit in, but he was nice. Is she doing better now?"

I offered a holovision smile. "I never terminate with a client if they're unhappy."

"That's good to hear. If your Marie Archer had done the same thing, we'd all be happy." I remembered that Marie's fiancé was Sean McBeadle. Mrs. McBeadle was pensive for a moment, then patted Chauncey on the cheek. "But then I never would have had Chauncey here to help me appreciate the theater."

"You're too kind," he said.

"Oh, before I forget, Chauncey, do you know those two men over there?"

She pointed at the two young men wearing sport coats and khaki slacks. They were getting drinks at the bar.

Chauncey shook his head.

"And you Rod?"

"Sorry."

"No one knows who they are. I just wondered if they were some of your people." She shook her head. "Now, Chauncey, will you go and get our coats? I don't want to be here when Sean shows up." She said to me, "Martha told me she wouldn't have invited him, but Sean gives so much to the Playhouse that she didn't see how she couldn't. Oh well. Life in Cleveland is so complex." Her companion had returned with their coats. "Let's say our thank you's, Chauncey, and go home."

They left me standing alone. I glanced around and didn't see Anna or hear her voice. Sophie wasn't to be seen or heard. Lang had finished telling his story with a clap of the hands, and his audience laughed. I thought of going off to find Anna. She wasn't supposed to be here, but I still wanted to see her.

I also wanted to see Marie. It had been so long since we'd sat around and chatted. Ever since the announcement of her impending marriage and her promotion, she had stopped showing up at the Cleaning Room. Aggie, for one, had been happy to see less of her; Aggie called her the biggest CT of them all. "You watch," Aggie had said four years ago when I'd transferred out of Direct Services. "You'll fall in love with her, just like a little puppy, and out of that she'll train you to be a wonderful little pony."

I finished off the beer in my glass. Sophie would probably want to leave before Marie showed up.

Standing by the sideboard, replete with candelabra and silver tray, stood a balding man in a tuxedo. He smiled at me. It was a moment before I recognized him: Joseph Megala, a servicer who had transferred to Cleveland from Houston. I was accustomed to seeing him in the Cleaning Room and wearing jeans and a golf shirt. I returned the smile. He elbowed a woman wearing a cotton skirt, a pink blouse, and a Beijing tie (in style for women, these days). She excused herself from the group she was involved with and turned to face me, following Joseph's signal. She smiled. Julie Staminsky: she had transferred from Direct Services about the same time I did, trained also with Marie. I thought of walking over and chatting when I became aware who was in the group of five or six people Julie had been talking with. Like an image fading onto a movie screen, their faces became clear in my mind and my memory. "They'll just dump you off like a horse tied up to a trough when they're tired of you," Aggie had said to me four years ago. "And they'll pick you up when they need you. Except for the free booze, it makes more sense to stay here. Let them come to you when they want you, and no head games to play." I finished off my beer, raised my empty glass for Joseph and Julie to see, to signal that I wasn't purposely avoiding them, and went up to the bar to be addressed as sir and have a new fresh glass with fresh, cool beer. *I thought they were just one of your people*, Chauncey's overweight and anxious jane had said. The dining room was filled with our people; there were at least ten of us, all dropped off to chat and sip something down while our janes and johns floated about.

"How you doing, Rod?" someone asked as she handed her glass to the bartender. "Another vodka martini," she said.

"I'm okay, Felice."

"I thought you were bound and determined not to work the Heights." She was wearing a dress of purple velvet. If that didn't make her stand out in the crowd, then the short length of the hem and the low cut of the dress did.

"Happens anyway," I said, feeling stupid. Joseph and Julie were walking over. I was anxious that Anna would walk in and see us all together. I felt ashamed, unworthy then; why should Anna not see me with the people I worked with, trained with? Why hadn't Anna come back? Why had Sophie left me behind?

"We'd given you up for dead," said Joseph.

"Or at least for someone bound for the straightworld," added Felice.

"With a monitor and a shitcollector, too."

I felt relieved enough that they were talking about Harry and Kevin—criticizing me for spending so much time with them—that I didn't feel insulted. "They're friends," I said.

"They're straight," said Felice.

"One of them," said Julie, "liked to come down to Prospect when I was working Direct."

"Kevin," I said. I guess she had trained with Marie a year after I did; that year after I transferred was when Kevin spent a lot of time down in the Prospect Neighborhood.

"That's the one," said Julie. "Tall husky guy. Soft voice. Always seemed bashful. Wanted to make it with more than one of us at a time. Nice enough guy."

"Still straight," said Felice.

"You could do worse for friends," said Joseph. He smiled at me again. "You're working that Greenspan woman now, aren't you?"

I nodded.

"That must be nice," said Julie.

"She's the only live one amongst this whole bunch," said Felice. "She's always talking up a storm or finding someone to get laid. She's too much of a free spirit for these people."

"Hey," said Joseph. "Steve over there is looking to set up a foursome for his john. The john wants at least one woman. Would your jane like that kind of thing?"

"I don't think so."

"You should try it," said Felice. "They always get a group together so there's a bunch of us. Some orgy. You hardly ever see the straights fucking the straights. Your jane is the only one who seems to enjoy that kind of risk."

"I think my client would pass."

Felice shook her head. "Rod, I think you're really straight on the inside. That's the kind of woman you keep attracting."

"There's nothing wrong with that," said Joseph. "It takes all kinds to keep this business going."

"Straight is as straight does."

"Felice, Marie was about as straight as a basketball hoop. And, look, she's the one—not Rod—who's going to get married."

"Anyway," Julie said to Felice, "Rod's heart is in the right place."

"And, sometimes," I said, "even my dick is." Julie laughed; Joseph smiled. Felice nodded. Before she could respond, I added, "I better find my jane."

"She'll find you when she wants you," said Felice. "Don't be in such a hurry to be with her."

"She's so lively," I said, "she might forget me."

I quickly walked away, carrying my glass filled with untouched, and by now, warm beer. I felt as if they were staring at my back, but when I turned, I saw that the three of them had melded back into their groups and were once again chatting away, letting the evening fade into their own kind of talk while the straights went on with their business.

I ended up in the front hall. It was like a large chamber lined with paintings and filled with people. Trudging up the front stairs was a silver-haired woman and two servicers. They moved as if they were weighed down by the alcohol and the evening. The male servicer had his arm hung over each woman's shoulders, both index fingers stretched out and brushing lightly back and forth across their breasts, moving rhythmically, like windshield wipers. Anna's blue dress with white scallops caught my attention. She stood at the top of a landing and stepped back to let the threesome pass. The silver-haired woman gestured for her to come along. Anna followed them with her eyes, hesitated, then followed with her feet. I reminded myself that the house was monitored, but I followed her anyway.

When I made it to the top of the stairs, I found that Anna had already walked down a well-lit hallway. All sorts of erotic paintings hung from the halls. According to Mary Hasselbacher, after the party was over, the paintings would be taken down and various family pictures would be hung in their place. Outside each door was a little stand supporting a nice square box with a plastic cover, the thirty-second test kit.

Anna was standing outside a closed door. The threesome must have already gone in. I wondered if they'd bothered with the test. As if in a daze Anna reached forward and flipped open the kit's plastic cover. She bowed over to get a closer look at something, most likely the instructions. She reached toward the back of the kit, withdrew a small sterilized packet. She ripped it open and placed the needle blood collector onto the appropriate slot. She stared at the kit for the longest time, and I couldn't help but watch her. Then, with a certain force, almost as if she were punishing herself, she pushed her thumb down onto the metal tip and held it there. She applied a bandage to her thumb while watching the screen for the results. The kit beeped its reassuring negative. It clicked a few times, then swallowed the test container into a bin that was full of chlorine bleach.

Anna stared at the machine a while longer, then turned her gaze to the closed door. I was too far away to hear whatever Anna heard within the room. She looked down at herself, reached up to cup her breasts as if that might give her some reassurance, then extended her hand to the doorknob.

"Anna," I whispered.

She jerked the hand away as if the doorknob had been electrified. She faced me, her hand now to her breast. "You scared me," she said.

I walked over to her. "Do you want to have a drink with me?"

She raised her bandage-covered thumb for me to see. "Do you want to do this, too? There's an empty room down the hall."

Through the door came the sound of a man groaning, a woman giggling, someone speaking in a hushed voice.

"I have a client," I said.

"Invite her up, too," she said.

"How about Uncle Ed?"

That seemed to bring her back to some sort of reality. She shook her head. "He wouldn't appreciate it."

"But he's down there, and you're up here," I said, "and what would he think when he saw the bandage on your thumb?"

"Are you going to bring Sophie up here?" she asked.

I shook my head.

"Sophie likes that kind of thing, you know. It would improve your image back at work."

"Let's go downstairs," I said. "Your Uncle Ed's telling all sorts of nice stories."

"He's telling stories about the war in Spain. I've heard all of them."

The door opened, and a naked woman with silver hair and flabby thighs looked out at us, squinting at the sudden light. "Will you guys join us or take your conversation elsewhere?"

I half-expected Anna to step forward, but instead she shook her head, firmly, as if she was denying some horrendous temptation. I smiled at the woman, took Anna by the arm, and led her down the stairs. Several people looked up from their conversations to watch us descend. Anna became aware of them, shook off my arm, and marched away.

I was left standing alone at the foot of the stairs. All the conversations seemed to be nothing more than one long, continuous sound. A waitress walked by, as if I wasn't there, and lowered a tray of hor d'oeuvres for a nearby couple to chose from. The woman, old, wrinkled, brightly dressed in an African robe, said, "Try this," and lifted a stuffed mushroom to the old man's lips, playfully pushing the vegetable into the man's mouth. He smiled and offered a cracker with pâté to the woman. She took a bite of the offering. His hand glided over her gray hair and traced the expanse of it. She smiled at him.

Leaning against a nearby doorpost stood Martha Milanes. She noticed me at the stairs, smiled, and returned her attention to the clutter of people around her. Maybe I'd be better off back at the water trough with my own, a fresh beer in hand. But I didn't want Felice to call me straight again. I didn't want to be reminded that I spent too much time away from the business. I didn't want to think of Marie getting married. I didn't want to see Uncle Ed Lang.

The old woman raised herself up on her toes and brushed her lips against the old man's. He smiled, something bright and alive in his eyes. I wanted to go to a mirror and conjure up the same brightness in my eyes. I headed for the dining room, when I saw Lang in the library, telling more stories. Anna had an arm entwined around one of his. She leaned up to him and whispered something in his ear. She whispered a lot, and it started to look like she was nibbling at his earlobe. Lang wrapped an arm around her shoulder and looked around. He was blushing. He became all eyes for Anna. The New Puritan falls to temptation, I thought. Straight is as straight does, Felice had said. They use each other, Aggie had said. When Marie got here, there finally would be someone I could talk with.

I made my way to the dining room. Joseph talked to Steven, emphasizing his points, hands slicing through air. Felice was listening to four others, nodding her head with mock-seriousness, giggling every now and then. In the corner, beside the bar, Julie was embracing a woman in a silvery gown. They were kissing, the woman's hand resting upon Julie's breast.

I stepped out into the hallway. The old couple had their coats on and were thanking Martha Milanes. Anna and Lang, holding coats over arms, stood in line behind the old couple. I visualized Sophie's flirtatious kiss, and I wondered if someone had told Anna.

A waitress walked by, offered me an hor d'oeuvre and no smile. She gave her smiles to two of the better-dressed guests. Marie would be here soon, I told myself. Anna was gone. I had let her go. It didn't matter. Maybe she wouldn't show up at the Playhouse tomorrow. Maybe she wouldn't want to get together next week. Maybe I'd never have to crawl back into the gutter I'd crawled out of.

I wanted to find Sophie. Why had she left me alone for

so long? Did she think I'd be more comfortable drinking beer among my own kind? I walked in and out of the large rooms of the Milanes mansion, trying to pick out Sophie's form among the couples and the groups, my ears straining to hear her voice, her laughter, but all I heard was talk about how this company was in trouble, how the president was alienating the Brazilians, how the Kansas City Black Out was a blessing in disguise because it would induce all sorts of new R and D. One or two people nodded in acknowledgment as I walked by. Several said, "Hi, Roderick," but when I asked if they'd seen Sophie, they offered me a quizzical glance, as if they weren't sure why I was looking for her. One terribly thin man with a nose of broken veins suggested she might have gone upstairs, if he knew his Sophie.

I went into the dining room and got another beer. Julie and the woman in the silvery gown were still kissing. The "middle-aged" woman with the prosthesis and the rejuvenated skin was caressing Joseph's face with her real hand. I held the glass bottle tightly in my hand; my fingers turned white.

When Marie got here, there would be someone to talk with.

I remembered Sophie from the footage. She was straddling a man, almost faceless in the image, her hands upon his cheeks, her eyes closed, her hips gyrating. Anna took hold of my mind, and smiled, her face lighting up, her eyes twinkling like the old man's eyes. Marie, now, held me gently, my head against her breasts, telling me a lot of young trainees felt this way, that I'd get over it. My stomach felt far too empty. My temples pounded like the timpani in Sophie's classical music.

Joseph and Julie and Felice had all disappeared. Other colleagues, my own kind, one by one, were leaving the watering trough with their janes and johns, all seemingly electrified by the pervasive erotic tension in the air—or was that just me?—with Anna, Marie, Sophie in my head, because it couldn't be the servicers who felt the tension: each one too busy calculating what should be done for the rest of the evening (and I should have taken Anna into that room upstairs and with the other three, Anna and I would prove that we'd both crawled out of the same self-destructive gutter), each servicer thinking out what their client would like, if it was time for this position, that kiss, these compliments, those suggestions, or if it was time to start a termination pattern because things were getting too close, or was this the time to take advantage of it all and cut down on all those calculations, all those feigned responses, cut all ties like Marie had cut her ties because each Friday there was one more blood test and all the negatives didn't add up against the warmth and the smiles.

"Rod?"

I turned, relief filling all those empty spots of my body, and pulled Sophie to me. Her lips opened to mine, and with more passion than tenderness I let my tongue find hers. I heard someone mutter something behind me, but this time I wasn't going to pay attention, I wasn't going to calculate, I was just going to let my senses lose themselves in the feeling of Sophie's warmth against me, the smell of her perfume lightly entwining itself into everything else I breathed, my blood-tight penis pressing heavy against her abdomen.

Sophie abruptly stepped back, out of my embrace, and examined my face, her eyes narrowed, her lips pursed. "Rod?" she said.

My hands held her arms. I became aware of my erection, and, my face growing hot and flushed, I let go of her.

"I thought you didn't like public places?"

I nodded and glanced around. A couple who had been staring at us immediately turned away.

"Do you want to go home?" she asked, her voice soft with concern. Did I look like something was wrong with me?

I nodded. "Let's get out of here."

"Let me say thank you to a few people, and we'll leave."

"Okay," I said. "I'll meet you at the door."

She started to say something, thought better of it, then smiled. I couldn't read the look in her face. She quickly kissed me on the lips, her lips pausing a moment against mine, transforming the gesture into something tender.

Sophie then walked off to say her good-byes. Ignoring everyone else, I made my way through the various couples, their conversations flooding my ears like alien sounds, and waited for her at the doorway.

"Okay, fleshpot," I finally heard Sophie say, "let's head home."

We stepped out into the cold May air, a chill finding its way into my bones. The air was damp with the coming morning's dew. Just as we were about to step out past the lions and into the driveway, a car softly glided up, its heavy lights slicing the air. A valet rushed up and opened the passenger door while the driver got out under his own power.

"Come on," Sophie said, tugging at my arm.

I watched the woman rise, barely noticing the valet at her side. She wore some sort of fur coat. Her hair was blond and done up in an elaborate style. Small gems hung from her ears.

"Marie!" I called out to her.

She looked at me from across the hood of the car. She didn't seem to recognize me, and momentarily I thought I'd made a mistake. "Oh, hi, Rod," she said. She smiled: no invite, no RSVP; we were in a different world. Marie walked around the car, took the arm of the car's driver—a stout man with heavy jowls—and the two of them walked into the Milanes's house.

Sophie softly hugged my arm, pressing her face against my shoulder. "Shall we head home?" Her voice was soft, not at all insistent.

"Sure," I said.

45

THE STREETLIGHTS THAT cast Fairmount Boulevard into a faintly silver aura now began to dim. It was one A.M. The monitors had infrared lenses to spot any trouble, and the Conservation Acts required some sort of early-morning cutbacks in light, heat, and water. The night and the houses sliding past were ghostly. The silence in the car, exaggerated by the continual exhaling of the defroster, reminded me of the taut silence in which Artie and I would await my father's ghost stories when we were on the beach in Michigan. The fine sand was pale white, in contrast to the stark black and bright reds of burnt logs surrounding a low, fading fire. The stars were clear, and the night's stillness held them. A fresh breeze—I could almost smell the clear air—rushed through the leaves of the nearby hill and rustled the towels we had brought down, in case we dared the ice-cold water for a skinny-dip. The waves regularly lapped at the shore, whispering against the sands and pebbles it drew back out into the lake. Now was the perfect time, and my father would lean forward.

"You seem pensive tonight," said Sophie.

The effects of the afternoon K-pill had faded completely, and the beer was taking over.

"I'm sorry about all the teasing," she said. "I just couldn't resist. You look good in that suit."

"Oh. Thanks."

The defroster filled in the spaces with sound. Sophie drove past her house. My head rotated to the right to watch the house slide by, its visibility quickly eclipsed by other homes. Our favorite story had been about the Flying Dutchman, and so my father brought him and his ship to float above the waters of Grand Traverse Bay. We were too young to mock the incongruity, and we loved how the Dutchman would stop at Gull Island, with its single crumbling house inhabited by gulls and the ghosts of the people who used to live there before the house was abandoned and the screeching of gulls took over.

"Rod, I'm sorry about the woman who snubbed you."

"That's okay."

"Was she a former lover of yours?"

"Not really."

"Do you feel like talking about it?"

"Sophie, you know you drove by your house."

"I know. Let's drive for a while. Something nice about it. It's like we're separate from the world. Perpetual motion as long as there's methane in the tank. I'd hate to have the whole process computerized like in L.A., where you're hooked into some electrical track. I like it this way. You can drive forever, like in a dream, but part of you is in control."

Same dream, different vehicles, I thought.

"Now tell me about this woman who can't appreciate your talents and your warmth."

I thought of kissing Sophie. "It's too long a story, and I don't know where to start."

"With her name?"

"Marie Archer."

"And where did you meet her?"

"Uh, she was my trainer. When I transferred from Direct Services to Leisure Services."

"Oooh, this sounds like a juicy story; just the kind I like."

The car dropped down the hill at the end of Fairmount, and she shot too quickly under the Cedar-Fairmount shopping center.

"Training is sort of tedious. You learn dos and don'ts. You role-play a variety of situations. Dinner, breakfast, your client drunk, your client depressed, your client hinting that she's falling in love. Learning how to read different kinds of files prepared by the AI. How to make judgments based on what you see in the footage of your clients."

"And a lot of fucking?"

"Yeah. A lot of that. Mostly because it's different. In Direct Services it doesn't matter too much how involved you are. You have to act somewhat receptive, feign a little pleasure, but you don't really have to be there emotionally. Just as long as your body makes the right moves. And you never kiss anyone."

We had been speeding down Cedar Hill, the lights of the University Circle mini-Construct already visible up ahead.

"I don't get that," she said while concentrating on several curves in the road. At a light, Sophie turned a corner and took the road under the mini-Construct.

"When you're working Direct, you just don't kiss. That's all. A friend of mine says that once you start kissing people, everything gets confused."

"So this Marie Archer taught you how to kiss so it would seem as if you weren't faking it."

"I guess that would explain it best," I said.

"And she was gentle and nice, and you fell in love."

I smiled. "That's pretty much it." I glanced out the window. The wrecking crews on this part of Euclid had been active; everything looked like the result of some war I'd seen pictures of while in school.

"I know the story," she said. "I fell in love with my first director. He'd treat me today the same way the Archer woman treated you. They're afraid you're still after them, so they snub you to stay safe."

"Yeah, but she's supposedly still a friend."

"I hear some bitterness there," she said. "Are you really talking about your trainer, or are you talking about Anna?"

"I don't want to talk about either," I said.

"Shall we head home?"

"I'm getting tired," I said. I remembered Sophie's kiss, and it had happened too quickly. My suit coat was good for hiding a lot of feelings.

We returned home, and Sophie asked me if I'd like a glass of brandy before we went to bed. I politely declined and said I'd like to read for a while. I grabbed a copy of *Romeo and Juliet* from her library and took it upstairs.

The book spent most of its time on my lap while I stared out the windows opposite the bed. The windows felt like night eyes looking in on me, and I felt myself becoming lost in the labyrinths the darkness held. I saw myself in a friend's apartment, one of the cheap, ramshackle buildings right outside the concrete of the University Circle Construct. The friend, an ex-Havenite, had gone out for several drinks, and I was fucking Susie Sundai. It was the fourth time, we were bathed with sweat, and it seemed as if it would last forever. Her vagina was drenched with semen, and there was so little friction tugging at my penis. "I can't believe we're doing it again," she kept saying. There was no true concrete desire; it was a larger need that kept us going for one more sweaty round. I wondered what we were going to do about the drenched sheets, how we would explain them. "This is better than the woods," I said. She told me she loved me. I felt scared. A month later she told me she wanted to have a baby. A month after that she threatened to kill herself. A month later I told her I wouldn't touch her unless she . . . and *I didn't want to think about that*. I instead wanted to tell Marie that I loved her. We weren't naked. We were sipping coffee in a nearby café because Marie hated the Cleaning Room and all its gossip. I wanted to explain to her how I felt . . . and *I didn't want to think about that* so I shook my head clear, and the night eyes looking in were attractive and a bit frightening. Arthur and I had loved my father's stories, loved all the things the Flying Dutchman did, and while we lay in bed and the night wind rustled leaves and brought in the waves, we imagined we heard his ship approaching the beach; when the house settled and the stairs creaked, we imagined the sounds were his approaching steps up the stairs, along the hall, toward our door. We relished our fear. And eyes closed, floating between wakefulness and sleep, I placed myself aboard that ship. The wood creaked. Water rushed below the ship. A hand gripped my shoulder, and I couldn't quite turn enough to get a look at his face, but I knew he was the Dutchman, which Dutchman he was. He led me downstairs, and instead of a mess room there was an empty, dark chamber, with a pallet that was bathed in dim light. Susie Sundai was skin and shadows. I was naked. The hand gave a little shove, and I went to Susie, who opened her arms. The Dutchman led me to the next pallet and Aggie. She looped her arms around me, told me to place my cheek against her ear, that way a jane would have to turn her head for a kiss, then I could place my head against her other ear, tactfully avoiding the kiss, always ready to whisper anything that occurred to me. The hand on the shoulder, and Aggie's light dimmed, and Marie's brightened. A new pallet. Marie embraced me as if she meant it, and she described exactly how each move I made felt, so I'd know for sure, could apply the training later, and she kissed me as if she wanted to kiss forever. The hand on the shoulder, and Anna awaited me. She had her knees pulled up to her breasts, said she didn't want to make love. The ship creaked; the hand touched my shoulder; the wooden hull was cold against my back. I expected Sophie next, and as the dim light glowed upon her skin, I didn't recognize her at first in all the shadows. Her breasts were lined with red. She held open her arms and seemed to be smiling. The hand against my shoulder urged me forward. I tried to look again, but the Dutchman's face was cast in shadow. I turned toward the woman, and the flow of blood downward drew me to her. She had let her red hair down, and her smile was generous, and I knew who she was and why she beckoned toward me, and I began to kiss the deep red line along her neck when a sound drew my attention away from her.

The light on the night table was on. There was a tapping on the guest-room door. "Rod?" Sophie's voice was a barely audible whisper. I became aware of just how naked I was under the sheet and blanket, and I raised my knees to obscure the persistent erection that had been tugging at me since I'd been in the car. I held up the book like I was reading it.

"I'm awake," I said.

"Can I come in?"

"Sure."

The door opened, the carpeting rustling audibly as the door slid across it. Sophie was wearing a loose-fitting brown bathrobe. The casualness of it made it seem even more sexual.

"What's up?" I said.

She stepped up to the front of the bed, took hold of one of the bedposts, then let it go, as if grasping it contained some sort of innate symbolism. "I feel as if something went unsaid that should have been said."

"We don't have to talk about it. I understand."

"Rod, I don't think so." She looked down at the floor. It was disheartening to see her at a loss for words, without a role to play. "Was that kiss . . . the one at the end of the party . . . was that . . . ?"

"It wasn't for the monitors."

She considered that for a moment, then said, "Was it for Anna?"

I didn't know what to say; I wanted to be honest with Sophie because I had always been honest with her.

She sat down on the edge of the other bed. "I won't be hurt. It wasn't fair of me to kiss you like that earlier. Were you trying to get back at her?"

That didn't sound true, so I shook my head.

"You can't really blame Anna," Sophie said. It sounded like a prepared line, the introduction to an explanation. "Anna is confused."

"I don't want to hear about this."

"She told you about Lang?"

I tried to remember if she'd mentioned Lang at all. "No," I said.

"I'm surprised," she said. Sophie looked out the window, as if an answer could be found out there. She looked as if she were sorry she'd come in. "I don't know if I should tell you this," she said, "but it makes tonight look a lot worse if you don't know."

"Know what?"

"Anna was half in love with Ed Lang when she was a teenager. He was like a carbon copy of her father, but he'd gone off and done all the heroic things. He even got her mother to convert, you know, become a New Puritan. He probably politicized Anna more than Sauro ever did."

"She didn't have to go home with him."

"You didn't let me finish. Ed Lang was—oh, Anna should really tell you this. It's not my business."

"Sophie, are you going to tell me?"

"Ed Lang is to Anna what the director was to me, and your trainer was to you. He was also the first man Anna slept with. She was eighteen and a good girl just like her parents wanted. The parents were out one night, and Ed Lang came over, and they had some drinks."

"And one thing led to another. I've heard this kind of story before."

"Listen, my little dumpling, and try to be sympathetic. It wasn't much of a moment, as sex goes, at least that's what Anna said. But she was instantly in love with him for risking that kind of thing in her parents' house. He apologized afterwards and couldn't look her in the eye for weeks. She learned early what most people learn later on—the men who talk most about honor are usually the least honorable in their own lives. She was terribly disillusioned, and I think she's always wanted the illusion back."

I found it hard to care about Anna's pains. "Do you think they're sleeping together now?"

"I wish I could say they weren't." She bent forward to pat my hand. "And, to be honest, I wish I could say they were."

Her robe had opened enough for me to see her breasts, hanging a bit with their weight, one nipple hidden by the bathrobe, the profile of the other visible against the outline of fabric. We sat like that in silence. I had trouble swallowing. I knew all I had to do was reach over to the night table and turn off the light.

"I'm sorry," she said and sat up. The fabric of her bathrobe closed around her breasts. "I didn't mean to make this so complex."

I didn't know how to speak.

"I'll see you in the morning," she said. She stopped at the door and asked me if I wanted it shut. I nodded, and she closed it behind her, the old latch clicking easily into place.

46

I WOKE UP the next morning resenting everyone. Resentment was an occupational hazard, so I followed training and went through all the names in order to convince myself that my feelings were petty. Marie, Anna, Sophie, Lang, Papa Bear, the men who'd killed Dorothy. Only in Marie's case could I convince myself that my feelings were petty.

To make matters worse, I made the society page for the first time in my life. Mary Hasselbacher gushed that Sophie Greenspan was seen with her new companion, that they were spotted kissing passionately, and that they left the party in a hurry. Sophie thought it was amusing, until I reminded her that Anna would probably read the same thing. "Remember," I said, "you gave us comps for tonight's show. We'll be sitting next to each other."

Sophie's newborn frown didn't last long—the *PD*'s review of the play was a good one, and Sophie got a rave. "Chicago," shouted out Sophie, the actress in her overwhelmed by the emotion, "here I come!"

"*Do you think* Anna will come?" I asked, just before she stepped out the door to run some errands. I had told her I was going to stay in the house and reread *Romeo and Juliet*.

"You mean to the play?"

I nodded.

"Do you want me to give her a call and clear things up?"

"Don't bother," I said. "I only want her to come if she really wants to."

I wished for a while that I were Philip Marlowe with a photostat license. There would be no monitors. I could ask everybody—Anna, Sophie, Sauro's family, Sauro's ASD friends—all sorts of questions, and all my prying would be considered professional.

I wasn't Philip Marlowe. I was a private dick, but for a different age. But I could search Sophie's house. I had to know about Sophie—if, as Lang had hinted, she was as involved as her cousin.

I started with her computer. Her personal crystals were stored in a carved wooden box she kept right by the set-up. I examined each crystal as if it were a diamond and I was looking for a flaw. I had no right to go through any of this.

Once I started, however, it was easy to forget my reluctance. I went through each one, and every file had open access. Nothing was privatized. I found computer-stored photos of theater programs. I found copies of letters, of letters to the editor at the *PD*, of some handbills on refugees, of saved transcripts of the bulletin board, where she'd logged on to talk with other users about sexual independence, about Nigerian boat people, about the nature of American society.

I found a copy of the petition Lang had mentioned. It had a long preamble about how there was fine balance between protecting the general welfare and creating a police state to eliminate crime. Liberty came with responsibility, and monitoring promised a shelter from violence but not from the state's eyesight. "We have created a vast panopticon. Personal choice is no longer a product of free will. It is influenced by the state's vision. The possibility for democratic liberties are limited, and all it will take is the right corrupt people at the right corrupt moment to eliminate all our freedoms in the name of safety."

Sophie had gotten a lot of people to sign the petition. Sauro Contini had signed first, Stuart Greenspan the second. Papa Bear had scrawled in the margin, *what about the camps?* Many of the names I recognized from the party

Sophie had held what seemed like months ago. Many were from the party we were at last night. Martha Milanes had signed her name. Husband Herbert had not. There was an adjacent file, which listed all the places that Sophie had sent the list of names and a cross-reference to the TV time she'd been given on the local news to promote the petition. The date of the last signature was last November. Sophie had single-handedly, without ASD promotion, gotten three thousand signatures. It sure looked like a UHL recruiting front to me. I was sure that two months later all three thousand were on the UHL mailing list for their January Manifesto.

I gave up on the computer and tried her bedroom. The drawers had nothing but clothes, underclothes, pajamas, and some sexy things that looked like they'd never been worn. I held a large garter and told myself that none of this was my business. The bookshelves had books. None of the books had hidden papers or compartments. The bathroom had toiletries. I looked through an adjoining study and found marked-up scripts.

I thought of something and headed back downstairs to the East Room and the computer. I went through the crystals until I found the one where she recorded her finances. I was going through those, trying to find an irregularity in spending, a sign that she was paying for gun shipments or extra computer use or something, when I heard her car pull up in the driveway.

I panicked. I adiosed the computer and hurried from the East Room into the pantry to the dining room and across a small hallway into the library. I had some book open in my lap when I heard the heavy squeak of the front door opening. I put the book down to go help Sophie, returning with dry cleaning and champagne for the opening.

The sun had had come out that afternoon, and the temperature rose slowly enough that Sophie and I weren't aware of the heat until we were sweating. We went over her scenes, but I found it hard to sit still with her in the same room. Several times I leaned forward and almost told her everything.

A shower cooled me off, but I longed for some sort of

climate control as I dressed. I velcroed up my shirt, and the collar was damp. I hesitated to loop the tie around my neck.

There was a curt knock on the door. Before I could answer, Sophie had marched into the room. This time her bathrobe was belted tightly. "You've been through my clothes."

I tried to act surprised. "No. I haven't."

"And I suppose you also didn't go through my financial records and forgot to take the crystal out of the computer."

I didn't say anything.

"I wouldn't have thought it was you. But I couldn't understand how you got to page 200 in *The Republic* while I was gone. You've never touched my philosophy books. You know, if you'd never asked me all those questions about that woman, I wouldn't have become suspicious. If you'd just told me you'd gone out for a walk, I'd have convinced myself that someone else had sneaked in and looked through my stuff."

"Who?"

"The people you work for. Are you FBI or UHL?"

I stared at her, measuring each gesture, each expression. I didn't want to lie, not to Sophie.

"Rod, I want to know why you went through my stuff. I want to know who put you up to this."

"No one."

"You're just naturally nosey?"

"No."

"Are you FBI or UHL?"

"Sort of."

"Sort of *what?*"

"I'm kind of an informer," I said, although I had done nothing more than identify a few photos.

"I didn't figure you for a special agent. Who's got you on the line?"

"Lang, for one."

That surprised her. She could only whisper, "And for two?"

"Your cousin."

"Oh, God." I barely heard her say it. She turned away from me, grabbed a bedpost, and held on for a while. We both listened to her breathe, long, heavy breaths, which she finally gained control of. "I always knew it, but I didn't know it. So that's why he was talking so long with you the other night."

I nodded.

"Do they each know you're informing for the enemy?"

"They suspect."

"Does Anna know?"

"No. I'm informing on her. They both think she's important."

"You're not telling me something, Rod. Anna hung out and helped out, but she was never as political as Sauro. And neither of them was political enough to be terrorists or to inform on old friends for the FBI. That takes a certain kind of righteousness or greed that both of them were, thank God, too lazy to possess."

"They just wanted me to keep an eye out," I said.

"For Anna? Or for her father? He's the important one. He's the one who claims to run the company that built the camps. He's Mr. Morality. He's the type who just might close the door to his daughter and then show up when he hears about what his daughter's up to. You're not the informer, Rod. You're the bait."

I shook my head. I felt like I had when all the lights went out in the Construct. Or when the hand had grabbed my arm, placed the knife to my throat. Everything had been much quicker for Dorothy Souto.

"You have to do something, you know," Sophie said. "After the play, I'll use some connections at the *PD* to get a story going. You can talk to your friend who works at Monitoring. Maybe he can get some footage out for you." The excitement of the idea dissipated from her face. She had solved everything, and I wasn't responding. "What's wrong with that? You just can't sit around and wait to end up dead or in jail."

"I think you're blowing this all out of proportion," I managed to say.

"Then you tell me what to do. You've lied to Anna about your past. You've spied on her. You've spied on me. I'm trusting you anyway. I'm asking you to give up your complacency and help me. For Anna's sake."

"Lang warned me to watch out for you."

"Of course he would. Someone who disagrees is someone dangerous."

"Your cousin thinks Sauro was pushed," I said. "Maybe your cousin pushed Sauro. Somebody took a knife to Dorothy Souto."

"So?"

"I had a knife to my throat once. It's not going to happen again."

"I don't know who killed the Souto woman, but it sure is working if it was meant to scare you. And I knew Sauro a whole lot better than you, or my cousin. My cousin will do anything to convince you of his cause. Sauro probably jumped on his own, the poor boy. It was the only way he had left to make Anna love him again."

47

ACT 1, SCENE 4: Romeo and some other Montagues were heading uninvited to a party thrown by Juliet's father, old man Capulet; Mercutio was ranting and raving about some obscure gods; and Anna hadn't shown up yet. I had waited for her in the lobby, a pair of comps in hand, occasionally glancing up at the monitor, knowing our little subterfuge was more than obvious. When the lights were dimmed several times in succession and those milling by the bar began to file in, I wrote Anna's name on the envelope that held her ticket and handed it to the man at the ticket booth. During the first few scenes I found myself glancing up continually at the entrance, but no sign of Anna; maybe she wasn't coming, maybe an evening with Lang was enough to convince her that it just wasn't worth all the trouble. Maybe Lang had explained it all to her while they rested in each other's arms in the same bed Anna had shared with Sauro and with me. Maybe Sophie had called her and warned her. Maybe she'd read Mary Hasselbacher's column about the kiss. Maybe she was late, and I was trying too hard for an early ulcer.

Scenery slid across the stage; a street scene became the interior of a brightly decorated castle.

Nearby some clothes rustled, someone muttered an excuse, somebody else grumbled, and Anna stepped on a few toes before she collapsed into her seat next to me. I turned to look at her, and I felt a smile crease my face. She winked at me, her eyes bright, and I wanted to kiss her. I remembered the monitors and thought better of it. "I thought you'd never make it," I whispered.

"I messed up on my rapid schedules." Her voice was barely audible.

I didn't know if I believed her. "The play's going better tonight."

She nodded. She faced the stage, but her eyes were unfocused. I wondered what she was thinking, what she'd never tell me. On the stage Romeo had found Juliet amidst the entire mass of people at the party.

"Have not saints lips," said Romeo, "and holy palmers, too?" *Palmers are pilgrims,* Sophie had explained to me. *They're called that because they pray with their palms together.*

"Ay, pilgrim," said Juliet, "lips that they must use in prayer."

"Oh, then, dear saint, let lips do what hands do! They pray; grant thou, lest faith turn to despair."

"Saints do not move, though grant for prayer's sake."

"Then move not while my prayer's effect I take. Thus from my lips, by thine my sin is purged." Romeo managed to smile nervously as if he were truly fourteen, leaned forward and kissed Juliet upon the lips.

"Then have my lips the sin that they have took," said Juliet.

"Sin from my lips?" Romeo asked. "O trespass sweetly urged. Give me my sin again."

Romeo boldly stepped forward for his second kiss. The audience laughed as if at a well-remembered joke. I felt comfortable, and I placed my hand upon Anna's. Her hand shot away and trembled for a moment as if it had been electrocuted.

I barely heard anything as the nurse explained to Juliet who Romeo really was. Why don't they both just shake their heads, I thought, say they blew it, and search for better options? Why did Romeo risk ascending the balcony, kissing Juliet's hands, vowing things that could mean his death?

Juliet's words seemed remote, like a rite practiced by some forgotten African tribe that you only read about in books.

> *Three words, dear Romeo, and good night indeed.*
> *If that thy bent of love be honorable,*
> *Thy purpose marriage, send me word to-morrow,*
> *By one that I'll procure to come to thee,*
> *Where and what time thou wilt perform the rite;*
> *And all my fortunes at thy foot I'll lay*
> *And follow thee my lord throughout the world.*

Juliet's nurse called out to her.

How is it, I wondered, that after one meeting they can be so assured of their love that they can risk so much? Is it risk that increases passion—the secrets and the things unsaid? Or is it just the crying out of skins that have yet to touch? The walls Romeo climbed were the walls around cities, around estates. What walls do we climb?

Both of us were staring at the same play, and somehow it should bring us together. Like Romeo, we should be oblivious to practicalities, or, like Juliet, we should argue them away.

We watched helplessly as all the arrangements were made, as Romeo and Juliet were secretly married, as Tybalt, a nephew of Lady Capulet, slew Mercutio, and as Romeo, in a surge of emotion, slew Tybalt. We watched quietly, the dead upon the stage shocking each of us as the feud endangered everything, and we quietly urged, along with Benvolio's spoken words, for Romeo to flee from the scene before he was captured, and we watched him flee, already knowing that he'd started his final run toward death.

It was a relief for the inevitable to be cut off by the falling of the curtain.

The intermission was worse than the first half of the play. Two-hundred-dollar cokes in hand, we stood against a stone pillar as people mingled, buying drinks and cigarettes, looking about for recognizable faces. There were more suits and fur coats tonight than last night. Martha Milanes, wearing a yellow gown studded with jewels, smiled at me, then at Anna, and seemed about to approach us until her husband grabbed her arm and politely pulled her in another direction. Stuart Greenspan was off in the corner chatting with Timothy Molina and Bill O'Brien. He made an effort not to look in our direction.

Anna kept looking around like she was surveilling the place, who was where, who was noticing us, who was putting two and two together. I restrained myself from looking at a monitor and figuring out who else might be putting two and two together.

"I've got to make a call," Anna said. She talked to me as if I were a business companion. She left me there with my coke. I wondered if she was going to call Lang, tell him everything between us was dead, and set up a time to see him later.

"Who'd you call?" I asked when she returned, her face taut, her lips pursed, as if on the point of being forced open into a smile. Her eyes slid back and forth as if looking for someone.

"A friend," she said, "wanted to get a drink after the play."

"Why don't you get one with Sophie and me?"

"Is that her idea or yours?" she said, then shook her head. "I'm sorry to be so bitchy; it's been a bad day."

"Still recataloging those paintings for your boss?"

"Did I tell you about that?" Anna looked down at her coke and frowned. "We should have spent the extra money and put some alcohol in this."

"I can get you one."

She shook her head and looked at me wistfully. "It's not worth the trouble."

"Anna, what is it?"

"Nothing." Her favorite word with Sauro. It meant: a lot is wrong, and if you love me, you'll figure it out.

I searched for another topic. "You left the party early."

"I heard about you and Sophie. I thought you didn't like public displays of emotion?"

"You had a few public displays of your own," I said.

"You're being petty."

"I'm being petty. You left with your father's best friend."

"You abandoned me," she said. It came out hoarsely.

"I don't want to lose my job," I said. I wanted to tell her about all the other things I could lose, too.

"You can't have it both ways. And I can't wait for you to decide."

I tried to read the thoughts behind her eyes and tried to frame some sort of response. The lights dimmed, and we filed back into the theater.

Mercutio and Tybalt were still dead upon the stage. The prince decided to exile Romeo, upon pain of death, from Verona. Juliet was torn by the news, and Romeo believed all was lost until the nurse, meeting him in Friar Lawrence's cell, told him differently. And once again Romeo must have scaled the deathly wall, for he now shared a bed with Juliet, who was asking him not to leave. I could see her clearly, sitting up in the hotel bed: "Is there anywhere you have to be; is there anyone expecting you?" Romeo fled the dawn with the sound of Juliet's mother knocking upon her door. Her parents filed in and told her to prepare for happiness and marriage to young Count Paris, a kinsman of the prince.

Anna leaned over and whispered, "Things would be much simpler if she just told them the truth. That would avert the tragedy."

I wondered which truth she meant. "Well, have you told your parents about your latest love?"

Her eyes narrowed. "That's not fair. And besides, they're in Pakistan."

In a seat in front of us, a woman turned and raised a finger to her lips.

The play continued, one misunderstanding after another. If two teenagers weren't about to die, it would have been a comedy of errors.

I watched and tried desperately to understand if it was love or honor that brought Romeo to the tomb, a vial of poison ready. Was this all wishful thinking, or had there once been a time when love was so vital and passionate that it lasted beyond death itself? "Don't listen to all that romantic nonsense," Aggie once said, "about love and all the rest. They'll just be planning their next best move. You can talk all you want about fixing hearts, but listen, in today's world, to ache is just that, to ache." But if one was willing to climb walls, visit an apothecary who listens to his poverty rather than his will and sells poison, to descend into a tomb and expect a reunion beyond a meaningless life. . . . Were we treating life as if it had too much meaning? Is that why we hesitate each time our passion and our love demand we do something more? What walls do you climb when all of them are invisible? Romeo, thinking Juliet dead, swallowed the poison. Too soon and too late afterward, Juliet awakened from her drug-induced slumber by the friar who had married them. At the sound of people approaching, Friar Lawrence fled, leaving Juliet to discover Romeo in his timeless sleep, an empty vial in his hand. "I will kiss thy lips; happ'ly some poison yet doth hang on them. . . ." And she found his lips too warm, and heard the sounds of others approaching and reached for his dagger and it all came to me in a rush—the man who grabbed me in a Coventry alleyway and the too many showers that didn't cleanse and all the morphine and all the illegal tricks and all the training that made me safe and life painless without morphine and—I realized that now Juliet had a dagger to her breast and the sounds of people outside the tomb were prompting her. There was a way over the walls.

I leaned toward Anna, placing my lips to her ear. "I'm going to ask Sophie to terminate our contract tomorrow. Our month is up on Wednesday. I'll see you first thing that morning . . . if you want."

The woman in front of us turned and glared. I helplessly slid back into my seat. Juliet was sprawled across the stage as others rushed in. I turned my eyes to Anna's face, expecting some response. She turned to me, her expression thoughtful. Then she nodded, and, for a moment, I felt truly free.

48

EVERYONE APPLAUDED, and the cast took their bows, and it seemed like this was the way to convert our despair into joy. Then, like it had all never really happened, we all began to file out of the theater.

"Do you want to get a drink with Sophie and me?" I asked.

"I wouldn't want to get in the way," she said. Whatever I'd promised her for Wednesday didn't seem to matter anymore.

"It'll be fun," I said.

"Let me make another call," she said.

"Were you going to see Uncle Ed?" I asked.

"Until Wednesday it's none of your business." She kept looking straight ahead. She didn't bother to gauge my reaction.

"Do you want to meet at her dressing room?"

"I know where it is."

"It's actually right next door. They gave her her own room to impress the Chicago people."

"I know. She told both of us, remember?"

We made our way back into the lobby. I gave Anna a quick kiss on the cheek and pushed through the crowd to the doors leading backstage. Once I was in the concrete corridor, the heavy metal door shut, one set of noises was replaced by another: laughter, shouts, and catcalls. The cast was happy.

I wanted to feel as happy. Anna and I would be back

together on Wednesday, I told myself. But I feared that Sophie would insist on telling Anna everything, on going to the *PD* and getting something started. And, of course, I would go along. It would all be over soon.

The door to Sophie's dressing room had a black tile with her name printed in white. Below that someone had pasted on a star cut out of yellow construction paper. I knocked several times, and she didn't answer. The door was locked.

The actor who played Romeo stuck his head out an open door. "Are you looking for Sophie?"

"Yeah. We were supposed to meet here. She locked her door on me."

"That's odd."

A woman who was still dressed as the nurse walked up and tried the door. "I saw her with some guy. I think she left with him."

The heavy door at the end of the corridor opened, and the murmur of the crowd echoed off concrete. The door slammed shut. "Where's my cousin Sophie?" someone shouted.

Romeo glared at Stuart who was walking arm in arm with a pudgy Timothy Molina. I wondered where Bill O'Brien, Timothy's spouse was. Several other actors stepped out into the hall, probably to find out what loudmouth dimwit had invaded their celebration.

"She's not here," I said.

"Oh. Are you sure?"

"We're sure," said the nurse. "Her horse just knocked, and there's no answer."

Stuart shrugged, thought a moment, then waved goodbye. "She's probably out with the crowd. Tell her I loved her performance. She'll make it to Chicago yet." He headed for the door, passing Anna on his way out. They chatted for a second, then parted.

"Who was the guy Sophie was with?" I asked. "One of the scouts from Chicago?"

"Gosh, no," said Romeo. "The scouts are both women. They're upstairs with Dolores."

"Everything's set," said Anna. She smiled as if she'd

just put down a heavy burden. "No one's expecting me. Where's Sophie?"

"She's not here," said the nurse.

"Did you see her out in the lobby?" I asked Anna.

"She wouldn't be out there," said Anna. "Sophie hates mixing performance and reality."

"That's for sure," said Romeo. He sounded like Sophie didn't want to mix performance and him.

I turned back to her door and knocked again. I kept thinking that this was all wrong, that we shouldn't be so casually standing here, wondering where Sophie was. But no one else seemed to think anything was wrong.

"She's obviously not in there," said somebody else.

"Just open the door, Rod," said Anna, "and take a look."

"It's locked," I said.

"Sophie would only lock it if she was fucking someone," said Anna. "And you're out here."

I told myself that if I was wrong, I'd only look foolish. Three shoves with all my weight behind my shoulder did it. Cheap wood cracked, and the door swung open. Someone else must have reached in to hit the light switch, because the ones lined over her mirror flashed on so suddenly that I squinted, and lost my orientation.

Whoever had gotten to her hadn't used a knife. There was no blood. I pumped her chest, breathed into her mouth while holding her nose, barely hearing the shouting that had erupted as I kept going at it, hoping I was remembering the first aid and the CPR right because it had been a while since my last refresher course, and I kept going at it, yelling at her to be okay until somebody took firm hold of my arms and told me that he was a doctor and that she was dead. I told him they must have poisoned her, and he looked at me in disbelief. I sat back against the wall and watched everybody else swarm around Sophie. She was lying on the concrete floor, still in her costume. Her head was still tilted back, her eyes open. I wished, for the briefest of moments, that there had been enough poison on her lips for my own.

Part 4

termination

I hold that a little rebellion now and then is a good thing, and as necessary in the political world as storms in the physical. Unsuccessful rebellions indeed generally establish the incroachments on the rights of the people which had produced them.
—THOMAS JEFFERSON

49

ANNA'S COMPUTER HAD *PD* subscription service, and the paper was full of the information that had come to the forefront during the last six hours. The FBI had lent the use of their updated labs to the Cleveland Police, and their doctors of forensic medicine found that Ms. Sophie Greenspan had been killed by a synthetic nerve drug developed by the military during the Cocaine Wars last century. But it was reported that the United States, per treaty agreement, no longer manufactured any nerve drugs of this order. A spokesman for the Department of Defense said the United States did have samples in high-security storage; but that those samples were untouched. Edward Lang stated that Greenspan had been running front activities for the UHL and might have been executed by the organization for trying to break away.

In the Arts and Living section of the *PD* was an overview of Sophie's career, highlighting her performances at the Playhouse over the past year. One of the women from Chicago said Ms. Greenspan would have been an asset to the Chicago production of the play this fall. An editorial summarized Sophie's several forays into politics and saluted her for never compromising the art of her performance with her political beliefs. The editorial never doubted Lang's evaluation. In all the coverage, analysis, and opinions, the Union for Human Liberation was mentioned twenty times, according to the computer count I did. There was no mention of the UHL goals, or of the living (if you could call them that) conditions in the camps.

Last night, we had been held at the theater for hours after the discovery of Sophie's body. The cops, led by a hyperactive woman by the name of Ibarra, took forever to do the necessary mopping up. They questioned us together. They questioned us separately. Some officer must have been calling up public right to know info, because the detectives' questions kept getting more personal. They fed the Playhouse design software into the terminal, and came up with time charts and movement diagrams. When the footage from Monitoring had been transferred, they discovered that Adolf, for unknown reasons, had erased all coverage of Sophie from curtain call to discovery of the body. Flustered by that discrepancy, Ibarra became visibly angry after a phone call from Ohls, who told her that I had some connection with the Dorothy Souto murder. That's when Ibarra took Anna and me into a rather large office and locked the door behind her. Her face red, her body in constant motion with pent up emotion, Ibarra grilled me about my politics, grilled Anna about hers, and grilled us about our relationship until Anna admitted everything, which only made a frustrated Ibarra suspicious.

They finally let us go. It was three A.M. when I got Anna home. The place was as spotless as an apartment waiting to be rented, and the air was just as stale. It was as if she had spent the last three nights here without once opening a window. I opened all the windows while Anna, moving like an automaton, much like the first day I'd met her, undressed and searched for a nightgown. Her body looked sexless. She bent over to open a drawer, and her belly creased into tiny little rolls. I couldn't imagine ever having been attracted to her. She found a nightgown, raised it to her face, and sniffed. "It smells like something at a funeral parlor," she said.

It was then, after she'd put on the nightgown, that it came back to her, what had been so easily buried during the too many questions and time charts and movement diagrams. We couldn't go back to Sophie's door immediately after the curtain call and knock it down with our first suspicions. Anna let go of whatever had built up inside her, and it came out as a wail. She pounded her feet on the floor, pulled at her hair, and her rage did nothing. It was an hour before she was willing to cry in my arms, another before she'd lie down. I massaged her to sleep.

The lessening gray of early morning woke me. I showered and got back into the slacks and shirt I had on last night. Hungry for some food, I opened the refrigerator, and it smelled like food that had been there a month too long. I slammed the door, fled the apartment, and took a walk through the neighborhood. The sun on my skin made me feel like I had a hangover. I watched my shadow as I walked to an early morning store. I bought eggs, orange juice, coffee, milk, and bread. Back at the apartment I cleared the refrigerator of once-upon-a-time food and tried to relax by cooking. I scrambled some eggs, adding onion, garlic, and sharp cheddar cheese.

I didn't want to wake Anna. It was Saturday; she didn't have to work. I didn't know what to tell her about Sophie. Sophie had wanted me to tell everything to Anna, and to the *PD*. What could I tell them that could be proven?

Around ten o'clock, the vidphone started to chirp. I considered not answering, then changed my mind. Joan from the gallery called and said she'd call back later to see what she could do. Martha Milanes called to express her condolences and looked surprised to see me. Norman and Emma White called. Timothy Molina and Bill O'Brien called. Aunt Lorena Smith called.

"Who might you be?" she asked, even though she had to have known.

"Rod Lawrence," I said. "I'm a friend of your grand-niece."

"Yes," she said. She was too refined to say *I bet*. "I saw your picture in today's *Plain Dealer;* it said you had taken her home. You were employed by Anna's *friend,* weren't you?"

"Yes, ma'am." The ma'am slipped out. She commanded that sort of authority.

"And before that, by my grand-niece?"

I nodded.

I couldn't read the expression on her face. "When Anna wakes up," she said, "will you ask her to call me first thing?" I told her Anna would call her, and she said good-bye. The screen went gray.

The floor creaked, and I turned. Anna wearing her nightgown, her face puffy with sleep, shuffled into the living room. She looked at me as if I belonged there, like a piece of the furniture. "I thought I heard Aunt Lorena's voice," she said. She yawned, gave me a perfunctory hug, and before I could envelop myself in her warmth, she had broken away and headed over to the couch.

"Yeah. She wants you to call first thing."

"I'm so tired." She collapsed on the couch and looked up at me.

"I'll make you some coffee and eggs."

"Would you?" she smiled dreamily, as if she were about to fall back asleep."

"Scrambled or fried?"

"Are they any good? I haven't been here in weeks. The place smells sort of musty."

I had trouble talking. Where had she been the last few nights, if not here? "I bought some stuff this morning."

I made coffee for both of us and scrambled the eggs the same way I had earlier.

"Could you get me some aspirin?" she asked when I handed her the plate.

When I returned from the bathroom, Anna was sitting by the vidphone, punching out a number. She had left her plate of eggs by the coffee table. "Sit down somewhere she can't see you," she said, her back to me. "Hi, Rosa. Could I speak to my aunt, please?" Aunt Lorena's live-in servant, Rosa, told Anna how sorry she was to hear about Anna's friend, then left to get Mrs. Smith. "Hi, Aunt Lorena," Anna finally said.

"Why, hello, I didn't expect to hear from you so soon." The anger in Lorena's voice was gone, or well controlled. "You look as if you could use some more sleep."

"I didn't sleep very well."

"I'm sure. I am terribly sorry for what happened to your friend. I always did enjoy her company when you brought her over for dinner. I do hope that what the papers say isn't true."

"I haven't seen the paper."

"You might not want to read it. It's all pretty ghastly. Now, the reason I wanted you to call is because I wanted to talk with you about your father's plans."

"My father?" Anna glanced at me as if I would be able to explain it.

"Yes. Your father was in Karachi when word broke out. It was ten-thirty in the morning their time when someone gave him the unfortunate news. A little later he was told about your *friend,* the one who answered your phone, and about all the other rumors. He got on the first plane out, and he'll be here tonight. The rest of your family will follow tomorrow."

"My father will be here tonight." She repeated it, like an incantation.

"Yes. He'll be very tired, but he would like you to dine with us at my house. He will be staying with me, of course."

"I don't have a car."

"You have a license. You can rent one. If you can spend monies from your trust fund on having a friend, you can afford renting a car for an evening to come out and see your father. It's about time the two of you got back together."

"What time should I come?"

"Around seven will do."

Anna looked at me. I felt she was going to invite me while Aunt Lorena looked on.

"And, Anna dear, I think it's best if you come alone. For your father's sake."

Anna nodded helplessly. Aunt Lorena gave her the number of the hotel in Karachi where Anna's mother and two sisters were staying so Anna could call and tell them she was all right. Aunt Lorena then asked if there was anything she could do. Perhaps, she suggested, Anna should call George and Joan from the Gallery. They'd be happy to help out and look after her. Anna could spend the night with them, or out in Hunting Valley with her.

"I'm okay," Anna said. "I'll see you tonight."

They said good-bye, and Anna turned off the phone.

"She's probably scared that I'm charging overtime," I said.

It was the wrong thing to say. Anna glared at me and said, "She's doing her best."

Anna headed out of the living room when I took hold of her arm. "Can I go to the bathroom?" she asked.

"Do you want me to stay?"

"That's up to you. You can come back on Wednesday. If you want."

"I'm here now. I brought you back last night. I want to be with you."

She looked at me as if she didn't believe me.

"I love you," I said.

"I do, too." She didn't sound too sure about that, and she looked at the wood floor for a while. "But my best friend's dead, and I keep wanting it to be a dream, and you're here, but it's because she's dead you're here. I have a headache bigger than my head, and my father's coming to see me and tell me about everything wrong I've ever done. I don't know what you want from me."

"A hug and a kiss?"

"Is that all?"

"That would be a start."

"Then what? We make love like none of this ever happened?"

"No. Another hug would do."

She embraced me, brushed her lips against mine. She left me for the bedroom, then turned around and marched back. "Remember, I had the locks set for your print. I'm not going to change that. I do want you with me. I at least want you here after I see my father. But I need some time alone. Could you go out for a while and, maybe, come back later?"

I nodded, kissed her, and left her there. The stone stairway was drafty, and my footsteps echoed. I wished her locks were as old-fashioned as the building. I longed for something tangible like keys in my pocket. I felt as if I'd left a dream. I could return to the Construct and act as if it never had happened.

Meanwhile, Papa Baxter was coming to Cleveland, just like Papa Bear had wanted.

50

FOR FOUR QUARTERS—only one hundred dollars—you can spend the rest of your life underground on the RTA. I got on at West 25th, intending to head home, but I stayed on long past my stop. Just before we swept out from under the Construct and into daylight, I transferred to a rapid heading in a different direction. At all the silver-lit stops, I watched the people: the synthetic clothes, or the 100 percent cotton; the cheap precut, or the Democracy Now careful fit; the old worn-out, or the bright and colorful new; the short, cropped hairstyles and the hair spiraled atop, the blond, brown, black, and red hair, the pale white skin, the shades of olive, the shades of brown, the jet black, all the while listening to the different languages and dialects. For brief moments Cleveland contained the entire miserable world underground. Between stops, listening to the faint electric hum, I stared through my reflection into the sparsely lit darkness and watched for gnomes.

I finally ended up at Personal Services. I considered a massage parlor that provided more than a rubdown. Or maybe Direct Services would have someone who'd tell me how wonderful I was. Or at the Sensory Arcades Julius could recommend some Experience that left you feeling peaceful and content. As usual, I settled for the swimming pool and kicked and pulled away at the excess energy. In the steambath afterward I felt sick and exhausted.

I was going to skip the Cleaning Room, but I ran into

Julie Staminsky in the locker room. "You look like you need a beer. Let me buy you one." She squeezed my arm and didn't mention the party at Herbert Milanes'.

We ended up sitting with Eric, Aggie, and Henry. Henry turned away from me as if I had done something wrong. "Sorry to hear about your jane," Eric said.

Aggie sipped coffee. "Suburban life is more interesting than I thought."

"Aggie!" Julie hissed.

"Rod can handle it," Aggie said. "His picture made the paper. He's big time now."

I finished my beer. "Maybe I better go."

Julie implored me to stay. "They're just upset about Cindy."

Aggie shook her head. "That's not it. Personally, I am upset with Rod here. It's the first one, isn't it? You're in love with her."

I nodded.

"I saw that train coming a mile away, and if I saw it coming, I know you must've seen it coming, too. Why didn't you just step off the tracks and get out of the way?"

"Aggie," I said, "if you were in love, wouldn't you do the same thing?"

"Hell no. Not with two people dead."

"Oh, come on, Aggie," said Julie, "tell the truth."

"Okay," she said, "you want the truth. Here's the flat-out truth. I'd do it for my kid. And maybe I'd do it for a man the first one or two weeks I was in love with him. But I've been in love before. After a while being in love doesn't stop you from being alone. So what's the use? Use your brains, Rod, the ones in your big head," she tapped her temple, "and get off this sinking ship before you go under."

On the bulletin board someone had posted the departure time for Cindy's train on Monday morning. She was bound for Camp Seven. Maybe I could ask Luis to give her words of advice.

Next to that was hardcopy of all the articles about Sophie that mentioned me. Someone had programmed Tricky Dick to boldface my name whenever it appeared. It didn't appear that often. However, there was a picture from the Arts and Living section that hadn't been there in the earlier edition I had read. It was an enlarged section of a monitor-eye view of the theater seats. Anna and I were holding hands. Two people sitting directly behind us looked familiar. Two men, holding hands, fitting into the crowd as two lovers watching *Romeo and Juliet*. The other night they had been wearing blue blazers and khaki pants like a couple out of the twentieth century. They were the two who had crashed Milanes's party. Now they were sitting behind Anna and me.

I tore the picture off the bulletin board, folded it, and shoved it into my pocket. I turned away from the bulletin board. Everyone in the Cleaning Room was busy eating, drinking, or chatting. No one seemed to have noticed. Except, of course, the monitor.

I almost made it out of Personal Services, but Joseph found me, told me that Fred had heard I was in and wanted to see me.

Fred was slouched in his chair. His face was pale, and his dark circles were becoming pouches. The last time I had seen him like this was the last time a servicer had come back with bad blood.

"You look tired," I said and sat down.

"You don't look too hot yourself." His voice was hoarse, a cross between a whisper and a croak. "I'm sorry to hear about your jane. It's too bad she had to get involved with those kind of people."

If he hadn't looked so horrible, I would have asked him what kind of people he meant.

"I wanted to touch base with you, since you were here. Palaez came to tell me this morning that you broke our agreement last night. As if we didn't have enough problems."

"I take it Palaez wants my neck."

"She's bought the rope and she's building the scaffold right now."

"Glad to hear she's getting some pleasure out of life."

Neither of us said anything. We sat in our respective chairs as if we'd be better off if sleep overtook us.

I finally said, "Do you want me to resign?"

Fred looked surprised. "Is the Baxter woman going to put you up?"

"I doubt it."

"Do you still want to be here?"

I nodded.

"Marketing people came to me this morning with an idea I thought a bit crass, but it could save your neck." His voice became a croak. He swallowed some water and sprayed the back of his throat with some medication he had on his desk. "That's a little better. Marketing wants you transferred to media for a bit, to capitalize on the publicity. They feel they could adapt a script to you by Wednesday, and have shooting finished within a week, and something out by the end of the month. They're also thinking of going through your past files and putting together a montage of you with some of your shift-janes. Tricky Dick could have it edited by Tuesday, Palaez could have legal clearances by Friday, and the video would be out a week from Monday. It should help cut our losses, and it would make some great advertising for you. It could make you one of the hottest numbers in the Heights in a month or so." He was talking quickly, as if he were selling the idea to both of us. His voice became softer, squeakier, and his last words were barely audible, and he sprayed his throat again. "They gave me a flatscreen of all your previous clients, and they wanted you to delete the ones you thought wouldn't go for the idea. We'll do a credit search and make our first offers to those who could use a little help paying off their balances due."

Before I could say anything, he passed me the flatscreen. The whole proposal was written out and then followed by a list of names. The list seemed too long; I couldn't possibly have taken care of this many in the last three years.

"I can't think about this right now," I said.

"Your name's going to be in the newspapers for a while. You'll probably have reporters calling you soon. They spent all morning calling me. I got more calls about you than I did about Cindy."

"They're shits," I said.

"They're doing their job. And Marketing is doing its job. They want to capitalize on your notoriety. It would put you right with Palaez, because she'd get a cut for the extra legal work. It would help us with projections."

"Do you want me to do it?"

"I sort of think it stinks. But the Marketing people say it's just fucking. What does it matter if the audience is one, two, or thousands?"

I stared at the names and wondered if Anna would want to buy a copy, maybe share it with her father. I deleted Sophie's and Anna's names. I then deleted Beatrice Knecivic. I thumbprinted the appropriate spot for approval and tossed it onto Fred's desk. "Can I take a week's vacation? I'm thinking of visiting my brother."

"Sure," he said. "Media can wait a week. And Marketing can get together this other crystal on its own. You look like you need a rest. When will you leave?"

"I don't know. Maybe tomorrow. Maybe after Sophie's funeral. Well, at least not until Cindy leaves."

I got home and Harry turned out to be right. There were over a dozen messages on the computer. The *Plain Dealer*, *The New York Times*, *Time*, the *Nation*, the *Way of Christ*, AP, UPI, and some I'd never heard of. The reporters' names were a mix of nationalities, and I felt as if the whole world were intruding. Along with that was a message from Harry: *We'll be at the Admiral at 15 hours if you want some company*.

I wondered if they'd bury me next to Sophie if Lang or Papa Bear or Angel took exception to a press conference. Cheetah screeched. It was Stuart Greenspan. He looked worse than Fred. Lang claimed that Stuart's people killed his cousin. Did guilt rob a face of life the way grief did?

"Hi, Rod," he said. "You look the way I feel."

"I'm sorry about Sophie," I said.

"We all are. And we're angry, too. Look, I'm at her place. Sophie's mother and sister are making funeral arrangements. If you want to take the rapid out to University Circle, I'll pick you up and bring you here to get your stuff. Anna has some stuff here, too."

I'd forgotten I'd had stuff there. I'd forgotten that Sophie had a sister, a half sister really. She must have flown in. Everybody, it seemed, was flying in. I wondered if Artie would fly in if I asked him to.

"Can you make it?" he said. "You can come out tomorrow, if you prefer."

I told him I'd come. I called up an RTA schedule, then told Stuart to pick me up in forty-five minutes.

After we'd disconnected, I called up yesterday's *PD* and located the review of *Romeo and Juliet*. I got the name of the actor who played the nurse from the cast list, and I called up Directory for a number. Her phone had a nice old-fashioned ring to it. By the tenth ring I had almost given up. She answered.

Her face filled the screen. Her eyes grew wide when she saw who I was.

"I'm sorry to bother you," I said.

"You're the guy who found Sophie, right?"

"Yeah. My name's Rod Lawrence. I was her companion."

She wasn't sure if she should offer condolences or not to a companion, so she just looked confused.

"Yesterday, just before I knocked the door in, you said some guy had come to see Sophie."

"Yeah. The police already got a description from me. They said they'd relay it to Monitoring."

"Did you see this picture in the *PD* this morning?"

I felt around for the hardcopy I'd pulled off the Cleaning Room Bulletin Board. I was sure I'd laid it out somewhere.

I reached into my pocket and found I'd never taken it out. I unfolded the paper and held the picture up to the phone lens. "I'm in the middle of the picture. I'm sitting with Sophie's friend Anna Baxter."

"Okay. I see you."

"Right behind us are two men holding hands. Do you recognize either of them?"

She said nothing for a while. Then, "Yeah, the guy on the right looks familiar. I think he's the one I saw last night." She sounded suspicious.

"I have to give this info to the police," I said. "I'll call you back later." The nurse disappeared.

I held the *PD* photo in front of me. The man on the

right had been the man at the party who'd argued against nudity in the theater. His clothes had been a little rumpled. His friend had called him Ken. Now I knew he'd spoken to Sophie after the play. I waited for some inspiration to connect it all. None came. Ken had been at the play. So had Stuart Greenspan. One had worked hard to be inconspicuous. The other had worked hard to be noticed.

I headed for the RTA, to see the one who had worked hard to be noticed.

51

STUART GREENSPAN CARRIED himself as if his stocky frame were heavier than usual. He talked pleasantly, but sadly; his grief was apparent, and I regretted my previous suspicions. "I had expected to find your stuff in Sophie's room," he said. "I figured the stuff about you and Anna was something Lang had put together as bait."

He helped me gather my clothes from the guest room and place them in my Democracy Now suitcase. Then we packed the clothes Anna had left behind in one of Sophie's suitcases.

"The funeral will be on Wednesday," he said, finally. "The FBI will be done with the body, and the funeral home will have it dressed and ready for a closed-casket service." He smiled grimly. "Too bad. It would have been my first time in a temple since my bar mitzvah."

"You're not going?"

"Let me show you something." He led me to Sophie's bedroom and picked up a small remote-control box with lots of lights. "I think I told you about this at the party. It finds listening devices. Luis and I spent hours going over the house this morning. We found only two. One in her bedroom, and one in yours. They were well designed and well planted. You had to have this thing aimed directly at them to find them. Someone heard you tell Sophie that I was your contact for the UHL."

My belly dropped into my bowels.

"An inside source told me that they're using that

information, gathered illegally, to try to put together enough legal evidence to get a warrant for my arrest. It would be a real coup for Edward Lang if he could arrest a top terrorist and bring him to trial. It would get him out of Cleveland and back in Washington."

"How can he tie you into Kansas City?"

"He can't. I wasn't there; I wasn't part of it."

I must have looked as if I didn't believe him.

"There are certain things we can cover up, but to get people from Cleveland to Kansas City without anyone noticing some anomalies is close to impossible. Kansas City people did Kansas, just as Cleveland people will do Cleveland, if Angel decides that Cleveland is the city to hit."

"Then what can he arrest you for?"

"The train-bombing in December. I planned it, and I guess some info that would tie me to it has leaked."

"You did that?"

"Yeah. I planned it. The train car that would take people to the camps was the only thing destroyed. No one was injured. And the effort was a failure. All it got was bad publicity and Edward Lang. So my career is over."

"You're going underground? Like Luis?"

"Something like that. But Luis really escaped; he's officially dead: A body was planted with his ID, enough remains to verify the ID, and now he's pretty much a ghost. He has a new name, a false bancard, and the rest. I, on the other hand, exist. And, unfortunately, the police investigation is catching up with Lang's."

"Where do I stand in all of this?"

"James Baxter's coming to town, I hear."

I nodded.

"Maybe we can still have that meeting. I want to talk with him, one on one. It would be nice if it was some place quiet, maybe even monitored. You could see me in the restaurant and invite me over to Anna's apartment, and it would be like inviting an old friend. I want a dialogue, not an assassination or kidnapping."

"Right," I said.

He ignored the sarcasm in my voice. "I think you can help make a meeting happen."

I couldn't help but laugh. Not because it was funny, but because it was so serious. "I won't even see him. He's here to rescue his daughter."

"And his daughter is in love with you. He's gotta know what will happen if he asks her to choose. He lost that gamble last June. I think you'll meet him, and we'll want to be part of that meeting."

I started to shake my head before I knew it.

"It has to happen, or there'll be worse things in the making. Remember what I told you about Angel. She'll black out as many Constructs, blow up as many police, assassinate as many politicians as possible. Make it so terrible that freeing the hivers will look like a pleasant alternative."

"Sounds like a nifty plan to win friends."

"Isn't it? That's why this meeting has to happen. And don't forget you owe us. For Dorothy and Sophie, you owe us."

"Sophie wasn't one of you," I said.

"But they still killed her."

"They say *you* did."

"Of course, they would say that."

"You would have, if you thought it necessary. Plenty of innocents died in the Kansas City Black Out."

"And plenty of innocents die in the camps every day."

"What makes you so different from them?"

"The cause. The cause is what makes us different. They want safety and order and cleanliness. We want human liberty."

"Bullshit."

"Let's put it on a down-to-earth level. Let's not talk about order and liberty. It's probably wrong to kill in the name of either. How about in the name of Cindy Molero, who is being shipped off to the camps on Monday? How about in the name of Luis, who was sent to die there? How about in the name of children who are born, grow, watch their parents die, and then die themselves? Is that down to earth enough for you?"

"I want no part of it."

"You are part of it, whether you like it or not. If you

enjoy living, you'll be part of it. If you like to see Anna Baxter living, you'll be part of it."

"Anna was ASD; she was part of the cause."

"You got the past tense right. Now she's screwing Edward Lang when she's not screwing you."

"What the fuck does that mean?"

"It means just what I said. She left Sophie's house on Tuesday and skipped work that day. She went straight to Lang's apartment. She stayed there Wednesday and Thursday night, too. Maybe she set up Sauro."

"I can't believe that."

"Then find me a better explanation."

"Maybe Sauro jumped on his own."

Greenspan raised his hands in surrender.

"Lang told me Anna might be one of you," I continued. "He said you're the one who suggested that Anna hire a servicer."

"Lang's been manipulating you."

"And you haven't?"

"I'd better take you to the rapid."

"Was Sophie one of you?"

"No."

"Is Anna?"

"No."

"But Sauro was, right?"

"To a point."

"But he had nothing to do with Kansas City."

"That's a joke. Only two people here knew about Kansas City before it happened, and Luis was the other one."

I eyed him for a second. "I know enough law to know that if I don't turn you in, you've made me liable for aiding and abetting."

Greenspan nodded, a faint grimace on his face as if he found the whole thing distasteful.

"How do you know I won't tell Lang?"

"Because you'll make a meeting happen."

"You don't know that."

"I think it's time to take you back to the rapid." He stepped forward, then stopped. "You know, two suitcases is a lot to carry on the rapid. Why don't I drop them off at your place later this afternoon, after my cousin and I have closed up the house?"

"I can handle them."

"Let me drop off Anna's, then. It'd probably look better if you took yours with you."

He placed the bug detector in his jacket pocket and started for the door, as if everything were settled and there was nothing more to discuss. I took hold of his arm. He faced me.

"Let's say Sophie was a threat to you. Would you have killed her?"

Greenspan had to think about it, then he nodded. He didn't look too happy with the idea, but he had no problem nodding.

"What if the entire city of Cleveland was a threat?"

"They aren't. They're the ones who can get our people out, who can demand justice for us." He flexed his arm, and I dropped my hand. "But I'll tell you this. If the only way to end the horror of the camps was to kill every single person in the city, we'd do it, without compunction, with as little sympathy as the majority of the people here felt for us when we were condemned to die alone."

I stared with what must have been disbelief. I tried to understand who the "us" was. The people who were sent to the camps had nothing more in common than a virus and their humanity.

"But remember this, Lang's people would probably do the exact same thing if they thought it would rid the world forever of evil terrorists." He smiled then. "But, you do understand, in real life, no one is going to wipe out Cleveland, or any other city. Now let me take you to the rapid. There's a lot I have to do here."

We walked away from the bedroom almost gingerly, as if stepping away from the ghosts of our imagined apocalypse.

When I got out of the car at University Circle, Papa Bear promised he'd see me again.

52

THE ADMIRAL OF the Port was empty except for a bunch of regulars. All of them looked at me; none of them said anything. My face must have been on the holo. Bernardo, the bartender, saw me, got out a Thirty-Three, and poured a shot of dark rum. "It's on the house," he said in a low voice.

Harry wasn't there, but Kevin was. He sat on a bar stool. In front of him were arrayed the empty bottles to mark the time he'd been here. He'd been here for six beers. He was almost finished with the seventh. I sat on the stool next to his. I said hello and downed the shot. "Where's Harry?" I asked.

"They called him in at Monitoring," Kevin said. "They got the FBI or somebody in there going through everybody's clearance. They're giving Harry a rough time because he showed you some stuff."

Kevin watched the holo—an Indians game was on— and finished off the beer. He lined the green bottle up with the others. "Your client's murder didn't get saved by Adolf, so they know there's a terrorist working Monitoring. They're trying to weed him out."

I sipped my beer.

"You know, you could have told us some of it."

"She wasn't UHL. They're lying."

Bernardo handed Kevin a new beer. Kevin drank some before speaking. "Why would they lie?"

"I don't know. I just know my client wasn't a terrorist."

"There were a bunch of reporters all over Harry this morning. They came looking for you."

"I was out," I said.

"They asked if you'd be with that Baxter woman. We didn't know what to say. You hadn't bothered to fill your friends in on the situation."

"I'm with her."

Kevin smiled. It was an ironic smile. "After we got rid of the reporters, your brother called. He sounded like he'd heard the news."

We said nothing for the longest time. I wanted to tell him about Anna, but I couldn't think of any way to start. I finished the beer and told him I had to get going.

"Going out to Ohio City?"

"Yeah."

"I liked her the one time I met her. Give her my best." He saluted me with his empty beer bottle. "And good luck with the reporters." He turned back to the bar and cocked his head a bit to watch the holo. It was as if I'd never been there.

There were no reporters lurking outside my door, just a monitor to greet me when I walked in. There *were* messages from journalists to call. Several, working for slick printouts with pictures and all, offered cash for an exclusive. There was a message from Artie—*Please call. Mom and I are worried*. There was a message from Anna—*I didn't access the lock to your print to keep you away*. I called up the yellow file and picked out the name of a travel agent. I called them up and made a reservation for tomorrow, Sunday at 1435, a one-way ticket to Traverse City. I then called Anna and told her I'd be right over after I shaved and showered. She didn't invite me over to share a shower. She offered a very formal, "I'll be looking forward to seeing you."

Parked near the brownstone where Anna lived was a deep red SEAT that I'd never seen before. Dowdy but reputable, the Spanish import looked like the kind of car Anna would rent. Parked on the front steps, and a little less reputable, were a few reporters. They knew my name and started asking questions.

"I see you rented some friends along with your car," I said to Anna after she had kissed me. She was wearing a white skirt and a frilly red blouse. I wondered if she'd picked the colors on purpose to reflect her contradictory feelings.

"Did you tell them anything?" she asked.

"I told them I was madly in love with you."

She turned pale. "Great. That's all my father needs to see."

"That sounds fair. I tell them at work that we're together, and you don't tell your father anything." I shook my head. "It was just a joke. I didn't tell them anything."

Anna tried hard not to look relieved. She left the living room and came back with a glass of water and two aspirin. I pictured her lining glass bottles of aspirin along the top of the medicine cabinet.

She looked at her watch. "I gotta go. I'll be late."

"I just got here."

"I'm sorry. But I have to be there by seven. I waited for you all afternoon."

"Do you really even want me here?"

"Your thumbprint got you in, didn't it?"

"Then why are you leaving so soon?"

"I don't want to be late. I haven't seen my father in almost a year. I want to make a good impression."

I couldn't imagine my presence here as much help. "Do you want me here when you come back?"

"Do what you want. You obviously did all afternoon."

"I spent a good part of my afternoon packing up the stuff you left behind at Sophie's. Didn't Stuart Greenspan drop it off?"

"No. Was he supposed to?" She leaned forward and kissed my lips. "I'll try to be back early."

I watched her leave. I almost left with her to head back to the Construct. But she turned her head and smiled. "I do want you here. And you're right. I will tell my father about you, if he asks."

The evening stretched out, and it took forever for the grays of approaching night to creep in. I paced the apartment, listening to Sauro's jazz crystals until the music frayed my nerves. I tried some classical, but it reminded me of Sophie. Anna's music made me nostalgic and resentful. I tried silence instead, and my mind worked overtime. I pulled out various books and could not get past page two of any of them. I made it to page ten of Chandler's *The Long Good-bye*, but honorable, friendless Philip Marlowe was just too depressing.

I looked through the bookshelves again. There were all of Sauro's ASD books on the Relocation Camps. That would liven me up. There was also a notebook. It held together hardcopies of Sauro's poetry. I carried it to the couch and opened it. All the poems were neatly printed and centered, like pages for a book. All the poems ended with the name of a city and a date. I skimmed through them. Most of them I didn't understand. The political ones were too easy to understand. An idea came to me, and I flipped to the end of the notebook. There were no poems dated March 15. There was a poem about a friend who offered more than friendship, and it seemed really to be about sex and politics. I yawned. I read the other ones. There were no references to the Kansas City Black Out, no strongly worded poem about the great blow for justice. There was a poem about searching through all of Anna's stuff, taking the clothes and refolding them, sorting through papers, going through computer files, seeking some sign that love was still there in the everyday things. The rest were all poems about silences in the house, about Anna's eyes and how he couldn't understand what she was thinking as her eyes watched him. The last poem, dated March 31, was three bare lines:

Alone means dead
Alone means alive
Courage.

Sauro's last three lines got to me, and I dropped the notebook on the coffee table. Vinyl against wood resounded much too loudly in the quiet apartment. Maybe Sophie was right; maybe a plunge downward was the only way to recapture Anna's love.

I thought about Anna sitting with her father, maybe deciding that too much had gone wrong in Cleveland with Sauro dead, then Sophie dead. Perhaps she'd go back to Boston, enter business school, join Baxter Construction, and press the up button on the corporate elevator.

I leaned back in the couch and stared at the bookshelves and the stereo. I turned back the clock in my head. I tell Anna, just as she is leaving, that I want to ride with her in the car, just part of the way. We take the highway to Chagrin Road, and from there cut over to where Lorena Smith lives. Once we reach unmonitored roads, I tell her to pull over. She is surprised. In a blur of words I explain everything. I tell her that her father's in danger, that he should get out of town. Anna isn't shocked that she's discovered one more set of lies surrounding our relationship. She is happy that I'm truthful. Together we agree to save her father, head off the UHL's evil plans. Then I ask her why she slept with Lang, and the whole fantasy shatters.

Papa Bear had told me that Anna was CIA. Lang had told me she might be UHL. And I didn't want her to be innocent anymore. I wanted her to be someone who'd chosen a side, who knew with certainty what she believed, what risks she was willing to take.

The night dragged on. Was father lecturing daughter? Was daughter explaining herself to father? Were they making small talk, talking circles around the issues? Did Aunt Lorena preside? I began to feel that I'd wait forever. Anna would decide to spend the night out there, and she would call me in the morning, informing me of her decision to leave for Boston.

For a moment I felt free.

Then my stomach turned.

I wanted familiar company, so I pulled the tiny television out of the corner and switched stations until I found a movie I had seen before, about an evil hives case who'd escaped the camps. He carried around a case of syringes and tracked down everyone who'd put him in the camp. He then withdrew some of his blood and injected it into his victim. I had liked the movie when I had first seen it. Now the malevolence of the hiver and the bureaucratic goodness of the people who'd sent him away were sickening. I didn't wait for the good guys to kill him.

I fled the TV, fled Anna's apartment, and before I knew what I was doing, I found myself standing on the roof.

I stood in the doorway and surveyed the area. A stone wall enclosed the large rectangular area. The night air was chilly. The occasional sound of a passing car floated upward. The sky had an orange hue, and the stars, which had been visible from Sophie's backyard, were only imaginary here. Across the river the Construct spread away from the Terminal Tower in awkward blockings. Lights upon the Construct's roof made it look like a runway designed by a five year old, spreading out toward the horizon. Within the hour, the lights would shut down. After cloudy days lights would shut down sooner, preserving the battery reserves for emergencies.

I walked from the doorway to the wall. I placed my hands upon the stone. It came up to my waist. I could easily lean over, lose balance. I looked down toward the street. Five flights of lighted windows down. Streetlights gave the street itself a silver, ghostly hue. It wouldn't be too hard to lift a leg over the wall. It would make a lot of things easier. Neither of my feet left the rooftop. They remained planted more firmly than my thoughts. I wondered how well planted Sauro's thoughts had been. Had someone come up here to meet him, to chat with him? Perhaps Someone closed in, knife in hand, and Sauro stepped too far back, lost his balance, and Someone made only a halfhearted, unsuccessful effort to reel Sauro back in. Or perhaps Someone had found out all he wanted to know.

If I jumped, if they found me splattered on the street, would they call it suicide or murder? Would the papers blame the UHL and the UHL blame the CIA?

I turned away from my view of the street and the Construct. The stair turret housing the rooftop doorway seemed almost alive in the city night glow. I stared at it, staring at what had been so obvious that I hadn't even thought of it. How could there have been any question in anyone's mind what had happened to Sauro? There was the monitor that hung above the doorway, its tiny red light beneath the lens reminding me it was on. I walked to the other side of the stair turret to confirm what I already knew. Embedded in the stone was another monitor. Its red light was on. Sauro's death should be in his file, his very classified file.

53

ANNA WAS SITTING on the couch when I walked in. Sauro's notebook was open on the coffee table, where I had left it, and Anna was bent over, reading through it. At the sound of my entrance, she gave a start, recognized who it was, and offered me a smile, followed by a hug. "I'm upset with you. You gave me a scare. You were reading Sauro's poems about me, and then you were gone."

"Where did you think I'd gone?"

"Home." She kissed me. It was a nice kiss, but it was the wrong kiss for the wrong moment. I felt as if I were being rewarded for staying, or maybe being made comfortable for some bad news. "Do you want to pour us some brandy and I'll tell you about my big evening?"

"Sure."

She reshelved Sauro's poems while I tracked down the brandy and the two brandy snifters she and Sauro owned. She was sitting on the couch when I returned. I sat in the adjoining chair. We drank the brandy, and she recounted her evening: the stilted cocktail conversation, her father's doctrinaire observations about Pakistan. Over dinner he caught her up on who had done what in Boston. It wasn't until Aunt Lorena had retired early for bed to read a book that father sat down with daughter in the living room and got down to the matter at hand. Anna played out the roles, and in the way she gesticulated, the way she tried to capture others' style of speech, I was reminded that Anna had once been Sophie's drama student. There was a moment when Anna gestured and spoke exactly like Sophie, and I suddenly felt very empty, that this whole conversation was meaningless, a verbal dance over Sophie's yet-to-be-dug grave.

"The long and the short of it, my father concluded, was that he wants me back in the family. Everything will be water under the bridge, as if none of it ever happened." She sounded a bit doubtful because, of course, it all did happen. "He wants me to come back, go to business school, and then start working someplace I'd enjoy. He'd really like to see me at Baxter Construction, but he'd be just as happy if I had a job with any other major firm."

"How do you feel about that?" It was a nice, neutral question.

"The art gallery is a dead-end job. It only really made sense when I was here with Sauro. We were living for a cause, and all that."

"What about getting licensed to run an art gallery?"

"That was just a dream. I had to tell your friends something."

"Do you really want to go into business?"

She looked unsure of herself. It reminded me of when she tried to explain to Sauro why she'd interviewed with the CIA back in college. "I don't know." She took too big a swallow of brandy and coughed. "I'm just weary of life in Cleveland. There're all my ASD friends, and they just make me feel as if everything's so hopeless. And all my socialite friends—the ones at *that* party—" She shook her head. "Sauro died. Now Sophie's dead. I don't want to stay here anymore."

What about me? I wanted to say, but I couldn't bring myself to ask her.

"Would you come with me to Boston?" she asked.

The question caught me off guard, and I didn't know what to say. I'd been bracing myself for the exact opposite. "What about your father?"

"What about him?"

"I can't see him sending you to business school if you're still with me."

"I didn't have a right to, but I told him you'd probably transfer to Boston if I moved. He got angry, but for the first time in years, I saw him fight it back. He thought about it and all, and then he told me to invite you to dinner tomorrow. If he likes you, he'll offer you a job."

Anna put on a crystal, and we slow-danced to some of her Beautiful-Woman-without-a-Personality music. I reminded her that we never got out to dance, and she assured me that I could show her how good a dancer I was once we got to Boston. As we danced, I tried to imagine life in Boston. Boston was a dot on a map. I tried to picture Anna going to school, working her way up in Baxter Construction, and living with one of the workers. It wasn't quite the straight life Aggie had imagined, but it was straight. I pulled Anna closer, to make the future more tangible, to negate my years of training. Her body was warm. Her skin smelled clean and wonderful. I let a hand slide down back, to lower back, across the bigger-than-necessary curves. Blood flowed easily into place, and I was willing to lose myself in any kind of belief.

"Why does it always have to be this way?" Her voice was plaintive. "Why can't we just dance for dancing's sake."

I wondered what else her father had said to her. I returned my hand to her shoulder blades and bent my body away from hers. We danced like that until the crystal started to replay, and Anna said she was tired. "Can we just cuddle in bed?" she asked.

She wore her nightgown. I kept my underwear on. "Stuart didn't come with our stuff?" she asked as she maneuvered herself close to me, arm over chest, leg over thigh.

"No. Unless he came while I was on the roof." I wanted to tell her that he'd gone underground, that her father's friend—her friend—was busy getting a warrant for his arrest. But the hearing range of the living-room monitor had been extended; her father's friend had gotten a warrant for that.

"Would you stay with your job in Boston?"

"If your father offers me a real job, I'll take it."

She pulled herself closer to me. Her body was warm, and I wanted her warmth that much closer. She slid her leg off my erection and farther down my thigh. "Sorry," she whispered.

"That's okay."

"If you quit your job, would you get your vasectomy reversed?"

"I don't know. There's a ten percent chance it's not reversible."

"Wasn't that something of a gamble, getting one?"

"It comes with the job."

"What about children?"

"I never expected to have any."

She was silent for a moment. I thought of the silences that may have driven Sauro to the roof. I liked how easy it was to blame Sauro's death on other people.

"Do you ever want to have children?" she asked.

"Would you want a child?" I asked.

"Yeah. Someday. Sooner if things work out between me and you."

"Why?"

"I'm not sure how to put it in words. I want to see something grow, you know, from the beginning."

"I could buy you a plant," I said, and immediately regretted it.

"You think I'm being silly." There was hurt and anger in her voice.

"No, but Boston and children won't be enough. There's gotta be more. There's going to be old friends who are going to wonder what you've dragged in with you. There's your New Puritan mother. There'll be your job, which will be very different from mine."

"Life isn't easy," she said, as if that explained everything. "Life wasn't meant to be easy. But you sound as if you're trying to talk yourself out of it. Can't you look a little bit forward? Can't you see all that love—all that life coming together?"

I couldn't see it at all, but I found myself enveloped by the warmth of her dream.

"And you know," she said, "if it was tonight, the child would be a girl. I know."

She brought her lips to mine, and I returned her fragile kiss. I touched her face with care, as if too much pressure, too much haste would break the crystalline image she had formed in our minds. We made love as if the intersection of our two bodies would indeed bring about something new to our lives. Our touches, our movements, were slow and studied. We were carrying out a ritual. We were sea and deeper sea, one sliding silent across the other. We were fertile land awaiting seed to sprout roots that would grow and wind their way up through dirt and moisture until plant and land are almost one. Almost.

"Anna?" I whispered, much later, thinking she must be asleep. We had pulled off her nightgown during our lovemaking, and I was lying beside her, tracing patterns around and across her breasts, my fingertips attracted by their warmth and softness. "Does this feel good?"

"Mmmmmmmm."

"If I quit my job, but had to stay in Cleveland, would you stay with me?"

"You don't want to go to Boston?"

"Yeah. I do. But that's not it." My hand halted, my fingers poised. "It's just, if I stayed, would you stay with me?"

"In Cleveland?"

"Yeah."

She didn't answer. My fingers touched the curve of her breast. The quiet bred honesty. "I don't know," she whispered.

Everything fell into place at that point. The love she had demanded from me was not the love she returned.

Now it should have been easy to leave her there. Lang and Papa Bear had lost their hold over me. But I didn't leave. We fell asleep in each other's arms.

54

ANNA CALLED STUART Greenspan's home the next day to find out when he'd bring over the suitcase with her stuff. His phone played the "Internationale," and Anna gave up after the first chorus. "I want to know what he's done with my stuff."

She printed up the *PD* while I made waffles, and we found out why Stuart hadn't delivered the luggage. His body had been discovered in Public Square, along with the body of Regina Huddleston, an employee of Monitoring Services. It was another internal battle in the UHL, said Edward Lang. There was a picture: the clothes were bloodied: they'd both been tortured like Dorothy Souto. Both their throats had met the edge of a knife. Anna handed me the page with the photo before scrambling to the bathroom. I listened to her vomit while I stared at the picture.

Regina Huddleston had been a tall, bony woman. Her hair was white. Her eyes were wide open. The blouse and slacks didn't conceal the blood that had been drawn. Papa Bear had been wearing his leather jacket. The blood was so dark and caked that it looked like part of the leather's aging process.

Anna returned to pick up her plate. "I can't eat anymore," she said. She pointed at the picture. "And you want to stay in Cleveland?"

"Did you know Stuart was UHL?" I asked.

"They said Sophie was UHL. I didn't believe that, either."

"This is your Uncle Ed saying it."

"My Uncle Ed is trying to save his career." She sounded bitter.

"Sophie said he's CIA."

"That's what Stuart probably told her."

I felt she was being evasive. I wanted to ask where she had spent the last three nights, whom she had called before Sophie had been killed. "You don't look too hot," she said. "Maybe you should lie down for a while."

I shook my head. "I just need to get out for a bit."

"Oh."

"I think I'm going to take a walk, maybe go to the apartment."

"You are coming back, aren't you?"

"Of course."

"You've seemed upset ever since I said I didn't want to live in Cleveland. I'll live anywhere with you, but here."

I let that pronouncement make me feel a little bit better. "I'll be back this afternoon. What should I wear to dinner?"

"Something nice. You know, like the jacket you had on the first time we met."

"Sure."

"And bring a suitcase with you. You're living with me now, right?" She said it as if she didn't quite believe it was true.

"Right."

Harry was sitting in the TV room, drinking a Thirty-Three. On the TV a man was driving a wooden stake through a vampire's heart. It looked like a terribly easy thing to do.

I walked to the study and flipped on the terminal. More messages from newspapers and one from Showtime News. Another message from my brother Artie. There were no messages from Stuart Greenspan. Or the police.

In the kitchen I got out two beers and joined Harry back in the TV room. I handed the other beer to him. "I heard about your colleague this morning," I said.

"Regina?" He eyed me as if I were somehow involved.

"Did you know her well?"

The vampire killer on TV had a new stake and a new adversary.

"She and I were working the same shift Thursday night, while you were out riding with the rich folks."

"Do you think she was UHL?"

"She was as UHL as I am. Every once in a while she'd give out a piece of footage to the press. I think she copied some fuck footage to take home to her husband. But it wasn't like she was the only one who did that sort of thing. I copied some footage, but all it got me was an interview with the FBI."

We sipped beers in silence for a while.

"She was the one who discovered you having lunch with our good friend Eddy Lang." Harry finished off his beer and went to the kitchen for another. The vampire killer was making love to a beautiful brunette woman. He had his face buried in her neck and hair, and he was breathing loudly. She had her hands pressed against his shoulder blades, holding him in place. She opened her mouth, revealing two sharp little teeth.

I looked away. Harry returned and handed me an opened beer. The vampire killer must have suspected something, because now he was struggling with her.

"Did something happen to Regina at work?" I said, almost as if it were a statement and not a question.

Harry nodded. "Ask your buddy Lang what happened."

"Lang?"

"He called her in for questioning yesterday afternoon. He had these two clones with him, a regular Humpty and Dumpty pair. She didn't even come back. This kind of thing isn't supposed to happen in our country. I know we do stuff like this to other people, but it shouldn't happen to our own."

"What did Lang talk to her about?"

"I wasn't there."

"Look, Harry, Lang's on my ass. He thinks Anna is UHL. I'm supposed to keep an eye on her."

"Are you being compensated or threatened?"

"I'm not being paid."

Harry had started to smile. It was a wry smile, revealing all his teeth, but it lacked warmth. "Edward Lang took your Baxter woman to her place Thursday night. Regina just happened upon it. She called me over to watch, you know, see the big New Puritan consultant in action. But Adolf started to erase it immediately, right while we watched, wiped it right off the screens. We tried to get into the progamming, but couldn't. Monitoring isn't supposed to do that. We're all equally monitored. As long as all the systems work. I told Regina to forget about it. But this was the second time Adolf's progamming had been fucked with, so on Friday she told our supervisor. On Saturday, Lang wanted to see her. And today she makes the front page of the *Plain Dealer*. How's that for Justice and the American Way?"

On the TV the vampire killer was fighting off three vampires. I never did see what happened to the woman who had tried to bite him.

I walked a total of two meters into our spacious study, and sat down in front of Albert Einstein. I called up Tricky Dick. It wasn't too late to catch a rapid to the airport. I had several hours before my flight left for Michigan. Artie would greet me like the prodigal son. My mother would be happy enough to see me that it would be days before she needed to know how she'd failed me so miserably. Sophie had said I was bait. I couldn't imagine fish in Cleveland taking the trouble to kill off a worm in Traverse City.

I turned the screen away from the monitor's angle of vision. I had to lean a bit awkwardly to my left to read the menu, but that was fine. If the privacy of user lines was still protected, no one but Tricky could know what I was calling up. And I took care of Tricky Dick's silence by calling for a confidential file. I accessed my meeting with Fred and documented the demotion. I accessed my earlier meeting with Palaez and Fred and related the demotion to my relationship with Anna Elizabeth Baxter. Next, I registered a complaint: my below-standard servicing of Anna Elizabeth Baxter was due to accessible information that Tricky Dick had not included in his file on her. I provided the time and date. If Adolf had provided Tricky Dick with the footage and Tricky Dick had edited from the file, then I would have it in several minutes.

Harry's hand grasped my shoulder. "You'll get a crick in your neck doing that."

"I like this angle."

He leaned his body against the desk to get a look at the screen. "What are you calling up?"

"Wait and see."

Harry went to the kitchen and came back with two more beers.

"Are you off for the rest of the day?" I asked.

"I'm on duty tonight. Nothing ever happens Sunday night."

"Do they know you saw the same thing Regina did?"

"They did as soon as I told you. I'm thinking of calling in sick. I like knives to cut steak, and that's about it."

The screen flashed with footage of the street outside Anna's apartment building. There were an ambulance and two police cars, plus a crowd. A covered body carried by gurney into the ambulance. Anna bent over crying. Stooped over her was a man in a London Fog coat, patting her back. I didn't have to wait for him to look up to know that it was Edward Lang. I stilled the image, took out the second crystal in Anna's old file, and called up the time of Sauro's death. I compared that with the counter number on the stilled image. Lang had arrived at Bridge and 28th within fifteen minutes.

"He got there pretty quick," said Harry.

"I know."

I rewound, found the counter numbers, and had that section saved in the complaint file. I identified the man in the footage as X and suggested to Tricky Dick that Anna might have been seeing X when she was not with me. I asked him to look for any signs of X in any of the dailies. Harry and I waited. I glanced at my watch. You were supposed to meet domestic flights an hour in advance for security clearances. I had a half hour to get to the airport. Harry brought out the last two beers. I didn't know why I was drinking so much. Tonight I was supposed to meet James Baxter. I didn't need a head foggy with beer.

Tricky Dick finished: Anna and X did not meet again.

"Maybe there's nothing in it," I said. I went to the kitchen and programmed the synthesizer to brew up some coffee.

"How about this?" said Harry. "Get Tricky Dick to go through the same memory and look for holes in timing, see if there's anything strange that Adolf edited out before the file was transferred to Tricky Dick."

"I don't know about this, Harry. A file is full of holes. It's not like Adolf saves everything."

"No," Harry said, already seated and typing away. "But she went out to lunch a lot, and Tricky Dick saved that in the dailies so you could watch her at work in a social setting. Every daily listed what she did. Let's see what's missing."

I was on my second cup of coffee by the time Harry had scrolled through everything. "Okay, on Tuesday, April twentieth, there's no record of what Anna did that afternoon. On Tuesday April twentieth and on Saturday April twenty-fourth, we have a listing that she ate at the Arcade, but we don't have a listing for the restaurant or her lunch companions. Mean anything?"

"It was just the first week we were together, that's all," I said, but I was already trying to remember. On Saturday, she'd been upset and wondered if I had a girlfriend. I had given her a yellow carnation, but she had preferred (now I remembered) yellow roses. On Tuesday, it had been Maureen and Maggie's anniversary, and Anna called up late. Tuesday was the afternoon that Anna's whereabouts were unknown. Lang had told Fred, Fred had told me, and Lang had never brought it up again. Is that when I had stopped trusting her?

"Wake up, Rod. I said: did you want to look for signs of negotiated editing?"

"What?"

"Tricky Dick doesn't have that footage because Adolf didn't turn it over to him, which is a possibility. Or Adolf turned it over to your AI, then later requested that it be edited out. You never notice, because it hasn't been in your file. Negotiated editing."

I had finished a roll and a third cup of coffee when Harry looked up. "It was there. The table of contents for those days was reformatted twice. Someone came in and changed things, so the directory listing had to be changed. No record of the previous contents is there. It was sloppy work—someone good wouldn't have left a record that there had been a previous entry. Ring any bells?"

I shook my head again. Lang lived near the Arcade. Would it make sense for Anna to see him the afternoon after we met? Why again the following Saturday? Lang had been there to help clean up after Sauro's death. Lang had been there the day after she had hired me. Lang had been there two days before Anna and I had first slept together.

"What are you going to do with this?" Harry asked.

"Nothing. Nothing here you can take to court."

"No. It just looks funny. You know, you look pretty strung out. Maybe you should get some rest."

I tried to follow Harry's advice. The walls of the bedroom seemed to close in on me in the darkness. The bed was too small and too hard. I tried to go through a series of relaxation exercises, but I couldn't concentrate on them. Everytime I felt I was drifting off to sleep, I snapped awake. I felt like I was floating above my bed when the phone screeched, and Harry answered. I overheard him say things like "he's not available," so I guessed he was talking to reporters. Everything spun slowly. Dorothy Souto was dead. Sophie Greenspan was dead. I had died once. Papa Bear had wanted to meet Papa Baxter. I was going to dine with father and daughter tonight. Papa Bear and Regina Huddleston were dead. There had been knives at their throats. Once, there had been a knife at my throat. Maybe I'd died twice.

I hit the bedroom light on and checked the clock. My plane left for Traverse City in ten minutes. I felt relieved.

I padded out of my bedroom through the TV room, and into the study. "You look pretty pale," Harry said.

"I feel pale." I flipped on the vidphone and pressed out the seven digits Pilar had made me memorize. Lang's face appeared on the screen. He looked tired, the way he had when he took me to lunch at the Spanish restaurant. "We need to talk," I said.

"Yes. We do. Can I expect to see you in forty-five minutes?"

"Sure." My plane for Traverse City should be out on the runway by now. The screen went gray.

"What are you seeing Lang about?"

"You don't want to know."

Harry looked me squarely in the eye.

"Okay," I said. "Anna's father wants to meet me for dinner. I've been told by Anna that if he likes me, he'll give me a job."

"Impressive. Do you want it?"

"It gets me out of this mess, doesn't it?"

"Not if Lang knows. Isn't Baxter the UHL nominee for Mr. Immorality in Business?"

"Yeah."

"Rod . . . leave town."

"I can't."

"Is she worth it? That's all I've ever asked. Is she worth it?"

"I don't know," I said, and felt as if Harry had asked the wrong question. I found that Albert was still on, and I accessed our *PD* subscription and called up large articles on ASD rallies and events. I scrolled through, until reports on the Camp Seven riots caught my eye. I scanned the first paragraph of each article. *Inmates at Camp Seven lead a violent riot,* said one. *Camp conditions were the fuel to fire the violence,* said another. *A ragged group of several hundred protestors joined the rioters. Some ASD protestors expressed a hope that their efforts would claim the attention of the caring world. Governor Oya called in the National Guard to maintain order. Local Clevelanders expressed outrage at the quarantine of friends and relatives who had been killed, wounded, or placed in quarantine after the riots at Camp Seven culminated with the National Guard's efforts to stop the violence with tear gas and rifle fire.*

There had been two writers who had covered the riots at Camp Seven. John Tassel, who had traveled out there, sounded the most sympathetic. I adiosed the *PD,* and accessed a brand-new confidential diary, and hoped there wasn't some warrant to tap our lines. I wrote:

> Harry:
> James Baxter, Anna, and I will be having dinner at Murmuring Brooks at Bridge and W. 30th in Ohio City. Record it. If anything should happen, keep recording and try to feed the info to John Tassel at the PD. If anything big should happen, you can feed footage to one of the TV stations. Just in case, I want a record for afterwards. The UHL will be there. I know.

I stepped aside so Harry could read it. He swallowed hard, eyed me for a minute, and reread it. Just in case, I deleted the entry, then adiosed Albert. Harry said nothing for a while.

"Steamy diary entry," he said.

I washed up and got ready to see Lang.

Harry was drinking coffee as I headed for the door. "Need the caffeine," he said. "You never know when a Sunday night will take you by surprise."

55

LANG WAS ALONE in his large apartment. The lights were off, and the midafternoon sun made everything seem terribly still. Lang was holding a Bible in his hand, his finger inserted between the pages he must have been reading when I'd arrived. "Come in," he said softly. He led me down the bare hallway to his study, and gestured toward the usual chair. He found a bookmark, placed it where his finger had been, then set the book down on the fireplace mantel. He looked at the book for a moment, perhaps expecting some sort of instruction. He then walked to the chair facing me and sat down. He didn't shake my hand, offer me coffee, or pretend that I was one of his students. He held his back straight and held my eyes with a steady gaze. His wife, a son, and his parents, stared me down from the holocubes.

"What can I do for you?" he asked.

"I want to cut a deal with you."

"Because you saw Stuart Greenspan yesterday," he said.

"Yeah."

Lang nodded, as if he hadn't expected any other answer. He looked like he was tired of being right. "You read today's *Plain Dealer*?"

"Yes."

"Then you know he's dead. And you also know he was killed by terrorists. Our guess is that it was the same splinter group that killed Souto and Sophie Greenspan."

"Not by the splinter group," I said. "Stuart Greenspan was part of the splinter group."

"Meaning?"

"He didn't want to black out cities or assassinate people. He wanted some kind of propaganda victory."

"Like the train bombing in December." Lang's smile was almost malicious.

"No one was injured," I said.

"Not that time. But accidents do happen. People show up unexpectedly. Someone could have been hurt or killed. Tell me more about this splinter group."

"I want a deal first."

"I take it your deal will have to do with your dinner tonight."

I nodded. "I'll give you the information I have in return for your promise that this is it."

"Meaning?"

"You declassify our files and find someone else to monitor. You let us step out of the spotlight and go to Boston. Just leave us alone. For that, I'll tell you what I know."

"I wish I could go with that, but you're not in a position to state terms." Lang reached over to his desk, cleared some papers that covered the computer keyboard, and punched a single button. He must have prepared this moment, because over the terminal speaker came voices:

—Are you FBI or UHL? —came Sophie's voice.

The recording was perfect. I felt as if she were in the room, and I suddenly longed to bring her back to life.

—Rod, I want to know why you went through my stuff. I want to know who put you up to this.

—No one.

"Turn it off," I said.

"I think you should listen to a little more."

—I'm an informer.

—I didn't figure you for a special agent. Who's got you on the line?

—Lang, for one.

(Pause)—And for two?

—Your cousin.

—Oh, God.

I closed my eyes and could see her reaching for the bedpost. Even though Stuart had told me the conversation had been bugged, I hadn't been prepared for this.

—I always knew it, but I didn't know it. So that's why he was talking so long with you the other night.

I opened my eyes. Lang was smiling wanly, as if he'd known all along and he was sorry that he was right.

—Do they each know you're informing for the enemy?
—They suspect.

Lang reached for the keyboard, pressed another button. The tape fast-forwarded for the briefest moment, then Sophie's voice returned:

—. . . takes a certain kind of righteousness that both of them were, thank God, too lazy to possess.

—They just wanted me to keep an eye out.

—For Anna? Or for her father? He's the important one. He's the one who claims to run the company that built the camps. He's Mr. Morality. He's the type who just might close the door on his daughter and then show up when he hears about what his daughter's up to. You're not the informer, Rod. You're the bait.

Lang hit another button, and silence returned. I wanted to hear Sophie's voice again. Lang leaned forward, as if he were going to share a secret with me. "What did Stuart Greenspan want to talk about?"

I was shaken. I opened my mouth to ask him about the deal.

"Rod, we've gone over the legalities of this before. This tape is not admissible evidence. And I assure you, you will not be able to prove that it exists. We have enough to go on to collect all sorts of evidence. I know we can convict you for the crime of accessory to terrorism. The minimum sentence is twenty years, no probation. If we turn up enough evidence, we could even try you for treason." He sounded as if he regretted bringing it up.

I hesitated.

He sat back and waited.

I could go along. It wouldn't be anything new. I said, "You saw Contini die."

He watched me expectantly.

"You were there awful quick after Contini jumped. So

quick you'd have to have been in the area. You forgot to edit that part out when you cut out your lunch meetings with Anna at the Arcade."

He was nodding, and I felt as if he'd heard this all before. "And your evidence?"

"The roof of Anna's apartment building is monitored. Sauro's jump is in the file. Show it to me. And while you're at it, let's take a look at the footage of you and Anna together Thursday night after the party. Let's raise some questions in the *Plain Dealer* and see how they stick to your career. Or do you want to find some quote in Thomas Jefferson that justifies getting rid of me, too?"

His voice was so soft I almost couldn't hear him: "There's no such quote."

"You didn't push Sauro. Who did?"

"He didn't get pushed. We approached him. We wanted to ask him about his whereabouts on March fifteenth. He ran to the roof, and before we could stop him, he jumped." He paused to let it sink in. "We've wanted to know ever since why he ran . . . why he jumped. We've wanted to know why there's no record of him on March fifteenth. Can you answer that?"

I shook my head.

"And you want me to trust you and Anna, to just leave you alone."

"Yes. Because you know we're innocent."

"No. I don't."

"Then tell me why you took her home with you. Most people don't sleep with people they're investigating."

"I didn't sleep with her."

"That's why Adolf erased the footage? That's why Regina Huddleston, who saw it and reported it, ended up dead?"

"You've been misinformed."

"Of course I have. And since you've classified every document possible, how is anyone going to be properly informed? You're protecting something, Lang. I couldn't care less what it is. But I want out. I'll give you the information you want, if you just let us out of this little mess."

He said nothing for the longest time. "Okay, let's hear it."

"There's a woman called the Angel. I've never met her. I don't know what she looks like. All I know is that she and Greenspan knew each other in grad school. She plotted the Kansas City Black Out. She plotted the assassinations of the Baxter Construction VPs. She plans to use whatever violence it will take to get the camps opened. Greenspan thought that was the wrong way to go about it. He said he wanted a propaganda victory. He wanted to join James Baxter for dinner tonight. He wanted the meeting to be monitored."

"How did he plan to arrange this?"

"He told me he'd contact me sometime beforehand."

"How would he contact you?"

"He didn't say."

"That's not enough."

"That's all I know."

"Was Greenspan always your contact?"

"Yes."

"And Dorothy Souto worked with him."

"I think so."

"You met three people the morning of May seventh. I take it Greenspan called himself Papa Bear."

"No. He called himself Papa."

"Have you seen Mama or Baby since?"

"No."

"Do you know who they are?"

"No."

"I showed you some pictures almost three weeks ago. Let's go through them again. I want these people identified so we can keep an eye out for them."

He handed me the bound set of pictures, and I dutifully went through them, already knowing in advance that there would be no Mama Bear or Baby Bear. "They're not here," I said.

"Here are the people other than Stuart Greenspan who visited Sophie Greenspan's house yesterday." He handed me one picture. It had been shot with a high-powered lens from the house next door. They caught only her face, because she happened to have pointed something out to Stuart, who was standing with her.

"This is Sophie's half sister. I recognize her from Sophie's file."

He handed me another. It was Sophie's director, Dolores. The next one was Sophie's mother, who was stepping out of Bill O'Brien's car. The next person I didn't recognize, and that was followed by a profile view of Luis. I couldn't help but recognize the way he carried his emaciated body, the way he'd slicked back his blond hair. I thought of Cindy Molero, who'd be on her way to Camp Seven tomorrow.

"I met him at Sophie's party," I said, amazed at how easily the lie came out, "but I don't remember his name."

"You recognized him pretty readily."

"He looks really sick. I couldn't help but notice him."

Lang looked again at the picture, then at me. "Describe the other two, the ones that were with Greenspan." He placed the picture on top of the others.

I described a male version of Aggie. He listened, his fingers rifling through the pictures. I described an effeminate version of Henry. He absentmindedly shuffled the pictures into a different order. "I can sketch them for you on a flatscreen," I said. Compsketching had been part of our training. It developed visual memory.

"I was hoping you would." He stood up and placed the photos, face down, on his chair. "In fact, I took the liberty of prepping a flatscreen with the software you trained with. I hope I got the right one." He fished through his papers, found the flatscreen, and handed it to me.

It was the correct software.

"We'll need two sketches."

He paced the room while I sketched. Every now and then he picked the Bible up off the mantel, then replaced it. It took me ten minutes, and he looked at the sketches for all of ten seconds. He shook his head, and I knew he didn't believe me.

He picked up the photos before sitting down and placed them in his lap. He reached onto the desk and slid one more photo off his papers. "I was sort of expecting it to be these two." The picture was of Ken and his buddy standing outside the door to Sophie's house. They weren't wearing matching khaki slacks and blue blazers; instead they were wearing Democracy Now jeans and short sleeve shirts. Harry had talked about Lang being with Humpty and Dumpty, and I had pictured Ken and his buddy being CIA, not UHL. Maybe they worked for Angel. "No," I said. "I've never seen these two with Stuart."

"But you've seen them before, right?"

"I saw them at Herbert Milanes's party," I said. "They came without an invitation. I also saw them in a picture in the *Plain Dealer*. This one here called the other one Ken. They sat behind Anna and me during the play."

"Is that all?"

"Yeah," I said, testing the waters.

The waters were hot. "We have it on record that you talked with someone about this matter."

"Okay. I talked with the actress who played the nurse in the play. She said she saw this one, Ken, talking to Sophie right after the curtain went down."

"According to the police report, the one you called Ken was the last person to see Sophie alive." He'd made his point. "That's all for the pictures." He gave them a light toss onto his desk, and they spread out like a hand of cards. "And in exchange for this information, you want to be left alone."

"Anna and I both."

"You want to have dinner with James Baxter, and you plan to accept the job he'll offer you, in Boston, so you can stay with Anna." He didn't sound too pleased with the idea. "Where you want to be left alone."

"Yes."

"You haven't given me enough information to do anything. To get what you want, you're going to have to pay a price."

"What kind of price?"

"I expect you to show up to dinner tonight, be terribly polite, and, if Baxter offers you a job, accept it."

"That's easy enough."

"I figured you might like it. I don't think your relationship with Anna will last, but it would do you good to get a secure job with Baxter Construction."

"Maybe I should become a New Puritan?"

"It's an idea." He leaned forward, stopped, rubbed a hand across his face, as if that could wipe away the exhaustion. "If the UHL contacts you before dinner tonight, I want you to call. Agreed?"

I nodded.

"Now, they may well wait to contact you at the restaurant. If you see someone you recognize, someone who isn't in one of these photos, get to a pay phone and call. If that's not possible, I want you to pull at your right earlobe and then rub the back of your neck." He had me do it ten times until it looked like a natural gesture. "That looks passable," he said. "Once you do that, we'll take it from there." He misinterpreted my look of disbelief. "I know it's a bit unconventional," he explained. "We should wire you for sound and everything else. I don't mind if they're suspicious of a trap, but if they detect that we have you rigged, things will get out of control."

"In all the traps I know, the bait usually doesn't make it out alive. Why not tell your friend James that he's in danger, and get him on the next plane home?"

"If you do everything right, all three of you will be on the next plane to Boston. If you play games with me, if you don't stick to your promise, this will go wrong. And if this goes wrong, there are people I work with who will want to turn it into a shooting contest. I want to take these people to trial. I want to make it clear that our way works. This is a law and order issue. This is how a society proves itself to God, with rational, law-abiding conduct."

"Does Baxter know he's helping prove the American Way to God?"

"Don't worry. James Baxter will be fine. They want him alive. If they had wanted him dead, they could have killed him years ago."

"Maybe they'll change their minds."

"If you do your job, every one who counts will walk out smiling. James Baxter is my friend. Anna Baxter is his daughter. I wouldn't risk either of their lives unduly." He looked away from me with his final words. The *unduly* put everything else in perspective.

He escorted me to the door. Before opening it, he put

a hand on my shoulder, as if our encounter had somehow made us closer. "If you just had tried to understand," he said, "you would be on our side. I hate to make deals. I hate to use threats. Threats make people angry, and they forget their own best interests."

"I want to walk out of the restaurant alive," I said.

"You will. And if you do everything right, you will be on a plane to Boston with Anna Baxter. Remember that." It was meant as fatherly advice. I tried to imagine the Edward Lang who had attracted young Anna Baxter's love and awe. I pictured a man who loved to give out fatherly advice, who loved to promise great ideas to fight for. He didn't look too much like the Edward Lang who was patting my shoulder, promising me that everything would be all right.

56

I ARRIVED IN Ohio City late that afternoon, my Democracy Now suitcase in hand. In it were some clothes, neatly folded slacks, jacket and Beijing tie, toiletries. Under the clothes I had hidden my ChemKit and a palm-size flatscreen with the Chandler novel I was reading. The air around the RTA platform closed in around me, and I felt as if I wore a sheen of sweat beneath my clothes. Everything within me had felt like spaghetti when I had boarded the rapid, and now it felt as if someone had left only the sauce. Sauce was red; blood was red. And I couldn't face Anna.

I walked, shifting the suitcase back and forth in my hands. Everything on West 25th Street was closed for the day. Only restaurants and a few bars with extra-expensive liquor licenses would open for the evening. I stopped at the brownstone where Anna lived, thumbed open the second door, and found I couldn't handle the four flights of stairs yet. Leaving my suitcase there, I left the brownstone, walked past them all, and the wall where Sauro had chiseled his only lasting work of art.

I stopped at the corner of Bridge and West 30th and looked across the street. There stood the facsimile Victorian house that contained Murmuring Brooks. A specially licensed truck was parked on West 30th, and a man and a woman in blue overalls were carrying boxes of fish to an open metal door. I looked in, a curious visitor. This was where the fresh meat and the catch of the day were kept. A chill escaped into the moist air. The man and woman were finished as soon as they started, and a woman wearing white stared at me until I got out of the way. She shut the door; I heard a bolt slide into place.

I followed West 30th to Jay, where the row of brick apartment buildings ran parallel to the brownstones on Bridge. I walked around the neighborhood, along little streets with renovated clapboard houses and dilapidated clapboard houses, and I heard children calling out in English and in Spanish and in Arabic. It was like an upscale shackville. I walked back toward West 28th and wandered through the alleyways between the brownstones and the brick apartment buildings. Invisible to the main streets, fire escapes zigzagged their way up the buildings, all the way to the roofs. A few had been recently painted, shiny black or gray. Most were dulled black with grit.

When I had been hustling illegally on Coventry, while they were building the mini-Construct there, I had worked up and down Hampshire and Lancashire, along Euclid Heights Boulevard, dodging through little alleyways of the slowly growing mini-Construct. I had learned how to hide from the uniforms who never troubled to learn the nooks and crannies of the construction sites, the darkened alleys and their easy fire escapes: the stairs leading to rooftops.

It was a long walk, and it left me feeling disheartened. This wasn't Coventry. I wasn't hustling ass for money. If I walked out of the restaurant alive, it would be because Lang's plan had worked, or because with Papa Bear dead, the UHL never showed up.

Anna was taking a shower. I called out, "It's me," and she called back, "You're late." I nodded to myself, as if her words had more than one meaning. Suitcase in hand, I stood by the doorway and found I couldn't move. The monitor watched me, and I wondered who was watching the monitor.

I geared myself up to tell Anna, explain everything, take her anger in stride, tell her after a second set of lies that sure, she could trust me, just like I could trust her after all the things she might have left unspoken, unpromised. I could explain everything, the UHL wouldn't show up, and all would be lost for nothing. Lang had said it would be safe. Two simple gestures, they'd take care of everything.

"Rod?" Anna was standing in the tiny hallway. "Why are you standing there?"

"Just thinking."

"You look a little uneasy there. You shouldn't worry. My father is a master of charm. Remember, he wants me home, so he wants you home, too."

"You'll go without me," I said.

"No. I said I'd go anywhere. I just won't stay in Cleveland."

I wanted to believe in her and in forever, so I embraced her. Her skin smelled fresh; her body felt warm. I protracted the embrace, and I told myself again to tell her everything.

She pressed fingers against chest and stepped back. "We're going to be late," she said. "Get naked and get a shower." She took the suitcase from my hand. "I better de-wrinkle your clothes."

The water's warmth was fading. I washed my hair, rubbed soap over my body, and rinsed off before the water became too cold. Anna was naked when I walked into the bedroom. She had laid out her clothes and mine on the bed. She picked a garter belt out of her bureau dresser and held it between thumb and forefinger for inspection. It was the white frilly one, part of the outfit she'd bought before our stay at the Democracy Now Hotel.

"I won't be able to concentrate," I said.

She put it away. "I wouldn't want that."

"But then again, it might keep me in the right frame of mind."

She closed the bureau drawer just a bit too hard. "I hope you have other frames of mind that are equally appealing."

"You know I do," I said. I finished drying off and slipped on underwear and slacks. The slacks and jacket looked as if they'd been freshly pressed. I wonder what gizmo Anna had been given once upon a time for Christmas that could do this.

Anna put on a sedate blue dress that covered everything and went down past the knees. I was sure Donna Palaez had one exactly like it, in a shade of provocative gray.

"I wish this headache would go away," Anna said. "I feel like I'm back home."

"Did you take some aspirin?"

"Just before you got here. When my head's like this, nothing will do it any good."

"Maybe we should get the blood flowing."

"Is that all you think about?"

"No. I was going to suggest that we go dancing after dinner. We haven't gone dancing once since we met."

"We did last night." She made it sound nostalgic, like it had happened too long ago.

"You know what I mean."

"I don't know," she said. "Let's get going, we'll be late."

This is my last chance, I kept thinking while we finished our grooming, brushing our hair, cleaning our teeth, straightening out our clothes. In the camps you got so weak that someone else had to do this for you. The humidity and something rooted deep within me had drawn out sweat, covering me like a thin coat of varnish. I felt a bit shaky and excited, as if I had drunk far too much coffee.

The door closed, and the sound echoed briefly against the stone. We headed down the stairs, our footsteps repeating in the air. I was going to say something about Stuart, but other words emerged:

"You know, you never told me that your Uncle Ed showed up here when Sauro died."

She twisted her head to watch me as we walked down the steps to the sidewalk. "What does that have to do with anything?"

"It just seemed odd to me that he got here so quickly."

"I don't see why. He works just across the river."

"How did he end up here?"

"I called him. What's all this to you? Are you jealous because I brought him to a party?"

"You went home with him afterward," I said. "In fact, you never came home after you left Sophie's. I think you went to his place and stayed there."

"You *are* jealous," she said.

"You never told me about him."

"You never told me about Beatrice What's-her-face."

"Knecivic."

"Whatever. Why do you want to spoil our evening now?" She stopped in front of the doorway and looked at me. "Hasn't enough happened? Is it really that important if I had a fling with Ed Lang? You had yours with Sophie."

She pushed open the door, marched through the entranceway, pushed open the second, and was down the steps on the sidewalk before I could get hold of her elbow. The sky outside was pale blue, the early evening heat a residue of the day. "I didn't have a fling with Sophie."

She shook off my hand and kept walking. "That's not what I saw in the paper."

"I kissed her that night. But I never slept with her."

"Well, if you didn't, it wasn't because she didn't want it."

"That's a hell of a thing to say about your best friend."

She stopped, turned on her heel. "Yeah. She was my best friend. But she couldn't control herself, she was so lonely. She and Sauro were going to get something for my birthday, and they ended up in bed together. Sauro was going to take me out dancing. I was going to be twenty-three." She made it sound as if her birthday had never happened.

"Are you sure they were together?"

"Sauro could never lie about anything. Not really. Unlike other people I know." Murmuring Brooks was across the street, and the Sunday's quiet surrounded us. Anna faced me, took my hand in hers. "Please . . . can't we make this a pleasant evening?"

"Can you tell me about Lang?"

"If it'll make you happy, I'll tell you everything tonight, okay?"

I shook my head. "Your father's about to offer me a job. It's only fair that I know now."

"It's not that important."

"When Sauro died, he was the one you called, not Sophie, or your aunt Lorena."

"See what I mean? I did call them. Sophie wasn't at home. My aunt was in bed, sick, and she told me to call Uncle Ed. She said he was in town, so I should take advantage of it."

I waited for more.

"I had to call someone."

"But you were in love with him once."

"Who told you that? Sophie?"

I nodded.

"I'm not in love with him anymore. Can we go in now?"

"But you saw him for lunch. The day after we met: you saw him for lunch and spent the whole afternoon with him."

"So? I wanted some comfort, and he represented home. He was nice, strong, honorable, and I wanted to fall in love with him again. He talked me out of that, and when he found out I'd hired you, he tried talking me out of *that*."

"Did you talk politics?"

"What?"

"Stuart thought you were Lang's informant."

"Stuart would think that."

"What did you talk about?"

"I don't know."

"What about Wednesday night—or Thursday—or Friday? You were with him until the play."

"I didn't have anywhere else to go."

"What did he talk about?"

"What the hell is it to you?"

"Okay, Mr. Serviceman, you really want to know. He wanted me to leave Cleveland. He thought all my friends were getting into too much trouble. He especially thought it'd be best if I break away from you. Satisfied?"

"He's getting half his wish. You're leaving Cleveland."

"He's not going to get the second, unless you want to stay here."

"Why did you hire me in the first place?"

"Why the hell are you so suspicious all of a sudden? You had that file on me. You should be able to read me like a book."

"You hired me to get your father back, didn't you? He couldn't come back over Sauro, but maybe if you went too far, he'd come back for you."

"I thought you knew me."

"I do, Anna. There are people who think you're Lang's informant. Lang thinks you're hooked up with terrorists. Your father's here to save you."

"And everyone I care about is dead. Sauro's dead. Sophie's dead."

"And me?"

"I don't know, Rod. What do you want? You seem to want to turn me into something. What is it you want me to be?"

I shook my head and said nothing.

"Look, Rod, I slept with Ed Lang. I can't change that. You hurt me, too. You can't change that."

I hesitated, considered telling her everything. But then Lang would always be there, keeping an eye on us, editing Anna's file into a redundant innocence. And the UHL would be there, too, looking for a way to get to her father, who had built some of the camps.

"My father's waiting," she said.

It seemed impossible that anything could really happen in the stillness of this Sunday heat.

"Do you still want me to meet your father?"

"Yes." She took me by the arm, and we walked into the restaurant. Its single monitor hung just above the doorway's exit sign. The sun had begun its late-afternoon swing toward the horizon, but its rays were cool. The sound of the water rushing through the holographic brooks should have been tranquilizing.

The maître d' led us to James Baxter, seated in the last table against the real wood wall, just before the doorway that led to kitchen and bathrooms. He was sitting with his back to the restaurant, which surprised me. I would have expected him to sit where he could have a view of the entire restaurant and everyone in it.

James Baxter turned his head, saw us coming, and rose from his chair. He held himself professionally, but there was a certain anxiety in his smile. "I love you," Anna whispered under her breath.

We passed a table, and the two people sitting there caught my eye. I twisted my head to catch a glimpse. A young man, whom I had seen in a subway four weeks ago, was wearing a jacket and tie and was lifting an expensive hamburger to his mouth. Sitting across from him, thin face pale, blond hair slicked back, looking weak enough to collapse headfirst into his pasta, sat Luis.

I tried to look away before he could see me, but I had caught his eye, and he winked. Then Mama Bear smiled, as if a smile would reassure me that everything would be all right.

57

IN PHOTOS AND footage James Baxter had an aura that made him seem physically larger than he actually was. He was a bit shorter than me with a minor pot belly that the high school and college letterman had insisted he'd never have. His dark hair, contrasting with Anna's lighter hair, was cut short and combed back in a style that would have been appropriate ten years ago. His cheeks bulged, the same baby fat that gave Anna's face a cherubic quality. The father's cheeks would eventually be the heavy jowls of a bulldog, gravity and rich food filling in the true character of his face. But cutting through the implied friendliness of his build were two dark eyes that commanded attention and imbued his half smiles with a certain dark irony. When he saw us—and Anna dropped her arm to her side—he rose and stepped forward, carrying his weight with the grace of the twenty-year old athlete that still lived within.

"Hi, Dad," Anna said and hugged him.

He kissed her on the cheek. "It's good to see you, Na-Na." Her youngest sister, as a baby, had tried to say Anna and came out with nah-nah, a double-sound soon appropriated by her father as a term of endearment and exasperation.

Anna stood back from her father and replaced her hand on my arm. "And, Dad, I'd like you to meet Roderick Lawrence, my beau."

Baxter half smiled at the final word, but he held out his hand. His grip was tight, and his eyes bore into mine. I held his hand firmly, maintained eye contact. "It's nice to meet you, sir."

"How do you do. I'm always interested in meeting Anna's friends." He said it pleasantly enough, but his eyes confirmed that he and Anna defined the word *friend* differently.

"It's awfully kind of you to invite me."

He smiled more than a half smile, and I caught myself feeling at ease. Anna had once told me that her father was so charming that he could stick a knife in you and you wouldn't know it until you saw the blood. Baxter gestured us to sit. I sat against the real wood wall, opposite him; Anna sat between us. The fourth chair, the one closest to the exit, was empty and with no place setting. Like always, an arrangement of flowers and a lit white candle sat in the middle of the table. The table was set with cloth napkins, a complete set of silverware, and three different-sized glasses. The arrangement didn't seem as intimidating as it had way back in April.

"Anyway," Baxter said to me, "you're the one I want to talk with. I've heard a lot about you." The eyes cheerfully expressed his double meaning. "Most of it surprisingly good. It seems that you've treated my daughter quite well during some very disturbing times."

"It's difficult not to treat her well."

The discussed party didn't say anything.

A waitress brought us the menus etched in wood and offered to take our cocktail orders.

Anna's father nodded to her. "Anna?"

"A glass of white wine, please."

"Are you sure?" he asked. "We'll probably have some wine with the meal. Wouldn't you like something else?"

"I guess I will," she said to the waitress. "How about an Orgasm? Please."

Baxter rolled his eyes and looked at me. "Is that another of those sweet drinks?"

I grimaced and nodded seriously. With my conspiratorial nod a minor bond had been established. Anna drank sweet drinks with silly names, whereas Anna's father and I would never do that.

"And you, sir?" the waitress said to Baxter, who, in turn, nodded in my direction.

I wanted a beer, to quench my thirst while keeping my head clear. A waiter was clearing the plates off Luis and Baby Bear's table. More than half of Luis's plate was still covered with pasta. I decided on Scotch and knew I needed a brand name. "Dewars, on the rocks, please." Anna seemed surprised by my order, but she didn't say anything.

"And I'll have a dry vodka martini straight up," said Baxter. "Make that with Stoly."

The waitress nodded and said, "I'll be right back with your drinks."

"That's a nice touch," Anna's father said, watching the waitress leave, his eyes following the swaying of her ass. Mr. Morality, I guess, liked to watch temptation. "That's what I like about coming to Cleveland. Those nice little personal touches. In Boston you get those damn Chinese robots or some Palestinian who can barely speak English."

Sauro would have risen to the bait. "This is a nice place," I said.

Anna and her father talked. They talked about various neighbors and Baxter Construction employees, what their children were doing now. They talked about Baxter Construction projects, and Anna seemed to know a lot more than she'd ever let on. I could picture her as a child, going to work with her father on a day school was closed, being shown off around the office, and I remembered my father taking me around the bank, when he'd worked there. To look more grown up, she would ask all sorts of questions about work at the dinner table, and Baxter wouldn't reply with the one sentence dead-end, but would go on at length, as if his oldest daughter had every right to know whatever she wanted about the company. There had been a part of her that had always been ready to return to Boston.

With our permission, Baxter ordered filet mignon and rice for the three of us. Over dinner, Anna and her father kept talking about the political situations in the countries where Baxter Construction was rebuilding or revising cities. I was amazed at the nonchalance with which Baxter talked of rebuilding cultures as well as places, and I could understand how easy it had been for Sauro to leave a negative impression over that Thanksgiving weekend when he had stayed with the Baxters. Accustomed to talking openly with his own parents about whatever subject came up, he must have snapped at the controversy like a famished dog pouncing on motionless steak.

The waiter at the other end of the room brought cake and coffee for Baby Bear and Luis. Baby Bear, fork in hand, started to devour the cake. Luis took a long, slow sip at his coffee. I wondered how painful it was for him to swallow. He didn't look in our direction. Above the exit sign the single monitor surveyed the room. In the low lighting and shadows, the multifaceted lens was invisible. Only the curve of black, a point of red light, gave away its presence. I surveyed the entire restaurant. I half expected to see Lang, but, of course, I didn't.

Baxter must have noticed my wandering eye, because he started including me in the conversation. I worked hard to agree with him, always ending with polite pleasantries: "Yes, it's a sad situation" or "Things always seem to get more complex" or, and just once, "You've visited there, so you're better qualified to evaluate the situation than I am." His questions were a culling device, first to establish if Anna had found another Sauro, then to test my intelligence, my education, to show Anna how well I thought on my feet, to establish if I was someone who would be worthy of her time.

"Tell me," he said, a new kind of smile, almost mischievous, forming, "what do you think of the Construct?"

"The one here in Cleveland?"

"Rod knows," said Anna, "what company built half the Construct here. It's not like that's a fair question."

"Rod's entitled to an opinion," said Anna's father.

Anna leaned forward, hesitated, then said, "Sauro certainly never was."

"Your Sauropod, Na-Na, didn't have opinions. He had answers. For everything. Whether or not he knew anything about the subject."

Anna turned away. "I won't argue with you about Sauro."

"You know," I said, hoping to diffuse things. "Sauro just may have been trying to get a reaction."

"And he got a reaction!" A deep and negative enthusiasm resounded through his voice. I was beginning to get a glimpse of how Baxter enjoyed himself. "I had to sit at my own dinner table and listen to this horse-wally come spewing out. But I put up with it, and do you know why?"

I shook my head.

"Because I believe that there should always be a certain courtesy offered in your house to guests, whether they are welcome or not. So I let him sit with us in our living room; I let him sit at my table. And I listened to him say what he wanted in the language he wanted. And I put up with it.

Anna patted my hand. "Maybe we should change the subject," she said. "You know, Rod here likes to read."

"Oh, and what have you read recently that you liked?"

"Jude the Obscure."

"But his favorite is Raymond Chandler," Anna said.

"I like Chandler, too," said Anna's father, and he made it sound like an important declaration. "I didn't expect to be, but I really am impressed with you, young man."

If I had captained several teams, graduated magna cum laude from Harvard, and worked for an archrival company, he really would have meant it. But he did *sound* sincere. He was more convincing than some servicers I had trained with.

"What sort of work did your father do?" came the inevitable question. Now he was checking my pedigree.

I told him the Ivy League college where my father had taught math. Anna's father looked suitably impressed. "But he got tired of all the academic work—the publish-or-perish aspect—and he decided to teach kids. So we moved to Cleveland, where my parents had grown up and my father taught at Heights High."

"I taught for a while, too," Baxter said. "Boy, did I love it. I taught biology, but I enjoyed the hell out of it when they let me teach prehistory as a January mini-course. I loved to teach about the dinosaurs."

"My brother used to collect dinosaurs," I said.

"Dad still does."

Anna's father looked a bit embarrassed. "Anna's exaggerating."

"No. I'm not."

"I just collect them. There's nothing like a dinosaur to make a great paperweight."

"The paper certainly won't move," I said. Another bond, however minor, had been created. I wouldn't join with his daughter's teasing.

After dinner came dessert and coffee. Luis and Baby Bear were still there. The waiter had brought Baby Bear a coke. Luis stared at his coffee cup. As far as I could tell, he hadn't touched his cake. Anna and her father were comparing Cleveland and Boston weather, with the same seriousness with which they'd talked about politics. The maître d' led two men to a table across from us, near the exit. A holographic brook ran right by their table. Humpty wore a blue suit so well pressed that the creases looked as if they could cut butter; Dumpty, Ken, wore a gray suit a half size too big. Dumpty had been the last person to see Sophie alive. I tried not to pay attention to them, but I couldn't focus on talk of snowstorms and cloud cover. Luis was saying something to Baby Bear while Baby Bear finished off his cola. Neither of them had paid much attention to Humpty and Dumpty's entrance.

"Have you talked with Uncle Ed?" Anna asked her father, avoiding my gaze.

"This morning. We're going to have an early breakfast tomorrow morning before I head back to Boston. Which reminds me, I had him get hold of that detective, the one who's investigating your friend Sophie's death. I think her name is Ibarra. She told Ed that she'd let you leave Cleveland in a day or two. She'd have things wrapped up by then as far as you're concerned. When can your mother and I expect you home?"

"Rod and I would probably need a week to straighten things out here."

Humpty, in the blue suit, caught my eye and smiled at me. UHL or CIA, I didn't think he would let us have a week to get out of town. Dumpty was placing his hand in the brook next to their table and watched the image of water run along his skin.

"And with that in mind," said Anna's father, "we should probably bring dinner to the business at hand. If you don't mind, Anna, I'd like to have a few words with Rod here."

Anna glanced over at me, then faced her father. "I think I should stay, Dad. This does concern me, you know."

Baxter sat back with one of his half smiles. "To be perfectly honest, Anna, this doesn't."

"Dad, I'm not leaving. This is a dinner, not a business meeting."

Baxter's left hand had reached into his jacket pocket, probably to press a call button. A compact, tight-faced man who would probably scare a gang of thugs in spite of the shortness of his shadow rose from a nearby table and joined us. He was wearing a light gray suit. The man sitting at the table next to us, eating alone, his back to Anna, was wearing the exact same suit.

"Frederico . . . would you mind escorting my daughter home?"

"No. Not at all, sir."

I must have looked surprised to see Frederico standing there because Anna said to me, "Don't worry. There are three other bodyguards here, all dressed like Frederico." The second one sat by the entranceway, the third two tables away from Humpty and Dumpty.

"I'm not overly fond of it all," said Anna's father, "but it comes with the territory."

Frederico didn't say anything—that came with his territory.

"Thank you, Frederico," said Anna, "but I'm not going home quite yet."

Baxter looked exasperated, but he nodded. Frederico said "Yes, sir," and turned away.

Luis watched him return to his table. Anna glanced over in Luis's direction, and Mama Bear returned his attention to his untouched cake. He should have been dead and buried in Camp Seven, not here. Across from us Humpty must have been watching Frederico return to his seat because his eyes had stopped midway between us and Frederico's table. He started at the sight of Luis, then tried to cover up his surprise by returning to his meal. Dumpty was too busy cutting into a steak to pay attention.

Anna's father signaled for the waitress and ordered

three brandies, Torres Reserva. "Unless," he said to me, "you'd prefer something different."

"No. Brandy'll be fine."

Anna nodded.

Baxter watched the waitress's swaying rear disappear behind the bar. He looked back at me. "I do like those personal touches. No robot would move like that."

"Unfortunately," I said, "there's a difference between personal touches and touching personally."

Baxter laughed—a quick outburst like the release of something that had been longing to escape—and abruptly stopped. He must have remembered what I did for a living. He looked uncomfortable with the ensuing silence, and he caught himself looking back and forth between me and Anna. Baby Bear stood up and walked past us to the exit, where arrows pointed one way to the kitchen and another to the rest rooms, telephones, and the exit.

"Rod, I can guess some of the things Anna here, or her friends, might have told you about me. But I want you to know that I do the best a man can do to be principled."

"Dad, I have never said anything to the contrary."

"Fine, Na-Na, but I want to tell him." He returned his gaze to me. "I *am* a principled man, and there is money I don't have because of those principles. Baxter Construction has not built anything in Los Angeles, San Francisco, or Managua, nor any place else where there might be a major earthquake. But just because the company has my family name and by sheer willpower my family possesses a majority share of the stock, it doesn't mean I have total control. There are stockholders, a board of trustees, employees, powerful unions in China and Russia, clients who give you a budget. There are government regulations and lobbyists and competitors."

"And there are relocation camps," I said.

He eyed me for a moment, as if suddenly discovering that I was Sauro in disguise. "Yes. And they're a product of shoddy workmanship. Congress designed them, gave me the specifications, and gave me the budget. We took a loss on each camp we built, and each camp we built was better than any made by our competitors. I spent a week of my life last year and a million dollars out of my own pocket lobbying for a larger budget for the relocation camps. But her Sauropod and his friends condemned my every effort." Anna was about to say something, but his palm slapped the table. The remaining silverware rattled. Luis, conspicuously enough, remained intent on his coffee cup.

"You're not running for office, Dad." Baxter looked a bit sheepish.

Anna's father said something I didn't hear: Baby Bear was returning to his seat, then leaning over to tell Luis something. In the dim light just before sunset, Luis's nod was barely discernible.

"Rod, I want you to understand some things before I ask you an important question. There's something gratifying about being the kind of person you say a person should be. It provides a kind of energy. You're certain of things the way a good athlete is. I used to play sports when I was in school. Soccer in the fall, I swam in the winter, and I played tennis in the spring. I kept in shape, did what was necessary, but after a while other things got in the way—business decisions, family decisions; business trips, family vacations—and you run out of time for that kind of dedication. And then you find your body slowing down, and you find yourself in a little less of a rush. You start to take a look at what you've done and what people have done for you. And you begin to wonder. You wonder if you chose the right job. If you treated your wife with enough love. If you raised your children the right way. You wonder if you protected them too much from the world's cruelty. You wonder if you put too much emphasis on prayer. You think that you gave them too many things one day, and the next you think that you refused them too many. I should have let them work for money and take a lot more risks, so they would have fallen flat on their faces more often as children and less as adults."

"You know," Anna said, "I'm twenty-three, and I'm not a piece of steak to be cut up in front of the two of you."

Baxter nodded.

"Well . . . ?"

"Anna, I had hoped originally to have this discussion with Rod, alone, so there wouldn't be someone monitoring his every reaction."

"Mr. Baxter," I said. "If Anna's any reflection of the way you raised her, I'd say you did pretty well."

Anna smiled shyly, but her father didn't seem to hear me. "Rod, it was my intent to be a principled father. The way you lead your life reflects your character, and I was upset, to say the least, that Anna chose to go on living the sort of life that Sauropod led. I decided, I thought quite fairly, that if she wanted to lead her own life, she would have to lead it on her own. And make it on her own. I always felt that class would win out in the end. I thought that Anna would see that there was a difference in character between herself and that Sauropod, or between herself and her friend Sophie."

Anna was already shaking her head. This is not what she'd come to hear. The two of them were dead, and her father hadn't seemed to notice.

He finished off his brandy. "So, you see, it's my fault, in a way. I let my principles destroy my family, and that was the most unprincipled thing of all." Anna's eyes were on her father; this was the closest he'd come to an apology. "My daughter has suffered enough tragedy on her own, and I don't want to wait two years for her to grow tired of Cleveland. I want to make it possible for her to return home."

I had been dreading this moment and already knew, deep down, that he wasn't really going to offer me a job. I didn't know how he was going to do it in front of Anna, but there would be a bribe and a plea for me to stay away from Anna, for Anna's sake. With Humpty across from us, wearing his crisp blue suit and carefully cutting into his steak as if it were a work of art, it would be hard to disagree.

"I know what sort of work you do," he said, "and I don't like it. I don't know how you ended up in such a career, if you can call it that, and I don't want to know. My daughter thinks she loves you."

"I do," she said.

I hesitated, then said, "I love her."

"I know. You could become rather wealthy falling in love with a woman like my daughter."

"Your daughter can stay here in Cleveland," I said. "My job pays better than her current one does."

"Touché," he said.

"This is enough, Dad, make your point."

He picked up his brandy snifter, realized it was empty, and replaced it on the table. "You graduated from high school?"

"I passed the equivalency test."

"No college?"

"Rod, I'm sorry. I told him all of this last night. Why, Dad, do you have to drag Rod through this?"

"Anna's right. I'm not being fair. But the media won't be, either. You're intelligent. According to the Public Files I had called up, you are a hard worker. Would you be willing to apply your intelligence to some hard work in another profession, say in Boston, for Baxter Construction?"

I didn't know how to answer.

"I can offer you a low-level job, but with night school and discipline, there would be plenty of room for advancement. It can't be anything special. We'll have to handle the PR on this just right, or I will look like a moral hypocrite. We'll market you as a male Fanny Hill that Anna fell in love with and reformed. It puts you in the spotlight for a while, but . . . does this sound at all agreeable?"

I was overwhelmed, confused. Things didn't work out this way, this neatly. As if to remind me of that, Humpty took a bite of steak and winked. At the other end of the room, a waiter was pouring more coffee for Luis. "Will you excuse me for a moment?"

"Why of course."

I stepped away from the table—Anna looking insecure why hadn't I said yes, and Baxter looking certain of himself—and headed for the rest rooms. I had to pass Humpty and Dumpty's table. I kept my head up, tried to act as if they weren't there.

"Hi, Rod," Humpty said.

I couldn't help but turn. Humpty was holding up his steak knife. He ran his finger along the knife's edge. His smile was sincere and friendly.

Sharp edges are for dull wits, but I only thought of that

while standing at the urinal in the bathroom. My legs trembled, and I didn't know whom I was betraying anymore. I velcroed my fly together and went to sit on the toilet. I locked the thin metal door. What was I to do now? Why hadn't I seen any of Lang's men? Was anybody there to do something when I pulled on my earlobe, then rubbed the back of my neck? A chill swept my skin, and I became aware of how much I had sweated, how damp my clothes were. How did you conquer the fear? How did you die with dignity?

I thought of calling Harry, see if he was getting this. Or maybe I'd call John Tassel at the *PD*, or maybe I'd accept Baxter's offer and see if we could make it out of here alive and to Boston, and I'd start over with everything. If I had been happy before I met Anna, why did I want her so badly now?

The bathroom door opened with a whoosh of air and a moment of restaurant noise. The door shut, and feet approached the closed toilet door. The feet were wearing running shoes. A hand knocked on the door. "How long are you going to be?" The voice sounded tired. I didn't recognize it. It would be nice to see someone I didn't recognize.

"I'm coming out," I said. I stood up, opened the door.

Mama Bear grinned at me. "Fancy meeting you here," he said. He stepped aside and gestured toward the sink.

I slipped past him, turned on the cold water, and splashed it onto my face.

"I haven't seen you around in a while. It was too bad about Stuart, wasn't it?" Anger slipped into his voice. I looked up. His face was pale, his blond hair slicked back, his two eyes reminding me of Detective Ohls's eyes, tired with the effort of it all. Close up I realized that there was some makeup on his face, to cover his blotches. His smile was forced.

"Yeah," I said. It was too bad about Stuart. I hit the button of a dryer and let air blow over face and hands.

"My friend has to go soon. Would you mind if I dropped by your table and joined you for a chat?" There was that fourth chair, with no place setting, just waiting for him.

The bathroom had no monitor, but I wondered if it had been bugged or if Baby Bear on his most recent trip, had scanned the place. If Lang had someone listening, the name Stuart would have caught his attention, and he would be hastily replaying our conversation, looking for some coded meaning. The hot air rushing over my hands stopped.

"You set up Sauro," I said.

"Sauro who?" he asked. He turned up the water and pressed his palm against the dryer's on button. How long would it take them to filter out the sound from the recording in order to make out our voices?

"Sauro's the guy who jumped off a roof to celebrate April Fool's Day. On March fifteenth he was fucking Stuart's cousin. He wasn't anywhere near Kansas City. No one was. But you had somebody erase all footage of him that day. It was enough to make Lang suspicious and send him off on a wild-goose chase. Sauro had done just enough UHL work to keep Lang curious. Or maybe you wanted Lang to worry enough about Anna that he'd use his connections to get Baxter here. Poor Sauro thought he knew enough about the UHL to jump."

"No one asked him to jump. No one's asking you to jump. You have someone in Monitoring. And we have someone in Monitoring. This will be a monitored dialogue between Baxter and me. That's all. All three of you will walk out of here alive. Unless Evan didn't clean out all the bugs they might have planted in here. Then you and I both have numbered days. Remember, you never turned in Stuart. That makes you an accessory. It's not like they'll let you go home to Boston with her."

The dryer shut off, and Luis turned off the running water. His hands turned each knob with exquisite care, as if each motion were a conscious decision. I wondered how long his nerves had been degenerating. "See you soon," he said, and locked himself into the cubicle.

I stepped out of the bathroom. The sun was setting, giving everything a pale orange cast. The candles seemed brighter than before. I walked past Humpty and Dumpty, who were busy with pie and coffee. If they were UHL, as Lang had claimed when he showed me that photo of them standing outside Sophie's house, why had they made such a point of recognizing me? If they were Lang's men, waiting for me to pull my earlobe, rub my neck, then why were they being so conspicuous? Why had Luis's presence surprised Humpty? I sat down opposite Baxter.

"Well?" he said.

I didn't know what to say, or do. For Edward Lang and for Stuart Greenspan, the answer was always a moral one, armed to the hilt. For me?

My lack of response let Baxter settle into other, more comfortable expectations. "You don't want the job, do you? You were expecting another kind of offer." I wasn't sure if he was relieved or disgusted.

Anna stared at the candle flame, shaking her head. Her father must have told her to expect this. While I was in the bathroom, he must have laid it out for her, how once again she'd been used. I should have answered immediately.

"Can I ask you a question?" I said.

At this point he had stopped caring. "Why not?"

Luis walked past us to his table. Humpty followed him with his eyes. Lang had had a picture of Luis at Sophie's house on Saturday. Dumpty, the last person who had seen Sophie alive, was busy with a second helping of ice cream. Luis picked up his coffee, stared at the cup, then returned it to its saucer. He signaled to the waiter to bring his check. There was a bolt on the cooler door. I wondered if you could make it from the kitchen to the cooler and out the door, if somehow three people could run down the alleyways, up fire escapes, and hide until it was all over.

Baxter had built some of the camps. A majority of them. Cindy was leaving by train on Monday. Did I want him to escape?

"Well?" said Baxter. "You had a question."

"It's a hypothetical question."

"Having to do with money." He offered me his half smile, like he'd known it all along.

"No. It's truly hypothetical. Let's assume that your daughter's friends in ASD are right. Let's assume there should be no relocation camps."

Baxter was already shaking his head.

"Rod, my father just offered you a job. What's going on?"

I held up my hand before he could speak. The waiter had yet to bring Luis and Baby Bear their check. "Let's try a different tack. It's one hundred years into the future. There has been a cure for all forms of hives, in fact for all disease transmitted sexually." Baxter frowned; I was beginning to fear that he had stopped listening. "People have discovered how to live sexually free lives without jealousy or guilt. They have found a way to manage their feelings, and pleasure has become another way of sharing. No one is obsessed with it. No one is put off by it."

"Not only is that utopian," Baxter blurted out, "it's preposterous."

Anna took my hand and glared at me. "I think we should change the subject."

The waiter was handing Luis his check. Luis already had his bancard out, and he gave it to the waiter. Mama Bear would be here any moment to join us. Maybe that would be for the best, at least for Cindy who had only been doing her job.

"I just don't think it would happen," Baxter was saying.

"Look," I said, and the anger somehow freed me. "You went to college. You know what a hypothesis is. It's not real. It's an experiment in thought. Let's just assume that one hundred years from now, true personal and sexual freedom is the way things work. Can you and your Harvard degree manage that?"

"I will not abide by such treatment."

Anna glared at me. "What's gotten into you today?"

"We're talking about your life."

That stopped him.

"We have sexual freedom. A historian from that time period looks back at our time. He looks at Baxter Construction. He looks at the camps your company built, financial loss and all. He doesn't believe the inmates did anything wrong. How will that historian portray you?"

I wasn't sure how well he had heard me. Halfway through he had started to shake his head. "You're not UHL," he said. It had been meant as a statement, but it came out as a question. Anna looked at me as if something she'd been wondering about had started to make sense.

The waiter walked over to Luis and Baby Bear's table and handed Luis the bancard. He looked as if he were explaining some sort of problem. He was all bows and flourishes of hands until Baby Bear handed the waiter his card.

"No," I said. "I'm not UHL. What will that historian write?"

Baxter sat back, lifted his empty brandy snifter. "Hypothetically?"

I nodded.

"If that was to happen, if such freedom could exist in human beings without being so destructive, then I'm wrong. I don't think I am. I think desires must always be watched and controlled. But if your scenario was to happen, then I would be the villain of the piece."

I had expected a different answer. I had expected it to be easy, then, to wait for Luis, or to pull at my earlobe. The waiter was returning with Baby Bear's bancard. Luis and Baby Bear were already shaking hands, ready to part. Humpty looked up from his coffee, turned his gaze on me.

"Here's the situation," I said. "There are UHL people here who want to talk with you tonight. I'm not sure what they plan to have happen. Lang has some men here to keep an eye on us."

"What are you saying?"

I repeated myself.

"Then," he said, trying to act calm, as if making an executive decision he had control over, "I think we can trust Ed Lang to take care of things."

"Ed Lang," I said, "set you up. He knew this was going to happen, and he let it."

Baxter turned to Anna as if she might know anything about this.

"Your buddy Ed Lang had Sophie Greenspan killed."

"I can't believe that."

"Both sides are here," I said. "I want us out of the cross fire. There's another exit, one they might not be watching. Maybe if there's some kind of diversion, you can make it to the kitchen. There's a cooler with a door that leads to the outside."

Baxter looked as if he'd stopped believing me. Anna

watched me; I had no idea what she believed. Baby Bear was walking toward the entranceway up front.

"Call your bodyguards over," I whispered.

But it was too late. Luis pulled the fourth chair away from the table, and sat down. His right hand covered Baxter's left. Anna watched him, her head shaking at first, then frozen, as she recognized him and remembered why she shouldn't have. "You're dead."

"Dying," Luis said.

"I have four bodyguards," Baxter said.

The bodyguard sitting alone at the next table, the one behind Anna, had already turned in his chair to face us. "My gun is aimed at your daughter, sir. Please, don't call anyone."

Humpty was watching, but Luis had his back to him. If he was one of Lang's, then all I had to do was raise my hand to earlobe then neck. But there was a gun at Anna's back.

"You've got me here," Baxter finally said.

Luis nodded. "And Jacob *will* shoot your daughter, if necessary. Four people died so this meeting could happen."

Anna shifted her eyes to mine, probing, trying to figure out what role I had played in this.

"What," said Baxter, "would it take to keep my daughter out of this?"

"I'm staying," said Anna. Her voice was hoarse, each word a struggle.

"We're all staying," said Jacob.

Humpty was looking to Jacob, then to me. Something was wrong, but he didn't know what. Standing by the exit that led to kitchen and rest rooms, conversing with the maître d', was Bill O'Brien trying to look inconspicuous.

"If Stuart were still alive," Luis said, his voice soft, almost reasonable, "he'd really want to talk with you. He'd want to ask you why, why've you done what you've done, when you've been a decent, honorable person in your private life?"

Baxter almost started to answer.

"But we just don't have time."

I closed my eyes for a moment, wished it were over, then opened them. The restaurant had become a deep twilight blue. Candles made everyone's faces glow. Luis, in awkward little jerks, shrugged off his jacket. He was wearing a short-sleeved shirt. Pockmarks heightened the whiteness of his skin. He closed his right hand into a fist, lowered his arm out of sight below the table. His left hand picked up a table knife, lowered it out of sight. One arm slid above the other, and Luis closed his eyes. He looked surprised by the pain. This close, in the dim twilight, Baxter and I could see the blood veil his arm. The sound of running water, the murmur of dinner conversation, pervaded the room.

Luis faced Baxter. "Take off your jacket. Cut your arm, too. Then we'll place your arm against my arm. It will be a bond, like we're blood brothers, or something."

"Dad . . . don't."

Baxter removed his jacket, spread the shoulders carefully across the chair, and rolled up the sleeves of his shirt. He reached his hand out for the knife. In candlelight the blood on the knife was barely visible. "Don't wipe it clean," said Luis.

Humpty looked to me for some sort of signal. Dumpty rose from their table and made his way to the back of the restaurant, perhaps for the phones. Luis had his back to both of them. O'Brien, standing at the kitchen door, watched Dumpty, in his baggy gray suit, leave. The knife in Baxter's hand was below the table, out of sight, but he was looking at Luis.

"It's Hives Twelve and Seventeen," said Luis. "Chemicals keep me going. There's no vaccine and no cure. Maybe they'll find you an experimental drug that'll work. Maybe they'll modify one of your camps for you, make it a little more humane. You get the point."

Baxter's face was pale, and the flabbiness in his jowls made him look old. Anna was staring at me, waiting for me to do something. Then she turned to Luis, her mouth opened, about to say something.

"I'll count to ten," said Luis, "and Jacob will shoot Anna."

Baxter shook his head. He stared at the knife under the table, gritted his teeth. I felt as if the dull blade was tearing my own skin.

"Now," said Luis, "raise your arm."

Anna had her eyes shut, closing this out: it just couldn't really be happening. Frederico was standing up, then making his way toward us. Baxter raised his arm, blood flowing down toward the elbow. Humpty stood, his head darting back and forth as if to get a better look. His eyes almost fastened on Baxter's bloody arm, then Luis's arm, raised as if in salute.

"Our arms will touch," Luis said, "and it'll all be over."

Humpty's gun was out, blood exploded from Luis's head, and the shot was heard, followed by the dull sound of Luis's head hitting the hardwood table. Jacob was already up and aiming at Humpty, O'Brien was reaching into his jacket, Frederico was running forward, and I grabbed Anna, who pulled away from me. Shots went off. Screams erupted. "Get that gun," somebody yelled. Chairs scraped the floor, people shouted. I pushed Anna to the floor, heard her hit, then scrambled over to cover her with my body. Another shot, and Baxter toppled. There were two more shots, then nothing.

The silence lasted forever.

Anna was curled on the floor, trembling, in shock. I tried to help her up, but she slid away from me. Somebody was helping Baxter sit up. Blood soaked through his shirt around the shoulder. Two men and a woman shouted that they were police and approached us slowly, weapons raised, announcing that it was over, that nobody should move.

Jacob lay next to us, his body twisted. Humpty lay against the wall, the water of the holographic brook drowning him in ghostly light. Standing yards apart, Bill O'Brien and Frederico faced each other, their pistols raised, their stances frozen, as if they would face each other off like that forever.

Among the swarm of paramedics, police, journalists, and special agents from this agency and that who overtook the restaurant within the next thirty minutes, Lang was nowhere to be seen. We found out days later that two hours after Lang and I had met, the operation had been taken out of his hands.

58

ON MONDAY MORNING Cindy Molero, carrying two bags of luggage, boarded a well-marked train car while eight of us stared at each other in a security holding cell at the Cleveland Justice Center. Cindy's husband, holding their baby in his arms, watched the train pull out. Sally Kim and Norman White stood with him, waving to the receding train, unsure after all of these years of seeing off such trains if it was appropriate to wave. And, in our cell, the eight of us were silent, except for the occasional banality about when they'd let us out.

The cell was white linoleum, like the cells where they kept the Kansas City Five. There were six chairs, four cots, a sink, a toilet, and a monitor. We all looked away whenever Anna went pee. Frederico and the two surviving bodyguards had taken over the cots, every now and then asking Anna if she wanted to sleep in the fourth one. Evan Christopher—Baby Bear—and Bill O'Brien sat next to each other and stared at the floor. At midnight the police had brought in Timothy Molina, who'd been home alone watching the whole thing on the late-night news. Molina had moved his chair as far away from O'Brien as he could. Anna and I sat next to each other, our heads turned away, watching nothing happen in opposite directions. She'd spent most of the night crying, wetting the cell's one towel and trying to rid her blouse of Luis's and Jacob's blood.

In what I guess was the morning—they'd taken our watches and refused to tell us the time—four guards, dressed up and armed for a third-rate war, opened the thick metal door and brought us what looked like scrambled eggs, potatoes, and coffee. Without ever looking at her, the first guard told Anna that her father was in stable condition and would be released from the hospital that afternoon. Anna thanked him; she didn't ask about the result of her father's blood test.

"Can you get her a clean shirt?" Frederico asked.

The second guard started to nod, but the one standing in the door shook her head.

After the guards had left, the door slammed shut, Timothy rose from his chair and sat down on Anna's other side. "They'll probably let you out this afternoon," he said.

Anna nodded.

"Maybe you should get some sleep. You've been up all night. Now that you know, for sure, that your father's fine . . ."

"Thank you . . . no." She looked down at her feet, her hair slipping down over her shoulders, veiling her profile.

When they brought us lunch, they told us two guys from Monitoring were being held for questioning in the next room. "One of them got the news to the *Plain Dealer*, and the other got it to Showtime News."

"Good for them," muttered Bill.

"When do we get to see a lawyer?" asked Molina.

The guard standing in the door tried to stare Molina down. "When someone wants to ask you some questions, you'll get a lawyer."

The tumblers of the door's lock shift into place with an electronic whine that echoed in the room.

"Look," Timothy said, "they're waiting for one of us to break. They want someone to say something they can make use of." He shifted his gaze to Bill O'Brien, who was pointedly staring at one of the overhead monitors. "Maybe something can be said so those of us who are a little less involved can be even less involved."

Bill continued gazing at the monitor. "Tim, they have to charge us in forty-eight hours or let us go. Let's keep it that way."

Timothy reached for his ring finger, pulled off his

wedding band, and threw it at O'Brien, hitting him in cheek. The ring clattered on the linoleum floor. O'Brien rubbed his cheek, but refused to look at his spouse.

Timothy turned to me. "I thought you were apolitical. I thought you didn't vote."

"I don't."

"Rod set us up." Anna had said that. She was looking at me now, awaiting a reaction. Thin red lines cut through the whites of her eyes like shattered glass.

"Ask your Uncle Ed about that, why don't you?"

"And he's going to tell me he killed Sophie, right?"

I considered the monitors' presence, and I liked that they were there. Somebody important could hear this. I didn't know that Lang had resigned his position and was already on his way back to Boston, taking the morning flight James Baxter would have been on. "He didn't do it with his own hands."

"Why would he?" Her face was puffy, pale, her hair in tangles hanging over her shoulders.

"To protect you, Anna."

"Me? From what?"

"From yourself. He thought you were UHL, or about to be. Everything you did must have made him more suspicious. You hired a servicer. You told him to get the Experience. You introduced him to Stuart Greenspan. You hid out with him in an unmonitored house."

"You're making this up."

"Maybe. I don't know." I considered it for a moment: maybe it had all been done by Angel's people, trying to cut Stuart off; maybe Stuart had made Angel up to win over my sympathy; or maybe Angel was still in Kansas City and couldn't care less. "But, you know, every connection that could get you or him in trouble ended up dead. Dorothy Suoto gave me the Experience. Tortured and dead. Regina Huddleston saw you and Lang sleeping together and was going to report it to her superiors. Tortured and dead. Stuart Greenspan goes without saying. Then there's Sophie Greenspan. She was going to take me to the *PD*, have me tell them everything I knew about what Lang wanted, about what Stuart wanted. It would have blown the whole thing.

Because the UHL never would have come out into the open. I wonder how all of it looked on the news."

"Were you well paid for all of this?"

"I didn't get paid at all."

"Then why? You let it happen. Why?"

I shook my head. Not because I didn't know, but because I didn't know how to say it.

"You must have been paid off," she said. She glared at me, waiting for me to deny it.

Tuesday afternoon Evan Christopher, otherwise known as Baby Bear, and Bill O'Brien were charged with premeditated murder in commission of terrorist activities, a charge that would call for the death penalty if they were found guilty. By the end of the week, a grand jury had indicted each of them on twenty counts of terrorist conspiracy and violence. Their faces and names had appeared enough in the papers and on the holo to insure the real trials Lang had wanted.

Within a week the ACLU was suing the state on our behalf for violating our Miranda rights by forbidding us contact with lawyers while we were kept in the white room. Several newspapers called for boards of inquiry to investigate Edward Lang and Cuyahoga Monitoring Services' involvement in the deaths of Dorothy Suoto, Sophie Greenspan, Regina Huddleston, and Stuart Greenspan. But Humpty was dead, shot by Frederico, who thought Humpty's gun had been aimed for Baxter and not for Luis. And Dumpty was dead, garroted by Bill O'Brien on his way back from the telephones. With those two gone I didn't think the inquiry would get very far.

The same afternoon they charged Baby Bear and Bill O'Brien with murder, they fed us lunch, then let us go. Except for Anna. They had released her before breakfast so she could accompany her father back to Boston on a late morning flight. With the thick metal door open, four guards standing in the doorway, she stood up and turned to me. I rose and faced her. She looked like she had when Sauro had died—the swollen cheeks, the dark circles under bloodshot eyes, the hair out of place. But she held her body with a kind of determination that hadn't been there in April, and there was a hardness in her eyes. I waited for one of us to say something, but she saw whatever she'd wanted to see and left with the guards. Needless to say, she never wrote.

But Anna had been right about one thing: I did get paid. The money Lang had promised me, the money I'd never agreed to. Two weeks later it appeared in my account, enough to take a substantial leave of absence, to think things out, to decide what I wanted to do.

I found out the name of the free clinic that Beatrice Knecivic worked for, the one whose doctor did all the work in the shackvilles. I transferred the money to them, and for five minutes I felt better about everything.

ACKNOWLEDGMENTS

Jay Parini, Stephen Geller, and, most of all, Tony Geist gave important advice when this was a project called *Winter Kept Us Warm*.

Lucius Shepard, with the help of Kate Wilhelm and Damon Knight, gave the advice that transformed this novel into *Sheltered Lives*. Lou Aronica shepherded the project from a proposal to its current form. April Bernard helped me rethink important sections of this novel and trimmed down my verbal excesses. Lise Rodgers caught mistakes that everyone else missed.

Bob Morgan, Bill Johnson, Karen Fowler, Patrick Delahunt, Ralph Vicinanza, and my family supplied the necessary encouragement. UPB supplied several days off. Pat McDonnell supplied the tour.

My grandmother, Mary Louise Vail, provided the tools and the working space.

Kevin Ho and Veronica Lee answered medical questions and made other important suggestions.

The following wrote books invaluable to my research for this novel: Jeanne Wahatshui and James D. Houston, Ross Macdonald, Primo Levi, Paul Monette, Philip Slater, Susan Sontag, William Whyte, Howard Zinn, and Soshana Zuboff

Special thanks to James Bresnicky and his red pen, and to April Stewart-Oberndorf for service beyond the call of duty.

ABOUT THE AUTHOR

CHARLES STEWART–OBERNDORF is a native Clevelander who has studied in New Hampshire, Granada, Spain, and the Clarion Writer's Workshop (1987). He currently lives in Cleveland Heights with his wife and four year old son. When he's not with them, he teaches English and social studies at University School. When he can, he works on his second novel.

Bantam Spectra Special Editions

A program dedicated to masterful works of fantastic fiction by many of today's most visionary writers.

◆

Full Spectrum 2 edited by Lou Aronica, Shawna McCarthy, and Amy Stout
No Enemy But Time by Michael Bishop
Mindplayers by Pat Cadigan
Synners by Pat Cadigan
Great Work of Time by John Crowley
Little, Big by John Crowley
Stars In My Pocket Like Grains Of Sand by Samuel R. Delany
The Difference Engine by William Gibson and Bruce Sterling
Through the Heart by Richard Grant
Winterlong by Elizabeth Hand
Cloven Hooves by Megan Lindholm
Desolation Road by Ian McDonald
King of Morning, Queen of Day by Ian McDonald
Out On Blue Six by Ian McDonald
Points of Departure by Pat Murphy
Sheltered Lives by Charles Oberndorf
Emergence by David R. Palmer
Life During Wartime by Lucius Shepard
Beauty by Sheri S. Tepper

PROOF OF PURCHASE

S P E C T R A

Special Editions

SHELTERED LIVES